A TALE
OF TWO CITIES

WITH READER'S GUIDE

AMSCO LITERATURE PROGRAM

WILBERT J. LEVY, *Program Editor*

Motif page—
mni-me; Lucyand mom

Charles Dickens

A TALE OF
TWO CITIES

Amsco Literature Program

When ordering this book, you may specify:
R 108 ALP (Paperback)
R 108 H (Hardbound)

WITH READER'S GUIDE

Henry I. Christ

Amsco School Publications, Inc.

315 HUDSON STREET NEW YORK, N.Y. 10013

Please visit our Web site at:

www.amscopub.com

ISBN 978-0-87720-813-6

A Tale of Two Cities with Reader's Guide

CONTENTS

Book the First: Recalled to Life

Book the Second: the Golden Thread

Book the Third: The Track of a Storm

BOOK THE FIRST: RECALLED TO LIFE

Chapter 1. The Period

It was the best of times, it was the worst of times, it was the age of wisdom, it was the age of foolishness, it was the epoch of belief, it was the epoch of incredulity, it was the season of Light, it was the season of Darkness, it was the spring of hope, it was the winter of despair, we had everything before us, we had nothing before us, 5 we were all going direct to Heaven, we were all going direct the other way—in short, the period was so far like the present period, that some of its noisiest authorities insisted on its being received, for good or for evil, in the superlative degree of comparison only.

There were a king with a large jaw, and a queen with a plain face, on the throne of England; there were a king with a large jaw, and a queen with a fair face, on the throne of France. In both countries it was clearer than crystal to the lords of the State preserves of loaves and fishes, that things in general were settled for ever.

It was the year of Our Lord one thousand seven hundred and 15 seventy-five. Spiritual revelations were conceded to England at that favoured period, as at this. Mrs. Southcott had recently attained her five-and-twentieth blessed birthday, of whom a prophetic private in the Life Guards had heralded the sublime appearance by announcing that arrangements were made for the swallowing up of London and Westminster. Even the Cock-lane ghost had been laid only a round dozen of years, after rapping out its messages, as the spirits of this very year last past (supernaturally deficient in originality) rapped out theirs. Mere messages in the earthly order of events had lately come to the English Crown and People, from a congress of 25

1

British subjects in America: which, strange to relate, have proved more important to the human race than any communications yet received through any of the chickens of the Cock-lane brood.

France, less favoured on the whole as to matters spiritual than her sister of the shield and trident, rolled with exceeding smoothness down hill, making paper money and spending it. Under the guidance of her Christian pastors, she entertained herself, besides, with such humane achievements as sentencing a youth to have his hands cut off, his tongue torn out with pincers, and his body burned alive, because he had not kneeled down in the rain to do honour to a dirty procession of monks which passed within his view, at a distance of some fifty or sixty yards. It is likely enough that, rooted in the woods of France and Norway, there were growing trees, when that sufferer was put to death, already marked by the Woodman, Fate, to come down and be sawn into boards, to make a certain movable framework with a sack and a knife in it, terrible in history. It is likely enough that in the rough outhouses of some tillers of the heavy lands adjacent to Paris, there were sheltered from the weather that very day, rude carts, bespattered with rustic mire, snuffed about by pigs, and roosted in by poultry, which the Farmer, Death, had already set apart to be his tumbrils of the Revolution. But that Woodman and that Farmer, though they work unceasingly, work silently, and no one heard them as they went about with muffled tread: the rather, forasmuch as to entertain any suspicion that they were awake, was to be atheistical and traitorous.

In England, there was scarcely an amount of order and protection to justify much national boasting. Daring burglaries by armed men, and highway robberies, took place in the capital itself every night; families were publicly cautioned not to go out of town without removing their furniture to upholsterers' warehouses for security; the highwayman in the dark was a City tradesman in the light, and, being recognised and challenged by his fellow-tradesman whom he stopped in his character of "the Captain," gallantly shot him through the head and rode away; the mail was waylaid by seven robbers, and the guard shot three dead, and then got shot dead himself by the other four, "in consequence of the failure of his ammunition": after which the mail was robbed in peace; that magnificent potentate, the Lord Mayor of London, was made to stand and deliver on Turnham Green by one highwayman, who despoiled the illustrious creature in sight of all his retinue; prisoners in London gaols fought battles with their turnkeys, and the majesty of the law fired blunderbusses in among them, loaded with rounds of shot and ball; thieves snipped off diamond crosses from the necks of noble lords at Court drawing-rooms; musketeers went into St. Giles's, to search for contraband goods, and the mob fired on the musketeers, and the musketeers fired on the mob, and nobody thought any of these occurrences much out of the common way. In the midst of them, the hangman, ever busy and ever worse than useless, was in constant requisition; now, stringing up long rows of miscellaneous criminals; now, hanging a housebreaker on Saturday who had been taken on Tuesday; now, burning people in the hand at Newgate by the dozen, and now, burning pamphlets at the door of Westminister Hall; to-day, taking the life of an atrocious murderer, and to-morrow of a wretched pilferer who had robbed a farmer's boy of sixpence.

All these things, and a thousand like them, came to pass in and close upon the dear old year one thousand seven hundred and seventy-five. Environed by them, while the Woodman and the Farmer worked unheeded, those two of the large jaws, and those other two of the plain and the fair faces, trod with stir enough, and carried their divine rights with a high hand. Thus did the year one thousand seven hundred and seventy-five conduct their Greatnesses, and myriads of small creatures—the creatures of this chronicle among the rest—along the roads that lay before them.

Chapter 2. The Mail

It was the Dover road that lay, on a Friday night late in November, before the first of the persons with whom this history has business. The Dover road lay, as to him, beyond the Dover mail, as it lumbered up Shooter's Hill. He walked uphill in the mire by the side of the mail, as the rest of the passengers did; not because they had the least relish for walking exercise, under the circumstances, but because the hill, and the harness, and the mud,

and the mail, were all so heavy, that the horses had three times already come to a stop, besides once drawing the coach across the road, with the mutinous intent of taking it back to Blackheath. Reins and whip and coachman and guard, however, in combina-
5   tion, had read that article of war which forbade a purpose otherwise strongly in favour of the argument, that some brute animals are endued with Reason; and the team had capitulated and returned to their duty.

With drooping heads and tremulous tails, they mashed their way through the thick mud, floundering and stumbling between whiles, as if they were falling to pieces at the larger joints. As often as the driver rested them and brought them to a stand, with a wary "Wo-ho! so-ho then!" the near leader violently shook his head and everything upon it—like an unusually emphatic horse, denying that
15 the coach could be got up the hill. Whenever the leader made this rattle, the passenger started, as a nervous passenger might, and was disturbed in mind.

There was a steaming mist in all the hollows, and it had roamed in its forlornness up the hill, like an evil spirit, seeking rest and finding none. A clammy and intensely cold mist, it made its slow way through the air in ripples that visibly followed and overspread one another, as the waves of an unwholesome sea might do. It was dense enough to shut out everything from the light of the coach-lamps but these its own workings, and a few yards of road; and the
25 reek of the labouring horses steamed into it, as if they had made it all.

Two other passengers, besides the one, were plodding up the hill by the side of the mail. All three were wrapped to the cheek-bones and over the ears, and wore jack-boots. Not one of the three could have said, from anything he saw, what either of the other two was like; and each was hidden under almost as many wrappers from the eyes of the mind, as from the eyes of the body, of his two companions. In those days, travellers were very shy of being confidential on a short notice, for anybody on the road might be a
35 robber or in league with robbers. As to the latter, when every posting-house and ale-house could produce somebody in "the Captain's" pay, ranging from the landlord to the lowest stable nondescript, it was the likeliest thing upon the cards. So the guard of the Dover mail thought to himself, that Friday night in

November, one thousand seven hundred and seventy-five, lumbering up Shooter's Hill, as he stood on his own particular perch behind the mail, beating his feet, and keeping an eye and a hand on the arm-chest before him, where a loaded blunderbuss lay at the top of six or eight loaded horse-pistols, deposited on a substratum of cutlass.

The Dover mail was in its usual genial position that the guard suspected the passengers, the passengers suspected one another and the guard, they all suspected everybody else, and the coachman was sure of nothing but the horses; as to which cattle he could with a clear conscience have taken his oath on the two Testaments that they were not fit for the journey.

"Wo-ho!" said the coachman. "So, then! One more pull and you're at the top and be damned to you, for I have had trouble enough to get you to it!—Joe!"

"Halloa!" the guard replied.

"What o'clock do you make it, Joe?"

"Ten minutes, good, past eleven."

"My blood!" ejaculated the vexed coachman, "and not atop of Shooter's yet! Tst! Yah! Get on with you!"

The emphatic horse, cut short by the whip in a most decided negative, made a decided scramble for it, and the three other horses followed suit. Once more, the Dover mail struggled on, with the jack-boots of its passengers squashing along by its side. They had stopped when the coach stopped, and they kept close company with it. If any one of the three had had the hardihood to propose to another to walk on a little ahead into the mist and darkness, he would have put himself in a fair way of getting shot instantly as a highwayman.

The last burst carried the mail to the summit of the hill. The horses stopped to breathe again, and the guard got down to skid the wheel for the descent, and open the coach-door to let the passengers in.

"Tst! Joe!" cried the coachman in a warning voice, looking down from his box.

"What do you say, Tom?"

They both listened.

"I say a horse at a canter coming up, Joe."

"*I* say a horse at a gallop, Tom," returned the guard, leaving his hold of the door, and mounting nimbly to his place. "Gentlemen! In the king's name, all of you!"

With this hurried adjuration, he cocked his blunderbuss, and stood on the offensive.

5   The passenger booked by this history was on the coach-step, getting in; the two other passengers were close behind him, and about to follow. He remained on the step, half in the coach and half out of it; they remained in the road below him. They all looked from the coachman to the guard, and from the guard to the coachman, and listened. The coachman looked back and the guard looked back, and even the emphatic leader pricked up his ears and looked back, without contradicting.

The stillness consequent on the cessation of the rumbling and labouring of the coach, added to the stillness of the night, made it 15   very quiet indeed. The panting of the horses communicated a tremulous motion to the coach, as if it were in a state of agitation. The hearts of the passengers beat loud enough perhaps to be heard; but at any rate, the quiet pause was audibly expressive of people out of breath, and holding the breath, and having the pulses quickened by expectation.

The sound of a horse at a gallop came fast and furiously up the hill.

"So-ho!" the guard sang out, as loud as he could roar. "Yo there! Stand! I shall fire!"

25   The pace was suddenly checked, and, with much splashing and floundering, a man's voice called from the mist, "Is that the Dover mail?"

"Never you mind what it is!" the guard retorted. "What are you?"

"*Is* that the Dover mail?"

"Why do you want to know?"

"I want a passenger, if it is."

"What passenger?"

"Mr. Jarvis Lorry."

35   Our booked passenger showed in a moment that it was his name. The guard, the coachman, and the two other passengers eyed him distrustfully.

"Keep where you are," the guard called to the voice in the mist, "because, if I should make a mistake, it could never be set right in your lifetime. Gentleman of the name of Lorry answer straight."

"What is the matter?" asked the passenger, then, with mildly quavering speech. "Who wants me? Is it Jerry?"

("I don't like Jerry's voice, if it is Jerry," growled the guard to himself. "He's hoarser than suits me, is Jerry.")

"Yes, Mr. Lorry."

"What is the matter?"

"A despatch sent after you from over yonder. T. and Co."

"I know this messenger, guard," said Mr. Lorry, getting down into the road—assisted from behind more swiftly than politely by the other two passengers, who immediately scrambled into the coach, shut the door, and pulled up the window. "He may come close; there's nothing wrong."

"I hope there ain't, but I can't make so 'Nation sure of that," said the guard, in gruff soliloquy. "Hallo you!"

"Well! And hallo you!" said Jerry, more hoarsely than before.

"Come on at a footpace, d'ye mind me? And if you've got holsters to that saddle o' yourn, don't let me see your hand go nigh 'em. For I'm a devil at a quick mistake, and when I make one it takes the form of Lead. So now let's look at you."

The figures of a horse and rider came slowly through the eddying mist, and came to the side of the mail, where the passenger stood. The rider stooped, and, casting up his eyes at the guard, handed the passenger a small folded paper. The rider's horse was blown, and both horse and rider were covered with mud, from the hoofs of the horse to the hat of the man.

"Guard!" said the passenger, in a tone of quiet business confidence.

The watchful guard, with his right hand at the stock of his raised blunderbuss, his left at the barrel, and his eye on the horseman, answered curtly, "Sir."

"There is nothing to apprehend. I belong to Tellson's Bank. You must know Tellson's Bank in London. I am going to Paris on business. A crown to drink. I may read this?"

"If so be as you're quick, sir."

He opened it in the light of the coach-lamp on that side, and read—first to himself and then aloud: " 'Wait at Dover for Mam'selle.' It's not long, you see, guard. Jerry, say that my answer was, RECALLED TO LIFE."

Jerry started in his saddle. "That's a Blazing strange answer, too," said he, at his hoarsest.

"Take that message back, and they will know that I received this, as well as if I wrote. Make the best of your way. Good night."

5   With those words the passenger opened the coach-door and got in; not at all assisted by his fellow-passengers, who had expeditiously secreted their watches and purses in their boots, and were now making a general pretence of being asleep. With no more definite purpose than to escape the hazard of originating any other kind of action.

The coach lumbered on again, with heavier wreaths of mist closing round it as it began the descent. The guard soon replaced his blunderbuss in his arm-chest, and, having looked to the rest of its contents, and having looked to the supplementary pistols that he

15   wore in his belt, looked to a smaller chest beneath his seat, in which there were a few smith's tools, a couple of torches, and a tinder-box. For he was furnished with that completeness that if the coach-lamps had been blown and stormed out, which did occasionally happen, he had only to shut himself up inside, keep the flint and steel sparks well off the straw, and get a light with tolerable safety and ease (if he were lucky) in five minutes.

"Tom!" softly over the coach-roof.

"Hallo, Joe."

"Did you hear the message?"

25   "I did, Joe."

"What did you make of it, Tom?"

"Nothing at all, Joe."

"That's a coincidence, too," the guard mused, "for I made the same of it myself."

Jerry, left alone in the mist and darkness, dismounted meanwhile, not only to ease his spent horse, but to wipe the mud from his face, and shake the wet out of his hat-brim, which might be capable of holding about half a gallon. After standing with the bridle over his heavily-splashed arm, until the wheels of the mail

35   were no longer within hearing and the night was quite still again, he turned to walk down the hill.

"After that there gallop from Temple Bar, old lady, I won't trust your fore-legs till I get you on the level," said this hoarse messenger, glancing at his mare. " 'Recalled to life.' That's a Blazing strange message. Much of that wouldn't do for you, Jerry! I say, Jerry! You'd be in a Blazing bad way, if recalling to life was to come into fashion, Jerry!"

Chapter 3. *The Night Shadows*

A wonderful fact to reflect upon, that every human creature is constituted to be that profound secret and mystery to every other. A solemn consideration, when I enter a great city by night, that every one of those darkly clustered houses encloses its own secret; that every room in every one of them encloses its own secret; that every beating heart in the hundreds of thousands of breasts there is, in some of its imaginings, a secret to the heart nearest it! Something of the awfulness, even of Death itself, is referable to this. No more can I turn the leaves of this dear book that I loved, and vainly hope in time to read it all. No more can I look into the depths of this unfathomable water, wherein, as momentary lights glanced into it, I have had glimpses of buried treasure and other things submerged. It was appointed that the book should shut with a spring, for ever and for ever, when I had read but a page. It was appointed that the water should be locked in an eternal frost, when the light was playing on its surface, and I stood in ignorance on the shore. My friend is dead, my neighbour is dead, my love, the darling of my soul, is dead; it is the inexorable consolidation and perpetuation of the secret that was always in that individuality, and which I shall carry in mine to my life's end. In any of the burial-places of this city through which I pass, is there a sleeper more inscrutable than its busy inhabitants are, in their innermost personality, to me, or than I am to them?

As to this, his natural and not to be alienated inheritance, the messenger on horseback had exactly the same possessions as the King, the first Minister of State, or the richest merchant in London. So with the three passengers shut up in the narrow compass of one lumbering old mail-coach; they were mysteries to one another, as complete as if each had been in his own coach and six, or his own coach and sixty, with the breadth of a county between him and the next.

The messenger rode back at an easy trot, stopping pretty often at ale-houses by the way to drink, but evincing a tendency to keep his own counsel, and to keep his hat cocked over his eyes. He had eyes that assorted very well with that decoration, being of a surface black, with no depth in the colour or form, and much too near together—as if they were afraid of being found out in something, singly, if they kept too far apart. They had a sinister expression, under an old cocked-hat like a three-cornered spittoon, and over a great muffler for the chin and throat, which descended nearly to the wearer's knees. When he stopped for drink, he moved this muffler with his left hand, only while he poured his liquor in with his right; as soon as that was done, he muffled again.

"No, Jerry, no!" said the messenger, harping on one theme as he rode. "It wouldn't do for you, Jerry. Jerry, you honest tradesman, it wouldn't suit *your* line of business! Recalled—! Bust me if I don't think he'd been a drinking!"

His message perplexed his mind to that degree that he was fain, several times, to take off his hat to scratch his head. Except on the crown, which was raggedly bald, he had stiff, black hair, standing jaggedly all over it, and growing downhill almost to his broad, blunt nose. It was so like smith's work, so much more like the top of a strongly spiked wall than a head of hair, that the best of players at leap-frog might have declined him, as the most dangerous man in the world to go over.

While he trotted back with the message he was to deliver to the night watchman in his box at the door of Tellson's Bank, by Temple Bar, who was to deliver it to greater authorities within, the shadows of the night took such shapes to him as arose out of the message, and took such shapes to the mare as arose out of *her* private topics of uneasiness. They seemed to be numerous, for she shied at every shadow on the road.

What time, the mail-coach lumbered, jolted, rattled, and bumped upon its tedious way, with its three fellow-inscrutables inside. To whom, likewise, the shadows of the night revealed themselves, in the forms their dozing eyes and wandering thoughts suggested.

Tellson's Bank had a run upon it in the mail. As the bank passenger—with an arm drawn through the leathern strap, which did what lay in it to keep him from pounding against the next passenger, and driving him into his corner, whenever the coach got a special jolt—nodded in his place, with half-shut eyes, the little coach-windows, and the coach-lamp dimly gleaming through them, and the bulky bundle of opposite passenger, became the bank, and did a great stroke of business. The rattle of the harness was the chink of money, and more drafts were honoured in five minutes than even Tellson's, with all its foreign and home connection, ever paid in thrice the time. Then the strong-rooms underground, at Tellson's, with such of their valuable stores and secrets as were known to the passenger (and it was not a little that he knew about them), opened before him, and he went in among them with the great keys and the feebly-burning candle, and found them safe, and strong, and sound, and still, just as he had last seen them.

But, though the bank was almost always with him, and though the coach (in a confused way, like the presence of pain under an opiate) was always with him, there was another current of impression that never ceased to run, all through the night. He was on his way to dig some one out of a grave.

Now, which of the multitude of faces that showed themselves before him was the true face of the buried person, the shadows of the night did not indicate; but they were all the faces of a man of five-and-forty by years, and they differed principally in the passions they expressed, and in the ghastliness of their worn and wasted state. Pride, contempt, defiance, stubbornness, submission, lamentation, succeeded one another; so did varieties of sunken cheek, cadaverous colour, emaciated hands and figures. But the face was in the main one face, and every head was prematurely white. A hundred times the dozing passenger inquired of this spectre:

"Buried how long?"

The answer was always the same: "Almost eighteen years."

"You had abandoned all hope of being dug out?"

"Long ago."

"You know that you are recalled to life?"

"They tell me so."

"I hope you care to live?"

"I can't say."

"Shall I show her to you? Will you come and see her?"

The answers to this question were various and contradictory.

5

15

25

35

Sometimes the broken reply was, "Wait! It would kill me if I saw her too soon." Sometimes, it was given in a tender rain of tears, and then it was, "Take me to her." Sometimes it was staring and bewildered, and then it was, "I don't know her. I don't understand."

After such imaginary discourse, the passenger in his fancy would dig, and dig, dig—now with a spade, now with a great key, now with his hands—to dig this wretched creature out. Got out at last, with earth hanging about his face and hair, he would suddenly fall away to dust. The passenger would then start to himself, and lower the window, to get the reality of mist and rain on his cheek.

Yet even when his eyes were opened on the mist and rain, on the moving patch of light from the lamps, and the hedge at the roadside retreating by jerks, the night shadows outside the coach would fall into the train of the night shadows within. The real banking-house by Temple Bar, the real business of the past day, the real strong-rooms, the real express sent after him, and the real message returned, would all be there. Out of the midst of them, the ghostly face would rise, and he would accost it again.

"Buried how long?"

"Almost eighteen years."

"I hope you care to live?"

"I can't say."

Dig—dig—dig—until an impatient movement from one of the two passengers would admonish him to pull up the window, draw his arm securely through the leathern strap, and speculate upon the two slumbering forms, until his mind lost its hold of them, and they again slid away into the bank and the grave.

"Buried how long?"

"Almost eighteen years."

"You had abandoned all hope of being dug out?"

"Long ago."

The words were still in his hearing as just spoken—distinctly in his hearing as ever spoken words had been in his life—when the weary passenger started to the consciousness of daylight, and found that the shadows of the night were gone.

He lowered the window, and looked out at the rising sun. There was a ridge of ploughed land, with a plough upon it where it had been left last night when the horses were unyoked; beyond, a quiet coppice-wood, in which many leaves of burning red and golden yellow still remained upon the trees. Though the earth was cold and wet, the sky was clear, and the sun rose bright, placid, and beautiful.

"Eighteen years!" said the passenger, looking at the sun. "Gra- 5
cious Creator of day! To be buried alive for eighteen years!"

Chapter 4. The Preparation

When the mail got successfully to Dover, in the course of the forenoon, the head drawer at the Royal George Hotel opened the coach-door as his custom was. He did it with some flourish of ceremony, for a mail journey from London in winter was an achieve-ment to congratulate an adventurous traveller upon.

By that time, there was only one adventurous traveller left to be congratulated; for the two others had been set down at their respective roadside destinations. The mildewy inside of the coach, with its damp and dirty straw, its disagreeable smell, and its 15
obscurity, was rather like a larger dog-kennel. Mr. Lorry, the passenger, shaking himself out of it in chains of straw, a tangle of shaggy wrapper, flapping hat, and muddy legs, was rather like a larger sort of dog.

"There will be a packet to Calais to-morrow, drawer?"

"Yes, sir, if the weather holds and the wind sets tolerable fair. The tide will serve pretty nicely at about two in the afternoon, sir. Bed, sir?"

"I shall not go to bed till night; but I want a bedroom, and a barber."

25

"And then breakfast, sir? Yes, sir. That way, sir, if you please. Show Concord! Gentleman's valise and hot water to Concord. Pull off gentleman's boots in Concord. (You will find a fine sea-coal fire, sir.) Fetch barber to Concord. Stir about there, now, for Concord!"

The Concord bedchamber being always assigned to a passenger by the mail, and passengers by the mail being always heavily wrapped up from head to foot, the room had the odd interest for the establishment of the Royal George, that although but one kind of man was seen to go into it, all kinds and varieties of men came out of it. Consequently, another drawer, and two porters, and several maids and the landlady, were all loitering by accident at various points of the road between the Concord and the coffee-room, when a gentleman of sixty, formally dressed in a brown suit of clothes, pretty well worn, but very well kept, with large square cuffs and large flaps to the pockets, passed along on his way to his breakfast.

The coffee-room had no other occupant, that forenoon, than the gentleman in brown. His breakfast-table was drawn before the fire, and as he sat, with its light shining on him, waiting for the meal, he sat so still, that he might have been sitting for his portrait.

Very orderly and methodical he looked, with a hand on each knee, and a loud watch ticking a sonorous sermon under his flapped waistcoat, as though it pitted its gravity and longevity against the levity and evanescence of the brisk fire. He had a good leg, and was a little vain of it, for his brown stockings fitted sleek and close, and were of a fine texture; his shoes and buckles, too, though plain, were trim. He wore an odd little sleek crisp flaxen wig, setting very close to his head; which wig, it is to be presumed, was made of hair, but which looked far more as though it were spun from filaments of silk or glass. His linen, though not of a fineness in accordance with his stockings, was as white as the tops of the waves that broke upon the neighbouring beach, or the specks of sail that glinted in the sunlight far at sea. A face habitually suppressed and quieted was still lighted up under the quaint wig by a pair of moist bright eyes that must have cost their owner, in years gone by, some pains to drill to the composed and reserved expression of Tellson's Bank. He had a healthy colour in his cheeks, and his face, though lined, bore few traces of anxiety. But, perhaps the confidential bachelor clerks in Tellson's Bank were principally occupied with the cares of other people; and perhaps second-hand cares, like second-hand clothes, come easily off and on.

Completing his resemblance to a man who was sitting for his portrait, Mr. Lorry dropped off to sleep. The arrival of his breakfast roused him, and he said to the drawer, as he moved his chair to it:

"I wish accommodation prepared for a young lady who may come here at any time to-day. She may ask for Mr. Jarvis Lorry, or she may only ask for a gentleman from Tellson's Bank. Please to let me know."

"Yes, sir. Tellson's Bank in London, sir?"

"Yes."

"Yes, sir. We have oftentimes the honour to entertain your gentlemen in their travelling backwards and forwards betwixt London and Paris, sir. A vast deal of travelling, sir, in Tellson and Company's House."

"Yes. We are quite a French House, as well as an English one."

"Yes, sir. Not much in the habit of such travelling yourself, I think, sir?"

"Not of late years. It is fifteen years since we—since I—came last from France."

"Indeed, sir? That was before my time here, sir. Before our people's time here, sir. The George was in other hands at that time, sir."

"I believe so."

"But I would hold a pretty wager, sir, that a House like Tellson and Company was flourishing, a matter of fifty, not to speak of fifteen years ago?"

"You might treble that, and say a hundred and fifty, yet not be far from the truth."

"Indeed, sir!"

Rounding his mouth and both his eyes, as he stepped backward from the table, the waiter shifted his napkin from his right arm to his left, dropped into a comfortable attitude, and stood surveying the guest while he ate and drank, as from an observatory or watch-tower, according to the immemorial usage of waiters in all ages.

When Mr. Lorry had finished his breakfast, he went out for a stroll on the beach. The little narrow, crooked town of Dover hid itself away from the beach, and ran its head into the chalk cliffs, like a marine ostrich. The beach was a desert of heaps of sea and stones tumbling wildly about, and the sea did what it liked, and what it liked was destruction. It thundered at the town, and thundered at the cliffs, and brought the coast down, madly. The air among the houses was of so strong a piscatory flavour that one might have supposed sick fish went up to be dipped in it, as sick people went down to be dipped in the sea. A little fishing was done in the port, and a quantity of strolling about by night, and looking seaward: particularly at those times when the tide made, and was near flood. Small tradesmen, who did no business whatever, sometimes unaccountably realised large fortunes, and it was remarkable that nobody in the neighbourhood could endure a lamplighter.

As the day declined into the afternoon, and the air, which had been at intervals clear enough to allow the French coast to be seen, became again charged with mist and vapour, Mr. Lorry's thoughts seemed to cloud too. When it was dark, and he sat before the coffee-room fire, awaiting his dinner as he had awaited his breakfast, his mind was busily digging, digging, digging, in the live red coals.

A bottle of good claret after dinner does a digger in the red coals no harm, otherwise than as it has a tendency to throw him out of work. Mr. Lorry had been idle a long time, and had just poured out his last glassful of wine with as complete an appearance of satisfaction as is ever to be found in an elderly gentleman of a fresh complexion who has got to the end of a bottle, when a rattling of wheels came up the narrow street, and rumbled into the inn-yard.

He set down his glass untouched. "This is Mam'selle!" said he.

In a very few minutes the waiter came in to announce that Miss Manette had arrived from London, and would be happy to see the gentleman from Tellson's.

"So soon?"

Miss Manette had taken some refreshment on the road, and required none then, and was extremely anxious to see the gentleman from Tellson's immediately, if it suited his pleasure and convenience.

The gentleman from Tellson's had nothing left for it but to empty his glass with an air of stolid desperation, settle his odd little flaxen wig at the ears, and follow the waiter to Miss Manette's apartment. It was a large, dark room, furnished in a funereal manner with black horsehair, and loaded with heavy dark tables. These had been oiled and oiled, until the two tall candles on the table in the middle of the room were gloomily reflected on every leaf; as if *they* were buried, in deep graves of black mahogany, and no light to speak of could be expected from them until they were dug out.

The obscurity was so difficult to penetrate that Mr. Lorry, picking his way over the well-worn Turkey carpet, supposed Miss

Manette to be, for the moment, in some adjacent room, until, having got past the two tall candles, he saw, standing to receive him by the table between them and the fire, a young lady of not more than seventeen, in a riding-cloak, and still holding her straw travelling-hat by its ribbon in her hand. As his eyes rested on a short, slight, pretty figure, a quantity of golden hair, a pair of blue eyes that met his own with an inquiring look, and a forehead with a singular capacity (remembering how young and smooth it was) of lifting and knitting itself into an expression that was not quite one of perplexity, or wonder, or alarm, or merely of a bright fixed attention, though it included all the four expressions—as his eyes rested on these things, a sudden vivid likeness passed before him, of a child whom he had held in his arms on the passage across that very Channel, one cold time, when the hail drifted heavily and the sea ran high. The likeness passed away, like a breath along the surface of the gaunt pier-glass behind her, on the frame of which, a hospital procession of Negro cupids, several headless and all cripples, were offering black baskets of Dead Sea fruit to black divinities of the feminine gender—and he made his formal bow to Miss Manette.

"Pray take a seat, sir." In a very clear and pleasant young voice; a little foreign in its accent, but a very little indeed.

"I kiss your hand, miss," said Mr. Lorry, with the manners of an earlier date, as he made his formal bow again, and took his seat.

"I received a letter from the Bank, sir, yesterday, informing me that some intelligence—or discovery—"

"The word is not material, miss; either word will do."

"—respecting the small property of my poor father, whom I never saw—so long dead—"

Mr. Lorry moved in his chair, and cast a troubled look towards the hospital procession of Negro cupids. As if *they* had any help for anybody in their absurd baskets!

"—render it necessary that I should go to Paris, there to communicate with a gentleman of the Bank, so good as to be despatched to Paris for the purpose."

"Myself."

"As I was prepared to hear, sir."

She curtseyed to him (young ladies made curtseys in those days), with a pretty desire to convey to him that she felt how much older and wiser he was than she. He made her another bow.

"I replied to the Bank, sir, that as it was considered necessary, by those who know, and who are so kind as to advise me, that I should go to France, and that as I am an orphan and have no friend who could go with me, I should esteem it highly if I might be permitted to place myself, during the journey, under that worthy gentleman's protection. The gentleman had left London, but I think a messenger was sent after him to beg the favour of his waiting for me here."

"I was happy," said Mr. Lorry, "to be entrusted with the charge. I shall be more happy to execute it."

"Sir, I thank you indeed. I thank you very gratefully. It was told me by the Bank that the gentleman would explain to me the details of the business, and that I must prepare myself to find them of a surprising nature. I have done my best to prepare myself, and I naturally have a strong and eager interest to know what they are."

"Naturally," said Mr. Lorry. "Yes—I—"

After a pause, he added, again settling the crisp flaxen wig at the ears:

"It is very difficult to begin."

He did not begin, but, in his indecision, met her glance. The young forehead lifted itself into that singular expression—but it was pretty and characteristic, besides being singular—and she raised her hand, as if with an involuntary action she caught at, or stayed some passing shadow.

"Are you quite a stranger to me, sir?"

"Am I not?" Mr. Lorry opened his hands, and extended them outwards with an argumentative smile.

Between the eyebrows and just over the little feminine nose, the line of which was as delicate and fine as it was possible to be, the expression deepened itself as she took her seat thoughtfully in the chair by which she had hitherto remained standing. He watched her as she mused, and the moment she raised her eyes again, went on:

"In your adopted country, I presume, I cannot do better than address you as a young English lady, Miss Manette?"

"If you please, sir."

"Miss Manette, I am a man of business. I have a business charge to acquit myself of. In your reception of it, don't heed me any more than if I was a speaking machine—truly, I am not much else. I will, with your leave, relate to you, miss, the story of one of our customers."

"Story!"

He seemed wilfully to mistake the word she had repeated, when he added, in a hurry, "Yes, customers; in the banking business we usually call our connection our customers. He was a French gentleman; a scientific gentleman; a man of great acquirements—a Doctor."

"Not of Beauvais?"

"Why, yes, of Beauvais. Like Monsieur Manette, your father, the gentleman was of Beauvais. Like Monsieur Manette, your father, the gentleman was of repute in Paris. I had the honour of knowing him there. Our relations were business relations, but confidential. I was at that time in our French House, and had been—oh! twenty years."

"At that time—I may ask, at what time, sir?"

"I speak, miss, of twenty years ago. He married—an English lady—and I was one of the trustees. His affairs, like the affairs of many other French gentlemen and French families, were entirely in Tellson's hands. In a similar way I am, or I have been, trustee of one kind or other for scores of our customers. These are mere business relations, miss; there is no friendship in them; no particular interest, nothing like sentiment. I have passed from one to another, in the course of my business life, just as I pass from one of our customers to another in the course of my business day; in short, I have no feelings; I am a mere machine. To go on—"

"But this is my father's story, sir; and I begin to think"—the curiously roughened forehead was very intent upon him—"that when I was left an orphan through my mother's surviving my father only two years, it was you who brought me to England. I am almost sure it was you."

Mr. Lorry took the hesitating little hand that confidingly advanced to take his, and he put it with some ceremony to his lips. He then conducted the young lady straightway to her chair again, and, holding the chairback with his left hand, and using his right by turns to rub his chin, pull his wig at the ears, or point what he said, stood looking down into her face while she sat looking up into his.

"Miss Manette, it *was* I. And you will see how truly I spoke of myself just now, in saying I had no feelings, and that all the relations I hold with my fellow-creatures are mere business relations, when you reflect that I have never seen you since. No; you have been the ward of Tellson's House since, and I have been busy with the other business of Tellson's House since. Feelings! I have no time for them, no chance of them. I pass my whole life, miss, in turning an immense pecuniary mangle."

After this odd description of his daily routine of employment, Mr. Lorry flattened his flaxen wig upon his head with both hands (which was most unnecessary, for nothing could be flatter than its shining surface was before), and resumed his former attitude.

"So far, miss (as you have remarked), this is the story of your regretted father. Now comes the difference. If your father had not died when he did— Don't be frightened! How you start!"

She did, indeed, start. And she caught his wrist with both her hands.

"Pray," said Mr. Lorry, in a soothing tone, bringing his left hand from the back of the chair to lay it on the supplicatory fingers that clasped him in so violent a tremble: "pray control your agitation—a matter of business. As I was saying—"

Her look so discomposed him that he stopped, wandered, and began anew:

"As I was saying; if Monsieur Manette had not died; if he had suddenly and silently disappeared; if he had been spirited away; if it had not been difficult to guess to what dreadful place, though no art could trace him; if he had an enemy in some compatriot who could exercise a privilege that I in my own time have known the boldest people afraid to speak of in a whisper, across the water there; for instance, the privilege of filling up blank forms for the consignment of any one to the oblivion of a prison for any length of time; if his wife had implored the king, the queen, the court, the clergy, for any tidings of him, and all quite in vain—then the history of your father would have been the history of this unfortunate gentleman, the Doctor of Beauvais."

"I entreat you to tell me more, sir."

"I will. I am going to. You can bear it?"

"I can bear anything but the uncertainty you leave me in at this moment."

"You speak collectedly, and you—*are* collected. That's good!"

(Though his manner was less satisfied than his words.) "A matter of business. Regard it as a matter of business—business that must be done. Now if this doctor's wife, though a lady of great courage and spirit, had suffered so intensely from this cause before her little child was born—"   5

"The little child was a daughter, sir?"

"A daughter. A—a—matter of business—don't be distressed. Miss, if the poor lady had suffered so intensely before her little child was born, that she came to the determination of sparing the poor child the inheritance of any part of the agony she had known the pains of, by rearing her in the belief that her father was dead —No, don't kneel! In Heaven's name why should you kneel to me?"

"For the truth. O dear, good, compassionate sir, for the truth!"

"A—a matter of business. You confuse me, and how can I transact business if I am confused? Let us be clear-headed. If you   15
could kindly mention now, for instance, what nine times ninepence are, or how many shillings in twenty guineas, it would be so encouraging. I should be so much more at my ease about your state of mind."

Without directly answering to this appeal, she sat so still when he had gently raised her, and the hands that had not ceased to clasp his wrists were so much more steady than they had been, that she communicated some reassurance to Mr. Jarvis Lorry.

"That's right, that's right. Courage! Business! You have business before you; useful business. Miss Manette, your mother took this   25
course with you. And when she died—I believe broken-hearted— having never slackened her unavailing search for your father, she left you, at two years old, to grow to be blooming, beautiful, and happy, without the dark cloud upon you of living in uncertainty whether your father soon wore his heart out in prison, or wasted there through many lingering years."

As he said the words he looked down, with admiring pity, on the flowing golden hair; as if he pictured to himself that it might have been already tinged with gray.

"You know that your parents had no great possession, and that   35
what they had was secured to your mother and to you. There has been no new discovery, of money, or of any other property; but—"

He felt his wrist held closer, and he stopped. The expression in the forehead, which had so particularly attracted his notice, and which was now immovable, had deepened into one of pain and horror.

"But he has been—been found. He is alive. Greatly changed, it is too probable; almost a wreck, it is possible; though we will hope the best. Still, alive. Your father has been taken to the house of an old servant in Paris, and we are going there: I, to identify him if I can: you, to restore him to life, love, duty, rest, comfort."

A shiver ran through her frame, and from it through his. She said, in a low, distinct, awe-stricken voice, as if she were saying it in a dream:

"I am going to see his ghost! It will be his ghost—not him!"

Mr. Lorry quietly chafed the hands that held his arm. "There, there, there! See now, see now! The best and the worst are known to you, now. You are well on your way to the poor wronged gentleman, and, with a fair sea voyage, and a fair land journey, you will be soon at his dear side."

She repeated in the same tone, sunk to a whisper, "I have been free, I have been happy, yet his ghost has never haunted me!"

"Only one thing more," said Mr. Lorry, laying stress upon it as a wholesome means of enforcing her attention. "He has been found under another name; his own, long forgotten or long concealed. It would be worse than useless now to inquire which; worse than useless to seek to know whether he has been for years overlooked, or always designedly held prisoner. It would be worse than useless now to make any inquiries, because it would be dangerous. Better not to mention the subject, anywhere or in any way, and to remove him—for a while at all events—out of France. Even I, safe as an Englishman, and even Tellson's, important as they are to French credit, avoid all naming of the matter. I carry about me not a scrap of writing openly referring to it. This is a secret service altogether. My credentials, entries, and memoranda are all comprehended in the one line, 'Recalled to Life,' which may mean anything. But what is the matter? She doesn't notice a word! Miss Manette!"

Perfectly still and silent, and not even fallen back in her chair, she sat under his hand, utterly insensible; with her eyes open and fixed upon him, and with that last expression looking as if it were carved or branded into her forehead. So close was her hold upon his arm, that he feared to detach himself lest he should hurt her;

therefore he called out loudly for assistance without moving.

A wild-looking woman, whom, even in his agitation, Mr. Lorry observed to be all of a red colour, and to have red hair, and to be dressed in some extraordinary tight-fitting fashion, and to have on her head a most wonderful bonnet like a Grenadier wooden measure, and good measure too, or a great Stilton cheese, came running into the room in advance of the inn servants, and soon settled the question of his detachment from the poor young lady, by laying a brawny hand upon his chest, and sending him flying back against the nearest wall.

("I really think this must be a man!" was Mr. Lorry's breathless reflection, simultaneously with his coming against the wall.)

"Why, look at you all!" bawled this figure, addressing the inn servants. "Why don't you go and fetch things, instead of standing there staring at me? I am not so much to look at, am I? Why don't you go and fetch things? I'll let you know, if you don't bring smelling-salts, cold water, and vinegar, quick, I will."

There was an immediate dispersal for these restoratives, and she softly laid the patient on a sofa, and tended her with great skill and gentleness: calling her "my precious!" and "my bird!" and spreading her golden hair aside over her shoulders with great pride and care.

"And you in brown!" she said, indignantly turning to Mr. Lorry; "couldn't you tell her what you had to tell her, without frightening her to death? Look at her, with her pretty pale face and her cold hands. Do you call *that* being a banker?"

Mr. Lorry was so exceedingly disconcerted by a question so hard to answer, that he could only look on, at a distance, with much feeble sympathy and humility, while the strong woman, having banished the inn servants under the mysterious penalty of "letting them know" something not mentioned if they stayed there, staring, recovered her charge by a regular series of gradations, and coaxed her to lay her drooping head upon her shoulder.

"I hope she will do well now," said Mr. Lorry.

"No thanks to you in brown, if she does. My darling pretty!"

"I hope," said Mr. Lorry, after another pause of feeble sympathy and humility, "that you accompany Miss Manette to France?"

"A likely thing, too!" replied the strong woman. "If it was ever intended that I should go across salt water, do you suppose Providence would have cast my lot in an island?"

This being another question hard to answer, Mr. Jarvis Lorry withdrew to consider it.

Chapter 5. The Wine-Shop

A large cask of wine had been dropped and broken, in the street. The accident had happened in getting it out of a cart; the cask had tumbled out with a run, the hoops had burst, and it lay on the stones just outside the door of the wine-shop, shattered like a walnut-shell.

All the people within reach had suspended their business, or their idleness, to run to the spot and drink the wine. The rough, irregular stones of the street, pointing every way, and designed, one might have thought, expressly to lame all living creatures that approached them, had dammed it into little pools; these were surrounded, each by its own jostling group or crowd, according to its size. Some men kneeled down, made scoops of their two hands joined, and sipped, or tried to help women, who bent over their shoulders, to sip, before the wine had all run out between their fingers. Others, men and women, dipped in the puddles with little mugs of mutilated earthenware, or even with handkerchiefs from women's heads, which were squeezed dry into infants' mouths; others made small mud embankments, to stem the wine as it ran; others, directed by lookers-on up at high windows, darted here and there, to cut off little streams of wine that started away in new directions; others devoted themselves to the sodden and lee-dyed pieces of the cask, licking, and even champing the moister wine-rotted fragments with eager relish. There was no drainage to carry off the wine, and not only did it all get taken up, but so much mud got taken up along with it, that there might have been a scavenger in the street, if anybody acquainted with it could have believed in such a miraculous presence.

A shrill sound of laughter and of amused voices—voices of men, women, and children—resounded in the street while this wine game lasted. There was little roughness in the sport, and much playfulness. There was a special companionship in it, an observable inclination on the part of every one to join some other one, which led, especially among the luckier or lighter-hearted, to froliscome embraces, drinking of healths, shaking of hands, and even joining of hands and dancing, a dozen together. When the wine was gone, and the places where it had been most abundant were raked into a gridiron pattern by fingers, these demonstrations ceased, as suddenly as they had broken out. The man who had left his saw sticking in the firewood he was cutting, set it in motion again; the woman who had left on a doorstep the little pot of hot ashes, at which she had been trying to soften the pain in her own starved fingers and toes, or in those of her child, returned to it; men with bare arms, matted locks, and cadaverous faces, who had emerged into the winter light from cellars, moved away, to descend again; and a gloom gathered on the scene that appeared more natural to it than sunshine.

The wine was red wine, and had stained the ground of the narrow street in the suburb of Saint Antoine, in Paris, where it was spilled. It had stained many hands, too, and many faces, and many naked feet, and many wooden shoes. The hands of the man who sawed the wood left red marks on the billets; and the forehead of the woman who nursed her baby was stained with the stain of the old rag she wound about her head again. Those who had been greedy with the staves of the cask, had acquired a tigerish smear about the mouth; and one tall joker so besmirched, his head more out of a long squalid bag of a nightcap than in it, scrawled upon a wall with his finger dipped in muddy wine-lees—BLOOD.

The time was to come, when that wine too would be spilled on the street-stones, and when the stain of it would be red upon many there.

And now that the cloud settled on Saint Antoine, which a momentary gleam had driven from his sacred countenance, the darkness of it was heavy—cold, dirt, sickness, ignorance, and want, were the lords in waiting on the saintly presence—nobles of great power all of them; but, most especially, the last. Samples of a people that had undergone a terrible grinding and re-grinding in the mill, and certainly not in the fabulous mill which ground old people young, shivered at every corner, passed in and out at every doorway, looked from every window, fluttered in every vestige of a garment that the wind shook. The mill which had worked them down was the mill that grinds young people old; the children had ancient faces and grave voices; and upon them, and upon the grown faces, and ploughed into every furrow of age and coming up afresh, was the sign, Hunger. It was prevalent everywhere. Hunger was pushed out of the tall houses, in the wretched clothing that hung upon poles and lines; Hunger was patched into them with straw and rag and wood and paper; Hunger was repeated in every fragment of the small modicum of firewood that the man sawed off; Hunger stared down from the smokeless chimneys, and started up from the filthy street that had no offal, among its refuse, of anything to eat. Hunger was the inscription on the baker's shelves, written in every small loaf of his scanty stock of bad bread; at the sausage-shop, in every dead-dog preparation that was offered for sale. Hunger rattled its dry bones among the roasting chestnuts in the turned cylinder; Hunger was shred into atomies in every farthing porringer of husky chips of potato, fired with some reluctant drops of oil.

Its abiding place was in all things fitted to it. A narrow winding street, full of offence and stench, with other narrow winding streets diverging, all peopled by rags and nightcaps, and all smelling of rags and nightcaps, and all visible things with a brooding look upon them that looked ill. In the hunted air of the people there was yet some wild-beast thought of the possibility of turning at bay. Depressed and slinking though they were, eyes of fire were not wanting among them; nor compressed lips, white with what they suppressed; nor foreheads knitted into the likeness of the gallows-rope they mused about enduring, or inflicting. The trade signs (and they were almost as many as the shops) were, all, grim illustrations of Want. The butcher and the porkman painted up only the leanest scrags of meat; the baker, the coarsest of meagre loaves. The people rudely pictured as drinking in the wine-shops, croaked over their scanty measures of thin wine and beer, and were gloweringly confidential together. Nothing was represented in a flourishing condition, save tools and weapons; but, the cutler's knives and axes were sharp and bright, the smith's hammers were heavy, and the gunmaker's stock was murderous. The crippling stones of the pavement, with their many little reservoirs of mud and water, had no footways, but broke off abruptly at the doors. The kennel, to make amends, ran down the middle of the street—when it ran at all: which was only after heavy rains, and then it ran, by many eccentric fits, into the houses. Across the streets, at wide intervals, one clumsy lamp was slung by a rope and pulley; at night, when the lamplighter had let these down, and lighted, and hoisted them again, a feeble grove of dim wicks swung in a sickly manner overhead, as if they were at sea. Indeed they were at sea, and the ship and crew were in peril of tempest.

For, the time was to come, when the gaunt scarecrows of that region should have watched the lamplighter, in their idleness and hunger, so long as to conceive the idea of improving on his method, and hauling up men by those ropes and pulleys, to flare upon the darkness of their condition. But, the time was not come yet; and every wind that blew over France shook the rags of the scarecrows in vain, for the birds, fine of song and feather, took no warning.

The wine-shop was a corner shop, better than most others in its appearance and degree, and the master of the wine-shop had stood outside it, in a yellow waistcoat and green breeches, looking on at the struggle for the lost wine. "It's not my affair," said he, with a final shrug of the shoulders. "The people from the market did it. Let them bring another."

There, his eyes happening to catch the tall joker writing up his joke, he called to him across the way:

"Say, then, my Gaspard, what do you do there?"

The fellow pointed to his joke with immense significance, as is often the way with his tribe. It missed its mark, and completely failed, as is often the way with his tribe too.

"What now? Are you a subject for the mad hospital?" said the wine-shop keeper, crossing the road, and obliterating the jest with a handful of mud, picked up for the purpose, and smeared over it. "Why do you write in the public streets? Is there—tell me thou—is there no other place to write such words in?"

In his expostulation he dropped his cleaner hand (perhaps accidentally, perhaps not) upon the joker's heart. The joker rapped it with his own, took a nimble spring upward, and came down in a fantastic dancing attitude, with one of his stained shoes jerked off his foot into his hand, and held out. A joker of an extremely, not to say wolfishly practical character he looked, under those circumstances.

"Put it on, put it on," said the other. "Call wine, wine; and finish there." With that advice, he wiped his soiled hand upon the joker's dress, such as it was—quite deliberately, as having dirtied the hand on his account; and then re-crossed the road and entered the wine-shop.

This wine-shop keeper was a bull-necked, martial-looking man of thirty, and he should have been of a hot temperament, for, although it was a bitter day, he wore no coat, but carried one slung over his shoulder. His shirt-sleeves were rolled up, too, and his brown arms were bare to the elbows. Neither did he wear anything more on his head than his own crisply-curling short dark hair. He was a dark man altogether, with good eyes and a good bold breadth between them. Good-humoured looking on the whole, but implacable-looking, too; evidently a man of a strong resolution and a set purpose; a man not desirable to be met, rushing down a narrow pass with a gulf on either side, for nothing would turn the man.

Madame Defarge, his wife, sat in the shop behind the counter as he came in. Madame Defarge was a stout woman of about his own age, with a watchful eye that seldom seemed to look at anything, a large hand heavily ringed, a steady face, strong features, and great composure of manner. There was a character about Madame Defarge, from which one might have predicated that she did not often make mistakes against herself in any of the reckonings over which she presided. Madame Defarge, being sensitive to cold, was wrapped in fur, and had a quantity of bright shawl twined about her head, though not to the concealment of her large earrings. Her knitting was before her, but she had laid it down to pick her teeth with a toothpick. Thus engaged, with her right elbow supported by her left hand, Madame Defarge said nothing when her lord came in, but coughed just one grain of cough. This, in combination with the lifting of her darkly defined eyebrows over her toothpick by the breadth of a line, suggested to her husband that he would do well to look round the shop among the customers, for any new customer who had dropped in while he stepped over the way.

The wine-shop keeper accordingly rolled his eyes about, until they rested upon an elderly gentleman and a young lady, who were seated in a corner. Other company were there: two playing cards, two playing dominoes, three standing by the counter lengthening out a short supply of wine. As he passed behind the counter, he took notice that the elderly gentleman said in a look to the young lady, "This is our man."

"What the devil do *you* do in that galley there?" said Monsieur Defarge to himself; "I don't know you."

But, he feigned not to notice the two strangers, and fell into discourse with the triumvirate of customers who were drinking at the counter.

"How goes it, Jacques?" said one of these three to Monsieur Defarge. "Is all the spilt wine swallowed?"

"Every drop, Jacques," answered Monsieur Defarge.

When this interchange of Christian name was effected, Madame Defarge, picking her teeth with her toothpick, coughed another grain of cough, and raised her eyebrows by the breadth of another line.

"It is not often," said the second of the three, addressing Monsieur Defarge, "that many of these miserable beasts know the taste of wine, or of anything but black bread and death. Is it not so, Jacques?"

"It is so, Jacques," Monsieur Defarge returned.

At this second interchange of the Christian name, Madame Defarge, still using her toothpick with profound composure, coughed another grain of cough, and raised her eyebrows by the breadth of another line.

The last of the three now said his say, as he put down his empty drinking vessel, and smacked his lips.

"Ah! So much the worse! A bitter taste it is that such poor cattle always have in their mouths, and hard lives they live, Jacques. Am I right, Jacques?"

"You are right, Jacques," was the response of Monsieur Defarge.

This third interchange of the Christian name was completed at the moment when Madame Defarge put her toothpick by, kept her eyebrows up, and slightly rustled in her seat.

"Hold then! True!" muttered her husband. "Gentlemen—my wife!"

The three customers pulled off their hats to Madame Defarge, with three flourishes. She acknowledged their homage by bending her head, and giving them a quick look. Then she glanced in a casual manner round the wine-shop, took up her knitting with great apparent calmness and repose of spirit, and became absorbed in it.

"Gentlemen," said her husband, who had kept his bright eye observantly upon her, "good day. The chamber, furnished bachelor-fashion, that you wished to see, and were inquiring for when I stepped out, is on the fifth floor. The doorway of the staircase gives on the little courtyard close to the left here," pointing with his hand, "near to the window of my establishment. But, now that I remember, one of you has already been there, and can show the way. Gentlemen, adieu!"

They paid for their wine, and left the place. The eyes of Monsieur Defarge were studying his wife at her knitting, when the elderly gentleman advanced from his corner, and begged the favour of a word.

"Willingly, sir," said Monsieur Defarge, and quietly stepped with him to the door.

Their conference was very short, but very decided. Almost at the first word, Monsieur Defarge started and became deeply attentive. It had not lasted a minute, when he nodded and went out. The gentleman then beckoned to the young lady, and they, too, went out. Madame Defarge knitted with nimble fingers and steady eyebrows, and saw nothing.

Mr. Jarvis Lorry and Miss Manette, emerging from the wine-shop thus, joined Monsieur Defarge in the doorway to which he had directed his other company just before. It opened from a stinking little black courtyard, and was the general public entrance to a great pile of houses, inhabited by a great number of people. In the gloomy tile-paved entry to the gloomy tile-paved staircase, Monsieur Defarge bent down on one knee to the child of his old master, and put her hand to his lips. It was a gentle action, but not at all gently done; a very remarkable transformation had come over him in a few seconds. He had no good-humour in his face, nor any openness of aspect left, but had become a secret, angry, dangerous man.

"It is very high; it is a little difficult. Better to begin slowly." Thus Monsieur Defarge, in a stern voice, to Mr. Lorry, as they began ascending the stairs.

"Is he alone?" the latter whispered.

"Alone! God help him, who should be with him?" said the other, in the same low voice.

"Is he always alone, then?"

"Yes."

"Of his own desire?"

"Of his own necessity. As he was, when I first saw him after they found me and demanded to know if I would take him, and, at my peril, be discreet—as he was then, so he is now." 5

"He is greatly changed?"

"Changed!"

The keeper of the wine-shop stopped to strike the wall with his hand, and mutter a tremendous curse. No direct answer could have been half so forcible. Mr. Lorry's spirits grew heavier and heavier, as he and his two companions ascended higher and higher.

Such a staircase, with its accessories, in the older and more crowded parts of Paris, would be bad enough now; but, at that time, it was vile indeed to unaccustomed and unhardened senses. Every little habitation within the great foul nest of one high 15 building—that is to say, the room or rooms within every door that opened on the general staircase—left its own heap of refuse on its own landing, besides flinging other refuse from its own windows. The uncontrollable and hopeless mass of decomposition so engendered would have polluted the air, even if poverty and deprivation had not loaded it with their intangible impurities; the two bad sources combined made it almost insupportable. Through such an atmosphere, by a steep dark shaft of dirt and poison, the way lay. Yielding to his own disturbance of mind, and to his young companion's agitation, which became greater every instant, Mr. 25 Jarvis Lorry twice stopped to rest. Each of these stoppages was made at a doleful grating, by which any languishing good airs that were left uncorrupted seemed to escape, and all spoilt and sickly vapours seemed to crawl in. Through the rusted bars, tastes, rather than glimpses, were caught of the jumbled neighbourhood; and nothing within range, nearer or lower than the summits of the two great towers of Notre Dame, had any promise on it of healthy life or wholesome aspirations.

At last, the top of the staircase was gained, and they stopped for the third time. There was yet an upper staircase, of a steeper 35 inclination and of contracted dimensions, to be ascended, before the garret story was reached. The keeper of the wine-shop, always going a little in advance, and always going on the side which Mr. Lorry took, as though he dreaded to be asked any questions by the

young lady, turned himself about here, and, carefully feeling in the
pockets of the coat he carried over his shoulder, took out a key.

"The door is locked then, my friend?" said Mr. Lorry, surprised.

"Ay. Yes," was the grim reply of Monsieur Defarge.

5   "You think it necessary to keep the unfortunate gentleman so
retired?"

"I think it necessary to turn the key." Monsieur Defarge whispered it closer in his ear, and frowned heavily.

"Why?"

"Why! Because he has lived so long, locked up, that he would be
frightened—rave—tear himself to pieces—die—come to I know
not what harm—if his door was left open."

"Is it possible?" exclaimed Mr. Lorry.

"Is it possible?" repeated Defarge, bitterly. "Yes. And a beautiful
15   world we live in, when it *is* possible, and when many other such
things are possible, and not only possible, but done—done, see
you!—under that sky there, every day. Long live the Devil. Let us
go on."

This dialogue had been held in so very low a whisper, that not a
word of it had reached the young lady's ears. But, by this time she
trembled under such strong emotion, and her face expressed such
deep anxiety, and, above all, such dread and terror, that Mr. Lorry
felt it incumbent on him to speak a word or two of reassurance.

"Courage, dear miss! Courage! Business! The worst will be over
25   in a moment; it is but passing the room-door, and the worst is over.
Then, all the good you bring to him, all the relief, all the happiness
you bring to him, begin. Let our good friend here assist you on that
side. That's well, friend Defarge. Come, now. Business, business!"

They went up slowly and softly. The staircase was short, and they
were soon at the top. There, as it had an abrupt turn in it, they
came all at once in sight of three men, whose heads were bent
down close together at the side of a door, and who were intently
looking into the room to which the door belonged, through some
chinks or holes in the wall. On hearing footsteps close at hand,
35   these three turned, and rose, and showed themselves to be the three
of one name who had been drinking in the wine-shop.

"I forgot them in the surprise of your visit," explained Monsieur
Defarge. "Leave us, good boys; we have business here."

The three glided by, and went silently down.

There appearing to be no other door on that floor, and the keeper of the wine-shop going straight to this one when they were left alone, Mr. Lorry asked him in a whisper, with a little anger:

"Do you make a show of Monsieur Manette?"

"I show him, in the way you have seen, to a chosen few."

"Is that well?"

"I think it is well."

"Who are the few? How do you choose them?"

"I choose them as real men, of my name—Jacques is my name—to whom the sight is likely to do good. Enough: you are English; that is another thing. Stay there, if you please, a little moment."

With an admonitory gesture to keep them back, he stooped, and looked in through the crevice in the wall. Soon raising his head again, he struck twice or thrice upon the door—evidently with no other object than to make a noise there. With the same intention, he drew the key across it, three or four times, before he put it clumsily into the lock, and turned it as heavily as he could.

The door slowly opened inward under his hand, and he looked into the room and said something. A faint voice answered something. Little more than a single syllable could have been spoken on either side.

He looked back over his shoulder, and beckoned them to enter. Mr. Lorry got his arm securely round the daughter's waist, and held her; for he felt that she was sinking.

"A—a—a—business, business!" he urged, with a moisture that was not of business shining on his cheek. "Come in, come in!"

"I am afraid of it," she answered, shuddering.

"Of it? What?"

"I mean of him. Of my father."

Rendered in a manner desperate, by her state and by the beckoning of their conductor, he drew over his neck the arm that shook upon his shoulder, lifted her a little, and hurried her into the room. He set her down just within the door, and held her, clinging to him.

Defarge drew out the key, closed the door, locked it on the inside, took out the key again, and held it in his hand. All this he did, methodically, and with as loud and harsh an accompaniment of noise as he could make. Finally, he walked across the room with a measured tread to where the window was. He stopped there, and faced around.

The garret, built to be a depository for firewood and the like, was dim and dark: for the window of dormer shape was in truth a door
5   in the roof, with a little crane over it for the hoisting up of stores from the street: unglazed, and closing up the middle in two pieces, like any other door of French construction. To exclude the cold, one half of this door was fast closed, and the other was opened but a very little way. Such a scanty portion of light was admitted through these means, that it was difficult, on first coming in, to see anything; and long habit alone could have slowly formed in any one, the ability to do any work requiring nicety in such obscurity. Yet, work of that kind was being done in the garret; for, with his back towards the door, and his face towards the window where the
15   keeper of the wine-shop stood looking at him, a white-haired man sat on a low bench, stooping forward and very busy, making shoes.

Chapter 6. The Shoemaker

"Good day!" said Monsieur Defarge, looking down at the white head that bent low over the shoemaking.

It was raised for a moment, and a very faint voice responded to the salutation, as if it were at a distance:

"Good day!"

"You are still hard at work, I see?"

After a long silence, the head was lifted for another moment, and the voice replied, "Yes—I am working." This time, a pair of haggard
25   eyes had looked at the questioner, before the face had dropped again.

The faintness of the voice was pitiable and dreadful. It was not the faintness of physical weakness, though confinement and hard fare no doubt had their part in it. Its deplorable peculiarity was, that it was the faintness of solitude and disuse. It was like the last feeble echo of a sound made long and long ago. So entirely had it lost the life and resonance of the human voice, that it affected the senses like a once beautiful colour faded away into a poor weak stain. So sunken and suppressed it was, that it was like a voice underground. So expressive it was, of a hopeless and lost creature, that a famished traveller, wearied out by lonely wandering in a wilderness, would have remembered home and friends in such a tone before lying down to die.

Some minutes of silent work had passed, and the haggard eyes had looked up again; not with any interest or curiosity, but with a dull mechanical perception, beforehand, that the spot where the only visitor they were aware of had stood, was not yet empty.

"I want," said Defarge, who had not removed his gaze from the shoemaker, "to let in a little more light here. You can bear a little more?"

The shoemaker stopped his work; looked with a vacant air of listening, at the floor on one side of him; then similarly, at the floor on the other side of him; then upward at the speaker.

"What did you say?"

"You can bear a little more light?"

"I must bear it, if you let it in." (Laying the palest shadow of a stress upon the second word.)

The opened half-door was opened a little further, and secured at that angle for the time. A broad ray of light fell into the garret, and showed the workman with an unfinished shoe upon his lap, pausing in his labour. His few common tools and various scraps of leather were at his feet and on his bench. He had a white beard, raggedly cut, but not very long, a hollow face, and exceedingly bright eyes. The hollowness and thinness of his face would have caused them to look large, under his yet dark eyebrows and his confused white hair, though they had been really otherwise; but, they were naturally large, and looked unnaturally so. His yellow rags of shirt lay open at the throat, and showed his body to be withered and worn. He, and his old canvas frock, and his loose stockings, and all his poor tatters of clothes, had, in a long seclusion from direct light and air, faded down to such a dull uniformity of parchment-yellow, that it would have been hard to say which was which.

He had put up a hand between his eyes and the light, and the very bones of it seemed transparent. So he sat, with a steadfastly vacant gaze, pausing in his work. He never looked at the figure before him, without first looking down on this side of himself, then on that, as if he had lost the habit of associating place with sound;

he never spoke, without first wandering in this manner, and forgetting to speak.

"Are you going to finish that pair of shoes to-day?" asked Defarge, motioning to Mr. Lorry to come forward.

5   "What did you say?"

"Do you mean to finish that pair of shoes to-day?"

"I can't say that I mean to. I suppose so. I don't know."

But, the question reminded him of his work, and he bent over it again.

Mr. Lorry came silently forward, leaving the daughter by the door. When he had stood, for a minute or two, by the side of Defarge, the shoemaker looked up. He showed no surprise at seeing another figure, but the unsteady fingers of one of his hands strayed to his lips as he looked at it (his lips and his nails were of the same 15   pale lead-colour), and then the hand dropped to his work, and he once more bent over the shoe. The look and the action had occupied but an instant.

"You have a visitor, you see," said Monsieur Defarge.

"What did you say?"

"Here is a visitor."

The shoemaker looked up as before, but without removing a hand from his work.

"Come!" said Defarge. "Here is monsieur, who knows a well-made shoe when he sees one. Show him that shoe you are working 25   at. Take it, monsieur."

Mr. Lorry took it in his hand.

"Tell monsieur what kind of shoe it is, and the maker's name."

There was a longer pause than usual, before the shoemaker replied:

"I forget what it was you asked me. What did you say?"

"I said, couldn't you describe the kind of shoe, for monsieur's information?"

"It is a lady's shoe. It is a young lady's walking-shoe. It is in the present mode. I never saw the mode. I have had a pattern in my 35   hand." He glanced at the shoe with some little passing touch of pride.

"And the maker's name?" said Defarge.

Now that he had no work to hold, he laid the knuckles of the right hand in the hollow of the left, and then the knuckles of the left hand in the hollow of the right, and then passed a hand across his bearded chin, and so on in regular changes, without a moment's intermission. The task of recalling him from the vacancy into which he always sank when he had spoken was like recalling some very weak person from a swoon, or endeavouring, in the hope of some disclosure, to stay the spirit of a fast-dying man.

"Did you ask me for my name?"

"Assuredly I did."

"One Hundred and Five, North Tower."

"Is that all?"

"One Hundred and Five, North Tower."

With a weary sound that was not a sigh, nor a groan, he bent to work again, until the silence was again broken.

"You are not a shoemaker by trade?" said Mr. Lorry, looking steadfastly at him.

His haggard eyes turned to Defarge as if he would have transferred the question to him: but as no help came from that quarter, they turned back on the questioner when they had sought the ground.

"I am not a shoemaker by trade? No, I was not a shoemaker by trade. I—I learnt it here. I taught myself. I asked leave to—"

He lapsed away, even for minutes, ringing those measured changes on his hands the whole time. His eyes came slowly back, at last, to the face from which they had wandered; when they rested on it, he started, and resumed, in the manner of a sleeper that moment awake, reverting to a subject of last night.

"I asked leave to teach myself, and I got it with much difficulty after a long while, and I have made shoes ever since."

As he held out his hand for the shoe that had been taken from him, Mr. Lorry said, still looking steadfastly in his face:

"Monsieur Manette, do you remember nothing of me?"

The shoe dropped to the ground, and he sat looking fixedly at the questioner.

"Monsieur Manette"—Mr. Lorry laid his hand upon Defarge's arm—"do you remember nothing of this man? Look at him. Look at me. Is there no old banker, no old business, no old servant, no old time, rising in your mind, Monsieur Manette?"

As the captive of many years sat looking fixedly, by turns, at Mr. Lorry and Defarge, some long-obliterated marks of an actively intent intelligence in the middle of the forehead, gradually forced themselves through the black mist that had fallen on him. They were overclouded again, they were fainter, they were gone; but they had been there. And so exactly was the expression repeated on the fair young face of her who had crept along the wall to a point where she could see him, and where she now stood looking at him, with hands which at first had been only raised in frightened compassion, if not even to keep him off and shut out the sight of him, but which were now extending towards him, trembling with eagerness to lay the spectral face upon her warm young breast, and love it back to life and hope—so exactly was the expression repeated (though in stronger characters) on her fair young face, that it looked as though it had passed like a moving light, from him to her.

Darkness had fallen on him in its place. He looked at the two, less and less attentively, and his eyes in gloomy abstraction sought the ground and looked about him in the old way. Finally, with a deep long sigh, he took the shoe up, and resumed his work.

"Have you recognised him, monsieur?" asked Defarge in a whisper.

"Yes; for a moment. At first I thought it quite hopeless, but I have unquestionably seen, for a single moment, the face that I once knew so well. Hush! Let us draw further back. Hush!"

She had moved from the wall of the garret, very near to the bench on which he sat. There was something awful in his unconsciousness of the figure that could have put out its hand and touched him as he stooped over his labour.

Not a word was spoken, not a sound was made. She stood, like a spirit, beside him, and he bent over his work.

It happened, at length, that he had occasion to change the instrument in his hand, for his shoemaker's knife. It lay on that side of him which was not the side on which she stood. He had taken it up, and was stooping to work again, when his eyes caught the skirt of her dress. He raised them, and saw her face. The two spectators started forward, but she stayed them with a motion of her hand. She had no fear of his striking at her with the knife, though they had.

He stared at her with a fearful look, and after a while his lips began to form some words, though no sound proceeded from them.

By degrees, in the pauses of his quick and laboured breathing, he was heard to say:

"What is this?"

With the tears streaming down her face, she put her two hands to her lips, and kissed them to him; then clasped them on her breast, as if she laid his ruined head there.

"You are not the gaoler's daughter?"

She sighed, "No."

"Who are you?"

Not yet trusting the tones of her voice, she sat down on the bench beside him. He recoiled, but she laid her hand upon his arm. A strange thrill struck him when she did so, and visibly passed over his frame; he laid the knife down softly, as he sat staring at her.

Her golden hair, which she wore in long curls, had been hurriedly pushed aside, and fell down over her neck. Advancing his hand by little and little, he took it up and looked at it. In the midst of the action he went astray, and, with another deep sigh, fell to work at his shoemaking.

But not for long. Releasing his arm, she laid her hand upon his shoulder. After looking doubtfully at it, two or three times, as if to be sure that it was really there, he laid down his work, put his hand to his neck, and took off a blackened string with a scrap of folded rag attached to it. He opened this, carefully, on his knee, and it contained a very little quantity of hair: not more than one or two long golden hairs, which he had, in some old day, wound off upon his finger.

He took her hair into his hand again, and looked closely at it. "It is the same. How can it be! When was it! How was it!"

As the concentrating expression returned to his forehead, he seemed to become conscious that it was in hers too. He turned her full to the light, and looked at her.

"She had laid her head upon my shoulder, that night when I was summoned out—she had a fear of my going, though I had none—and when I was brought to the North Tower they found these upon my sleeve. 'You will leave me them? They can never help me to escape in the body, though they may in the spirit.' Those were the words I said. I remember them very well."

He formed this speech with his lips many times before he could utter it. But when he did find spoken words for it, they came to him coherently, though slowly.

"How was this?—*Was it you?*"

Once more, the two spectators started, as he turned upon her with a frightful suddenness. But she sat perfectly still in his grasp, and only said, in a low voice, "I entreat you, good gentlemen, do not come near us, do not speak, do not move!"

"Hark!" he exclaimed. "Whose voice was that?"

His hands released her as he uttered this cry, and went up to his white hair, which they tore in a frenzy. It died out, as everything but his shoemaking did die out of him, and he refolded his little packet and tried to secure it in his breast; but he still looked at her, and gloomily shook his head.

"No, no, no; you are too young, too blooming. It can't be. See what the prisoner is. These are not the hands she knew, this is not the face she knew, this is not a voice she ever heard. No, no. She was—and he was—before the slow years of the North Tower—ages ago. What is your name, my gentle angel?"

Hailing his softened tone and manner, his daughter fell upon her knees before him, with her appealing hands upon his breast.

"O, sir, at another time you shall know my name, and who my mother was, and who my father, and how I never knew their hard, hard history. But I cannot tell you at this time, and I cannot tell you here. All that I may tell you, here and now, is, that I pray to you to touch me and to bless me. Kiss me, kiss me! O my dear, my dear!"

His cold white head mingled with her radiant hair, which warmed and lighted it as though it were the light of Freedom shining on him.

"If you hear in my voice—I don't know that it is so, but I hope it is—if you hear in my voice any resemblance to a voice that once was sweet music in your ears, weep for it, weep for it! If you touch, in touching my hair, anything that recalls a beloved head that lay on your breast when you were young and free, weep for it, weep for it! If, when I hint to you of a Home that is before us, where I will be true to you with all my duty and with all my faithful service, I bring back the remembrance of a Home long desolate, while your poor heart pined away, weep for it, weep for it!"

She held him closer round the neck, and rocked him on her breast like a child.

"If, when I tell you, dearest dear, that your agony is over, and
that I have come here to take you from it, and that we go to
England to be at peace and at rest, I cause you to think of your
useful life laid waste, and of our native France so wicked to you,
weep for it, weep for it! And if, when I shall tell you of my name,
and of my father who is living, and of my mother who is dead, you
learn that I have to kneel to my honoured father, and implore his
pardon for having never for his sake striven all day and lain awake
and wept all night, because the love of my poor mother hid his
torture from me, weep for it, weep for it! Weep for her, then, and
for me! Good gentlemen, thank God! I feel his sacred tears upon
my face, and his sobs strike against my heart. O, see! Thank God
for us, thank God!"

He had sunk in her arms, and his face dropped on her breast: a
sight so touching, yet so terrible in the tremendous wrong and
suffering which had gone before it, that the two beholders covered
their faces.

When the quiet of the garret had been long undisturbed, and his
heaving breast and shaken form had long yielded to the calm that
must follow all storms—emblem to humanity, of the rest and silence into which the storm called Life must hush at last—they
came forward to raise the father and daughter from the ground.
He had gradually dropped to the floor, and lay there in a lethargy,
worn out. She had nestled down with him, that his head might lie
upon her arm; and her hair drooping over him curtained him from
the light.

"If, without disturbing him," she said, raising her hand to Mr.
Lorry as he stooped over them, after repeated blowings of his nose,
"all could be arranged for our leaving Paris at once, so that, from
the very door, he could be taken away—"

"But, consider. Is he fit for the journey?" asked Mr. Lorry.

"More fit for that, I think, than to remain in this city, so
dreadful to him."

"It is true," said Defarge, who was kneeling to look on and hear.
"More than that; Monsieur Manette is, for all reasons, best out of
France. Say, shall I hire a carriage and post-horses?"

"That's business," said Mr. Lorry, resuming on the shortest
notice his methodical manners; "and if business is to be done, I had
better do it."

"Then be so kind," urged Miss Manette, "as to leave us here.

You see how composed he has become, and you cannot be afraid to leave him with me now. Why should you be? If you will lock the door to secure us from interruption, I do not doubt that you will find him, when you come back, as quiet as you leave him. In any case, I will take care of him until you return, and then we will remove him straight."

Both Mr. Lorry and Defarge were rather disinclined to this course, and in favour of one of them remaining. But, as there were not only carriage and horses to be seen to, but travelling papers; and as time pressed, for the day was drawing to an end, it came at last to their hastily dividing the business that was necessary to be done, and hurrying away to do it.

Then, as the darkness closed in, the daughter laid her head down on the hard ground close at the father's side, and watched him. The darkness deepened and deepened, and they both lay quiet, until a light gleamed through the chinks in the wall.

Mr. Lorry and Monsieur Defarge had made all ready for the journey, and had brought with them, besides travelling cloaks and wrappers, bread and meat, wine, and hot coffee. Monsieur Defarge put this provender, and the lamp he carried, on the shoemaker's bench (there was nothing else in the garret but a pallet bed), and he and Mr. Lorry roused the captive, and assisted him to his feet.

No human intelligence could have read the mysteries of his mind, in the scared blank wonder of his face. Whether he knew what had happened, whether he recollected what they had said to him, whether he knew that he was free, were questions which no sagacity could have solved. They tried speaking to him; but, he was so confused, and so very slow to answer, that they took fright at his bewilderment, and agreed for the time to tamper with him no more. He had a wild, lost manner of occasionally clasping his head in his hands, that had not been seen in him before; yet, he had some pleasure in the mere sound of his daughter's voice, and invariably turned to it when she spoke.

In the submissive way of one long accustomed to obey under coercion, he ate and drank what they gave him to eat and drink, and put on the cloak and other wrappings that they gave him to wear. He readily responded to his daughter's drawing her arm through his, and took—and kept—her hand in both his own.

They began to descend; Monsieur Defarge going first with the lamp, Mr. Lorry closing the little procession. They had not traversed many steps of the long main staircase when he stopped, and stared at the roof and round at the walls.

"You remember the place, my father? You remember coming up here?"   5

"What did you say?"

But, before she could repeat the question, he murmured an answer as if she had repeated it.

"Remember? No, I don't remember. It was so very long ago."

That he had no recollection whatever of his having been brought from his prison to that house was apparent to them. They heard him mutter, "One Hundred and Five, North Tower"; and when he looked about him, it evidently was for the strong fortress-walls which had long encompassed him. On their reaching the courtyard he instinctively altered his tread, as being in expectation of a draw-   15
bridge; and when there was no drawbridge, and he saw the carriage waiting in the open street, he dropped his daughter's hand and clasped his head again.

No crowd was about the door; no people were discernible at any of the many windows; not even a chance passer-by was in the street. An unnatural silence and desertion reigned there. Only one soul was to be seen, and that was Madame Defarge—who leaned against the door-post, knitting, and saw nothing.

The prisoner had got into a coach, and his daughter had followed him, when Mr. Lorry's feet were arrested on the step by his   25
asking, miserably, for his shoemaking tools and the unfinished shoes. Madame Defarge immediately called to her husband that she would get them, and went, knitting, out of the lamplight, through the courtyard. She quickly brought them down and handed them in—and immediately afterwards leaned against the door-post, knitting, and saw nothing.

Defarge got upon the box, and gave the word "To the Barrier!" The postilion cracked his whip, and they clattered away under the feeble over-swinging lamps.

Under the over-swinging lamps—swinging ever brighter in the   35
better streets, and ever dimmer in the worse—and by lighted shops, gay crowds, illuminated coffee-houses, and theatre-doors, to one of the city gates. Soldiers with lanterns, at the guard-house there. "Your papers, travellers!" "See here then, Monsieur the Officer,"

said Defarge, getting down and taking him gravely apart, "these are
the papers of monsieur inside, with the white head. They were
consigned to me, with him, at the—" He dropped his voice, there
was a flutter among the military lanterns, and one of them being
5   handed into the coach by an arm in uniform, the eyes connected
with the arm looked, not an every-day or an every-night look, at
monsieur with the white head. "It is well. Forward!" from the
uniform. "Adieu!" from Defarge. And so, under a short grove of
feebler and feebler over-swinging lamps, out under the great groves
of stars.

Beneath that arch of unmoved and eternal lights; some, so
remote from this little earth that the learned tell us it is doubtful
whether their rays have even yet discovered it, as a point in space
where anything is suffered or done: the shadows of the night were
15   broad and black. All through the cold and restless interval, until
dawn, they once more whispered in the ears of Mr. Jarvis Lorry—
sitting opposite the buried man who had been dug out, and
wondering what subtle powers were for ever lost to him, and what
were capable of restoration—the old inquiry:

"I hope you care to be recalled to life?"

And the old answer:

"I can't say."

BOOK THE SECOND: THE GOLDEN THREAD

Chapter 1. Five Years Later

Tellson's Bank by Temple Bar was an old-fashioned place, even in the year one thousand seven hundred and eighty. It was very small, very dark, very ugly, very incommodious. It was an old-fashioned place, moreover, in the moral attribute that the partners in the House were proud of its smallness, proud of its darkness, proud of its ugliness, proud of its incommodiousness. They were even boastful of its eminence in those particulars, and were fired by an express conviction that, if it were less objectionable, it would be less respectable. This was no passive belief, but an active weapon which they flashed at more convenient places of business. Tellson's, (they said) wanted no elbow-room, Tellson's wanted no light, Tellson's wanted no embellishment. Noakes and Co.'s might, or Snooks Brothers' might; but Tellson's, thank Heaven!—

Any one of these partners would have disinherited his son on the question of rebuilding Tellson's. In this respect the House was much on a par with the Country, which did very often disinherit its sons for suggesting improvements in laws and customs that had long been highly objectionable, but were only the more respectable.

Thus it had come to pass, that Tellson's was the triumphant perfection of inconvenience. After bursting open a door of idiotic obstinacy, with a weak rattle in its throat, you fell into Tellson's down two steps, and came to your senses in a miserable little shop, with two little counters, where the oldest of men made your cheque shake as if the wind rustled it, while they examined the signature by the dingiest of windows, which were always under a

45

shower-bath of mud from Fleet Street, and which were made the
dingier by their own iron bars proper, and the heavy shadow of
Temple Bar. If your business necessitated your seeing "the House,"
you were put into a species of Condemned Hold at the back, where
5　you meditated on a misspent life, until the House came with its
hands in its pockets, and you could hardly blink at it in the dismal
twilight. Your money came out of, or went into, wormy old
wooden drawers, particles of which flew up your nose and down
your throat when they were opened and shut. Your bank-notes had
a musty odour, as if they were fast decomposing into rags again.
Your plate was stowed away among the neighbouring cesspools, and
evil communications corrupted its good polish in a day or two.
Your deeds got into extemporised strong-rooms made of kitchens
and sculleries, and fretted all the fat out of their parchments into
15　the banking-house air. Your lighter boxes of family papers went
upstairs into a Barmecide room, that always had a great dining-table
in it and never had a dinner, and where, even in the year one
thousand seven hundred and eighty, the first letters written to you
by your old love, or by your little children, were but newly released
from the horror of being ogled through the windows, by the heads
exposed on Temple Bar with an insensate brutality and ferocity
worthy of Abyssinia or Ashantee.

But indeed, at that time, putting to death was a recipe much in
vogue with all trades and professions, and not least of all with
25　Tellson's. Death is Nature's remedy for all things, and why not
Legislation's? Accordingly, the forger was put to Death; the utterer
of a bad note was put to Death; the unlawful opener of a letter was
put to Death; the purloiner of forty shillings and sixpence was put
to Death; the holder of a horse at Tellson's door, who made off
with it, was put to Death; the coiner of a bad shilling was put to
Death; the sounders of three-fourths of the notes in the whole
gamut of Crime were put to Death. Not that it did the least good
in the way of prevention—it might almost have been worth remarking that the fact was exactly the reverse—but, it cleared off
35　(as to this world) the trouble of each particular case, and left nothing else connected with it to be looked after. Thus, Tellson's, in its
day, like greater places of business, its contemporaries, had taken
so many lives, that, if the heads laid low before it had been ranged
on Temple Bar instead of being privately disposed of, they would

probably have excluded what little light the ground floor had, in a rather significant manner.

Cramped in all kinds of dim cupboards and hutches at Tellson's, the oldest of men carried on the business gravely. When they took a young man into Tellson's London house, they hid him some- 5 where till he was old. They kept him in a dark place, like a cheese, until he had the full Tellson flavour and blue-mould upon him. Then only was he permitted to be seen, spectacularly poring over large books, and casting his breeches and gaiters into the general weight of the establishment.

Outside Tellson's—never by any means in it, unless called in—was an odd-job-man, an occasional porter and messenger, who served as the live sign of the house. He was never absent during business hours, unless upon an errand, and then he was represented by his son: a grisly urchin of twelve, who was his express image. 15 People understood that Tellson's, in a stately way, tolerated the odd-job-man. The house had always tolerated some person in that capacity, and time and tide had drifted this person to the post. His surname was Cruncher, and on the youthful occasion of his renouncing by proxy the works of darkness, in the easterly parish church of Hounsditch, he had received the added appellation of Jerry.

The scene was Mr. Cruncher's private lodging in Hangingsword Alley, Whitefriars: the time, half-past seven of the clock on a windy March morning, Anno Domini seventeen hundred and 25 eighty. (Mr. Cruncher himself always spoke of the year of our Lord as Anna Dominoes: apparently under the impression that the Christian era dated from the invention of a popular game, by a lady who had bestowed her name upon it.)

Mr. Cruncher's apartments were not in a savoury neighbourhood, and were but two in number, even if a closet with a single pane of glass in it might be counted as one. But they were very decently kept. Early as it was, on the windy March morning, the room in which he lay abed was already scrubbed throughout; and between the cups and saucers arranged for breakfast, and the lumbering deal 35 table, a very clean white cloth was spread.

Mr. Cruncher reposed under a patchwork counterpane, like a Harlequin at home. At first, he slept heavily, but, by degrees, began to roll and surge in bed, until he rose above the surface, with his spiky hair looking as if it must tear the sheets to ribbons. At which juncture, he exclaimed, in a voice of dire exasperation:

"Bust me, if she ain't at it agin!"

A woman of orderly and industrious appearance rose from her knees in a corner, with sufficient haste and trepidation to show that she was the person referred to.

"What!" said Mr. Cruncher, looking out of bed for a boot. "You're at it agin, are you?"

After hailing the morn with this second salutation, he threw a boot at the woman as a third. It was a very muddy boot, and may introduce the odd circumstance connected with Mr. Cruncher's domestic economy, that, whereas he often came home after banking hours with clean boots, he often got up next morning to find the same boots covered with clay.

"What," said Mr. Cruncher, varying his apostrophe after missing his mark, "what are you up to, Aggerawayter?"

"I was only saying my prayers."

"Saying your prayers! You're a nice woman! What do you mean by flopping yourself down and praying agin me?"

"I was not praying against you; I was praying for you."

"You weren't. And if you were, I won't be took the liberty with. Here! Your mother's a nice woman, young Jerry, going a praying agin your father's prosperity. You've got a dutiful mother, you have, my son. You've got a religious mother, you have, my boy: going and flopping herself down, and praying that the bread-and-butter may be snatched out of the mouth of her only child."

Master Cruncher (who was in his shirt) took this very ill, and, turning to his mother, strongly deprecated any praying away of his personal board.

"And what do you suppose, you conceited female," said Mr. Cruncher, with unconscious inconsistency, "that the worth of *your* prayers may be? Name the price that you put *your* prayers at!"

"They only come from the heart, Jerry. They are worth no more than that."

"Worth no more than that," repeated Mr. Cruncher. "They ain't worth much, then. Whether or no, I won't be prayed agin, I tell you. I can't afford it. I'm not a-going to be made unlucky by *your* sneaking. If you must go flopping yourself down, flop in favour of your husband and child, and not in opposition to 'em. If I had had any but a unnat'ral wife, and this poor boy had had any but a

unnat'ral mother, I might have made some money last week instead
of being counterprayed and countermined and religiously circum-
wented into the worst of luck. B-u-u-ust me!" said Mr. Cruncher,
who all this time had been putting on his clothes, "if I ain't, what
with piety and one blowed thing and another, been choused this   5
last week into as bad luck as ever a poor devil of a honest tradesman met with! Young Jerry, dress yourself, my boy, and while I
clean my boots keep a eye upon your mother now and then, and if
you see any signs of more flopping, give me a call. For, I tell you,"
here he addressed his wife once more, "I won't be gone agin, in
this manner. I am as rickety as a hackney-coach, I'm as sleepy as
laudanum, my lines is strained to that degree that I shouldn't
know, if it wasn't for the pain in 'em, which was me and which
somebody else, yet I'm none the better for it in pocket; and it's
my suspicion that you've been at it from morning to night to pre-   15
vent me from being the better for it in pocket, and I won't put up
with it. Aggerawayter, and what do you say now!"

Growling, in addition, such phrases as "Ah! yes! You're religious,
too. You wouldn't put yourself in opposition to the interests of
your husband and child, would you? Not you!" and throwing off
other sarcastic sparks from the whirling grindstone of his indignation, Mr. Cruncher betook himself to his boot-cleaning and his
general preparation for business. In the meantime, his son, whose
head was garnished with tenderer spikes, and whose young eyes
stood close by one another, as his father's did, kept the required   25
watch upon his mother. He greatly disturbed that poor woman at
intervals, by darting out of his sleeping closet, where he made his
toilet, with a suppressed cry of "You are going to flop, Mother.
Halloa, Father!" and, after raising this fictitious alarm, darting in
again with an undutiful grin.

Mr. Cruncher's temper was not at all improved when he came to
his breakfast. He resented Mrs. Cruncher's saying grace with
particular animosity.

"Now, Aggerawayter! What are you up to? At it agin?"

His wife explained that she had merely "asked a blessing."   35

"Don't do it!" said Mr. Cruncher, looking about, as if he rather
expected to see the loaf disappear under the efficacy of his wife's
petitions. "I ain't a-going to be blest out of house and home. I
won't have my wittles blest off my table. Keep still!"

Exceedingly red-eyed and grim, as if he had been up all night at a party which had taken anything but a convivial turn, Jerry Cruncher worried his breakfast rather than ate it, growling over it like any four-footed inmate of a menagerie. Towards nine o'clock he smoothed his ruffled aspect, and, presenting as respectful and business-like an exterior as he could overlay his natural self with, issued forth to the occupation of the day.

It could scarcely be called a trade, in spite of his favourite description of himself as "a honest tradesman." His stock consisted of a wooden stool, made out of a broken-backed chair cut down, which stool young Jerry, walking at his father's side, carried every morning to beneath the banking-house window that was nearest Temple Bar; where, with the addition of the first handful of straw that could be gleaned from any passing vehicle to keep the cold and wet from the odd-job-man's feet, it formed the encampment for the day. On this post of his, Mr. Cruncher was as well known to Fleet Street and the Temple as the Bar itself—and was almost as ill-looking.

Encamped at a quarter before nine, in good time to touch his three-cornered hat to the oldest of men as they passed into Tellson's, Jerry took up his station on this windy March morning, with young Jerry standing by him, when not engaged in making forays through the Bar, to inflict bodily and mental injuries of an acute description on passing boys who were small enough for his amiable purpose. Father and son, extremely like each other, looking silently on at the morning traffic in Fleet Street, with their two heads as near to one another as the two eyes of each were, bore a considerable resemblance to a pair of monkeys. The resemblance was not lessened by the accidental circumstance, that the mature Jerry bit and spat out straw, while the twinkling eyes of the youthful Jerry were as restlessly watchful of him as of everything else in Fleet Street.

The head of one of the regular indoor messengers attached to Tellson's establishment was put through the door, and the word was given:

"Porter wanted!"

"Hooray, Father! Here's an early job to begin with!"

Having thus given his parent God speed, young Jerry seated himself on the stool, entered on his reversionary interest in the straw his father had been chewing, and cogitated.

"Al-ways rusty! His fingers is al-ways rusty!" muttered young Jerry. "Where does my father get all that iron rust from? He don't get no iron rust here!"

Chapter 2. A Sight

"You know the Old Bailey well, no doubt?" said one of the oldest of clerks to Jerry the messenger. 5

"Yes, sir," returned Jerry, in something of a dogged manner. "I *do* know the Bailey."

"Just so. And you know Mr. Lorry."

"I know Mr. Lorry, sir, much better than I know the Bailey. Much better," said Jerry, not unlike a reluctant witness at the establishment in question, "than I, as a honest tradesman, wish to know the Bailey."

"Very well. Find the door where the witnesses go in, and show the doorkeeper this note for Mr. Lorry. He will then let you in."

"Into the court, sir?"

"Into the court." 15

Mr. Cruncher's eyes seemed to get a little closer to one another, and to interchange the inquiry, "What do you think of this?"

"Am I to wait in the court, sir?" he asked, as the result of that conference.

"I am going to tell you. The doorkeeper will pass the note to Mr. Lorry, and do you make any gesture that will attract Mr. Lorry's attention, and show him where you stand. Then what you have to do is to remain there until he wants you."

"Is that all, sir?"

"That's all. He wishes to have a messenger at hand. This is to tell him you are there." 25

As the ancient clerk deliberately folded and superscribed the note, Mr. Cruncher, after surveying him in silence until he came to the blotting-paper stage, remarked:

"I suppose they'll be trying Forgeries this morning?"

"Treason!"

"That's quartering," said Jerry. "Barbarous!"

"It is the law," remarked the ancient clerk, turning his surprised spectacles upon him. "It is the law."

"It's hard in the law to spile a man, I think. It's hard enough to kill him, but it's wery hard to spile him, sir."

"Not at all," returned the ancient clerk. "Speak well of the law. Take care of your chest and voice, my good friend, and leave the law to take care of itself. I give you that advice."

"It's the damp, sir, what settles on my chest and voice," said Jerry. "I leave you to judge what a damp way of earning a living mine is."

"Well, well," said the old clerk; "we all have our various ways of gaining a livelihood. Some of us have damp ways, and some of us have dry ways. Here is the letter. Go along."

Jerry took the letter, and, remarking to himself with less internal deference than he made an outward show of, "You are a lean old one, too," made his bow, informed his son, in passing, of his destination, and went his way.

They hanged at Tyburn, in those days, so the street outside Newgate had not obtained one infamous notoriety that has since attached to it. But, the gaol was a vile place in which most kinds of debauchery and villainy were practised, and where dire diseases were bred, that came into court with the prisoners, and sometimes rushed straight from the dock at my Lord Chief Justice himself, and pulled him off the bench. It had more than once happened, that the Judge in the black cap pronounced his own doom as certainly as the prisoner's, and even died before him. For the rest, the Old Bailey was famous as a kind of deadly inn-yard, from which pale travellers set out continually, in carts and coaches, on a violent passage into the other world: traversing some two miles and a half of public street and road, and shaming few good citizens, if any. So powerful is use, and so desirable to be good use in the beginning. It was famous, too, for the pillory, a wise old institution, that inflicted a punishment of which no one could foresee the extent; also, for the whipping-post, another dear old institution, very humanising and softening to behold in action; also, for extensive transactions in blood-money, another fragment of ancestral wisdom, systematically leading to the most frightful mercenary crimes that could be committed under Heaven. Altogether, the Old Bailey, at that date, was a choice illustration of the precept that "Whatever is, is right"; an aphorism that would be as final as it is lazy, did it not include the troublesome consequence, that nothing that ever was, was wrong.

Making his way through the tainted crowd, dispersed up and down this hideous scene of action, with the skill of a man accustomed to make his way quietly, the messenger found out the door he sought, and handed in his letter through a trap in it. For people then paid to see the play at the Old Bailey, just as they paid to see the play in Bedlam—only the former entertainment was much the dearer. Therefore, all the Old Bailey doors were well guarded—except, indeed, the social doors by which the criminals got there, and those were always left wide open.

After some delay and demur, the door grudgingly turned on its hinges a very little way, and allowed Mr. Jerry Cruncher to squeeze himself into court.

"What's on?" he asked, in a whisper, of the man he found himself next to.

"Nothing yet."

"What's coming on?"

"The treason case."

"The quartering one, eh?"

"Ah!" returned the man, with a relish; "he'll be drawn on a hurdle to be half hanged, and then he'll be taken down and sliced before his own face, and then his inside will be taken out and burnt while he looks on, and then his head will be chopped off, and he'll be cut into quarters. That's the sentence."

"If he's found guilty you mean to say?" Jerry added, by way of proviso.

"Oh! they'll find him guilty," said the other. "Don't you be afraid of that."

Mr. Cruncher's attention was here diverted to the doorkeeper, whom he saw making his way to Mr. Lorry, with the note in his hand. Mr. Lorry sat at a table, among the gentlemen in wigs: not far from a wigged gentleman, the prisoner's counsel, who had a great bundle of papers before him: and nearly opposite another wigged gentleman with his hands in his pockets, whose whole attention, when Mr. Cruncher looked at him then or afterwards, seemed to be concentrated on the ceiling of the court. After some gruff coughing and rubbing of his chin and signing with his hand, Jerry attracted the notice of Mr. Lorry, who had stood up to look at him, and who quietly nodded and sat down again.

"What's *he* got to do with this case?" asked the man he had spoken with.

"Blest if I know," said Jerry.

"What have *you* got to do with it, then, if a person may inquire?"

"Blest if I know that either," said Jerry.

The entrance of the judge, and a consequent great stir and settling down in the court, stopped the dialogue. Presently, the dock became the central point of interest. Two gaolers, who had been standing there, went out, and the prisoner was brought in, and put to the bar.

Everybody present, except the one wigged gentleman who looked at the ceiling, stared at him. All the human breath in the place rolled at him, like a sea, or a wind, or a fire. Eager faces strained round pillars and corners, to get a sight of him; spectators in back rows stood up, not to miss a hair of him; people on the floor of the court laid their hands on the shoulders of the people before them, to help themselves, at anybody's cost, to a view of him— stood a-tiptoe, got upon ledges, stood upon next to nothing, to see every inch of him. Conspicuous among these latter, like an animated bit of the the spiked wall of Newgate, Jerry stood: aiming at the prisoner the beery breath of a whet he had taken as he came along, and discharging it to mingle with the waves of other beer, and gin, and tea, and coffee, and what not that flowed at him, and already broke upon the great windows behind him in an impure mist and rain.

The object of all this staring and blaring was a young man of about five-and-twenty, well-grown and well-looking, with a sunburnt cheek and a dark eye. His condition was that of a young gentleman. He was plainly dressed in black, or very dark gray, and his hair, which was long and dark, was gathered in a ribbon at the back of his neck; more to be out of his way than for ornament. As an emotion of the mind will express itself through any covering of the body, so the paleness which his situation engendered came through the brown upon his cheek, showing the soul to be stronger than the sun. He was otherwise quite self-possessed, bowed to the judge, and stood quiet.

The sort of interest with which this man was stared and breathed at was not a sort that elevated humanity. Had he stood in peril of a less horrible sentence—had there been a chance of any one of its savage details being spared—by just so much would he have lost in his fascination. The form that was to be doomed to be so shame- 5 fully mangled was the sight; the immortal creature that was to be so butchered and torn asunder, yielded the sensation. Whatever gloss the various spectators put upon the interest, according to their several arts and powers of self-deceit, the interest was, at the root of it, ogreish.

Silence in the court! Charles Darnay had yesterday pleaded not guilty to an indictment denouncing him (with infinite jingle and jangle) for that he was a false traitor to our serene, illustrious, excellent, and so forth, prince, our Lord the King, by reason of his having, on divers occasions, and by divers means and ways, assisted 15 Lewis, the French King, in his wars against our said serene, illus- trious, excellent, and so forth; that was to say, by coming and going, between the dominions of our said serene, illustrious, excel- lent, and so forth, and those of the said French Lewis, and wick- edly, falsely, traitorously, and otherwise evil-adverbiously, reveal- ing to the said French Lewis what forces our said serene, illustrious, excellent, and so forth, had in preparation to send to Canada and North America. This much, Jerry, with his head becoming more and more spiky as the law terms bristled it, made out with huge satisfaction, and so arrived circuitously at the understanding that 25 the aforesaid, and over and over again aforesaid, Charles Darnay, stood there before him upon his trial; that the jury were swearing in; and that Mr. Attorney-General was making ready to speak.

The accused, who was (and who knew he was) being mentally hanged, beheaded, and quartered, by everybody there, neither flinched from the situation, nor assumed any theatrical air in it. He was quiet and attentive; watched the opening proceedings with a grave interest; and stood with his hands resting on the slab of wood before him, so composedly, that they had not displaced a leaf of the herbs with which it was strewn. The court was all bestrewn with 35 herbs and sprinkled with vinegar, as a precaution against gaol air and gaol fever.

Over the prisoner's head there was a mirror, to throw the light down upon him. Crowds of the wicked and the wretched had been reflected in it, and had passed from its surface and this earth's together. Haunted in a most ghastly manner that abominable place would have been, if the glass could ever have rendered back its reflections, as the ocean is one day to give up its dead. Some passing thought of the infamy and disgrace for which it had been reserved may have struck the prisoner's mind. Be that as it may, a change in his position making him conscious of a bar of light across his face, he looked up; and when he saw the glass his face flushed, and his right hand pushed the herbs away.

It happened, that the action turned his face to that side of the court which was on his left. About on a level with his eyes, there sat, in that corner of the Judge's bench, two persons upon whom his look immediately rested; so immediately, and so much to the changing of his aspect, that all the eyes that were turned upon him, turned to them.

The spectators saw in the two figures, a young lady of little more than twenty, and a gentleman who was evidently her father; a man of a very remarkable appearance in respect of the absolute white- ness of his hair, and a certain indescribable intensity of face: not of an active kind, but pondering and self-communing. When this expression was upon him, he looked as if he were old; but when it was stirred and broken up—as it was now, in a moment, on his speaking to his daughter—he became a handsome man, not past the prime of life.

His daughter had one of her hands drawn through his arm, as she sat by him, and the other pressed upon it. She had drawn close to him, in her dread of the scene, and in her pity for the prisoner. Her forehead had been strikingly expressive of an engrossing terror and compassion that saw nothing but the peril of the accused. This had been so very noticeable, so very powerfully and naturally shown, that starers who had had no pity for him were touched by her; and the whisper went about: "Who are they?"

Jerry, the messenger, who had made his own observations, in his own manner, and who had been sucking the rust off his fingers in his absorption, stretched his neck to hear who they were. The crowd about him had pressed and passed the inquiry on to the nearest attendant, and from him it had been more slowly pressed and passed back; at last it got to Jerry:

"Witnesses."

"For which side?"

"Against."

"Against what side?"

"The prisoner's."

The Judge, whose eyes had gone in the general direction, recalled them, leaned back in his seat, and looked steadily at the man whose   5
life was in his hand, as Mr. Attorney-General rose to spin the rope, grind the axe, and hammer the nails into the scaffold.

Chapter 3. A Disappointment

Mr. Attorney-General had to inform the jury that the prisoner before them, though young in years, was old in the treasonable practices which claimed the forfeit of his life. That this correspondence with the public enemy was not a correspondence of to-day, or of yesterday, or even of last year, or of the year before. That it was certain the prisoner had, for longer than that, been in the habit of passing and repassing between France and England, on secret business of which he could give no honest account. That, if it were   15
in the nature of traitorous ways to thrive (which happily it never was), the real wickedness and guilt of his business might have remained undiscovered. That Providence, however, had put it into the heart of a person who was beyond fear and beyond reproach, to ferret out the nature of the prisoner's schemes, and, struck with horror, to disclose them to his Majesty's Chief Secretary of State and most honourable Privy Council. That this patriot would be produced before them. That his position and attitude were, on the whole, sublime. That he had been the prisoner's friend, but, at once in an auspicious and an evil hour detecting his infamy, had   25
resolved to immolate the traitor he could no longer cherish in his bosom, on the sacred altar of his country. That, if statues were decreed in Britain, as in ancient Greece and Rome, to public benefactors, this shining citizen would assuredly have had one. That, as they were not so decreed, he probably would not have one. That Virtue, as had been observed by the poets (in many passages which he well knew the jury would have, word for word, at the tips of their tongues; whereat the jury's countenances displayed a guilty

consciousness that they knew nothing about the passages), was in a manner contagious; more especially the bright virtue known as patriotism, or love of country. That the lofty example of this immaculate and unimpeachable witness for the Crown, to refer to

5 whom however unworthily was an honour, had communicated itself to the prisoner's servant, and had engendered in him a holy determination to examine his master's table-drawers and pockets, and secrete his papers. That he (Mr. Attorney-General) was prepared to hear some disparagement attempted of this admirable servant; but that, in a general way, he preferred him to his (Mr. Attorney-General's) brothers and sisters, and honoured him more than his (Mr. Attorney-General's) father and mother. That he called with confidence on the jury to come and do likewise. That the evidence of these two witnesses, coupled with the documents of

15 their discovering that would be produced, would show the prisoner to have been furnished with lists of his Majesty's forces, and of their disposition and preparation, both by sea and land, and would leave no doubt that he had habitually conveyed such information to a hostile power. That these lists could not be proved to be in the prisoner's handwriting; but that it was all the same; that, indeed, it was rather the better for the prosecution, as showing the prisoner to be artful in his precautions. That the proof would go back five years, and would show the prisoner already engaged in these pernicious missions, within a few weeks before the date of

25 the very first action fought between the British troops and the Americans. That, for these reasons, the jury, being a loyal jury (as he knew they were), and being a responsible jury (as *they* knew they were), must positively find the prisoner guilty, and make an end of him, whether they liked it or not. That they never could lay their heads upon their pillows; that they never could tolerate the idea of their wives laying their heads upon their pillows; that they could never endure the notion of their children laying their heads upon their pillows; in short, that there never more could be, for them or theirs, any laying of heads upon pillows at all, unless the

35 prisoner's head was taken off. That head Mr. Attorney-General concluded by demanding of them, in the name of everything he could think of with a round turn in it, and on the faith of his solemn asseveration that he already considered the prisoner as good as dead and gone.

When the Attorney-General ceased, a buzz arose in the court as if a cloud of great blue-flies were swarming about the prisoner, in anticipation of what he was soon to become. When toned down again, the unimpeachable patriot appeared in the witness-box.

Mr. Solicitor-General then, following his leader's lead, examined the patriot: John Barsad, gentleman, by name. The story of his pure soul was exactly what Mr. Attorney-General had described it to be—perhaps, if it had a fault, a little too exactly. Having released his noble bosom of its burden, he would have modestly withdrawn himself, but that the wigged gentleman with the papers before him, sitting not far from Mr. Lorry, begged to ask him a few questions. The wigged gentleman sitting opposite still looked at the ceiling of the court.

Had he ever been a spy himself? No, he scorned the base insinuation. What did he live upon? His property. Where was his property? He didn't precisely remember where it was. What was it? No business of anybody's. Had he inherited it? Yes, he had. From whom? Distant relation. Very distant? Rather. Ever been in prison? Certainly not. Never in a debtor's prison? Didn't see what that had to do with it. Never in a debtor's prison?—Come, once again. Never? Yes. How many times? Two or three times. Not five or six? Perhaps. Of what profession? Gentleman. Ever been kicked? Might have been. Frequently? No. Ever kicked downstairs? Decidedly not; once received a kick on the top of a staircase, and fell downstairs of his own accord. Kicked on that occasion for cheating at dice? Something to that effect was said by the intoxicated liar who committed the assault, but it was not true. Swear it was not true? Positively. Ever live by cheating at play? Never. Ever live by play? Not more than other gentlemen do. Ever borrow money of the prisoner? Yes. Ever pay him? No. Was not this intimacy with the prisoner, in reality a very slight one, forced upon the prisoner in coaches, inns, and packets? No. Sure he saw the prisoner with these lists? Certain. Knew no more about the lists? No. Had not procured them himself, for instance? No. Expect to get anything by this evidence? No. Not in regular government pay and employment to lay traps? Oh dear no. Or to do anything? Oh dear no. Swear that? Over and over again. No motives but motives of sheer patriotism? None whatever.

The virtuous servant, Roger Cly, swore his way through the case at a great rate. He had taken service with the prisoner, in good faith and simplicity, four years ago. He had asked the prisoner, aboard the Calais packet, if he wanted a handy fellow, and the prisoner had engaged him. He had not asked the prisoner to take the handy fellow as an act of charity—never thought of such a thing. He began to have suspicions of the prisoner, and to keep an eye upon him, soon afterwards. In arranging his clothes, while travelling, he had seen similar lists to these in the prisoner's pockets, over and over again. He had taken these lists from the drawer of the prisoner's desk. He had not put them there first. He had seen the prisoner show these identical lists to French gentlemen at Calais, and similar lists to French gentlemen, both at Calais and Boulogne. He loved his country, and couldn't bear it, and had given information. He had never been suspected of stealing a silver teapot; he had been maligned respecting a mustard-pot, but it turned out to be only a plated one. He had known the last witness seven or eight years; that was merely a coincidence. He didn't call it a particularly curious coincidence; most coincidences were curious. Neither did he call it a curious coincidence that true patriotism was *his* only motive too. He was a true Briton, and hoped there were many like him.

The blue-flies buzzed again, and Mr. Attorney-General called Mr. Jarvis Lorry.

"Mr. Jarvis Lorry, are you a clerk in Tellson's Bank?"

"I am."

"On a certain Friday night in November one thousand seven hundred and seventy-five, did business occasion you to travel between London and Dover by the mail?"

"It did."

"Were there any other passengers in the mail?"

"Two."

"Did they alight on the road in the course of the night?"

"They did."

"Mr. Lorry, look upon the prisoner. Was he one of those two passengers?"

"I cannot undertake to say that he was."

"Does he resemble either of these two passengers?"

"Both were so wrapped up, and the night was so dark, and we were all so reserved, that I cannot undertake to say even that."

"Mr. Lorry, look again upon the prisoner. Supposing him wrapped up as those two passengers were, is there anything in his bulk and stature to render it unlikely that he was one of them?"

"No."

"You will not swear, Mr. Lorry, that he was not one of them?"   5

"No."

"So at least you say he may have been one of them?"

"Yes. Except that I remember them both to have been—like myself—timorous of highwaymen, and the prisoner has not a timorous air."

"Did you ever see a counterfeit of timidity, Mr. Lorry?"

"I certainly have seen that."

"Mr. Lorry, look once more upon the prisoner. Have you seen him, to your certain knowledge, before?"

"I have."   15

"When?"

"I was returning from France a few days afterwards, and at Calais, the prisoner came on board the packet-ship in which I returned, and made the voyage with me."

"At what hour did he come on board?"

"At a little after midnight."

"In the dead of the night. Was he the only passenger who came on board at that untimely hour?"

"He happened to be the only one."

"Never mind about 'happening,' Mr. Lorry. He was the only   25 passenger who came on board in the dead of the night?"

"He was."

"Were you travelling alone, Mr. Lorry, or with any companion?"

"With two companions. A gentleman and lady. They are here."

"They are here. Had you any conversation with the prisoner?"

"Hardly any. The weather was stormy, and the passage long and rough, and I lay on a sofa, almost from shore to shore."

"Miss Manette!"

The young lady, to whom all eyes had been turned before, and were now turned again, stood up where she had sat. Her father   35 rose with her, and kept her hand drawn through his arm.

"Miss Manette, look upon the prisoner."

To be confronted with such pity, and such earnest youth and beauty, was far more trying to the accused than to be confronted with all the crowd. Standing, as it were, apart with her on the edge of his grave, not all the staring curiosity that looked on could, for the moment, nerve him to remain quite still. His hurried right hand parcelled out the herbs before him into imaginary beds of flowers in a garden: and his efforts to control and steady his breathing shook the lips from which the colour rushed to his heart. The buzz of the great flies was loud again.

"Miss Manette, have you seen the prisoner before?"

"Yes, sir."

"Where?"

"On board of the packet-ship just now referred to, sir, and on the same occasion."

"You are the young lady just now referred to?"

"O! most unhappily, I am."

The plaintive tone of her compassion merged into the less musical voice of the judge, as he said something fiercely: "Answer the questions put to you, and make no remark upon them."

"Miss Manette, had you any conversation with the prisoner on that passage across the Channel?"

"Yes, sir."

"Recall it."

In the midst of a profound stillness, she faintly began: "When the gentleman came on board—"

"Do you mean the prisoner?" inquired the judge, knitting his brows.

"Yes, my Lord."

"Then say the prisoner."

"When the prisoner came on board, he noticed that my father," turning her eyes lovingly to him as he stood beside her, "was much fatigued and in a very weak state of health. My father was so reduced that I was afraid to take him out of the air, and I had made a bed for him on the deck near the cabin steps, and I sat on the deck at his side to take care of him. There were no other passengers that night, but we four. The prisoner was so good as to beg permission to advise me how I could shelter my father from the wind and weather, better than I had done. I had not known how to do it well, not understanding how the wind would set when we were out of the harbour. He did it for me. He expressed great gentleness and kindness for my father's state, and I am sure he felt it. That was the manner of our beginning to speak together."

"Let me interrupt you for a moment. Had he come on board alone?"

"No."

"How many were with him?"

"Two French gentlemen."

"Had they conferred together?"

"They had conferred together until the last moment, when it was necessary for the French gentlemen to be landed in their boat."

"Had any papers been handed about among them, similar to these lists?"

"Some papers had been handed about among them, but I don't know what papers."

"Like these in shape and size?"

"Possibly, but indeed I don't know, although they stood whispering very near to me: because they stood at the top of the cabin steps to have the light of the lamp that was hanging there; it was a dull lamp, and they spoke very low, and I did not hear what they said, and saw only that they looked at papers."

"Now, to the prisoner's conversation, Miss Manette."

"The prisoner was as open in his confidence with me—which arose out of my helpless situation—as he was kind, and good, and useful to my father. I hope," bursting into tears, "I may not repay him by doing him harm to-day."

Buzzing from the blue-flies.

"Miss Manette, if the prisoner does not perfectly understand that you give the evidence which it is your duty to give—which you must give—and which you cannot escape from giving—with great unwillingness, he is the only person present in that condition. Please to go on."

"He told me that he was travelling on business of a delicate and difficult nature which might get people into trouble, and that he was therefore travelling under an assumed name. He said that this business had, within a few days, taken him to France, and might, at intervals, take him backwards and forwards between France and England for a long time to come."

"Did he say anything about America, Miss Manette? Be particular."

"He tried to explain to me how that quarrel had arisen, and he said that, so far as he could judge, it was a wrong and foolish one on England's part. He added, in a jesting way, that perhaps George Washington might gain almost as great a name in history as George the Third. But there was no harm in his way of saying this: it was said laughingly, and to beguile the time."

Any strongly marked expression of face on the part of a chief actor in a scene of great interest to whom many eyes are directed will be unconsciously imitated by the spectators. Her forehead was painfully anxious and intent as she gave this evidence, and, in the pauses when she stopped for the judge to write it down, watched its effect upon the counsel for and against. Among the lookers-on there was the same expression in all quarters of the court; insomuch, that a great majority of the foreheads there might have been mirrors reflecting the witness, when the judge looked up from his notes to glare at that tremendous heresy about George Washington.

Mr. Attorney-General now signified to my Lord, that he deemed it necessary, as a matter of precaution and form, to call the young lady's father, Doctor Manette. Who was called accordingly.

"Doctor Manette, look upon the prisoner. Have you ever seen him before?"

"Once. When he called at my lodgings in London. Some three years, or three years and a half ago."

"Can you identify him as your fellow-passenger on board the packet, or speak to his conversation with your daughter?"

"Sir, I can do neither."

"Is there any particular and special reason for your being unable to do either?"

He answered, in a low voice, "There is."

"Has it been your misfortune to undergo a long imprisonment, without trial, or even accusation, in your native country, Doctor Manette?"

He answered, in a tone that went to every heart, "A long imprisonment."

"Were you newly released on the occasion in question?"

"They tell me so."

"Have you no remembrance of the occasion?"

"None. My mind is a blank, from some time—I cannot even say what time—when I employed myself, in my captivity, in making shoes, to the time when I found myself living in London with my dear daughter here. She had become familiar to me, when a gracious God restored my faculties; but, I am quite unable even to say how she had become familiar. I have no remembrance of the process."

Mr. Attorney-General sat down, and the father and daughter sat down together.

A singular circumstamce then arose in the case. The object in hand being to show that the prisoner went down, with some fellow-plotter untracked, in the Dover mail on that Friday night in November five years ago, and got out of the mail in the night, as a blind, at a place where he did not remain, but from which he travelled back some dozen miles or more, to a garrison and dock-yard, and there collected information; a witness was called to identify him as having been at the precise time required, in the coffee-room of an hotel in that garrison-and-dockyard town, waiting for another person. The prisoner's counsel was cross-examining this witness with no result, except that he had never seen the prisoner on any other occasion, when the wigged gentleman who had all this time been looking at the ceiling of the court, wrote a word or two on a little piece of paper, screwed it up, and tossed it to him. Opening this piece of paper in the next pause, the counsel looked with great attention and curiosity at the prisoner."

"You say again you are quite sure that it *was* the prisoner?"

The witness was quite sure.

"Did you ever see anybody very like the prisoner?"

Not so like (the witness said) as that he could be mistaken.

"Look well upon that gentleman, my learned friend there," pointing to him who had tossed the paper over, "and then look well upon the prisoner. How say you? Are they very like each other?"

Allowing for my learned friend's appearance being careless and slovenly if not debauched, they were sufficiently like each other to surprise, not only the witness, but everybody present, when they were thus brought into comparison. My Lord being prayed to bid my learned friend lay aside his wig, and giving no very gracious consent, the likeness became much more remarkable. My Lord inquired of Mr. Stryver (the prisoner's counsel), whether they were next to try Mr. Carton (name of my learned friend) for treason? But, Mr. Stryver replied to my Lord, no; but he would ask the witness to tell him whether what happened once might happen

twice; whether he would have been so confident if he had seen this illustration of his rashness sooner, whether he would be so confident, having seen it; and more. The upshot of which was, to smash this witness like a crockery vessel, and shiver his part of the case to
5   useless lumber.

Mr. Cruncher had by this time taken quite a lunch of rust off his fingers in his following of the evidence. He had now to attend while Mr. Stryver fitted the prisoner's case on the jury, like a compact suit of clothes; showing them how the patriot, Barsad, was a hired spy and traitor, an unblushing trafficker in blood, and one of the greatest scoundrels upon earth since accursed Judas—which he certainly did look rather like. How the virtuous servant, Cly, was his friend and partner, and was worthy to be; how the watchful eyes of those forgers and false swearers had rested on the prisoner as a
15   victim, because some family affairs in France, he being of French extraction, did require his making those passages across the Channel—though what those affairs were, a consideration for others who were near and dear to him, forbade him, even for his life, to disclose. How the evidence that had been warped and wrested from the young lady, whose anguish in giving it they had witnessed, came to nothing, involving the mere little innocent gallantries and politenesses likely to pass between any young gentleman and young lady so thrown together—with the exception of that reference to George Washington, which was altogether too extravagant and
25   impossible to be regarded in any other light than as a monstrous joke. How it would be a weakness in the government to break down in this attempt to practise for popularity on the lowest national antipathies and fears, and therefore Mr. Attorney-General had made the most of it; how, nevertheless, it rested upon nothing, save that vile and infamous character of evidence too often disfiguring such cases, and of which the State Trials of this country were full. But, there my Lord interposed (with as grave a face as if it had not been true), saying that he could not sit upon that Bench and suffer those allusions.

35   Mr. Stryver then called his few witnesses, and Mr. Cruncher had next to attend while Mr. Attorney-General turned the whole suit of clothes Mr. Stryver had fitted on the jury inside out; showing how Barsad and Cly were even a hundred times better than he had thought them, and the prisoner a hundred times worse. Lastly,

came my Lord himself, turning the suit of clothes, now inside out, now outside in, but on the whole decidedly trimming and shaping them into grave-clothes for the prisoner.

And now, the jury turned to consider, and the great flies swarmed again.

Mr. Carton, who had so long sat looking at the ceiling of the court, changed neither his place nor his attitude, even in this excitement. While his learned friend, Mr. Stryver, massing his papers before him, whispered with those who sat near, and from time to time glanced anxiously at the jury; while all the spectators moved more or less, and grouped themselves anew; while even my Lord himself arose from his seat, and slowly paced up and down his platform, not unattended by a suspicion in the minds of the audience that his state was feverish; this one man sat leaning back, with his torn gown half off him, his untidy wig put on just as it had happened to light on his head after its removal, his hands in his pockets, and his eyes on the ceiling as they had been all day. Something especially reckless in his demeanour not only gave him a disreputable look, but so diminished the strong resemblance he undoubtedly bore to the prisoner (which his momentary earnestness, when they were compared together, had strengthened), that many of the lookers-on, taking note of him now, said to one another they would hardly have thought the two were so alike. Mr. Cruncher made the observation to his next neighbour, and added, "I'd hold half a guinea that *he* don't get no law work to do. Don't look like the sort of one to get any, do he?"

Yet, this Mr. Carton took in more of the details of the scene than he appeared to take in; for now, when Miss Manette's head dropped upon her father's breast, he was the first to see it, and to say audibly: "Officer! look to that young lady. Help the gentleman to take her out. Don't you see that she will fall!"

There was much commiseration for her as she was removed, and much sympathy with her father. It had evidently been a great distress to him to have the days of his imprisonment recalled. He had shown strong internal agitation when he was questioned, and that pondering or brooding look which made him old had been upon him, like a heavy cloud, ever since. As he passed out, the jury, who had turned back and paused a moment, spoke, through their foreman.

They were not agreed, and wished to retire. My Lord (perhaps with George Washington on his mind) showed some surprise that they were not agreed, but signified his pleasure that they should retire under watch and ward, and retired himself. The trial had lasted all day, and the lamps in the court were now being lighted. It began to be rumoured that the jury would be out a long while. The spectators dropped off to get refreshment, and the prisoner withdrew to the back of the dock, and sat down.

Mr. Lorry, who had gone out when the young lady and her father went out, now reappeared, and beckoned to Jerry: who, in the slackened interest, could easily get near him.

"Jerry, if you wish to take something to eat, you can. But, keep in the way. You will be sure to hear when the jury come in. Don't be a moment behind them, for I want you to take the verdict back to the bank. You are the quickest messenger I know, and will get to Temple Bar long before I can."

Jerry had just enough forehead to knuckle, and he knuckled it in acknowledgment of this communication and a shilling. Mr. Carton came up at the moment, and touched Mr. Lorry on the arm.

"How is the young lady?"

"She is greatly distressed; but her father is comforting her, and she feels the better for being out of court."

"I'll tell the prisoner so. It won't do for a respectable bank gentleman like you to be seen speaking to him publicly, you know."

Mr. Lorry reddened as if he were conscious of having debated the point in his mind, and Mr. Carton made his way to the outside of the bar. The way out of court lay in that direction, and Jerry followed him, all eyes, ears, and spikes.

"Mr. Darnay!"

The prisoner came forward directly.

"You will naturally be anxious to hear of the witness, Miss Manette. She will do very well. You have seen the worst of her agitation."

"I am deeply sorry to have been the cause of it. Could you tell her so for me, with my fervent acknowledgments?"

"Yes, I could. I will, if you ask it."

Mr. Carton's manner was so careless as to be almost insolent. He stood, half turned from the prisoner, lounging with his elbow against the bar.

"I do ask it. Accept my cordial thanks."

"What," said Carton, still only half turned towards him, "do you expect, Mr. Darnay?"

"The worst."

"It's the wisest thing to expect, and the likeliest. But I think their withdrawing is in your favour." 5

Loitering on the way out of court not being allowed, Jerry heard no more: but left them—so like each other in feature, so unlike each other in manner—standing side by side, both reflected in the glass above them.

An hour and a half limped heavily away in the thief-and-rascal crowded passages below, even though assisted off with mutton pies and ale. The hoarse messenger, uncomfortably seated on a form after taking that refection, had dropped into a doze, when a loud murmur and a rapid tide of people setting up the stairs that led to the court carried him along with them. 15

"Jerry, Jerry!" Mr. Lorry was already calling at the door when he got there.

"Here, sir. It's a fight to get back again. Here I am, sir!"

Mr. Lorry handed him a paper through the throng. "Quick! Have you got it?"

"Yes, sir."

Hastily written on the paper was the word "Acquitted."

"If you had sent the message, 'Recalled to life,' again," muttered Jerry, as he turned, "I should have known what you meant, this time." 25

He had no opportunity of saying, or so much as thinking, anything else, until he was clear of the Old Bailey; for, the crowd came pouring out with a vehemence that nearly took him off his legs, and a loud buzz swept into the street as if the baffled blue-flies were dispersing in search of other carrion.

Chapter 4. Congratulatory

From the dimly-lighted passages of the court, the last sediment of the human stew that had been boiling there all day was straining off, when Doctor Manette, Lucie Manette, his daughter, Mr. Lorry, the solicitor for the defence, and its counsel, Mr. Stryver, stood gathered round Mr. Charles Darnay—just released—congratulating him on his escape from death.

5   It would have been difficult, by a far brighter light, to recognise in Doctor Manette, intellectual of face and upright of bearing, the shoemaker of the garret in Paris. Yet, no one could have looked at him twice, without looking again: even though the opportunity of observation had not extended to the mournful cadence of his low grave voice, and to the abstraction that overclouded him fitfully, without any apparent reason. While one external cause, and that a reference to his long lingering agony, would always—as on the trial—evoke this condition from the depths of his soul, it was also in its nature to arise of itself, and to draw a gloom over him, as incomprehensible to those unacquainted with his story as if they
15 had seen the shadow of the actual Bastille thrown upon him by a summer sun, when the substance was three hundred miles away.

Only his daughter had the power of charming this black brooding from his mind. She was the golden thread that united him to a Past beyond his misery, and to a Present beyond his misery: and the sound of her voice, the light of her face, the touch of her hand, had a strong beneficial influence with him almost always. Not absolutely always, for she could recall some occasions on which her power had failed; but they were few and slight, and she believed them over.

25 Mr. Darnay had kissed her hand fervently and gratefully, and had turned to Mr. Stryver, whom he warmly thanked. Mr. Stryver, a man of little more than thirty, but looking twenty years older than he was, stout, loud, red, bluff, and free from any drawback of delicacy, had a pushing way of shouldering himself (morally and physically) into companies and conversations, that argued well for his shouldering his way up in life.

He still had his wig and gown on, and he said, squaring himself at his late client to that degree that he squeezed the innocent Mr. Lorry clean out of the group: "I am glad to have brought you off
35 with honour, Mr. Darnay. It was an infamous prosecution, grossly infamous; but not the less likely to succeed on that account."

"You have laid me under an obligation to you for life—in two senses," said his late client, taking his hand.

"I have done my best for you, Mr. Darnay; and my best is as

good as another man's, I believe."

It clearly being incumbent on someone to say, "Much better," Mr. Lorry said it; perhaps not quite disinterestedly, but with the interested object of squeezing himself back again.

"You think so?" said Mr. Stryver. "Well! you have been present   5
all day, and you ought to know. You are a man of business, too."

"And as such," quoth Mr. Lorry, whom the counsel learned in the law had now shouldered back into the group, just as he had previously shouldered him out of it, "as such I will appeal to Doctor Manette, to break up this conference and order us all to our homes. Miss Lucie looks ill, Mr. Darnay has had a terrible day, we are worn out."

"Speak for yourself, Mr. Lorry," said Stryver; "I have a night's work to do yet. Speak for yourself."

"I speak for myself," answered Mr. Lorry, "and for Mr. Darnay,   15
and for Miss Lucie, and—Miss Lucie, do you not think I may speak for us all?" He asked her the question pointedly, and with a glance at her father.

His face had become frozen, as it were, in a very curious look at Darnay: an intent look, deepening into a frown of dislike and distrust, not even unmixed with fear. With this strange expression on him his thoughts had wandered away.

"My father," said Lucie, softly laying her hand on his.

He slowly shook the shadow off, and turned to her.

"Shall we go home, my father?"

With a long breath, he answered, "Yes."   25

The friends of the acquitted prisoner had dispersed, under the impression—which he himself had originated—that he would not be released that night. The lights were nearly all extinguished in the passages, the iron gates were being closed with a jar and a rattle, and the dismal place was deserted until to-morrow morning's interest of gallows, pillory, whipping-post, and branding-iron should re-people it. Walking between her father and Mr. Darnay, Lucie Manette passed into the open air. A hackney-coach was called, and the father and daughter departed in it.   35

Mr. Stryver had left them in the passages, to shoulder his way back to the robing-room. Another person, who had not joined the group, or interchanged a word with any one of them, but who had been leaning against the wall where its shadow was darkest, had silently strolled out after the rest, and had looked on until the coach drove away. He now stepped up to where Mr. Lorry and Mr. Darnay stood upon the pavement.

"So, Mr. Lorry! Men of business may speak to Mr. Darnay now?"

5 Nobody had made any acknowledgment of Mr. Carton's part in the day's proceedings; nobody had known of it. He was unrobed, and was none the better for it in appearance.

"If you knew what a conflict goes on in the business mind, when the business mind is divided between good-natured impulse and business appearances, you would be amused, Mr. Darnay."

Mr. Lorry reddened, and said, warmly, "You have mentioned that before, sir. We men of business, who serve a House, are not our own masters. We have to think of the House more than ourselves."

15 "I know, I know," rejoined Mr. Carton, carelessly. "Don't be nettled, Mr. Lorry. You are as good as another, I have no doubt: better, I dare say."

"And indeed, sir," pursued Mr. Lorry, not minding him, "I really don't know what you have to do with the matter. If you'll excuse me, as very much your elder, for saying so, I really don't know that it is your business."

"Business! Bless you, I have no business," said Mr. Carton.

"It is a pity you have not, sir."

"I think so, too."

25 "If you had," pursued Mr. Lorry, "perhaps you would attend to it."

"Lord love you, no!—I shouldn't," said Mr. Carton.

"Well, sir!" cried Mr. Lorry, thoroughly heated by his indifference, "business is a very good thing, and a very respectable thing. And, sir, if business imposes its restraints and its silences and impediments, Mr. Darnay as a young gentleman of generosity knows how to make allowance for that circumstance. Mr. Darnay, good-night, God bless you, sir! I hope you have been this day preserved for a prosperous and happy life.—Chair there!"

35 Perhaps a little angry with himself, as well as with the barrister, Mr. Lorry bustled into the chair, and was carried off to Tellson's. Carton, who smelt of port wine, and did not appear to be quite sober, laughed then, and turned to Darnay.

"This is a strange chance that throws you and me together. This must be a strange night to you, standing alone here with your counterpart on these street stones?"

"I hardly seem yet," returned Charles Darnay, "to belong to this world again."

"I don't wonder at it; it's not so long since you were pretty far advanced on your way to another. You speak faintly."

"I begin to think I *am* faint."

"Then why the devil don't you dine? I dined, myself, while those numskulls were deliberating which world you should belong to— this, or some other. Let me show you the nearest tavern to dine well at."

Drawing his arm through his own, he took him down Ludgate Hill to Fleet Street, and so, up a covered way, into a tavern. Here, they were shown into a little room, where Charles Darnay was soon recruiting his strength with a good plain dinner and good wine: while Carton sat opposite to him at the same table, with his separate bottle of port before him, and his fully half-insolent manner upon him.

"Do you feel, yet, that you belong to this terrestrial scheme again, Mr. Darnay?"

"I am frightfully confused regarding time and place; but I am so far mended as to feel that."

"It must be an immense satisfaction!"

He said it bitterly, and filled up his glass again: which was a large one.

"As to me, the greatest desire I have is to forget that I belong to it. It has no good in it for me—except wine like this—nor I for it. So we are not much alike in that particular. Indeed, I begin to think we are not much alike in any particular, you and I."

Confused by the emotion of the day, and feeling his being there with this double of coarse deportment to be like a dream, Charles Darnay was at a loss how to answer; finally, answered not at all.

"Now your dinner is done," Carton presently said, "why don't you call a health, Mr. Darnay; why don't you give your toast?"

"What health? What toast?"

"Why, it's on the tip of your tongue. It ought to be, it must be, I'll swear it's there."

"Miss Manette, then!"

"Miss Manette, then!"

Looking his companion full in the face while he drank the toast, Carton flung his glass over his shoulder against the wall, where it shivered to pieces; then rang the bell, and ordered in another.

"That's a fair young lady to hand to a coach in the dark, Mr. Darnay!" he said, filling his new goblet.

A slight frown and a laconic "Yes" were the answer.

"That's a fair young lady to be pitied by and wept for by! How does it feel? Is it worth being tried for one's life, to be the object of such sympathy and compassion, Mr. Darnay?"

Again Darnay answered not a word.

"She was mightily pleased to have your message, when I gave it her. Not that she showed she was pleased, but I suppose she was."

The allusion served as a timely reminder to Darnay that this disagreeable companion had, of his own free will, assisted him in the strait of the day. He turned the dialogue to that point, and thanked him for it.

"I neither want any thanks, nor merit any," was the careless rejoinder. "It was nothing to do, in the first place; and I don't know why I did it, in the second. Mr. Darnay, let me ask you a question."

"Willingly, and a small return for your good offices."

"Do you think I particularly like you?"

"Really, Mr. Carton," returned the other, oddly disconcerted, "I have not asked myself the question."

"But ask yourself the question now."

"You have acted as if you do; but I don't think you do."

"I don't think I do," said Carton. "I begin to have a very good opinion of your understanding."

"Nevertheless," pursued Darnay, rising to ring the bell, "there is nothing in that, I hope, to prevent my calling the reckoning, and our parting without ill-blood on either side."

Carton rejoining, "Nothing in life!" Darnay rang. "Do you call the whole reckoning?" said Carton. On his answering in the affirmative, "Then bring me another pint of this same wine, drawer, and come and wake me at ten."

The bill being paid, Charles Darnay rose and wished him good-night. Without returning the wish, Carton rose too, with something of a threat of defiance in his manner, and said, "A last word, Mr. Darnay: you think I am drunk?"

"I think you have been drinking, Mr. Carton."

"Think? You know I have been drinking."

"Since I must say so, I know it."

"Then you shall likewise know why. I am a disappointed drudge, sir. I care for no man on earth, and no man on earth cares for me."

"Much to be regretted. You might have used your talents better."

"May be so, Mr. Darnay; may be not. Don't let your sober face elate you, however; you don't know what it may come to. Good-night!"

When he was left alone, this strange being took up a candle, went to a glass that hung against the wall, and surveyed himself minutely in it.

"Do you particularly like the man?" he muttered, at his own image. "Why should you particularly like a man who resembles you? There is nothing in you to like; you know that. Ah, confound you! What a change you have made in yourself! A good reason for taking to a man, that he shows you what you have fallen away from, and what you might have been! Change places with him, and would you have been looked at by those blue eyes as he was, and commiserated by that agitated face as he was? Come on, and have it out in plain words! You hate the fellow."

He resorted to his pint of wine for consolation, drank it all in a few minutes, and fell asleep on his arms, with his hair straggling over the table, and a long winding-sheet in the candle dripping down upon him.

Chapter 5. The Jackal

Those were drinking days, and most men drank hard. So very great is the improvement Time has brought about in such habits, that a moderate statement of the quantity of wine and punch which one man would swallow in the course of a night, without any detriment to his reputation as a perfect gentleman, would seem, in these days, a ridiculous exaggeration. The learned profession of the law was certainly not behind any other learned profession in its Bacchanalian propensities; neither was Mr. Stryver, already fast shouldering his way to a large and lucrative practice, behind his compeers in this particular, any more than in the drier parts of the legal race.

5 A favourite at the Old Bailey, and eke at the Sessions, Mr. Stryver had begun cautiously to hew away the lower staves of the ladder on which he mounted. Sessions and Old Bailey had now to summon their favourite, specially, to their longing arms; and shouldering itself towards the visage of the Lord Chief Justice in the Court of King's Bench, the florid countenance of Mr. Stryver might be daily seen, bursting out of the bed of wigs, like a great sunflower pushing its way at the sun from among a rank garden full of flaring companions.

It had once been noted at the Bar, that while Mr. Stryver was a glib man, and an unscrupulous, and a ready, and a bold, he had not 15 that faculty of extracting the essence from a heap of statements, which is among the most striking and necessary of the advocate's accomplishments. But a remarkable improvement came upon him as to this. The more business he got, the greater his power seemed to grow of getting at its pith and marrow; and however late at night he sat carousing with Sydney Carton, he always had his points at his fingers' ends in the morning.

Sydney Carton, idlest and most unpromising of men, was Stryver's great ally. What the two drank together, between Hilary Term and Michaelmas, might have floated a king's ship. Stryver 25 never had a case in hand, anywhere, but Carton was there, with his hands in his pockets, staring at the ceiling of the court; they went the same circuit, and even there they prolonged their usual orgies late into the night, and Carton was rumoured to be seen at broad day, going home stealthily and unsteadily to his lodging, like a dissipated cat. At last, it began to get about, among such as were interested in the matter, that although Sydney Carton would never be a lion, he was an amazingly good jackal, and that he rendered suit and service to Stryver in that humble capacity.

"Ten o'clock, sir," said the man at the tavern, whom he had 35 charged to wake him—"ten o'clock, sir."

"*What's* the matter?"

"Ten o'clock, sir."

"What do you mean? Ten o'clock at night?"

"Yes, sir. Your honour told me to call you."

"Oh! I remember. Very well, very well."

After a few dull efforts to get to sleep again, which the man dexterously combated by stirring the fire continuously for five minutes, he got up, tossed his hat on, and walked out. He turned into the Temple, and, having revived himself by twice pacing the pavements of King's Bench Walk and Paper Buildings, turned into the Stryver chambers.

The Stryver clerk, who never assisted at these conferences, had gone home, and the Stryver principal opened the door. He had his slippers on, and a loose bed-gown, and his throat was bare for his greater ease. He had that rather wild, strained, seared marking about the eyes, which may be observed in all free livers of his class, from the portrait of Jeffries downward, and which can be traced, under various disguises of Art, through the portraits of every Drinking Age.

"You are a little late, Memory," said Stryver.

"About the usual time; it may be a quarter of an hour later."

They went into a dingy room lined with books and littered with papers, where there was a blazing fire. A kettle steamed upon the hob, and in the midst of the wreck of papers a table shone, with plenty of wine upon it, and brandy, and rum, and sugar, and lemons.

"You have had your bottle, I perceive, Sydney."

"Two to-night, I think. I have been dining with the day's client; or seeing him dine—it's all one!"

"That was a rare point, Sydney, that you brought to bear upon the identification. How did you come by it? When did it strike you?"

"I thought he was rather a handsome fellow, and I thought I should have been much the same sort of fellow, if I had had any luck."

Mr. Stryver laughed till he shook his precocious paunch.

"You and your luck, Sydney! Get to work, get to work."

Sullenly enough, the jackal loosened his dress, went into an adjoining room, and came back with a large jug of cold water, a basin, and a towel or two. Steeping the towels in the water, and partially wringing them out, he folded them on his head in a manner hideous to behold, sat down at the table, and said, "Now I am ready!"

"Not much boiling down to be done to-night, Memory," said Mr. Stryver, gaily, as he looked among his papers.

"How much?"

"Only two sets of them."

5 "Give me the worst first."

"There they are, Sydney. Fire away!"

The lion then composed himself on his back on a sofa on one side of the drinking-table, while the jackal sat at his own paper-be-strewn table proper, on the other side of it, with the bottles and glasses ready to his hand. Both resorted to the drinking-table without stint, but each in a different way; the lion for the most part reclining with his hands in his waistband, looking at the fire, or occasionally flirting with some lighter documents; the jackal, with knitted brows and intent face, so deep in his task, that his eyes did
15 not even follow the hand he stretched out for his glass—which often groped about, for a minute or more, before it found the glass for his lips. Two or three times the matter in hand became so knotty, that the jackal found it imperative on him to get up, and steep his towels anew. From these pilgrimages to the jug and basin, he returned with such eccentricities of damp head-gear as no words can describe; which were made the more ludicrous by his anxious gravity.

At length the jackal had got together a compact repast for the lion, and proceeded to offer it to him. The lion took it with care and caution, made his selection from it, and his remarks upon it,
25 and the jackal assisted both. When the repast was fully discussed, the lion put his hands in his waistband again, and lay down to meditate. The jackal then invigorated himself with a bumper for his throttle, and a fresh application to his head, and applied himself to the collection of a second meal; this was administered to the lion in the same manner, and was not disposed of until the clocks struck three in the morning.

"And now we have done, Sydney, fill a bumper of punch," said Mr. Stryver.

35 The jackal removed the towels from his head, which had been steaming again, shook himself, yawned, shivered, and complied.

"You were very sound, Sydney, in the matter of those crown witnesses to-day. Every question told."

"I always am sound; am I not?"

"I don't gainsay it. What has roughened your temper? Put some punch to it and smooth it again."

With a deprecatory grunt, the jackal again complied.

"The old Sydney Carton of old Shrewsbury School," said Stryver, nodding his head over him as he reviewed him in the present and the past, "the old seesaw Sydney. Up one minute and down the next; now in spirits and now in despondency!"

"Ah!" returned the other, sighing: "yes! The same Sydney, with the same luck. Even then, I did exercises for other boys, and seldom did my own."

"And why not?"

"God knows. It was my way, I suppose."

He sat, with his hands in his pockets, and his legs stretched out before him, looking at the fire.

"Carton," said his friend, squaring himself at him with a bullying air, as if the fire-grate had been the furnace in which sustained endeavour was forged, and the one delicate thing to be done for the old Sydney Carton of old Shrewsbury School was to shoulder him into it, "your way is, and always was, a lame way. You summon no energy and purpose. Look at me."

"Oh, botheration!" returned Sydney, with a lighter and more good-humoured laugh. "Don't *you* be moral!"

"How have I done what I have done?" said Stryver; "how do I do what I do?"

"Partly through paying me to help you, I suppose. But it's not worth your while to apostrophise me, or the air, about it; what you want to do, you do. You were always in the front rank, and I was always behind."

"I had to get into the front rank; I was not born there, was I?"

"I was not present at the ceremony; but my opinion is you were," said Carton. At this, he laughed again, and they both laughed.

"Before Shrewsbury, and at Shrewsbury, and ever since Shrewsbury," pursued Carton, "you have fallen into your rank, and I have fallen into mine. Even when we were fellow-students in the Student Quarter of Paris, picking up French, and French law, and other French crumbs that we didn't get much good of, you were always somewhere, and I was always—nowhere."

"And whose fault was that?"

"Upon my soul, I am not sure that it was not yours. You were

always driving and riving and shouldering and pressing, to that restless degree that I had no chance for my life but in rest and repose. It's a gloomy thing, however, to talk about one's own past, with the day breaking. Turn me in some other direction before I
5 go."

"Well then! Pledge me to the pretty witness," said Stryver, holding up his glass. "Are you turned in a pleasant direction?"

Apparently not, for he became gloomy again.

"Pretty witness," he muttered, looking down into his glass. "I have had enough of witnesses to-day and to-night; who's your pretty witness?"

"The picturesque doctor's daughter, Miss Manette."

"*She* pretty?"

"Is she not?"
15 "No."

"Why, man alive, she was the admiration of the whole court!"

"Rot the admiration of the whole court! Who made the Old Bailey a judge of beauty? She was a golden-haired doll!"

"Do you know, Sydney," said Mr. Stryver, looking at him with sharp eyes, and slowly drawing a hand across his florid face: "do you know, I rather thought, at the time, that you sympathised with the golden-haired doll, and were quick to see what happened to the golden-haired doll?"

"Quick to see what happened! If a girl, doll or no doll, swoons
25 within a yard or two of a man's nose, he can see it without a perspective-glass. I pledge you, but I deny the beauty. And now I'll have no more drink; I'll get to bed."

When his host followed him out on the staircase with a candle, to light him down the stairs, the day was coldly looking in through its grimy windows. When he got out of the house, the air was cold and sad, the dull sky overcast, the river dark and dim, the whole scene like a lifeless desert. And wreaths of dust were spinning round and round before the morning blast, as if the desert-sand had risen far away, and the first spray of it in its advance had begun to
35 overwhelm the city.

Waste forces within him, and a desert all around, this man stood still on his way across a silent terrace, and saw for a moment, lying in the wilderness before him, a mirage of honourable ambition, self-denial, and perseverance. In the fair city of this vision, there were airy galleries from which the loves and graces looked upon him, gardens in which the fruits of life hung ripening, waters of Hope that sparkled in his sight. A moment, and it was gone. Climbing into a high chamber in a well of houses, he threw himself down in his clothes on a neglected bed, and its pillow was wet with wasted tears. 5

Sadly, sadly, the sun rose: it rose upon no sadder sight than the man of good abilities and good emotions, incapable of their directed exercise, incapable of his own help and his own happiness, sensible of the blight on him, and resigning himself to let it eat him away.

Chapter 6. Hundreds of People

The quiet lodgings of Doctor Manette were in a quiet street-corner not far from Soho Square. On the afternoon of a certain fine Sunday when the waves of four months had rolled over the trial for treason, and carried it, as to the public interest and mem- 15 ory, far out to sea, Mr. Jarvis Lorry walked along the sunny streets from Clerkenwell, where he lived, on his way to dine with the Doc-tor. After several relapses into business-absorption, Mr. Lorry had become the Doctor's friend, and the quiet street-corner was the sunny part of his life.

On this certain fine Sunday, Mr. Lorry walked towards Soho, early in the afternoon, for three reasons of habit. Firstly, because, on fine Sundays, he often walked out, before dinner, with the Doctor and Lucie; secondly, because, on unfavourable Sundays, he was accustomed to be with them as the family friend, talking, reading, looking out of window, and generally getting through the day; thirdly, because he happened to have his own little shrewd doubts to solve, and knew how the ways of the Doctor's household pointed to that time as a likely time for solving them.

A quainter corner than the corner where the Doctor lived was not to be found in London. There was no way through it, and the front windows of the Doctor's lodging commanded a pleasant little vista of street that had a congenial air of retirement on it. There were few buildings then, north of the Oxford Road, and forest-trees flourished, and wild flowers grew, and the hawthorn blossomed in the now vanished fields. As a consequence, country airs circulated in Soho with vigorous freedom, instead of languishing into the parish like stray paupers without a settlement; and there was many a good south wall, not far off, on which the peaches ripened in their season.

The summer light struck into the corner brilliantly in the earlier part of the day; but, when the streets grew hot, the corner was in shadow, though not in shadow so remote but that you could see beyond it into a glare of brightness. It was a cool spot, staid but cheerful, a wonderful place for echoes, and a very harbour from the raging streets.

There ought to have been a tranquil bark in such an anchorage, and there was. The Doctor occupied two floors of a large still house, where several callings purported to be pursued by day, but whereof little was audible any day, and which was shunned by all of them at night. In a building at the back, attainable by a court-yard where a plane-tree rustled its green leaves, church-organs claimed to be made, and silver to be chased, and likewise gold to be beaten by some mysterious giant who had a golden arm starting out of the wall of the front hall—as if he had beaten himself precious, and menaced a similar conversion of all visitors. Very little of these trades, or of a lonely lodger rumoured to live upstairs, or of a dim coach-trimming maker asserted to have a counting-house below, was ever heard or seen. Occasionally, a stray workman, putting his coat on, traversed the hall, or a stranger peered about there, or a distant clink was heard across the courtyard, or a thump from the golden giant. These, however, were only the exceptions required to prove the rule that the sparrows in the plane-tree behind the house, and the echoes in the corner before it, had their own way from Sunday morning into Saturday night.

Doctor Manette received such patients here as his old reputation, and its revival in the floating whispers of his story, brought him. His scientific knowledge, and his vigilance and skill in conducting ingenious experiments, brought him otherwise into moderate request, and he earned as much as he wanted.

These things were within Mr. Jarvis Lorry's knowledge, thoughts, and notice, when he rang the door-bell of the tranquil house in the corner, on the fine Sunday afternoon.

"Doctor Manette at home?"

Expected home.

"Miss Lucie at home?"

Expected home.

"Miss Pross at home?"

Possibly at home, but of a certainty impossible for handmaid to anticipate intentions of Miss Pross, as to admission or denial of the fact.

"As I am at home myself," said Mr. Lorry, "I'll go upstairs."

Although the Doctor's daughter had known nothing of the country of her birth, she appeared to have innately derived from it that ability to make much of little means, which is one of its most useful and most agreeable characteristics. Simple as the furniture was, it was set off by so many little adornments, of no value but for their taste and fancy, that its effect was delightful. The disposition of everything in the rooms, from the largest object to the least; the arrangement of colours, the elegant variety and contrast obtained by thrift in trifles, by delicate hands, clear eyes, and good sense, were at once so pleasant in themselves, and so expressive of their originator, that, as Mr. Lorry stood looking about him, the very chairs and tables seemed to ask him, with something of that peculiar expression which he knew so well by this time, whether he approved.

There were three rooms on a floor, and, the doors by which they communicated being put open that the air might pass freely through them all, Mr. Lorry, smilingly observant of that fanciful resemblance which he detected all around him, walked from one to another. The first was the best room, and in it were Lucie's birds, and flowers, and books, and desk, and work-table, and box of water-colours; the second was the Doctor's consulting-room, used also as the dining-room; the third, changingly speckled by the rustle of the plane-tree in the yard, was the Doctor's bedroom, and there, in a corner, stood the disused shoemaker's bench and tray of tools, much as it had stood on the fifth floor of the dismal house by the wine-shop, in the suburb of Saint Antoine in Paris.

"I wonder," said Mr. Lorry, pausing in his looking about, "that he keeps that reminder of his sufferings about him!"

"And why wonder at that?" was the abrupt inquiry that made him start.

It proceeded from Miss Pross, the wild red woman, strong of

hand, whose acquaintance he had first made at the Royal George Hotel at Dover, and had since improved.

"I should have thought—" Mr. Lorry began.

"Pooh! You'd have thought!" said Miss Pross, and Mr. Lorry left

5 off.

"How do you do?" inquired that lady then—sharply, and yet as if to express that she bore him no malice.

"I am pretty well, I thank you," answered Mr. Lorry, with meekness; "how are you?"

"Nothing to boast of," said Miss Pross.

"Indeed?"

"Ah! Indeed!" said Miss Pross. "I am very much put out about my Ladybird."

"Indeed?"

15 "For gracious' sake say something else besides 'indeed,' or you'll fidget me to death," said Miss Pross: whose character (dissociated from stature) was shortness.

"Really, then?" said Mr. Lorry, as an amendment.

"Really is bad enough," returned Miss Pross, "but better. Yes, I am very much put out."

"May I ask the cause?"

"I don't want dozens of people who are not at all worthy of Ladybird, to come here looking after her," said Miss Pross.

"Do dozens come for that purpose?"

25 "Hundreds," said Miss Pross.

It was characteristic of this lady (as of some other people before her time and since) that whenever her original proposition was questioned, she exaggerated it.

"Dear me!" said Mr. Lorry, as the safest remark he could think of.

"I have lived with the darling—or the darling has lived with me, and paid me for it; which she certainly should never have done, you may take your affidavit, if I could have afforded to keep either myself or her for nothing—since she was ten years old. And it's

35 really very hard," said Miss Pross.

Not seeing with precision what was very hard, Mr. Lorry shook his head; using that important part of himself as a sort of fairy cloak that would fit anything.

"All sorts of people who are not in the least degree worthy of the pet are always turning up," said Miss Pross. "When you began it—"

"*I* began it, Miss Pross?"

"Didn't you? Who brought her father to life?"

"Oh! If *that* was beginning it—" said Mr. Lorry.   5

"It wasn't ending it, I suppose? I say, when you began it, it was hard enough; not that I have any fault to find with Doctor Manette, except that he is not worthy of such a daughter, which is no imputation on him, for it was not to be expected that anybody should be, under any circumstances. But it really is doubly and trebly hard to have crowds and multitudes of people turning up after him (I could have forgiven him), to take Ladybird's affections away from me."

Mr. Lorry knew Miss Pross to be very jealous, but he also knew   15
her by this time to be, beneath the surface of her eccentricity, one of those unselfish creatures—found only among women—who will, for pure love and admiration, bind themselves willing slaves, to youth when they have lost it, to beauty that they never had, to accomplishments that they were never fortunate enough to gain, to bright hopes that never shone upon their own sombre lives. He knew enough of the world to know that there is nothing in it better than the faithful service of the heart; so rendered and so free from any mercenary taint, he had such an exalted respect for it, that in the retributive arrangements made by his own mind—we all make   25
such arrangements, more or less—he stationed Miss Pross much nearer to the lower Angels than many ladies immeasurably better got up both by Nature and Art, who had balances at Tellson's.

"There never was, nor will be, but one man worthy of Ladybird," said Miss Pross; "and that was my brother Solomon, if he hadn't made a mistake in life."

Here again: Mr. Lorry's inquiries into Miss Pross's personal history had established the fact that her brother Solomon was a heartless scoundrel who had stripped her of everything she possessed, as a stake to speculate with, and had abandoned her in her poverty for evermore, with no touch of compunction. Miss Pross's   35
fidelity of belief in Solomon (deducting a mere trifle for this slight mistake) was quite a serious matter with Mr. Lorry, and had its weight in his good opinion of her.

"As we happen to be alone for the moment, and are both people of business," he said, when they had got back to the drawing-room and had sat down there in friendly relations, "let me ask you—does the Doctor, in talking with Lucie, never refer to the shoemaking time, yet?"

5   "Never."

"And yet keeps that bench and those tools beside him?"

"Ah!" returned Miss Pross, shaking her head. "But I don't say he don't refer to it within himself."

"Do you believe that he thinks of it much?"

"I do," said Miss Pross.

"Do you imagine—" Mr. Lorry had begun, when Miss Pross took him up short with:

"Never imagine anything. Have no imagination at all."

"I stand corrected; do you suppose—you go so far as to suppose,
15   sometimes?"

"Now and then," said Miss Pross.

"Do you suppose," Mr. Lorry went on, with a laughing twinkle in his bright eye, as it looked kindly at her, "that Doctor Manette has any theory of his own, preserved through all those years, relative to the cause of his being so oppressed; perhaps, even to the name of his oppressor?"

"I don't suppose anything about it but what Ladybird tells me."

"And this is—?"

"That she thinks he has."

25   "Now don't be angry at my asking all these questions; because I am a mere dull man of business, and you are a woman of business."

"Dull?" Miss Pross inquired, with placidity.

Rather wishing his modest adjective away, Mr. Lorry replied, "No, no, no. Surely not. To return to business—Is it not remarkable that Doctor Manette, unquestionably innocent of any crime as we are all well assured he is, should never touch upon that question? I will not say with me, though he had business relations with me many years ago, and we are now intimate; I will say with the fair daughter to whom he is so devotedly attached, and who is so devotedly attached to him? Believe me, Miss Pross, I don't
35   approach the topic with you, out of curiosity, but out of zealous interest."

"Well! To the best of my understanding, and bad's the best, you'll tell me," said Miss Pross, softened by the tone of the apology, "he is afraid of the whole subject."

"Afraid?"

"It's plain enough, I should think, why he may be. It's a dreadful remembrance. Besides that, his loss of himself grew out of it. Not knowing how he lost himself, or how he recovered himself, he may   5
never feel certain of not losing himself again. That alone wouldn't make the subject pleasant, I should think."

It was a profounder remark than Mr. Lorry had looked for. "True," said he, "and fearful to reflect upon. Yet, a doubt lurks in my mind, Miss Pross, whether it is good for Doctor Manette to have that suppression always shut up within him. Indeed, it is this doubt and the uneasiness it sometimes causes me that has led me to our present confidence."

"Can't be helped," said Miss Pross, shaking her head. "Touch that string, and he instantly changes for the worse. Better leave it   15
alone. In short, must leave it alone, like or no like. Sometimes, he gets up in the dead of the night, and will be heard, by us overhead there, walking up and down, walking up and down, in his room. Ladybird has learnt to know then that his mind is walking up and down, walking up and down, in his old prison. She hurries to him, and they go on together, walking up and down, walking up and down, until he is composed. But he never says a word of the true reason for his restlessness, to her, and she finds it best not to hint at it to him. In silence they go walking up and down together, walking up and down together, till her love and company have brought him   25
to himself."

Notwithstanding Miss Pross's denial of her own imagination, there was a perception of the pain of being monotonously haunted by one sad idea, in her repetition of the phrase, walking up and down, which testified to her possessing such a thing.

The corner has been mentioned as a wonderful corner for echoes; it had begun to echo so resoundingly to the tread of coming feet, that it seemed as though the very mention of that weary pacing to and fro had set it going. "Here they are!" said Miss Pross, rising to break up the confidence; "and now we shall have hundreds of   35
people pretty soon!"

It was such a curious corner in its acoustical properties, such a peculiar ear of a place, that as Mr. Lorry stood at the open window, looking for the father and daughter whose steps he heard, he fancied they would never approach. Not only would the echoes die away, as though the steps had gone; but, echoes of other steps that never came would be heard in their stead, and would die away for good when they seemed close at hand. However, father and daughter did at last appear, and Miss Pross was ready at the street door to receive them.

Miss Pross was a pleasant sight, albeit wild, and red, and grim, taking off her darling's bonnet when she came upstairs, and touching it up with the ends of her handkerchief, and blowing the dust off it, and folding her mantle ready for laying by, and smoothing her rich hair with as much pride as she could possibly have taken in her own hair if she had been the vainest and handsomest of women. Her darling was a pleasant sight too, embracing her and thanking her, and protesting against her taking so much trouble for her—which last she only dared to do playfully, or Miss Pross, sorely hurt, would have retired to her own chamber and cried. The Doctor was a pleasant sight too, looking on at them, and telling Miss Pross how she spoilt Lucie, in accents and with eyes that had as much spoiling in them as Miss Pross had, and would have had more if it were possible. Mr. Lorry was a pleasant sight too, beaming at all this in his little wig, and thanking his bachelor stars for having lighted him in his declining years to a Home. But, no Hundreds of people came to see the sights, and Mr. Lorry looked in vain for the fulfillment of Miss Pross's prediction.

Dinner-time, and still no Hundreds of people. In the arrangements of the little household, Miss Pross took charge of the lower regions, and always acquitted herself marvelously. Her dinners, of a very modest quality, were so well cooked and so well served, and so neat in their contrivances, half English and half French, that nothing could be better. Miss Pross's friendship being of the thoroughly practical kind, she had ravaged Soho and the adjacent provinces, in search of impoverished French, who, tempted by shillings and half-crowns, would impart culinary mysteries to her. From these decayed sons and daughters of Gaul, she had acquired such wonderful arts, that the woman and girl who formed the staff of domestics regarded her as quite a sorceress, or Cinderella's godmother: who would send out for a fowl, a rabbit, a vegetable or two from the garden, and change them into anything she pleased.

On Sundays, Miss Pross dined at the Doctor's table, but on other days persisted in taking her meals at unknown periods, either in the lower regions, or in her own room on the second floor—a blue chamber, to which no one but her Ladybird ever gained admittance. On this occasion, Miss Pross, responding to Ladybird's pleasant face and pleasant efforts to please her, unbent exceedingly; so the dinner was very pleasant, too.

It was an oppressing day, and, after dinner, Lucie proposed that the wine should be carried out under the plane-tree, and they should sit there in the air. As everything turned upon her, and revolved about her, they went out under the plane-tree, and she carried the wine down for the special benefit of Mr. Lorry. She had installed herself, some time before, as Mr. Lorry's cupbearer; and while they sat under the plane-tree, talking, she kept his glass replenished. Mysterious backs and ends of houses peeped at them as they talked, and the plane-tree whispered to them in its own way above their heads.

Still, the Hundreds of people did not present themselves. Mr. Darnay presented himself while they were sitting under the plane-tree, but he was only One.

Doctor Manette received him kindly, and so did Lucie. But, Miss Pross suddenly became afflicted with a twitching in the head and body, and retired into the house. She was not unfrequently the victim of this disorder, and she called it, in familiar conversation, "a fit of the jerks."

The Doctor was in his best condition, and looked specially young. The resemblance between him and Lucie was very strong at such times, and as they sat side by side, she leaning on his shoulder, and he resting his arm on the back of her chair, it was very agreeable to trace the likeness.

He had been talking all day, on many subjects, and with unusual vivacity. "Pray, Doctor Manette," said Mr. Darnay, as they sat under the plane-tree—and he said it in the natural pursuit of the topic in hand, which happened to be the old buildings of London—"have you seen much of the Tower?"

"Lucie and I have been there; but only casually. We have seen enough of it, to know that it teems with interest; little more."

"*I* have been there, as you remember," said Darnay, with a smile, though reddening a little angrily, "in another character, and not in a character that gives facilities for seeing much of it. They told me a curious thing when I was there."

"What was that?" Lucie asked.

"In making some alterations, the workmen came upon an old dungeon, which had been, for many years, built up and forgotten. Every stone of its inner wall was covered by inscriptions which had been carved by prisoners—dates, names, complaints, and prayers. Upon a corner stone in an angle of the wall, one prisoner, who seemed to have gone to execution, had cut, as his last work, three letters. They were done with some very poor instrument, and hurriedly, with an unsteady hand. At first, they were read as D.I.C.; but, on being more carefully examined, the last letter was found to be G. There was no record or legend of any prisoner with those initials, and many fruitless guesses were made what the name could have been. At length, it was suggested that the letters were not initials, but the complete word, DIG. The floor was examined very carefully under the inscription, and, in the earth beneath a stone, or tile, or some fragment of paving, were found the ashes of a paper, mingled with the ashes of a small leathern case or bag. What the unknown prisoner had written will never be read, but he had written something, and hidden it away to keep it from the gaoler."

"My father," exclaimed Lucie, "you are ill!"

He had suddenly started up, with his hand to his head. His manner and his look quite terrified them all.

"No, my dear, not ill. There are large drops of rain falling, and they made me start. We had better go in."

He recovered himself almost instantly. Rain was really falling in large drops, and he showed the back of his hand with rain-drops on it. But, he said not a single word in reference to the discovery that had been told of, and, as they went into the house, the business eye of Mr. Lorry either detected, or fancied it detected, on his face, as it turned towards Charles Darnay, the same singular look that had been upon it when it turned towards him in the passages of the Court House.

He recovered himself so quickly, however, that Mr. Lorry had doubts of his business eye. The arm of the golden giant in the hall was not more steady than he was, when he stopped under it to remark to them that he was not yet proof against slight surprises (if he ever would be), and that the rain had startled him.

Tea-time, and Miss Pross making tea, with another fit of the jerks upon her, and yet no Hundreds of people. Mr. Carton had lounged, but he made only Two.

The night was so very sultry, that although they sat with doors and windows open, they were overpowered by heat. When the tea-table was done with, they all moved to one of the windows, and looked out into the heavy twilight. Lucie sat by her father; Darnay sat beside her; Carton leaned against a window. The curtains were long and white, and some of the thunder-gusts that whirled into the corner caught them up to the ceiling, and waved them like spectral wings.

"The rain-drops are still falling, large, heavy, and few," said Doctor Manette. "It comes slowly."

"It comes surely," said Carton.

They spoke low, as people watching and waiting mostly do; as people in a dark room, watching and waiting for lightning, always do.

There was a great hurry in the streets, of people speeding away to get shelter before the storm broke; the wonderful corner for echoes resounded with the echoes of footsteps coming and going, yet not a footstep was there.

"A multitude of people, and yet a solitude!" said Darnay, when they had listened for a while.

"Is it not impressive, Mr. Darnay?" asked Lucie. "Sometimes, I have sat here of an evening, until I have fancied—but even the shade of a foolish fancy makes me shudder to-night, when all is so black and solemn—"

"Let us shudder too. We may know what it is."

"It will seem nothing to you. Such whims are only impressive as we originate them, I think; they are not to be communicated. I have sometimes sat alone here of an evening, listening, until I have made the echoes out to be the echoes of all the footsteps that are coming by and by into our lives."

"There is a great crowd coming one day into our lives, if that be so," Sydney Carton struck in, in his moody way.

The footsteps were incessant, and the hurry of them became more and more rapid. The corner echoed and re-echoed with the tread of feet; some, as it seemed, under the windows; some, as it seemed, in the room; some coming, some going, some breaking off, some stopping altogether; all in the distant streets, and not one within sight.

5   "Are all these footsteps destined to come to all of us, Miss Manette, or are we to divide them among us?"

"I don't know, Mr. Darnay; I told you it was a foolish fancy, but you asked for it. When I have yielded myself to it, I have been alone, and then I have imagined them the footsteps of the people who are to come into my life, and my father's."

"I take them into mine!" said Carton. "I ask no questions and make no stipulations. There is a great crowd bearing down upon us, Miss Manette, and I see them—by the lightning." He added the last words, after there had been a vivid flash which had shown him lounging in the window.

15   "And I hear them!" he added again, after a peal of thunder. "Here they come, fast, fierce, and furious!"

It was the rush and roar of rain that he typified, and it stopped him, for no voice could be heard in it. A memorable storm of thunder and lightning broke with that sweep of water, and there was not a moment's interval in crash, and fire, and rain, until after the moon rose at midnight.

The great bell of Saint Paul's was striking one in the cleared air, when Mr. Lorry, escorted by Jerry, high-booted and bearing a lantern, set forth on his return-passage to Clerkenwell. There were

25   solitary patches of road on the way between Soho and Clerkenwell, and Mr. Lorry, mindful of footpads, always retained Jerry for this service: though it was usually performed a good two hours earlier.

"What a night it has been! Almost a night, Jerry," said Mr. Lorry, "to bring the dead out of their graves."

"I never see the night myself, master—not yet I don't expect to—what would do that," answered Jerry.

"Good-night, Mr. Carton," said the man of business. "Good-night, Mr. Darnay. Shall we ever see such a night again, together!"

Perhaps. Perhaps, see the great crowd of people with its rush and

35   roar, bearing down upon them, too.

Chapter 7. Monseigneur in Town

Monseigneur, one of the great lords in power at the Court, held his fortnightly reception in his grand hotel in Paris. Monseigneur was in his inner room, his sanctuary of sanctuaries, the Holiest of Holiests to the crowd of worshippers in the suite of rooms without. Monseigneur was about to take his chocolate. Monseigneur could swallow a great many things with ease, and was by some few sullen minds supposed to be rather rapidly swallowing France; but, his morning's chocolate could not so much as get into the throat of Monseigneur without the aid of four strong men besides the cook.

Yes. It took four men, all four a-blaze with gorgeous decoration, and the chief of them unable to exist with fewer than two gold watches in his pocket, emulative of the noble and chaste fashion set by Monseigneur, to conduct the happy chocolate to Monseigneur's lips. One lacquey carried the chocolate-pot into the sacred presence; a second milled and frothed the chocolate with the little instrument he bore for that function; a third presented the favoured napkin; a fourth (he of the two gold watches) poured the chocolate out. It was impossible for Monseigneur to dispense with one of these attendants on the chocolate and hold his high place under the admiring Heavens. Deep would have been the blot upon his escutcheon if his chocolate had been ignobly waited on by only three men; he must have died of two.

Monseigneur had been out at a little supper last night, where the Comedy and the Grand Opera were charmingly represented. Monseigneur was out at a little supper most nights, with fascinating company. So polite and so impressible was Monseigneur, that the Comedy and the Grand Opera had far more influence with him in the tiresome articles of state affairs and state secrets, than the needs of all France. A happy circumstance for France, as the like always is for all countries ·similarly favoured!—always was for England (by way of example), in the regretted days of the merry Stuart who sold it.

Monseigneur had one truly noble idea of general public business, which was, to let everything go on in its own way; of particular public business, Monseigneur had the other truly noble idea that it must all go his way—tend to his own power and pocket. Of his pleasures, general and particular, Monseigneur had the other truly noble idea, that the world was made for them. The text of his order (altered from the original by only a pronoun, which is not much) ran: "The earth and the fulness thereof are mine, saith Monseigneur."

Yet, Monseigneur had slowly found that vulgar embarrassments crept into his affairs, both private and public; and he had, as to both classes of affairs, allied himself perforce with a Farmer-General. As to finances public, because Monseigneur could not make anything at all of them, and must consequently let them out to somebody who could; as to finances private, because Farmer-Generals were rich, and Monseigneur, after generations of great luxury and expense, was growing poor. Hence Monseigneur had taken his sister from a convent, while there was yet time to ward off the impending veil, the cheapest garment she could wear, and had bestowed her as a prize upon a very rich Farmer-General, poor in family. Which Farmer-General, carrying an appropriate cane with a golden apple on the top of it, was now among the company in the outer rooms, much prostrated before by mankind—always excepting superior mankind of the blood of Monseigneur, who, his own wife included, looked down upon him with the loftiest contempt.

A sumptuous man was the Farmer-General. Thirty horses stood in his stables, twenty-four male domestics sat in his halls, six body-women waited on his wife. As one who pretended to do nothing but plunder and forage where he could, the Farmer-General—howsoever his matrimonial relations conduced to social morality—was at least the greatest reality among the personages who attended at the hotel of Monseigneur that day.

For, the rooms, though a beautiful scene to look at, and adorned with every device of decoration that the taste and skill of the time could achieve, were, in truth, not a sound business; considered with any reference to the scarecrows in the rags and nightcaps elsewhere (and not so far off, either, but that the watching towers of Notre Dame, almost equi-distant from the two extremes, could see them both), they would have been an exceedingly uncomfortable business—if that could have been anybody's business, at the house of Monseigneur. Military officers destitute of military knowledge;

naval officers with no idea of a ship; civil officers without a notion
of affairs; brazen ecclesiastics, of the worst world worldly, with
sensual eyes, loose tongues, and looser lives; all totally unfit for their
several callings, all lying horribly in pretending to belong to them,
but all nearly or remotely of the order of Monseigneur, and   5
therefore foisted on all public employments from which anything
was to be got; these were to be told off by the score and the score.
People not immediately connected with Monseigneur or the State,
yet equally unconnected with anything that was real, or with lives
passed in travelling by any straight road to any true earthly end,
were no less abundant. Doctors who made great fortunes out of
dainty remedies for imaginary disorders that never existed, smiled
upon their courtly patients in the ante-chambers of Monseigneur.
Projectors who had discovered every kind of remedy for the little
evils with which the State was touched, except the remedy of   15
setting to work in earnest to root out a single sin, poured their
distracting babble into any ears they could lay hold of, at the
reception of Monseigneur. Unbelieving Philosophers who were
remodelling the world with words, and making card-towers of Babel
to scale the skies with, talked with Unbelieving Chemists who had
an eye on the transmutation of metals, at this wonderful gathering
accumulated by Monseigneur. Exquisite gentlemen of the finest
breeding, which was at that remarkable time—and has been
since—to be known by its fruits of indifference to every natural
subject of human interest, were in the most exemplary state of   25
exhaustion, at the hotel of Monseigneur. Such homes had these
various notabilities left behind them in the fine world of Paris, that
the spies among the assembled devotees of Monseigneur—forming
a goodly half of the polite company—would have found it hard to
discover among the angels of that sphere one solitary wife, who, in
her manners and appearance, owned to being a mother. Indeed,
except for the mere act of bringing a troublesome creature into this
world—which does not go far towards the realisation of the name
of mother—there was no such thing known to the fashion. Peasant
women kept the unfashionable babies close, and brought them up,   35
and charming grandmammas of sixty dressed and supped as at
twenty.

The leprosy of unreality disfigured every human creature in
attendance upon Monseigneur. In the outermost room were half a

dozen exceptional people who had had, for a few years, some vague misgiving in them that things in general were going rather wrong. As a promising way of setting them right, half of the half-dozen had become members of a fantastic sect of Convulsionists, and were even then considering within themselves whether they should foam, rage, roar, and turn cataleptic on the spot—thereby setting up a highly intelligible finger-post to the Future, for Monseigneur's guidance. Besides these Dervishes, were other three who had rushed into another sect, which mended matters with a jargon about "The Centre of Truth"; holding that Man had got out of the Centre of Truth—which did not need much demonstration—but had not got out of the Circumference, and that he was to be kept from flying out of the Circumference, and was even to be shoved back into the Centre, by fasting and seeing of spirits. Among these, accordingly, much discoursing with spirits went on—and it did a world of good which never became manifest.

But, the comfort was, that all the company at the grand hotel of Monseigneur were perfectly dressed. If the Day of Judgment had only been ascertained to be a dress day, everybody there would have been eternally correct. Such frizzling and powdering and sticking up of hair, such delicate complexions artificially preserved and mended, such gallant swords to look at, and such delicate honour to the sense of smell, would surely keep anything going, for ever and ever. The exquisite gentlemen of the finest breeding wore little pendent trinkets that chinked as they languidly moved; these golden fetters rang like precious little bells; and what with that ringing, and with the rustle of silk and brocade and fine linen, there was a flutter in the air that fanned Saint Antoine and his devouring hunger far away.

Dress was the one unfailing talisman and charm used for keeping all things in their places. Everybody was dressed for a Fancy Ball that was never to leave off. From the Palace of the Tuileries, through Monseigneur and the whole Court, through the Chambers, the Tribunals of Justice, and all society (except the scarecrows), the Fancy Ball descended to the Common Executioner; who, in pursuance of the charm, was required to officiate "frizzled, powdered, in a gold-laced coat, pumps, and white silk stockings." At the gallows and the wheel—the axe was a rarity—Monsieur Paris, as it was the episcopal mode among his brother professors of the provinces, Monsieur Orleans, and the rest, to call him, presided in this dainty dress. And who among the company at Monseigneur's reception in that seventeen hundred and eightieth year of our Lord, could possibly doubt that a system rooted in a frizzled hangman, powdered, gold-laced, pumped, and white-silk stockinged, would see the very stars out!   5

Monseigneur having eased his four men of their burdens and taken his chocolate, caused the doors of the Holiest of Holiests to be thrown open, and issued forth. Then, what submission, what cringing and fawning, what servility, what abject humiliation! As to bowing down in body and spirit, nothing in that way was left for Heaven—which may have been one among other reasons why the worshippers of Monseigneur never troubled it.

Bestowing a word of promise here and a smile there, a whisper on one happy slave and a wave of the hand on another, Monseigneur   15 affably passed through his rooms to the remote region of the Circumference of Truth. There, Monseigneur turned, and came back again, and so in the due course of time got himself shut up in his sanctuary by the chocolate sprites, and was seen no more.

The show being over, the flutter in the air became quite a little storm, and the precious little bells went ringing downstairs. There was soon but one person left of all the crowd, and he, with his hat under his arm and his snuffbox in his hand, slowly passed among the mirrors on his way out.

"I devote you," said this person, stopping at the last door on his   25 way, and turning in the direction of the sanctuary, "to the Devil!" With that, he shook the snuff from his fingers as if he had shaken the dust from his feet, and quietly walked downstairs.

He was a man of about sixty, handsomely dressed, haughty in manner, and with a face like a fine mask. A face of a transparent paleness; every feature in it clearly defined; one set expression on it. The nose, beautifully formed otherwise, was very slightly pinched at the top of each nostril. In those two compressions, or dints, the only little change that the face ever showed, resided. They persisted in changing colour sometimes, and they would be occasionally   35 dilated and contracted by something like a faint pulsation; then, they gave a look of treachery, and cruelty, to the whole counte-nance. Examined with attention, its capacity of helping such a look was to be found in the line of the mouth, and the lines of the orbits of the eyes, being much too horizontal and thin; still, in the effect the face made, it was a handsome face, and a remarkable one.

Its owner went downstairs into the courtyard, got into his carriage, and drove away. Not many people had talked with him at the reception; he had stood in a little space apart, and Monseigneur might have been warmer in his manner. It appeared, under the circumstances, rather agreeable to him to see the common people dispersed before his horses, and often barely escaping from being run down. His man drove as if he were charging an enemy, and the furious recklessness of the man brought no check into the face, or to the lips, of the master. The complaint had sometimes made itself audible, even in that deaf city and dumb age, that, in the narrow streets without footways, the fierce patrician custom of hard driving endangered and maimed the mere vulgar in a barbarous manner. But, few cared enough for that to think of it a second time, and, in this matter, as in all others, the common wretches were left to get out of their difficulties as they could.

With a wild rattle and clatter, and an inhuman abandonment of consideration not easy to be understood in these days, the carriage dashed through streets and swept round corners, with women screaming before it, and men clutching each other and clutching children out of its way. At last, swooping at a street corner by a fountain, one of its wheels came to a sickening little jolt, and there was a loud cry from a number of voices, and the horses reared and plunged.

But for the latter inconvenience, the carriage probably would not have stopped; carriages were often known to drive on, and leave their wounded behind, and why not? But the frightened valet had got down in a hurry, and there were twenty hands at the horses' bridles.

"What has gone wrong?" said Monsieur, calmly looking out.

A tall man in a nightcap had caught up a bundle from among the feet of the horses, and had laid it on the basement of the fountain, and was down in the mud and wet, howling over it like a wild animal.

"Pardon, Monsieur the Marquis!" said a ragged and submissive man, "it is a child."

"Why does he make that abominable noise? Is it his child?"

"Excuse me, Monsieur the Marquis—it is a pity—yes."

The fountain was a little removed; for the street opened, where it was, into a space some ten or twelve yards square. As the tall man suddenly got up from the ground, and came running at the carriage, Monsieur the Marquis clapped his hand for an instant on his sword-hilt.

"Killed!" shrieked the man, in wild desperation, extending both arms at their length above his head, and staring at him. "Dead!"

The people closed round, and looked at Monsieur the Marquis. There was nothing revealed by the many eyes that looked at him but watchfulness and eagerness; there was no visible menacing or anger. Neither did the people say anything; after the first cry, they had been silent, and they remained so. The voice of the submissive man who had spoken was flat and tame in its extreme submission. Monsieur the Marquis ran his eyes over them all, as if they had been mere rats come out of their holes.

He took out his purse.

"It is extraordinary to me," said he, "that you people cannot take care of yourselves and your children. One or the other of you is for ever in the way. How do I know what injury you have done my horses? See! Give him that."

He threw out a gold coin for the valet to pick up, and all the heads craned forward that all the eyes might look down at it as it fell. The tall man called out again with a most unearthly cry, "Dead!"

He was arrested by the quick arrival of another man, for whom the rest made way. On seeing him, the miserable creature fell upon his shoulder, sobbing and crying, and pointing to the fountain, where some women were stooping over the motionless bundle, and moving gently about it. They were as silent, however, as the men.

"I know all, I know all," said the last comer. "Be a brave man, my Gaspard! It is better for the poor little plaything to die so, than to live. It has died in a moment, without pain. Could it have lived an hour as happily?"

"You are a philosopher, you there," said the Marquis smiling. "How do they call you?"

"They call me Defarge."

"Of what trade?"

"Monsieur the Marquis, vendor of wine."

"Pick up that, philosopher and vendor of wine," said the Marquis throwing him another gold coin, "and spend it as you will. The horses there; are they right?"

5   Without deigning to look at the assemblage a second time, Monsieur the Marquis leaned back in his seat, and was just being driven away with the air of a gentleman who had accidentally broken some common thing, and had paid for it, and could afford to pay for it; when his ease was suddenly disturbed by a coin flying into his carriage, and ringing on its floor.

"Hold!" said Monsieur the Marquis. "Hold the horses! Who threw that?"

He looked to the spot where Defarge the vendor of wine had stood a moment before; but the wretched father was grovelling on his face on the pavement in that spot, and the figure that stood

15   beside him was the figure of a dark stout woman, knitting.

"You dogs!" said the Marquis, but smoothly, and with an unchanged front, except as to the spots on his nose. "I would ride over any of you very willingly, and exterminate you from the earth. If I knew which rascal threw at the carriage, and if that brigand were sufficiently near it, he should be crushed under the wheels."

So cowed was their condition, and so long and hard their experience of what such a man could do to them, within the law and beyond it, that not a voice, or a hand, or even an eye was raised. Among the men, not one. But the woman who stood

25   knitting looked up steadily, and looked the Marquis in the face. It was not for his dignity to notice it; his contemptuous eyes passed over her, and over all the other rats; and he leaned back in his seat again, and gave the word "Go on!"

He was driven on, and other carriages came whirling by in quick succession; the Minister, the State-Projector, the Farmer-General, the Doctor, the Lawyer, the Ecclesiastic, the Grand Opera, the Comedy, the whole Fancy Ball, in a bright continuous flow, came whirling by. The rats had crept out of their holes to look on, and they remained looking on for hours; soldiers and police often

35   passing between them and the spectacle, and making a barrier behind which they slunk, and through which they peeped. The father had long ago taken up his bundle and hidden himself away with it, when the women who had tended the bundle while it lay on the base of the fountain sat there watching the running of the

water and the rolling of the Fancy Ball—when the one woman who had stood conspicuous, knitting, still knitted on with the steadfastness of Fate. The water of the fountain ran, the swift river ran, the day ran into evening, so much life in the city ran into death according to rule, time and tide waited for no man, the rats were sleeping close together in their dark holes again, the Fancy Ball was lighted up at supper, all things ran their course. 5

Chapter 8. Monseigneur in the Country

A beautiful landscape, with the corn bright in it, but not abundant. Patches of poor rye where corn should have been, patches of poor peas and beans, patches of most coarse vegetable substitutes for wheat. On inanimate nature, as on the men and women who cultivated it, a prevalent tendency towards an appearance of vegetating unwillingly—a dejected disposition to give up, and wither away.

Monsieur the Marquis in his travelling carriage (which might have been lighter), conducted by four post-horses and two postilions, fagged up a steep hill. A blush on the countenance of Monsieur the Marquis was no impeachment of his high breeding; it was not from within; it was occasioned by an external circumstance beyond his control—the setting sun. 15

The sunset struck so brilliantly into the travelling carriage when it gained the hill-top, that its occupant was steeped in crimson. "It will die out," said Monsieur the Marquis, glancing at his hands, "directly."

In effect, the sun was so low that it dipped at the moment. When the heavy drag had been adjusted to the wheel, and the carriage slid down hill, with a cinderous smell, in a cloud of dust, the red glow departed quickly; the sun and the Marquis going down together, there was no glow left when the drag was taken off. 25

But, there remained a broken country, bold and open, a little village at the bottom of the hill, a broad sweep and rise beyond it, a church-tower, a windmill, a forest for the chase, and a crag with a fortress on it used as a prison. Round upon all these darkening objects as the night drew on, the Marquis looked, with the air of one who was coming near home.

The village had its one poor street, with its poor brewery, poor tannery, poor tavern, poor stable-yard for relay of post-horses, poor fountain, all usual poor appointments. It had its poor people too. All its people were poor, and many of them were sitting at their doors, shredding spare onions and the like for supper, while many were at the fountain, washing leaves, and grasses, and any such small yieldings of the earth that could be eaten. Expressive signs of what made them poor were not wanting; the tax for the state, the tax for the church, the tax for the lord, tax local and tax general, were to be paid here and to be paid there, according to solemn inscription in the little village, until the wonder was, that there was any village left unswallowed.

Few children were to be seen, and no dogs. As to the men and women, their choice on earth was stated in the prospect—Life on the lowest terms that could sustain it, down in the little village under the mill; or captivity and Death in the dominant prison on the crag.

Heralded by a courier in advance, and by the cracking of his postilions' whips, which twined snake-like about their heads in the evening air, as if he came attended by the Furies, Monsieur the Marquis drew up in his travelling carriage at the posting-house gate. It was hard by the fountain, and the peasants suspended their operations to look at him. He looked at them, and saw in them, without knowing it, the slow sure filing down of misery-worn face and figure that was to make the meagreness of Frenchmen an English superstition which should survive the truth through the best part of a hundred years.

Monsieur the Marquis cast his eyes over the submissive faces that drooped before him, as the like of himself had drooped before Monseigneur of the Court—only the difference was, that these faces drooped merely to suffer and not to propitiate—when a grizzled mender of the roads joined the group.

"Bring me hither that fellow!" said the Marquis to the courier.

The fellow was brought, cap in hand, and the other fellows closed round to look and listen, in the manner of the people at the Paris fountain.

"I passed you on the road?"

"Monseigneur, it is true. I had the honour of being passed on the road."

"Coming up the hill, and at the top of the hill, both?"

"Monseigneur, it is true."

"What did you look at, so fixedly?"

"Monseigneur, I looked at the man."

He stooped a little, and with his tattered blue cap pointed under   5
the carriage. All his fellows stooped to look under the carriage.

"What man, pig? And why look there?"

"Pardon, Monseigneur; he swung by the chain of the shoe—the
drag."

"Who?" demanded the traveller.

"Monseigneur, the man."

"May the Devil carry away these idiots! How do you call the
man? You know all the men of this part of the country. Who was
he?"

"Your clemency, Monseigneur! He was not of this part of the   15
country. Of all the days of my life, I never saw him."

"Swinging by the chain? To be suffocated?"

"With your gracious permission, that was the wonder of it,
Monseigneur. His head was hanging over—like this!"

He turned himself sideways to the carriage, and leaned back,
with his face thrown up to the sky, and his head hanging down;
then recovered himself, fumbled with his cap, and made a bow.

"What was he like?"

"Monseigneur, he was whiter than the miller. All covered with
dust, white as a spectre, tall as a spectre!"   25

The picture produced an immense sensation in the little crowd;
but all eyes, without comparing notes with other eyes, looked at
Monsieur the Marquis. Perhaps, to observe whether he had any
spectre on his conscience.

"Truly, you did well," said the Marquis, felicitously sensible that
such vermin were not to ruffle him, "to see a thief accompanying
my carriage, and not open that great mouth of yours. Bah! Put him
aside, Monsieur Gabelle!"

Monsieur Gabelle was the postmaster, and some other taxing
functionary united; he had come out with great obsequiousness to   35
assist at this examination, and had held the examined by the
drapery of his arm in an official manner.

"Bah! Go aside!" said Monsieur Gabelle.

"Lay hands on this stranger if he seeks to lodge in your village
to-night, and be sure that his business is honest, Gabelle."

"Monsieur, I am flattered to devote myself to your orders."

"Did he run away, fellow?—Where is that accursed?"

The accursed was already under the carriage with some half-dozen particular friends, pointing out the chain with his blue cap. Some half-dozen other particular friends promptly hauled him out, and presented him breathless to Monsieur the Marquis.

"Did the man run away, dolt, when we stopped for the drag?"

"Monseigneur, he precipitated himself over the hillside, head first, as a person plunges into a river."

"See to it, Gabelle. Go on!"

The half-dozen who were peering at the chain were still among the wheels, like sheep; the wheels turned so suddenly that they were lucky to save their skins and bones; they had very little else to save or they might not have been so fortunate.

The burst with which the carriage started out of the village and up the rise beyond was soon checked by the steepness of the hill. Gradually, it subsided to a foot-pace, swinging and lumbering upward among the many sweet scents of a summer night. The postilions, with a thousand gossamer gnats circling about them in lieu of the Furies, quietly mended the points to the lashes of their whips; the valet walked by the horses; the courier was audible, trotting on ahead into the dim distance.

At the steepest point of the hill there was a little burial-ground, with a Cross and a new large figure of Our Saviour on it; it was a poor figure in wood, done by some inexperienced rustic carver, but he had studied the figure from the life—his own life, maybe—for it was dreadfully spare and thin.

To this distressful emblem of a great distress that had long been growing worse, and was not at its worst, a woman was kneeling. She turned her head as the carriage came up to her, rose quickly, and presented herself at the carriage-door.

"It is you, Monseigneur! Monseigneur, a petition."

With an exclamation of impatience, but with his unchangeable face, Monseigneur looked out.

"How, then! What is it? Always petitions!"

"Monseigneur. For the love of the great God! My husband, the forester."

"What of your husband, the forester? Always the same with you people. He cannot pay something?"

"He has paid all, Monseigneur. He is dead."

"Well! He is quiet. Can I restore him to you?"

"Alas, no, Monseigneur! But he lies yonder, under a little heap of poor grass."

"Well?"

"Monseigneur, there are so many little heaps of poor grass."

"Again, well?"

She looked an old woman, but was young. Her manner was one of passionate grief; by turns she clasped her veinous and knotted hands together with wild energy, and laid one of them on the carriage-door—tenderly, caressingly, as if it had been a human breast, and could be expected to feel the appealing touch.

"Monseigneur, hear me! Monseigneur, hear my petition! My husband died of want; so many die of want; so many more will die of want."

"Again, well? Can I feed them?"

"Monseigneur, the good God knows; but I don't ask it. My petition is that a morsel of stone or wood, with my husband's name, may be placed over him to show where he lies. Otherwise, the place will be quickly forgotten, it will never be found when I am dead of the same malady, I shall be laid under some other heap of poor grass. Monseigneur, they are so many, they increase so fast, there is so much want. Monseigneur! Monseigneur!"

The valet had put her away from the door, the carriage had broken into a brisk trot, the postilions had quickened the pace, she was left far behind, and Monseigneur, again escorted by the Furies, was rapidly diminishing the league or two of distance that remained between him and his château.

The sweet scents of the summer night rose all around him, and rose, as the rain falls, impartially, on the dusty, ragged, and toil-worn group at the fountain not far away, to whom the mender of roads, with the aid of the blue cap without which he was nothing, still enlarged upon his man like a spectre, as long as they could bear it. By degrees, as they could bear no more, they dropped off one by one, and the lights twinkled in little casements; which lights, as the casements darkened, and more stars came out, seemed to have shot up into the sky instead of having been extinguished.

The shadow of a large high-roofed house, and of many overhanging trees, was upon Monsieur the Marquis by that time; and the shadow was exchanged for the light of a flambeau, as his carriage stopped, and the great door of his château was opened to him.

"Monsieur Charles, whom I expect; is he arrived from England?"

"Monseigneur, not yet."

Chapter 9. *The Gorgon's Head*

5   It was a heavy mass of building, that château of Monsieur the Marquis, with a large stone courtyard before it, and two stone sweeps of staircase meeting in a stone terrace before the principal door. A stony business altogether, with heavy stone balustrades, and stone urns, and stone flowers, and stone faces of men, and stone heads of lions, in all directions. As if the Gorgon's head had surveyed it, when it was finished, two centuries ago.

Up the broad flight of shallow steps, Monsieur the Marquis, flambeau preceded, went from his carriage, sufficiently disturbing the darkness to elicit loud remonstrance from an owl in the roof of

15   the great pile of stable building away among the trees. All else was so quiet, that the flambeau carried up the steps, and the other flambeau held at the great door, burnt as if they were in a close room of state, instead of being in the open night-air. Other sound than the owl's voice there was none, save the falling of a fountain into its stone basin; for, it was one of those dark nights that hold their breath by the hour together, and then heave a long low sigh, and hold their breath again.

The great door clanged behind him, and Monsieur the Marquis crossed a hall grim with certain old boar-spears, swords, and knives

25   of the chase; grimmer with certain heavy riding-rods and riding-whips, of which many a peasant, gone to his benefactor Death, had felt the weight when his lord was angry.

Avoiding the larger rooms, which were dark and made fast for the night, Monsieur the Marquis, with his flambeau-bearer going on before, went up the staircase to a door in a corridor. This thrown open, admitted him to his own private apartment of three rooms; his bedchamber and two others. High vaulted rooms with cool uncarpeted floors, great dogs upon the hearths for the burning of wood in winter time, and all luxuries befitting the state of a marquis in a luxurious age and country. The fashion of the last Louis but one, of the line that was never to break—the fourteenth Louis—was conspicuous in their rich furniture; but, it was diversified by many objects that were illustrations of old pages in the history of France.

A supper-table was laid for two, in the third of the rooms; a round room, in one of the château's four extinguisher-topped towers. A small lofty room, with its window wide open, and the wooden jalousie-blinds closed, so that the dark night only showed in slight horizontal lines of black, alternating with their broad lines of stone colour.

"My nephew," said Marquis, glancing at the supper preparation; "they said he was not arrived."

Nor was he; but, he had been expected with Monseigneur.

"Ah! It is not probable he will arrive to-night; nevertheless, leave the table as it is. I shall be ready in a quarter of an hour."

In a quarter of an hour Monseigneur was ready, and sat down alone to his sumptuous and choice supper. His chair was opposite to the window, and he had taken his soup, and was raising his glass of Bordeaux to his lips, when he put it down.

"What is that?" he calmly asked, looking with attention at the horizontal lines of black and stone colour.

"Monseigneur? That?"

"Outside the blinds. Open the blinds."

It was done.

"Well?"

"Monseigneur, it is nothing. The trees and the night are all that are here."

The servant who spoke had thrown the blinds wide, had looked out into the vacant darkness, and stood, with that blank behind him, looking round for instructions.

"Good," said the imperturbable master. "Close them again."

That was done too, and the Marquis went on with his supper. He was half-way through it, when he again stopped with his glass in his hand, hearing the sound of wheels. It came on briskly, and came up to the front of the château.

"Ask who is arrived."

It was the nephew of Monseigneur. He had been some few

leagues behind Monseigneur, early in the afternoon. He had diminished the distance rapidly, but not so rapidly as to come up with Monseigneur on the road. He had heard of Monseigneur, at the posting-houses, as being before him.

He was to be told (said Monseigneur) that supper awaited him then and there, and that he was prayed to come to it. In a little while he came. He had been known in England as Charles Darnay.

Monseigneur received him in a courtly manner, but they did not shake hands.

"You left Paris yesterday, sir?" he said to Monseigneur, as he took his seat at table.

"Yesterday. And you?"

"I come direct."

"From London?"

"Yes."

"You have been a long time coming," said the Marquis, with a smile.

"On the contrary; I come direct."

"Pardon me! I mean, not a long time on the journey; a long time intending the journey."

"I have been detained by"—the nephew stopped a moment in his answer—"various business."

"Without doubt," said the polished uncle.

So long as a servant was present, no other words passed between them. When coffee had been served and they were alone together, the nephew, looking at the uncle and meeting the eyes of the face that was like a fine mask, opened a conversation.

"I have come back, sir, as you anticipate, pursuing the object that took me away. It carried me into great and unexpected peril; but it is a sacred object, and if it had carried me to death I hope it would have sustained me."

"Not to death," said the uncle; "it is not necessary to say to death."

"I doubt, sir," returned the nephew, "whether, if it had carried me to the utmost brink of death, you would have cared to stop me there."

The deepened marks in the nose, and the lengthening of the fine straight lines in the cruel face, looked ominous as to that; the uncle made a graceful gesture of protest, which was so clearly a slight form of good breeding that it was not reassuring.

"Indeed, sir," pursued the nephew, "for anything I know, you may have expressly worked to give a more suspicious appearance to the suspicious circumstances that surrounded me."

"No, no, no," said the uncle, pleasantly.

"But, however that may be," resumed the nephew, glancing at him with deep distrust, "I know that your diplomacy would stop me by any means, and would know no scruple as to means."

"My friend, I told you so," said the uncle, with a fine pulsation in the two marks. "Do me the favour to recall that I told you so, long ago."

"I recall it."

"Thank you," said the Marquis—very sweetly indeed.

His tone lingered in the air, almost like the tone of a musical instrument.

"In effect, sir," pursued the nephew, "I believe it to be at once your bad fortune, and my good fortune, that has kept me out of a prison in France here."

"I do not quite understand," returned the uncle, sipping his coffee. "Dare I ask you to explain?"

"I believe that if you were not in disgrace with the Court, and had not been overshadowed by that cloud for years past, a letter *de cachet* would have sent me to some fortress indefinitely."

"It is possible," said the uncle, with great calmness. "For the honour of the family, I could even resolve to incommode you to that extent. Pray excuse me!"

"I perceive that, happily for me, the Reception of the day before yesterday was, as usual, a cold one," observed the nephew.

"I would not say happily, my friend," returned the uncle, with refined politeness; "I would not be sure of that. A good opportunity for consideration, surrounded by the advantages of solitude, might influence your destiny to far greater advantage than you influence it for yourself. But it is useless to discuss the question. I am, as you say, at a disadvantage. These little instruments of correction, these gentle aids to the power and honour of families, these slight favours that might so incommode you, are only to be obtained now by interest and importunity. They are sought by so many, and they are granted (comparatively) to so few! It used not to be so, but France in all such things is changed for the worse. Our not remote ancestors held the right of life and death over the surrounding vulgar. From this room, many such dogs have been taken out to be hanged; in the next room (my bedroom), one fellow, to our knowledge, was poniarded on the spot for professing some insolent delicacy respecting his daughter—*his* daughter? We have lost many privileges; a new philosophy has become the mode; and the assertion of our station, in these days, might (I do not go so far as to say would, but might) cause us real inconvenience. All very bad, very bad!"

The Marquis took a gentle little pinch of snuff, and shook his head; as elegantly despondent as he could becomingly be of a country still containing himself, that great means of regeneration.

"We have so asserted our station, both in the old time and in the modern time also," said the nephew, gloomily, "that I believe our name to be more detested than any name in France."

"Let us hope so," said the uncle. "Detestation of the high is the involuntary homage of the low."

"There is not," pursued the nephew, in his former tone, "a face I can look at, in all this country round about us, which looks at me with any deference on it but the dark deference of fear and slavery."

"A compliment," said the Marquis, "to the grandeur of the family, merited by the manner in which the family has sustained its grandeur. Hah!" And he took another gentle little pinch of snuff, and lightly crossed his legs.

But, when his nephew, leaning an elbow on the table, covered his eyes thoughtfully and dejectedly with his hand, the fine mask looked at him sideways with a stronger concentration of keenness, closeness, and dislike, than was comportable with its wearer's assumption of indifference.

"Repression is the only lasting philosophy. The dark deference of fear and slavery, my friend," observed the Marquis, "will keep the dogs obedient to the whip, as long as this roof," looking up to it, "shuts out the sky."

That might not be so long as the Marquis supposed. If a picture of the château as it was to be a very few years hence, and of fifty like it as they too were to be a very few years hence, could have been shown to him that night, he might have been at a loss to claim his own from the ghastly, fire-charred, plunder-wrecked ruins. As for the roof he vaunted, he might have found *that* shutting out the sky in a new way—to wit, for ever, from the eyes of the bodies into which its lead was fired, out of the barrels of a hundred thousand muskets.

"Meanwhile," said the Marquis, "I will preserve the honour and repose of the family, if you will not. But you must be fatigued. 5 Shall we terminate our conference for the night?"

"A moment more."

"An hour, if you please."

"Sir," said the nephew, "we have done wrong, and are reaping the fruits of wrong."

"*We* have done wrong?" repeated the Marquis, with an inquiring smile, and delicately pointing, first to the nephew, then to himself.

"Our family; our honourable family, whose honour is of so much account to both of us, in such different ways. Even in my father's time, we did a world of wrong, injuring every human creature who 15 came between us and our pleasure, whatever it was. Why need I speak of my father's time, when it is equally yours? Can I separate my father's twin brother, joint inheritor, and next successor, from himself?"

"Death has done that!" said the Marquis.

"And has left me," answered the nephew, "bound to a system that is frightful to me, responsible for it, but powerless in it; seeking to execute the last request of my dear mother's lips, and to obey the last look of my dear mother's eyes, which implored me to have mercy and to redress; and tortured by seeking assistance and 25 power in vain."

"Seeking them from me, my nephew," said the Marquis, touching him on the breast with his forefinger—they were now standing by the hearth—"you will for ever seek them in vain, be assured."

Every fine straight line in the clear whiteness of his face was cruelly, craftily, and closely compressed, while he stood looking quietly at his nephew, with his snuff-box in his hand.

Once again he touched him on the breast, as though his finger were the fine point of a small sword, with which, in delicate finesse, he ran him through the body, and said: 35

"My friend, I will die, perpetuating the system under which I have lived."

When he had said it, he took a culminating pinch of snuff, and put his box in his pocket.

"Better to be a rational creature," he added then, after ringing a small bell on the table, "and accept your natural destiny. But you are lost, Monsieur Charles, I see."

"This property and France are lost to me," said the nephew sadly; "I renounce them."

5 "Are they both yours to renounce? France may be, but is the property? It is scarcely worth mentioning; but, is it yet?"

"I had no intention, in the words I used, to claim it yet. If it passed to me from you, to-morrow—"

"Which I have the vanity to hope is not probable."

"—or twenty years hence—"

"You do me too much honour," said the Marquis; "still, I prefer that supposition."

"I would abandon it, and live otherwise and elsewhere. It is little to relinquish. What is it but a wilderness of misery and ruin?"

15 "Hah!" said the Marquis, glancing round the luxurious room.

"To the eye it is fair enough, here; but seen in its integrity, under the sky, and by the daylight, it is a crumbling tower of waste, mismanagement, extortion, debt, mortgage, oppression, hunger, nakedness, and suffering."

"Hah!" said the Marquis again, in a well-satisfied manner.

"If it ever becomes mine, it shall be put into some hands better qualified to free it slowly (if such a thing is possible) from the weight that drags it down, so that the miserable people who cannot leave it and who have been wrung to the last point of endurance 25 may, in another generation, suffer less; but it is not for me. There is a curse on it, and on all this land."

"And you?" said the uncle. "Forgive my curiosity; do you, under your new philosophy, graciously intend to live?"

"I must do, to live, what others of my countrymen, even with nobility at their backs, may have to do some day—work."

"In England, for example?"

"Yes. The family honour, sir, is safe from me in this country. The family name can suffer from me in no other, for I bear it in no other."

35 The ringing of the bell had caused the adjoining bed-chamber to be lighted. It now shone brightly, through the door of communication. The Marquis looked that way, and listened for the retreating step of his valet.

"England is very attractive to you, seeing how indifferently you have prospered there," he observed then, turning his calm face to his nephew with a smile.

"I have already said, that for my prospering there, I am sensible I may be indebted to you, sir. For the rest, it is my refuge."

"They say, those boastful English, that it is the refuge of many. You know a compatriot who has found a refuge there? A Doctor?"

"Yes."

"With a daughter?"

"Yes."

"Yes," said the Marquis. "You are fatigued. Good-night!"

As he bent his head in his most courtly manner, there was a secrecy in his smiling face, and he conveyed an air of mystery to those words, which struck the eyes and ears of his nephew forcibly. At the same time, the thin straight lines of the setting of the eyes, and the thin straight lips, and the markings in the nose, curved with a sarcasm that looked handsomely diabolic.

"Yes," repeated the Marquis. "A Doctor with a daughter. Yes. So commences the new philosophy! You are fatigued. Good-night!"

It would have been of as much avail to interrogate any stone face outside the château as to interrogate that face of his. The nephew looked at him in vain, in passing on to the door.

"Good-night!" said the uncle. "I look to the pleasure of seeing you again in the morning. Good repose! Light Monsieur my nephew to his chamber there!—And burn Monsieur my nephew in his bed, if you will," he added to himself, before he rang his little bell again, and summoned his valet to his own bedroom.

The valet come and gone, Monsieur the Marquis walked to and fro in his loose chamber-robe, to prepare himself gently for sleep, that hot still night. Rustling about the room, his softly-slippered feet making no noise on the floor, he moved like a refined tiger: looked like some enchanted marquis of the impenitently wicked sort, in story, whose periodical change into tiger form was either just going off, or just coming on.

He moved from end to end of his voluptuous bedroom, looking again at the scraps of the day's journey that came unbidden into his mind; the slow toil up the hill at sunset, the setting sun, the descent, the mill, the prison on the crag, the little village in the hollow, the peasants at the fountain, and the mender of roads with his blue cap pointing out the chain under the carriage. That fountain suggested the Paris fountain, the little bundle lying on the step, the women bending over it, and the tall man with his arms up, crying, "Dead!"

"I am cool now," said Monsieur the Marquis, "and may go to bed."

So, leaving only one light burning on the large hearth, he let his thin gauze curtains fall around him, and heard the night break its silence with a long sigh as he composed himself to sleep.

The stone faces on the outer walls stared blindly at the black night for three heavy hours; for three heavy hours the horses in the stables rattled at their racks, the dogs barked, and the owl made a noise with very little resemblance in it to the noise conventionally assigned to the owl by men-poets. But it is the obstinate custom of such creatures hardly ever to say what is set down for them.

For three heavy hours, the stone faces of the château, lion and human, stared blindly at the night. Dead darkness lay on all the landscape, dead darkness added its own hush to the hushing dust on all the roads. The burial-place had got to the pass that its little heaps of poor grass were undistinguishable from one another; the figure on the Cross might have come down, for anything that could be seen of it. In the village, taxers and taxed were fast asleep. Dreaming, perhaps, of banquets, as the starved usually do, and of ease and rest, as the driven slave and the yoked ox may, its lean inhabitants slept soundly, and were fed and freed.

The fountain in the village flowed unseen and unheard, and the fountain at the château dropped unseen and unheard—both melting away, like the minutes that were falling from the spring of Time—through three dark hours. Then, the gray water of both began to be ghostly in the light, and the eyes of the stone faces of the château were opened.

Lighter and lighter, until at last the sun touched the tops of the still trees, and poured its radiance over the hill. In the glow, the water of the château fountain seemed to turn to blood, and the stone faces crimsoned. The carol of the birds was loud and high, and, on the weather-beaten sill of the great window of the bed-chamber of Monsieur the Marquis, one little bird sang its sweetest song with all its might. At this, the nearest stone face seemed to stare amazed, and, with opened mouth and dropped under-jaw, looked awestricken.

Now, the sun was full up, and movement began in the village. Casement windows opened, crazy doors were unbarred, and people came forth shivering—chilled, as yet, by the new sweet air. Then began the rarely lightened toil of the day among the village population. Some, to the fountain; some, to the fields; men and women here, to dig and delve; men and women there, to see to the poor livestock, and lead the bony cows out, to such pasture as could be found by the roadside. In the church and at the Cross, a kneeling figure or two; attendant on the latter prayers, the led cow, trying for a breakfast among the weeds at its foot.

The château awoke later, as became its quality, but awoke gradually and surely. First, the lonely boar-spears and knives of the chase had been reddened as of old; then, had gleamed trenchant in the morning sunshine; now, doors and windows were thrown open, horses in their stables looked round over their shoulders at the light and freshness pouring in at doorways, leaves sparkled and rustled at iron-grated windows, dogs pulled hard at their chains, and reared impatient to be loosed.

All these trivial incidents belonged to the routine of life, and the return of morning. Surely, not so the ringing of the great bell of the château, nor the running up and down the stairs; nor the hurried figures on the terrace; nor the booting and tramping here and there and everywhere, nor the quick saddling of horses and riding away?

What winds conveyed this hurry to the grizzled mender of roads, already at work on the hilltop beyond the village, with his day's dinner (not much to carry) lying in a bundle that it was worth no cow's while to peck at, on a heap of stones? Had the birds, carrying some grains of it to a distance, dropped one over him as they sow chance seeds? Whether or no, the mender of roads ran, on the sultry morning, as if for his life, down the hill, knee-high in dust, and never stopped till he got to the fountain.

All the people of the village were at the fountain, standing about in their depressed manner, and whispering low, but showing no other emotions than grim curiosity and surprise. The led cows, hastily brought in and tethered to anything that would hold them, were looking stupidly on, or lying down chewing the cud of nothing particularly repaying their trouble, which they had picked up in their interrupted saunter. Some of the people of the château, and some of those of the posting-house, and all the taxing authori-

ties, were armed more or less, and were crowded on the other side
of the little street in a purposeless way, that was highly fraught with
nothing. Already, the mender of roads had penetrated into the
midst of a group of fifty particular friends, and was smiting himself
in the breast with his blue cap. What did all this portend, and
what portended the swift hoisting-up of Monsieur Gabelle behind
a servant on horseback, and the conveying away of the said Gabelle
(double-laden though the horse was), at a gallop, like a new version
of the German ballad of Leonora?

It portended that there was one stone face too many, up at the
château.

The Gorgon had surveyed the building again in the night, and
had added the one stone face wanting; the stone face for which it
had waited through about two hundred years.

It lay back on the pillow of Monsieur the Marquis. It was like a
fine mask, suddenly startled, made angry, and petrified. Driven
home into the heart of the stone figure attached to it was a knife.
Round its hilt was a frill of paper, on which was scrawled:

"*Drive him fast to his tomb. This, from* JACQUES."

Chapter 10. *Two Promises*

More months, to the number of twelve, had come and gone, and
Mr. Charles Darnay was established in England as a higher teacher
of the French language who was conversant with French literature.
In this age, he would have been a professor; in that age, he was a
tutor. He read with young men who could find any leisure and
interest for the study of a living tongue spoken all over the world,
and he cultivated a taste for its stores of knowledge and fancy. He
could write of them, besides, in sound English, and render them
into sound English. Such masters were not at that time easily
found; Princes that had been, and Kings that were to be, were not
yet of the teacher class, and no ruined nobility had dropped out of
Tellson's ledgers, to turn cooks and carpenters. As a tutor, whose
attainments made the student's way unusually pleasant and profit-
able, and as an elegant translator who brought something to his

work besides mere dictionary knowledge, young Mr. Darnay soon became known and encouraged. He was well acquainted, moreover, with the circumstances of his country, and those were of ever-growing interest. So, with great perseverance and untiring industry, he prospered.

In London, he had expected neither to walk on pavements of gold, nor lie on beds of roses; if he had had any such exalted expectation, he would not have prospered. He had expected labour, and he found it, and did it, and made the best of it. In this, his prosperity consisted.

A certain portion of his time was passed at Cambridge, where he read with undergraduates as a sort of tolerated smuggler who drove a contraband trade in European languages, instead of conveying Greek and Latin through the custom-house. The rest of his time he passed in London.

Now, from the days when it was always summer in Eden, to these days when it is mostly winter in fallen latitudes, the world of a man had invariably gone one way—Charles Darnay's way—the way of the love of a woman.

He had loved Lucie Manette from the hour of his danger. He had never heard a sound so sweet and dear as the sound of her compassionate voice; he had never seen a face so tenderly beautiful, as hers when it was confronted with his own on the edge of the grave that had been dug for him. But, he had not yet spoken to her on the subject; the assassination at the deserted château far away beyond the heaving water and the long, long, dusty roads—the solid stone château which had itself become the mere mist of a dream—had been done a year, and he had never yet, by so much as a single spoken word, disclosed to her the state of his heart.

That he had his reasons for this, he knew full well. It was again a summer day when, lately arrived in London from his college occupation, he turned into the quiet corner in Soho, bent on seeking an opportunity of opening his mind to Doctor Manette. It was the close of the summer day, and he knew Lucie to be out with Miss Pross.

He found the Doctor reading in his arm-chair at a window. The energy which had at once supported him under his old sufferings and aggravated their sharpness had been gradually restored to him. He was now a very energetic man indeed, with great firmness of purpose, strength of resolution, and vigour of action. In his recovered energy he was sometimes a little fitful and sudden, as he had at first been in the exercise of his other recovered faculties; but, this had never been frequently observable, and had grown more and more rare.

He studied much, slept little, sustained a great deal of fatigue with ease, and was equally cheerful. To him, now entered Charles Darnay, at sight of whom he laid aside his book and held out his hand.

"Charles Darnay! I rejoice to see you. We have been counting on your return these three or four days past. Mr. Stryver and Sydney Carton were both here yesterday, and both made you out to be more than due."

"I am obliged to them for their interest in the matter," he answered, a little coldly as to them, though very warmly as to the Doctor. "Miss Manette—"

"Is well," said the Doctor, as he stopped short, "and your return will delight us all. She has gone out on some household matters, but will soon be home."

"Doctor Manette, I knew she was from home. I took the opportunity of her being from home, to beg to speak to you."

There was a blank silence.

"Yes?" said the Doctor, with evident constraint. "Bring your chair here, and speak on."

He complied as to the chair, but appeared to find the speaking on less easy.

"I have had the happiness, Doctor Manette, of being so intimate here," so he at length began, "for some year and a half, that I hope the topic on which I am about to touch may not—"

He was stayed by the Doctor's putting out his hand to stop him. When he had kept it so a little while, he said, drawing it back:

"Is Lucie the topic?"

"She is."

"It is hard for me to speak of her at any time. It is very hard for me to hear her spoken of in that tone of yours, Charles Darnay."

"It is a tone of fervent admiration, true homage, and deep love, Doctor Manette!" he said deferentially.

There was another blank silence before her father rejoined:

"I believe it. I do you justice; I believe it."

His constraint was so manifest, and it was so manifest, too, that it originated in an unwillingness to approach the subject, that Charles Darnay hesitated.

"Shall I go on, sir?"

Another blank.

"Yes, go on."

"You anticipate what I would say, though you cannot know how earnestly I say it, how earnestly I feel it, without knowing my secret heart, and the hopes and fears and anxieties with which it has long been laden. Dear Doctor Manette, I love your daughter fondly, dearly, disinterestedly, devotedly. If ever there were love in the world, I love her. You have loved yourself; let your old love speak for me!"

The Doctor sat with his face turned away, and his eyes bent on the ground. At the last words, he stretched out his hand again, hurriedly, and cried:

"Not that, sir! Let that be! I adjure you, do not recall that!"

His cry was so like a cry of actual pain, that it rang in Charles Darnay's ears long after he had ceased. He motioned with the hand he had extended, and it seemed to be an appeal to Darnay to pause. The latter so received it, and remained silent.

"I ask your pardon," said the Doctor, in a subdued tone, after some moments. "I do not doubt your loving Lucie; you may be satisfied of it."

He turned towards him in his chair, but did not look at him, or raise his eyes. His chin dropped upon his hand, and his white hair overshadowed his face.

"Have you spoken to Lucie?"

"No."

"Nor written?"

"Never."

"It would be ungenerous to affect not to know that your self-denial is to be referred to your consideration for her father. Her father thanks you."

He offered his hand; but his eyes did not go with it.

"I know," said Darnay, respectfully, "how can I fail to know, Doctor Manette, I who have seen you together from day to day, that between you and Miss Manette there is an affection so unusual, so touching, so belonging to the circumstances in which it has been nurtured, that it can have few parallels, even in the tenderness between a father and child. I know, Doctor Manette —how can I fail to know—that, mingled with the affection and duty of a daughter who has become a woman, there is, in her heart, towards you, all the love and reliance of infancy itself. I know that, as in her childhood she had no parent, so she is now devoted to you with all the constancy and fervour of her present years and character, united to the trustfulness and attachment of the early days in which you were lost to her. I know perfectly well that if you had been restored to her from the world beyond this life, you could hardly be invested, in her sight, with a more sacred character than that in which you are always with her. I know that when she is clinging to you, the hands of baby, girl, and woman, all in one, are around your neck. I know that in loving you she sees and loves her mother at her own age, sees and loves you at my age, loves her mother brokenhearted, loves you through your dreadful trial and in your blessed restoration. I have known this, night and day, since I have known you in your home."

Her father sat silent, with his face bent down. His breathing was a little quickened; but he repressed all other signs of agitation.

"Dear Doctor Manette, always knowing this, always seeing her and you with this hallowed light about you, I have forborne, and forborne as long as it was in the nature of man to do it. I have felt, and do even now feel, that to bring my love—even mine—between you, is to touch your history with something not quite so good as itself. But I love her. Heaven is my witness that I love her!"

"I believe it," answered her father, mournfully. "I have thought so before now. I believe it."

"But, do not believe," said Darnay, upon whose ear the mournful voice struck with a reproachful sound, "that if my fortune were so cast as that, being one day so happy as to make her my wife, I must at any time put any separation between her and you, I could or would breathe a word of what I now say. Besides that I should know it to be hopeless. I should know it to be a baseness. If I had any such possibility, even at a remote distance of years, harboured in my thoughts, and hidden in my heart—if it ever had been there—if it ever could be there—I could not now touch this honoured hand."

He laid his own upon it as he spoke.

"No, dear Doctor Manette. Like you, a voluntary exile from France; like you, driven from it by its distractions, oppressions, and miseries; like you, striving to live away from it by my own exertions, and trusting in a happier future; I look only to sharing your fortunes, sharing your life and home, and being faithful to you to   5 the death. Not to divide with Lucie her privilege as your child, companion, and friend; but to come in aid of it, and bind her closer to you, if such a thing can be."

His touch still lingered on her father's hand. Answering the touch for a moment, but not coldly, her father rested his hands upon the arms of his chair, and looked up for the first time since the beginning of the conference. A struggle was evident in his face; a struggle with that occasional look which had a tendency in it to dark doubt and dread.

"You speak so feelingly and so manfully, Charles Darnay, that I   15 thank you with all my heart, and will open all my heart—or nearly so. Have any reason to believe that Lucie loves you?"

"None. As yet, none."

"Is it the immediate object of this confidence, that you may at once ascertain that, with my knowledge?"

"Not even so. I might not have the hopefulness to do it for weeks; I might (mistaken or not mistaken) have that hopefulness to-morrow."

"Do you seek any guidance from me?"

"I ask none, sir. But I have thought it possible that you might   25 have it in your power, if you should deem it right, to give me some."

"Do you seek any promise from me?"

"I do seek that."

"What is it?"

"I well understand that, without you, I could have no hope. I well understand that, even if Miss Manette held me at this moment in her innocent heart—do not think I have the presumption to assume so much—I could retain no place in it against her love for her father."   35

"If that be so, do you see what, on the other hand, is involved in it?"

"I understand equally well, that a word from her father in any suitor's favour would outweigh herself and all the world. For which reason, Doctor Manette," said Darnay, modestly but firmly, "I would not ask that word, to save my life."

"I am sure of it. Charles Darnay, mysteries arise out of close love, as well as out of wide division; in the former case, they are subtle and delicate, and difficult to penetrate. My daughter Lucie is, in this one respect, such a mystery to me; I can make no guess at the state of her heart."

"May I ask, sir, if you think she is—" As he hesitated her father supplied the rest.

"Is sought by any other suitor?"

"It is what I meant to say."

Her father considered a little before he answered:

"You have seen Mr. Carton here, yourself. Mr. Stryver is here too, occasionally. If it be at all, it can only be by one of these."

"Or both," said Darnay.

"I had not thought of both; I should not think either likely. You want a promise from me. Tell me what it is."

"It is, that if Miss Manette should bring to you at any time, on her own part, such a confidence as I have ventured to lay before you, you will bear testimony to what I have said, and to your belief in it. I hope you may be able to think so well of me, as to urge no influence against me. I say nothing more of my stake in this; this is what I ask. The condition on which I ask it, and which you have an undoubted right to require, I will observe immediately."

"I give the promise," said the Doctor, "without any condition. I believe your object to be, purely and truthfully, as you have stated it. I believe your intention is to perpetuate, and not to weaken, the ties between me and my other and far dearer self. If she should ever tell me that you are essential to her perfect happiness, I will give her to you. If there were—Charles Darnay, if there were—"

The young man had taken his hand gratefully; their hands were joined as the Doctor spoke:

"—any fancies, any reasons, any apprehensions, anything whatsoever, new or old, against the man she really loved—the direct responsibility thereof not lying on his head—they should all be obliterated for her sake. She is everything to me; more to me than suffering, more to me than wrong, more to me—Well! This is idle talk."

So strange was the way in which he faded into silence, and so strange his fixed look when he had ceased to speak, that Darnay felt his own hand turn cold in the hand that slowly released and dropped it.

"You said something to me," said Doctor Manette, breaking into a smile. "What was it you said to me?"

He was at a loss how to answer, until he remembered having spoken of a condition. Relieved as his mind reverted to that, he answered:

"Your confidence in me ought to be returned with full confidence on my part. My present name, though but slightly changed from my mother's, is not, as you will remember, my own. I wish to tell you what that is, and why I am in England."

"Stop!" said the Doctor of Beauvais.

"I wish it, that I may the better deserve your confidence, and have no secret from you."

"Stop!"

For an instant, the Doctor even had his two hands at his ears; for another instant even had his two hands laid on Darnay's lips.

"Tell me when I ask you, not now. If your suit should prosper, if Lucie should love you, you shall tell me on your marriage morning. Do you promise?"

"Willingly."

"Give me your hand. She will be home directly, and it is better she should not see us together to-night. Go! God bless you!"

It was dark when Charles Darnay left him, and it was an hour later and darker when Lucie came home; she hurried into the room alone—for Miss Pross had gone straight upstairs—and was surprised to find his reading-chair empty.

"My father!" she called to him. "Father dear!"

Nothing was said in answer, but she heard a low hammering sound in his bedroom. Passing lightly across the intermediate room, she looked in at his door and came running back frightened, crying to herself, with her blood all chilled, "What shall I do! What shall I do!"

Her uncertainty lasted but a moment; she hurried back, and tapped at his door, and softly called to him. The noise ceased at the sound of her voice, and he presently came out to her, and they walked up and down together for a long time.

She came down from her bed, to look at him in his sleep that night. He slept heavily, and his tray of shoemaking tools, and his old unfinished work, were all as usual.

Chapter 11. A Companion Picture

"Sydney," said Mr. Stryver, on that self-same night, or morning, to his jackal; "mix another bowl of punch; I have something to say
5   to you."

Sydney had been working double tides that night, and the night before, and the night before that, and a good many nights in succession, making a grand clearance among Mr. Stryver's papers before the setting in of the long vacation. The clearance was effected at last; the Stryver arrears were handsomely fetched up; everything was got rid of until November should come with its fogs atmospheric and fogs legal, and bring grist to the mill again.

Sydney was none the livelier and none the soberer for so much application. It had taken a deal of extra wet-towelling to pull him
15   through the night; a correspondingly extra quantity of wine had preceded the towelling; and he was in a very damaged condition, as he now pulled his turban off and threw it into the basin in which he had steeped it at intervals for the last six hours.

"Are you mixing that other bowl of punch?" said Stryver the portly, with his hands in his waistband, glancing round from the sofa where he lay on his back.

"I am."

"Now, look here! I am going to tell you something that will rather surprise you, and that perhaps will make you think me not
25   quite as shrewd as you usually do think me. I intend to marry."

"*Do* you?"

"Yes. And not for money. What do you say now?"

"I don't feel disposed to say much. Who is she?"

"Guess."

"Do I know her?"

"Guess."

"I am not going to guess, at five o'clock in the morning, with my brains frying and sputtering in my head. If you want me to guess, you must ask me to dinner."

"Well, then I'll tell you," said Stryver, coming slowly into a sitting posture. "Sydney, I rather despair of making myself intelligible to you, because you are such an insensible dog."

"And you," returned Sydney, busy concocting the punch, "are such a sensitive and poetical spirit."

"Come!" rejoined Stryver, laughing boastfully, "though I don't prefer any claim to being the soul of Romance (for I hope I know better), still I am a tenderer sort of fellow than *you*."

"You are a luckier, if you mean that."

"I don't mean that. I mean I am a man of more—more—"

"Say gallantry, while you are about it," suggested Carton.

"Well! I'll say gallantry. My meaning is that I am a man," said Stryver, inflating himself at his friend as he made the punch, "who cares more to be agreeable, who takes more pains to be agreeable, who knows better how to be agreeable, in a woman's society, than you do."   15

"Go on," said Sydney Carton.

"No; but before I go on," said Stryver, shaking his head in his bullying way, "I'll have this out with you. You've been at Doctor Manette's house as much as I have, or more than I have. Why, I have been ashamed of your moroseness there! Your manners have been of that silent and sullen and hang-dog kind, that, upon my life and soul, I have been ashamed of you, Sydney!"

"It should be very beneficial to a man of your practice at the bar, to be ashamed of anything," returned Sydney; "you ought to be   25 much obliged to me."

"You shall not get off in that way," rejoined Stryver, shouldering the rejoinder at him; "no, Sydney, it's my duty to tell you—and I tell you to your face to do you good—that you are a devilish ill-conditioned fellow in that sort of society. You are a disagreeable fellow."

Sydney drank a bumper of the punch he had made, and laughed.

"Look at me!" said Stryver, squaring himself; "I have less need to make myself agreeable than you have, being more independent in circumstances. Why do I do it?   35

"I never saw you do it yet," muttered Carton.

"I do it because it's politic; I do it on principle. And look at me! I get on!"

"You don't get on with your account of your matrimonial intentions," answered Carton, with a careless air; "I wish you would keep to that. As to me—will you never understand that I am incorrigible?"

He asked the question with some appearance of scorn.

"You have no business to be incorrigible," was his friend's answer, delivered in no very soothing tone.

"I have no business to be, at all, that I know of," said Sydney Carton. "Who is the lady?"

"Now, don't let my announcement of the name make you uncomfortable, Sydney," said Mr. Stryver, preparing him with ostentatious friendliness for the disclosure he was about to make, "because I know you don't mean half you say; and if you meant it all, it would be of no importance. I make this little preface, because you once mentioned the young lady to me in slighting terms."

"I did?"

"Certainly; and in these chambers."

Sydney Carton looked at his punch and looked at his complacent friend; drank his punch and looked at his complacent friend.

"You made mention of the young lady as a golden-haired doll. The young lady is Miss Manette. If you had been a fellow of any sensitiveness or delicacy of feeling in that kind of way, Sydney, I might have been a little resentful of your employing such a designation; but you are not. You want that sense altogether; therefore I am no more annoyed when I think of the expression, than I should be annoyed by a man's opinion of a picture of mine, who had no eye for pictures: or of a piece of music of mine, who had no ear for music."

Sydney Carton drank the punch at a great rate; drank it by bumpers, looking at his friend.

"Now you know all about it, Syd," said Mr. Stryver. "I don't care about fortune: she is a charming creature, and I have made up my mind to please myself: on the whole, I think I can afford to please myself. She will have in me a man already pretty well off, and a rapidly rising man, and a man of some distinction: it is a piece of good fortune for her, but she is worthy of good fortune. Are you astonished?"

Carton, still drinking the punch, rejoined, "Why should I be astonished?"

"You approve?"

Carton, still drinking the punch, rejoined, "Why should I not approve?"

"Well!" said his friend Stryver, "you take it more easily than I fancied you would, and are less mercenary on my behalf than I thought you would be; though, to be sure, you know well enough by this time that your ancient chum is a man of a pretty strong will. Yes, Sydney, I have had enough of this style of life, with no other 5 as a change from it; I feel that it is a pleasant thing for a man to have a home when he feels inclined to go to it (when he doesn't, he can stay away), and I feel that Miss Manette will tell well in any station, and will always do me credit. So I have made up my mind. And now, Sydney, old boy, I want to say a word to *you* about *your* prospects. You are in a bad way, you know; you really are in a bad way. You don't know the value of money, you live hard, you'll knock up one of these days, and be ill and poor; you really ought to think about a nurse."

The prosperous patronage with which he said it, made him look 15 twice as big as he was, and four times as offensive.

"Now, let me recommend you," pursued Stryver, "to look it in the face. I have looked it in the face, in my different way; look it in the face, you, in your different way. Marry. Provide somebody to take care of you. Never mind your having no enjoyment of women's society, nor understanding of it, nor tact for it. Find out somebody. Find out some respectable woman with a little property—somebody in the landlady way, or lodging-letting way—and marry her, against a rainy day. That's the kind of thing for *you*. Now think of it, Sydney." 25

"I'll think of it," said Sydney.

Chapter 12. The Fellow of Delicacy

Mr. Stryver having made up his mind to that magnanimous bestowal of good fortune on the Doctor's daughter, resolved to make her happiness known to her before he left town for the Long Vacation. After some mental debating of the point, he came to the conclusion that it would be as well to get all the preliminaries done with, and they could then arrange at their leisure whether he should give her his hand a week or two before Michaelmas Term, or in the little Christmas vacation between it and Hilary.

As to the strength of his case, he had not a doubt about it, but clearly saw his way to the verdict. Argued with the jury on substantial worldly grounds—the only grounds ever worth taking into account—it was a plain case, and had not a weak spot in it. He called himself for the plaintiff, there was no getting over his evidence, the counsel for the defendant threw up his brief, and the jury did not even turn to consider. After trying it, Stryver, C. J., was satisfied that no plainer case could be.

Accordingly, Mr. Stryver inaugurated the Long Vacation with a formal proposal to take Miss Manette to Vauxhall Gardens; that failing, to Ranelagh; that unaccountably failing too, it behoved him to present himself in Soho, and there declare his noble mind.

Towards Soho, therefore, Mr. Stryver shouldered his way from the Temple, while the bloom of the Long Vacation's infancy was still upon it. Anybody who had seen him projecting himself into Soho while he was yet on Saint Dunstan's side of Temple Bar, bursting in his full-blown way along the pavement, to the jostlement of all weaker people, might have seen how safe and strong he was.

His way taking him past Tellson's, and he both banking at Tellson's and knowing Mr. Lorry as the intimate friend of the Manettes, it entered Mr. Stryver's mind to enter the bank, and reveal to Mr. Lorry the brightness of the Soho horizon. So, he pushed open the door with the weak rattle in its throat, stumbled down the two steps, got past the two ancient cashiers, and shouldered himself into the musty back closet where Mr. Lorry sat at great books ruled for figures, with perpendicular iron bars to his window as if that were ruled for figures too, and everything under the clouds were a sum.

"Halloa!" said Mr. Stryver. "How do you do? I hope you are well!"

It was Stryver's grand peculiarity that he always seemed too big for any place, or space. He was so much too big for Tellson's, that old clerks in distant corners looked up with looks of remonstrance, as though he squeezed them against the wall. The House itself, magnificently reading the paper quite in the far-off perspective, lowered displeased, as if the Stryver head had been butted into its responsible waistcoat.

The discreet Mr. Lorry said, in a sample tone of the voice he would recommend under the circumstances, "How do you do, Mr.

Stryver? How do you do, sir?" and shook hands. There was a peculiarity in his manner of shaking hands, always to be seen in any clerk at Tellson's who shook hands with a customer when the House pervaded the air. He shook in a self-abnegating way, as one who shook for Tellson and Co.

"Can I do anything for you, Mr. Stryver?" asked Mr. Lorry, in his business character.

"Why, no, thank you; this is a private visit to yourself, Mr. Lorry; I have come for a private word."

"Oh indeed!" said Mr. Lorry, bending down his ear, while his eye strayed to the House afar off.

"I am going," said Mr. Stryver, leaning his arms confidentially on the desk: whereupon, although it was a large double one, there appeared to be not half desk enough for him: "I am going to make an offer of myself in marriage to your agreeable little friend, Miss Manette, Mr. Lorry."

"Oh dear me!" cried Mr. Lorry, rubbing his chin, and looking at his visitor dubiously.

"Oh dear me, sir?" repeated Stryver, drawing back. "Oh dear you, sir? What may your meaning be, Mr. Lorry?"

"My meaning," answered the man of business, "is, of course, friendly and appreciative, and that it does you the greatest credit, and—in short, my meaning is everything you could desire. But—really, you know, Mr. Stryver—" Mr. Lorry paused, and shook his head at him in the oddest manner, as if he were compelled against his will to add, internally, "you know there really is so much too much of you!"

"Well!" said Stryver, slapping the desk with his contentious hand, opening his eyes wider, and taking a long breath; "if I understand you, Mr. Lorry, I'll be hanged!"

Mr. Lorry adjusted his little wig at both ears as a means towards that end, and bit the feather of a pen.

"D——n it all, sir!" said Stryver, staring at him, "am I not eligible?"

"Oh dear yes! Yes. Oh yes, you're eligible!" said Mr. Lorry. "If you say eligible, you are eligible."

"Am I not prosperous?" asked Stryver.

"Oh! if you come to prosperous, you are prosperous," said Mr. Lorry.

"And advancing?"

"If you come to advancing, you know," said Mr. Lorry, delighted to be able to make another admission, "nobody can doubt that."

"Then what on earth is your meaning, Mr. Lorry?" demanded
5   Stryver, perceptibly crestfallen.

"Well! I— Were you going there now?" asked Mr. Lorry.

"Straight!" said Stryver, with a plump of his fist on the desk.

"Then I think I wouldn't, if I was you."

"Why?" said Stryver. "Now, I'll put you in a corner," forensically shaking a forefinger at him. "You are a man of business and bound to have a reason. State your reason. Why wouldn't you go?"

"Because," said Mr. Lorry, "I wouldn't go on such an object without having some cause to believe that I should succeed."

"D——n me!" cried Stryver, "but this beats everything."
15   Mr. Lorry glanced at the distant House, and glanced at the angry Stryver.

"Here's a man of business—a man of years—a man of experience—*in* a bank," said Stryver; "and having summed up three leading reasons for complete success, he says there's no reason at all! Says it with his head on!" Mr. Stryver remarked upon the peculiarity as if it would have been infinitely less remarkable if he had said it with his head off.

"When I speak of success, I speak of success with the young lady; and when I speak of causes and reasons to make success probable, I
25   speak of causes and reasons that will tell as such with the young lady. The young lady, my good sir," said Mr. Lorry, mildly tapping the Stryver arm, "the young lady. The young lady goes before all."

"Then you mean to tell me, Mr. Lorry," said Stryver, squaring his elbows, "that it is your deliberate opinion that the young lady at present in question is a mincing fool?"

"Not exactly so. I mean to tell you, Mr. Stryver," said Mr. Lorry, reddening, "that I will hear no disrespectful word of that young lady from any lips; and that if I knew any man—which I hope I do not—whose taste was so coarse, and whose temper was so over-
35   bearing, that he could not restrain himself from speaking disrespectfully of that young lady at this desk, not even Tellson's should prevent my giving him a piece of my mind."

The necessity of being angry in a suppressed tone had put Mr. Stryver's blood-vessels into a dangerous state when it was his turn to be angry; Mr. Lorry's veins, methodical as their courses could usually be, were in no better state now it was his turn.

"That is what I mean to tell you, sir," said Mr. Lorry. "Pray let there be no mistake about it."

Mr. Stryver sucked the end of a ruler for a little while, and then stood hitting a tune out of his teeth with it, which probably gave him the toothache. He broke the awkward silence by saying:

"This is something new to me, Mr. Lorry. You deliberately advise me not to go up to Soho and offer myself—myself, Stryver of the King's Bench bar?"

"Do you ask me for my advice, Mr. Stryver?"

"Yes, I do."

"Very good. Then I give it, and you have repeated it correctly."

"And all I can say of it is," laughed Stryver with a vexed laugh, "that this—ha, ha!—beats everything past, present, and to come."

"Now understand me," pursued Mr. Lorry. "As a man of business, I am not justified in saying anything about this matter, for, as a man of business, I know nothing of it. But, as an old fellow, who has carried Miss Manette in his arms, who is the trusted friend of Miss Manette and of her father too, and who has a great affection for them both, I have spoken. The confidence is not of my seeking, recollect. Now, you think I may not be right?"

"Not I!" said Stryver, whistling. "I can't undertake to find third parties in common sense; I can only find it for myself. I suppose sense in certain quarters; you suppose mincing bread-and-butter nonsense. It's new to me, but you are right, I dare say."

"What I suppose, Mr. Stryver, I claim to characterise for myself. And understand me, sir," said Mr. Lorry quickly flushing again, "I will not—not even at Tellson's—have it characterised for me by any gentleman breathing."

"There! I beg your pardon!" said Stryver.

"Granted. Thank you. Well, Mr. Stryver, I was about to say: it might be painful to you to find yourself mistaken, it might be painful to Doctor Manette to have the task of being explicit with you, it might be very painful to Miss Manette to have the task of being explicit with you. You know the terms upon which I have the honour and happiness to stand with the family. If you please, committing you in no way, representing you in no way, I will undertake to correct my advice by the exercise of a little new observation and judgment expressly brought to bear upon it. If you should then be dissatisfied with it, you can but test its soundness for yourself; if, on the other hand, you should be satisfied with it, and it should be what it now is, it may spare all sides what is best spared. What do you say?"

"How long would you keep me in town?"

"Oh! It is only a question of a few hours. I could go to Soho in the evening, and come to your chambers afterwards."

"Then I say yes," said Stryver. "I won't go up there now, I am not so hot upon it as that comes to; I say yes, and I shall expect you to look in to-night. Good-morning."

Then Mr. Stryver turned and burst out of the Bank causing such a concussion of air on his passage through, that to stand up against it bowing behind the two counters, required the utmost remaining strength of the two ancient clerks. Those vulnerable and feeble persons were always seen by the public in the act of bowing, and were popularly believed, when they had bowed a customer out, still to keep on bowing in the empty office until they bowed another customer in.

The barrister was keen enough to divine that the banker would not have gone so far in his expression of opinion on any less solid ground than moral certainty. Unprepared as he was for the large pill he had to swallow, he got it down. "And now," said Mr. Stryver, shaking his forensic forefinger at the Temple in general, when it was down, "my way out of this is to put you all in the wrong."

It was a bit of the art of an Old Bailey tactician, in which he found great relief. "You shall not put me in the wrong, young lady," said Mr. Stryver; "I'll do that for you."

Accordingly, when Mr. Lorry called that night as late as ten o'clock, Mr. Stryver, among a quantity of books and papers littered out for the purpose, seemed to have nothing less on his mind than the subject of the morning. He even showed surprise when he saw Mr. Lorry, and was altogether in an absent and preoccupied state.

"Well!" said that good-natured emissary, after a full half-hour of bootless attempts to bring him round to the question. "I have been to Soho."

"To Soho?" repeated Mr. Stryver, coldly. "Oh to be sure! What am I thinking of!"

"And I have no doubt," said Mr. Lorry, "that I was right in the conversation we had. My opinion is confirmed, and I reiterate my advice."

"I assure you," returned Mr. Stryver, in the friendliest way, " that I am sorry for it on your account, and sorry for it on the poor father's account. I know this must always be a sore subject with the family; let us say no more about it."

"I don't understand you," said Mr. Lorry.

"I dare say not," rejoined Stryver, nodding his head in a soothing and final way; "no matter, no matter."

"But it does matter," Mr. Lorry urged.

"No it doesn't; I assure you it doesn't. Having supposed that there was sense where there is no sense, and a laudable ambition where there is not a laudable ambition, I am well out of my mistake, and no harm is done. Young women have committed similar follies often before, and have repented them in poverty and obscurity often before. In an unselfish aspect, I am sorry that the thing is dropped, because it would have been a bad thing for me in a worldly point of view; in a selfish aspect, I am glad that the thing has dropped, because it would have been a bad thing for me in a worldly point of view—it is hardly necessary to say I could have gained nothing by it. There is no harm at all done. I have not proposed to the young lady, and, between ourselves, I am by no means certain, on reflection, that I ever should have committed my-self to that extent. Mr. Lorry, you can not control the mincing vanities and giddinesses of empty-headed girls; you must not ex-pect to do it, or you will always be disappointed. Now, pray say no more about it. I tell you, I regret it on account of others, but I am satisfied on my own account. And I am really very much obliged to you for allowing me to sound you, and for giving me your advice; you know the young lady better than I do; you were right, it never would have done."

Mr. Lorry was so taken aback, that he looked quite stupidly at Mr. Stryver shouldering him towards the door, with an appearance of showering generosity, forbearance, and good-will on his erring head. "Make the best of it, my dear sir," said Stryver; "say no more about it; thank you again for allowing me to sound you; good-night!"

Mr. Lorry was out in the night, before he knew where he was. Mr. Stryver was lying back on his sofa, winking at his ceiling.

Chapter 13. The Fellow of No Delicacy

If Sydney Carton ever shone anywhere, he certainly never shone in the house of Doctor Manette. He had been there often, during a whole year, and had always been the same moody and morose lounger there. When he cared to talk, he talked well; but, the cloud of caring for nothing, which overshadowed him with such a fatal darkness, was very rarely pierced by the light within him.

And yet he did care something for the streets that environed that house, and for the senseless stones that made their pavements. Many a night he vaguely and unhappily wandered there, when wine had brought no transitory gladness to him; many a dreary daybreak revealed his solitary figure lingering there, and still lingering there when the first beams of the sun brought into strong relief, removed beauties of architecture in spires of churches and lofty buildings, as perhaps the quiet time brought some sense of better things, else forgotten and unattainable, into his mind. Of late, the neglected bed in the Temple Court had known him more scantily than ever; and often when he had thrown himself upon it no longer than a few minutes, he had got up again, and haunted that neighbourhood.

On a day in August, when Mr. Stryver (after notifying to his jackal that "he had thought better of that marrying matter") had carried his delicacy into Devonshire, and when the sight and scent of flowers in the City streets had some waifs of goodness in them for the worst, of health for the sickliest, and of youth for the oldest, Sydney's feet still trod those stones. From being irresolute and purposeless, his feet became animated by an intention, and, in the working out of that intention, they took him to the Doctor's door.

He was shown upstairs, and found Lucie at her work, alone. She had never been quite at her ease with him, and received him with some little embarrassment as he seated himself near her table. But, looking up at his face in the interchange of the first few common-places, she observed a change in it.

"I fear you are not well, Mr. Carton!"

"No. But the life I lead, Miss Manette, is not conducive to health. What is to be expected of, or by, such profligates?"

"Is it not—forgive me; I have begun the question on my lips—a pity to live no better life?"

"God knows it is a shame!"

"Then why not change it?"

Looking gently at him again, she was surprised and saddened to see that there were tears in his eyes. There were tears in his voice too, as he answered:

"It is too late for that. I shall never be better than I am. I shall sink lower, and be worse."

He leaned an elbow on her table, and covered his eyes with his hand. The table trembled in the silence that followed.

She had never seen him softened, and was much distressed. He knew her to be so, without looking at her, and said:

"Pray forgive me, Miss Manette. I break down before the knowledge of what I want to say to you. Will you hear me?"

"If it will do you any good, Mr. Carton, if it would make you happier, it would make me very glad!"

"God bless you for your sweet compassion!"

He unshaded his face after a little while, and spoke steadily.

"Don't be afraid to hear me. Don't shrink from anything I say. I am like one who died young. All my life might have been."

"No, Mr. Carton. I am sure that the best part of it might still be; I am sure that you might be much, much worthier of yourself."

"Say of you, Miss Manette, and although I know better—although in the mystery of my own wretched heart I know better—I shall never forget it!"

She was pale and trembling. He came to her relief with a fixed despair of himself which made the interview unlike any other that could have been holden.

"If it had been possible, Miss Manette, that you could have returned the love of the man you see before you—self-flung away, wasted, drunken, poor creature of misuse as you know him to be—he would have been conscious this day and hour, in spite of his happiness, that he would bring you to misery, bring you to sorrow and repentance, blight you, disgrace you, pull you down with him. I know very well that you can have no tenderness for me; I ask for none; I am even thankful that it cannot be."

"Without it, can I not save you, Mr. Carton? Can I not recall you—forgive me again!—to a better course? Can I in no way repay your confidence? I know this is a confidence," she modestly said, after a little hesitation, and in earnest tears, "I know you would say this to no one else. Can I turn it to no good account for yourself, Mr. Carton?"

He shook his head.

"To none. No, Miss Manette, to none. If you will hear me through a very little more, all you can ever do for me is done. I wish you to know that you have been the last dream of my soul. In my degradation I have not been so degraded but that the sight of you with your father, and of this home made such a home by you, has stirred old shadows that I thought had died out of me. Since I knew you, I have been troubled by a remorse that I thought would never reproach me again, and have heard whispers from old voices impelling me upward, that I thought were silent forever. I have had unformed ideas of striving afresh, beginning anew, shaking off sloth and sensuality, and fighting out the abandoned night. A dream, all a dream, that ends in nothing, and leaves the sleeper where he lay down, but I wish you to know that you inspired it."

"Will nothing of it remain? O Mr. Carton, think again! Try again!"

"No, Miss Manette; all through it, I have known myself to be quite undeserving. And yet I have had the weakness, and have still the weakness, to wish you to know with what a sudden mastery you kindled me, heap of ashes that I am, into fire—a fire, however, inseparable in its nature from myself, quickening nothing, lighting nothing, doing no service, idly burning away."

"Since it is my misfortune, Mr. Carton, to have made you more unhappy than you were before you knew me—"

"Don't say that, Miss Manette, for you would have reclaimed me, if anything could. You will not be the cause of my becoming worse."

"Since the state of your mind that you describe, is, at all events, attributable to some influence of mine—this is what I mean, if I can make it plain—can I use no influence to serve you? Have I no power for good, with you, at all?"

"The utmost good that I am capable of now, Miss Manette, I have come here to realise. Let me carry through the rest of my misdirected life the remembrance that I opened my heart to you, last of all the world; and that there was something left in me at this time which you could deplore and pity."

"Which I entreated you to believe again and again, most fervently, with all my heart, was capable of better things, Mr. Carton!"

"Entreat me to believe it no more, Miss Manette. I have proved myself, and I know better. I distress you; I draw fast to an end. Will you let me believe, when I recall this day, that the last confidence of my life was reposed in your pure and innocent breast, and that it lies there alone, and will be shared by no one?"

"If that will be a consolation to you, yes."

"Not even by the dearest one ever to be known to you?"

"Mr. Carton," she answered, after an agitated pause, "the secret is yours, not mine; and I promise to respect it."

"Thank you. And again, God bless you."

He put her hand to his lips, and moved towards the door.

"Be under no apprehension, Miss Manette, of my ever resuming this conversation by so much as a passing word. I will never refer to it again. If I were dead, that could not be surer than it is henceforth. In the hour of my death, I shall hold sacred the one good remembrance—and shall thank and bless you for it—that my last avowal of myself was made to you, and that my name, and faults, and miseries were gently carried in your heart. May it otherwise be light and happy!"

He was so unlike what he had ever shown himself to be, and it was so sad to think how much he had thrown away, and how much he every day kept down and perverted, that Lucie Manette wept mournfully for him as he stood looking back to her.

"Be comforted!" he said. "I am not worth such feeling, Miss Manette. An hour or two hence, and the low companions and low habits that I scorn but yield to, will render me less worth such tears as those, than any wretch who creeps along the streets. Be comforted! But, within myself, I shall always be, towards you, what I am now, though outwardly I shall be what you have heretofore seen me. The last supplication but one I make to you, is, that you will believe this of me."

"I will, Mr. Carton."

"My last supplication of all is this; and with it, I will relieve you
of a visitor with whom I well know you have nothing in unison,
and between whom and you there is an impassable space. It is
useless to say it, I know, but it rises out of my soul. For you, and for
5   any dear to you, I would do anything. If my career were of that
better kind that there was any opportunity or capacity of sacrifice
in it, I would embrace any sacrifice for you and for those dear to
you. Try to hold me in your mind, at some quiet times, as ardent
and sincere in this one thing. The time will come, the time will not
be long in coming, when new ties will be formed about you—ties
that will bind you yet more tenderly and strongly to the home you
so adorn—the dearest ties that will ever grace and gladden you. O
Miss Manette, when the little picture of a happy father's face looks
up in yours, when you see your own bright beauty springing up
15 anew at your feet, think now and then that there is a man who
would give his life, to keep a life you love beside you!"

He said, "Farewell!" said a last "God bless you!" and left her.

Chapter 14. The Honest Tradesman

To the eyes of Mr. Jeremiah Cruncher, sitting on his stool in
Fleet Street with his grisly urchin beside him, a vast number and
variety of objects in movement were every day presented. Who
could sit upon anything in Fleet Street during the busy hours of
the day, and not be dazed and deafened by two immense proces-
sions, one ever tending westward with the sun, the other ever
tending eastward from the sun, both ever tending to the plains
25 beyond the range of red and purple where the sun goes down!

With his straw in his mouth, Mr. Cruncher sat watching the two
streams, like the heathen rustic who has for several centuries been
on duty watching one stream—saving that Jerry had no expectation
of their ever running dry. Nor would it have been an expectation of
a hopeful kind, since a small part of his income was derived from
the pilotage of timid women (mostly of a full habit and past the
middle term of life) from Tellson's side of the tides to the opposite
shore. Brief as such companionship was in every separate instance,

Mr. Cruncher never failed to become so interested in the lady as to express a strong desire to have the honour of drinking her very good health. And it was from the gifts bestowed upon him towards the execution of this benevolent purpose, that he recruited his finances, as just now observed.

Time was, when a poet sat upon a stool in a public place, and mused in the sight of men. Mr. Cruncher, sitting on a stool in a public place, but not being a poet, mused as little as possible, and looked about him.

It fell out that he was thus engaged in a season when crowds were few, and belated women few, and when his affairs in general were so unprosperous as to awaken a strong suspicion in his breast that Mrs. Cruncher must have been "flopping" in some pointed manner, when an unusual concourse, pouring down Fleet Street westward, attracted his attention. Looking that way, Mr. Cruncher made out that some kind of funeral was coming along, and that there was popular objection to this funeral, which engendered uproar.

"Young Jerry," said Mr. Cruncher, turning to his offspring, "it's a buryin'."

"Hooroar, Father!" cried Young Jerry.

The young gentleman uttered this exultant sound with mysterious significance. The elder gentleman took the cry so ill, that he watched his opportunity, and smote the young gentleman on the ear.

"What d'ye mean? What are you hooroaring at? What do you want to conwey to your own father, you young Rip? This boy is a getting too many for *me!*" said Mr. Cruncher, surveying him. "Him and his hooroars! Don't let me hear no more of you, or you shall feel some more of me. D'ye hear?"

"I warn't doing no harm," Young Jerry protested, rubbing his cheek.

"Drop it then," said Mr. Cruncher; "I won't have none of *your* no harms. Get atop of that there seat, and look at the crowd."

His son obeyed, and the crowd approached; they were bawling and hissing round a dingy hearse and dingy mourning coach, in which mourning coach there was only one mourner, dressed in the dingy trappings that were considered essential to the dignity of the position. The position appeared by no means to please him, however, with an increasing rabble surrounding the coach, deriding him, making grimaces at him, and incessantly groaning and calling out: "Yah! Spies! Tst! Yaha! Spies!" with many compliments too numerous and forcible to repeat.

5   Funerals had at all times a remarkable attraction for Mr. Cruncher; he always pricked up his senses, and became excited, when a funeral passed Tellson's. Naturally, therefore, a funeral with this uncommon attendance excited him greatly, and he asked of the first man who ran against him:

"What is it, brother? What's it about?"

"I don't know," said the man. "Spies! Yaha! Tst! Spies!"

He asked another man. "Who is it?"

"*I* don't know," returned the man, clapping his hands to his mouth nevertheless, and vociferating in a surprising heat and with 15   the greatest ardour, "Spies! Yaha! Tst, tst! Spi-ies!"

At length, a person better informed on the merits of the case, tumbled against him, and from this person he learned that the funeral was the funeral of one Roger Cly.

"Was *he* a spy?" asked Mr. Cruncher.

"Old Bailey spy," returned his informant. "Yaha! Tst! Yah! Old Bailey Spi-i-es!"

"Why, to be sure!" exclaimed Jerry, recalling the Trial at which he had assisted. "I've seen him. Dead, is he?"

"Dead as mutton," returned the other, "and can't be too dead. 25   Have 'em out, there! Spies! Pull 'em out, there! Spies!"

The idea was so acceptable in the prevalent absence of any idea, that the crowd caught it up with eagerness, and loudly repeating the suggestion to have 'em out, and to pull 'em out, mobbed the two vehicles so closely that they came to a stop. On the crowd's opening the coach doors, the one mourner scuffled out of himself and was in their hands for a moment; but he was so alert, and made such good use of his time, that in another moment he was scouring away up a by-street, after shedding his cloak, hat, long hatband, white pocket-handkerchief, and other symbolical tears.

35   These the people tore to pieces and scattered far and wide with great enjoyment, while the tradesmen hurriedly shut up their shops; for a crowd in those times stopped at nothing, and was a monster much dreaded. They had already got the length of opening the hearse to take the coffin out, when some brighter genius

proposed, instead, its being escorted to its destination amidst general rejoicing. Practical suggestions being much needed, this suggestion, too, was received with acclamation, and the coach was immediately filled with eight inside and a dozen out, while as many people got on the roof of the hearse as could by any exercise of ingenuity stick upon it. Among the first of these volunteers was Jerry Cruncher himself, who modestly concealed his spiky head from the observation of Tellson's, in the further corner of the mourning coach.

The officiating undertakers made some protest against these changes in the ceremonies; but, the river being alarmingly near, and several voices remarking on the efficacy of cold immersion in bringing refractory members of the profession to reason, the protest was faint and brief. The remodelled procession started, with a chimney-sweep driving the hearse—advised by the regular driver, who was perched beside him, under close inspection, for the purpose—and with a pieman, also attended by his cabinet minister, driving the mourning coach. A bear-leader, a popular street charac-ter of the time, was impressed as an additional ornament, before the cavalcade had gone far down the Strand; and his bear, who was black and very mangy, gave quite an undertaking air to that part of the procession in which he walked.

Thus, with beer-drinking, pipe-smoking, song-roaring, and infi-nite caricaturing of woe, the disorderly procession went its way, recruiting at every step, and all the shops shutting up before it. Its destination was the old church of Saint Pancras, far off in the fields. It got there in course of time; insisted on pouring into the burial-ground; finally accomplished the interment of the deceased Roger Cly in its own way, and highly to its own satisfaction.

The dead man disposed of, and the crowd being under the necessity of providing some other entertainment for itself, another brighter genius (or perhaps the same) conceived the humour of impeaching casual passers-by, as Old Bailey spies, and wreaking vengeance on them. Chase was given to some scores of inoffensive persons who had never been near the Old Bailey in their lives, in the realisation of this fancy, and they were roughly hustled and maltreated. The transition to the sport of window-breaking, and thence to the plundering of public-houses, was easy and natural. At last, after several hours, when sundry summer-houses had been pulled down, and some area-railings had been torn up, to arm the more belligerent spirits, a rumour got about that the Guards were coming. Before this rumour, the crowd gradually melted away, and perhaps the Guards came, and perhaps they never came, and this was the usual progress of a mob.

Mr. Cruncher did not assist at the closing sports, but had remained behind in the churchyard, to confer and condole with the undertakers. The place had a soothing influence on him. He procured a pipe from a neighbouring public-house, and smoked it, looking in at the railings and maturely considering the spot.

"Jerry," said Mr. Cruncher, apostrophising himself in his usual way, "you see that there Cly that day, and you see with your own eyes that he was a young 'un and a straight made 'un."

Having smoked his pipe out, and ruminated a little longer, he turned himself about, that he might appear, before the hour of closing, on his station at Tellson's. Whether his meditations on mortality had touched his liver, or whether his general health had been previously at all amiss, or whether he desired to show a little attention to an eminent man, is not so much to the purpose, as that he made a short call upon his medical adviser—a distinguished surgeon—on his way back.

Young Jerry relieved his father with dutiful interest, and reported no job in his absence. The bank closed, the ancient clerks came out, the usual watch was set, and Mr. Cruncher and his son went home to tea.

"Now, I tell you where it is!" said Mr. Cruncher to his wife, on entering. "If, as a honest tradesman, my wenturs goes wrong to-night, I shall make sure that you've been praying agin me, and I shall work you for it the same as if I seen you do it."

The dejected Mrs. Cruncher shook her head.

"Why, you're at it afore my face!" said Mr. Cruncher, with signs of angry apprehension.

"I am saying nothing."

"Well, then; don't meditate nothing. You might as well flop as meditate. You may as well go agin me one way as another. Drop it altogether."

"Yes, Jerry."

"Yes, Jerry," repeated Mr. Cruncher, sitting down to tea. "Ah! It is yes, Jerry. That's about it. You may say yes, Jerry."

Mr. Cruncher had no particular meaning in these sulky corrobo-rations, but made use of them, as people not unfrequently do, to express general ironical dissatisfaction.

"You and your yes, Jerry," said Mr. Cruncher, taking a bite out of his bread-and-butter, and seeming to help it down with a large invisible oyster out of his saucer. "Ah! I think so. I believe you."

"You are going out to-night?" asked his decent wife, when he took another bite.

"Yes, I am."

"May I go with you, father?" asked his son, briskly.

"No, you mayn't. I'm going—as your mother knows—a fishing. That's where I'm going to. Going a fishing."

"Your fishing-rod gets rayther rusty; don't it, Father?"

"Never you mind."

"Shall you bring any fish home, Father?"

"If I don't, you'll have short commons, to-morrow," returned the gentleman, shaking his head; "that's questions enough for you; I ain't a going out till you've been long a-bed."

He devoted himself during the remainder of the evening to keeping a most viligant watch on Mrs. Cruncher, and sullenly holding her in conversation that she might be prevented from meditating any petitions to his disadvantage. With this view, he urged his son to hold her in conversation also, and led the unfortunate woman a hard life by dwelling on any causes of complaint he could bring against her, rather than he would leave her for a moment to her own reflections. The devoutest person could have rendered no greater homage to the efficacy of an honest prayer than he did in this distrust of his wife. It was as if a professed unbeliever in ghosts should be frightened by a ghost story.

"And mind you!" said Mr. Cruncher. "No games tomorrow! If I, as a honest tradesman, succeed in providing a jinte of meat or two, none of your not touching of it, and sticking to bread. If I, as a honest tradesman, am able to provide a little beer, none of your declaring on water. When you go to Rome, do as Rome does. Rome will be a ugly customer to you, if you don't. I'm your Rome, you know."

Then he began grumbling again:

"With your flying into the face of your own wittles and drink! I don't know how scarce you mayn't make the wittles and drink here, by your flopping tricks and your unfeeling conduct. Look at your boy; he *is* your'n, ain't he? He's as thin as a lath. Do you call yourself a mother, and not know that a mother's first duty is to blow her boy out?"

This touched Young Jerry on a tender place; who adjured his mother to perform her first duty, and, whatever else she did or neglected, above all things to lay especial stress on the discharge of that maternal function so affectingly and delicately indicated by his other parent.

Thus the evening wore away with the Cruncher family, until Young Jerry was ordered to bed, and his mother, laid under similar injunctions, obeyed them. Mr. Cruncher beguiled the earlier watches of the night with solitary pipes, and did not start upon his excursion until nearly one o'clock. Towards that small and ghostly hour, he rose up from his chair, took a key out of his pocket, opened a locked cupboard, and brought forth a sack, a crowbar of convenient size, a rope and chain, and other fishing tackle of that nature. Disposing these articles about him in skilful manner, he bestowed a parting defiance on Mrs. Cruncher, extinguished the light, and went out.

Young Jerry, who had only made a feint of undressing when he went to bed, was not long after his father. Under cover of the darkness he followed out of the room, followed down the stairs, followed down the court, followed out into the streets. He was in no uneasiness concerning his getting into the house again, for it was full of lodgers, and the door stood ajar all night.

Impelled by a laudable ambition to study the art and mystery of his father's honest calling, Young Jerry, keeping as close to housefronts, walls, and doorways, as his eyes were close to one another, held his honoured parent in view. The honoured parent, steering northward, had not gone far, when he was joined by another disciple of Izaak Walton, and the two trudged on together.

Within half an hour from the first starting, they were beyond the winking lamps, and the more than winking watchmen, and were out upon a lonely road. Another fisherman was picked up here—and that so silently, that if Young Jerry had been superstitious, he might have supposed the second follower of the gentle craft to have, all of a sudden, split himself in two.

The three went on, and Young Jerry went on, until the three stopped under a bank overhanging the road. Upon the top of the bank was a low brick wall, surmounted by an iron railing. In the shadow of bank and wall the three turned out of the road, and up a blind lane, of which the wall—there, risen to some eight or ten feet high—formed one side. Crouching down in a corner, peeping up the lane, the next object that Young Jerry saw was the form of his honoured parent, pretty well defined against a watery and clouded moon, nimbly scaling an iron gate. He was soon over, and then the second fisherman got over, and then the third. They all dropped softly on the ground within the gate, and lay there a little—listening perhaps. Then, they moved away on their hands and knees.

It was now Young Jerry's turn to approach the gate: which he did, holding his breath. Crouching down again in a corner there, and looking in, he made out the three fishermen creeping through some rank grass, and all the gravestones in the churchyard—it was a large churchyard that they were in—looking on like ghosts in white, while the church tower itself looked on like the ghost of a monstrous giant. They did not creep far, before they stopped and stood upright. And then they began to fish.

They fished with a spade, at first. Presently the honoured parent appeared to be adjusting some instrument like a great corkscrew. Whatever tools they worked with, they worked hard, until the awful striking of the church clock so terrified Young Jerry, that he made off, with his hair as stiff as his father's.

But, his long-cherished desire to know more about these matters not only stopped him in his running away, but lured him back again. They were still fishing perseveringly, when he peeped in at the gate for the second time; but, now they seemed to have got a bite. There was a screwing and complaining sound down below, and their bent figures were strained, as if by a weight. By slow degrees the weight broke away the earth upon it, and came to the surface. Young Jerry very well knew what it would be; but, when he saw it, and saw his honoured parent about to wrench it open, he was so frightened, being new to the sight, that he made off again, and never stopped until he had run a mile or more.

He would not have stopped then for anything less necessary than breath, it being a spectral sort of race that he ran, and one highly desirable to get to the end of. He had a strong idea that the coffin he had seen was running after him; and, pictured as hopping on behind him, bolt upright, upon its narrow end, always on the point of overtaking him and hopping on at his side—perhaps taking his arm—it was a pursuer to shun. It was an inconsistent and ubiquitous fiend too, for, while it was making the whole night behind him dreadful, he darted out into the roadway to avoid dark alleys, fearful of its coming hopping out of them like a dropsical boy's-kite without tail and wings. It hid in doorways too, rubbing its horrible shoulders against doors, and drawing them up to its ears, as if it were laughing. It got into shadows on the road, and lay cunningly on its back to trip him up. All this time it was incessantly hopping on behind and gaining on him, so that when the boy got to his own door he had reason for being half dead. And even then it would not leave him, but followed him upstairs with a bump on every stair, scrambled into bed with him, and bumped down, dead and heavy, on his breast when he fell asleep.

From his oppressed slumber, Young Jerry in his closet was awakened after daybreak and before sunrise by the presence of his father in the family room. Something had gone wrong with him; at least, so Young Jerry inferred, from the circumstance of his holding Mrs. Cruncher by the ears, and knocking the back of her head against the headboard of the bed.

"I told you I would," said Mr. Cruncher, "and I did."

"Jerry, Jerry, Jerry!" his wife implored.

"You oppose yourself to the profit of the business," said Jerry, "and me and my partners suffer. You was to honour and obey; why the devil don't you?"

"I try to be a good wife, Jerry," the poor woman protested, with tears.

"Is it being a good wife to oppose your husband's business? Is it honouring your husband to dishonour his business? Is it obeying your husband to disobey him on the wital subject of his business?"

"You hadn't taken to the dreadful business then, Jerry."

"It's enough for you," retorted Mr. Cruncher, "to be the wife of an honest tradesman, and not to occupy your female mind with calculations when he took to his trade or when he didn't. A honouring and obeying wife would let his trade alone altogether. Call yourself a religious woman? If you're a religious woman, give me a irreligious one! You have no more nat'ral sense of duty than the bed of this here Thames River has of a pile, and similarly it must be knocked into you."

The altercation was conducted in a low tone of voice, and terminated in the honest tradesman's kicking off his clay-soiled boots, and lying down at his length on the floor. After taking a timid peep at him lying on his back, with his rusty hands under his head for a pillow, his son lay down too, and fell asleep again.

There was no fish for breakfast, and not much of anything else. Mr. Cruncher was out of spirits, and out of temper, and kept an iron pot-lid by him as a projectile for the correction of Mrs. Cruncher, in case he should observe any symptoms of her saying Grace. He was brushed and washed at the usual hour, and set off with his son to pursue his ostensible calling.

Young Jerry, walking with the stool under his arm at his father's side along sunny and crowded Fleet Street, was a very different Young Jerry from him of the previous night, running home through darkness and solitude from his grim pursuer. His cunning was fresh with the day, and his qualms were gone with the night—in which particulars it is not improbable that he had compeers in Fleet Street and the City of London, that fine morning.

"Father," said Young Jerry, as they walked along: taking care to keep at arm's length and to have the stool well between them: "what's a resurrection-man?"

Mr. Cruncher came to a stop on the pavement before he answered, "How should I know?"

"I thought you knowed everything, Father," said the artless boy.

"Hem! Well," returned Mr. Cruncher, going on again, and lifting off his hat to give his spikes free play, "he's a tradesman."

"What's his goods, Father?" asked the brisk Young Jerry.

"His goods," said Mr. Cruncher, after turning it over in his mind, "is a branch of scientific goods."

"Persons' bodies, ain't it, Father?" asked the lively boy.

"I believe it is something of that sort," said Mr. Cruncher.

"Oh, Father, I should so like to be a resurrection-man when I'm quite growed up!"

Mr. Cruncher was soothed, but shook his head in a dubious and moral way. "It depends upon how you dewelop your talents. Be careful to dewelop your talents, and never to say no more than you can help to nobody, and there's no telling at the present time what you may not come to be fit for." As Young Jerry, thus encouraged, went on a few yards in advance, to plant the stool in the shadow of the Bar, Mr. Cruncher added to himself: "Jerry, you honest tradesman, there's hopes wot that boy will yet be a blessing to you, and a recompense to you for his mother!"

Chapter 15. Knitting

There had been earlier drinking than usual in the wine-shop of Monsieur Defarge. As early as six o'clock in the morning, sallow faces peeping through its barred windows had descried other faces within, bending over measures of wine. Monsieur Defarge sold a very thin wine at the best of times, but it would seem to have been an unsuually thin wine that he sold at this time. A sour wine, moreover, or a souring, for its influence on the mood of those who drank it was to make them gloomy. No vivacious Bacchanalian flame leaped out of the pressed grape of Monsieur Defarge: but, a smouldering fire that burnt in the dark lay hidden in the dregs of it.

This had been the third morning in succession on which there had been early drinking at the wine-shop of Monsieur Defarge. It had begun on Monday, and here was Wednesday come. There had been more of early brooding than drinking; for, many men had listened and whispered and slunk about there from the time of the opening of the door, who could not have laid a piece of money on the counter to save their souls. These were to the full as interested in the place, however, as if they could have commanded whole barrels of wine; and they glided from seat to seat, and from corner to corner, swallowing talk in lieu of drink, with greedy looks.

Notwithstanding an unusual flow of company, the master of the wine-shop was not visible. He was not missed; for, nobody who crossed the threshold looked for him, nobody asked for him, nobody wondered to see only Madame Defarge in her seat, presiding over the distribution of wine, with a bowl of battered small coins before her, as much defaced and beaten out of their original impress as the small coinage of humanity from whose ragged pockets they had come.

A suspended interest and a prevalent absence of mind were perhaps observed by the spies who looked in at the wine-shop, as they looked in at every place, high and low, from the king's palace to the criminal's gaol. Games at cards languished, players at dominoes musingly built towers with them, drinkers drew figures on the tables with spilt drops of wine, Madame Defarge herself picked out the pattern on her sleeve with her toothpick, and saw and heard something inaudible and invisible a long way off.

Thus, Saint Antoine in this vinous feature of his, until midday. It was high noontide, when two dusty men passed through his streets and under his swinging lamps: of whom, one was Monsieur Defarge: the other a mender of roads in a blue cap. All adust and athirst, the two entered the wine-shop. Their arrival had lighted a kind of fire in the breast of Saint Antoine, fast spreading as they came along, which stirred and flickered in flames of faces at most doors and windows. Yet, no one had followed them, and no man spoke when they entered the wine-shop, though the eyes of every man there were turned upon them.

"Good-day, gentlemen!" said Monsieur Defarge.

It may have been a signal for loosening the general tongue. It elicited an answering chorus of "Good-day!"

"It is bad weather, gentlemen," said Defarge, shaking his head.

Upon which, every man looked at his neighbour, and then all cast down their eyes and sat silent. Except one man, who got up and went out.

"My wife," said Defarge aloud, addressing Madame Defarge; "I have travelled certain leagues with this good mender of roads, called Jacques. I met him—by accident—a day and a half's journey out of Paris. He is a good child, this mender of roads, called Jacques. Give him to drink, my wife!"

A second man got up and went out. Madame Defarge set wine before the mender of roads called Jacques, who doffed his blue cap to the company, and drank. In the breast of his blouse he carried some coarse dark bread; he ate of this between whiles, and sat munching and drinking near Madame Defarge's counter. A third man got up and went out.

Defarge refreshed himself with a draught of wine—but, he took

less than was given to the stranger, as being himself a man to whom
it was no rarity—and stood waiting until the countryman had
made his breakfast. He looked at no one present, and no one now
looked at him; not even Madame Defarge, who had taken up her
5 knitting, and was at work.

"Have you finished your repast, friend?" he asked, in due season.

"Yes, thank you."

"Come, then! You shall see the apartment that I told you you
could occupy. It will suit you to a marvel."

Out of the wine-shop into the street, out of the street into a
courtyard, out of the courtyard up a steep staircase, out of the
staircase into a garret—formerly the garret where a white-haired
man sat on a low bench, stooping forward and very busy, making
shoes.

15 No white-haired man was there now; but, the three men were
there who had gone out of the wine-shop singly. And between
them and the white-haired man afar off was the one small link, that
they had once looked in at him through the chinks in the wall.

Defarge closed the door carefully, and spoke in a subdued voice:

"Jacques One, Jacques Two, Jacques Three! This is the witness
encountered by appointment, by me, Jacques Four. He will tell you
all. Speak, Jacques Five!"

The mender of roads, blue cap in hand, wiped his swarthy
forehead with it, and said, "Where shall I commence, monsieur?"

25 "Commence," was Monsieur Defarge's not unreasonable reply,
"at the commencement."

"I saw him then, messieurs," began the mender of roads, "a year
ago this running summer, underneath the carriage of the Marquis,
hanging by the chain. Behold the manner of it. I leaving my work
on the road, the sun going to bed, the carriage of the Marquis
slowly ascending the hill, he hanging by the chain—like this."

Again the mender of roads went through the whole performance;
in which he ought to have been perfect by that time, seeing that it
had been the infallible resource and indispensable entertainment of
35 his village during a whole year.

Jacques One struck in, and asked if he had ever seen the man
before?

"Never," answered the mender of roads, recovering his perpendicular.

Jacques Three demanded how he afterwards recognized him then?

"By his tall figure," said the mender of roads, softly, and with his finger at his nose. "When Monsieur the Marquis demands that evening, 'Say, what is he like?' I make response, 'Tall as a spectre.'"

"You should have said, short as a dwarf," returned Jacques Two.

"But what did I know? The deed was not then accomplished, neither did he confide in me. Observe! Under those circumstances even, I do not offer my testimony. Monsieur the Marquis indicates me with his finger, standing near our little fountain, and says, 'To me! Bring that rascal!' My faith, messieurs, I offer nothing."

"He is right there, Jacques," murmured Defarge, to him who had interrupted. "Go on."

"Good!" said the mender of roads, with an air of mystery. "The tall man is lost, and he is sought—how many months? Nine, ten, eleven?"

"No matter the number," said Defarge. "He is well hidden, but at last he is unluckily found. Go on!"

"I am again at work upon the hillside, and the sun is again about to go to bed. I am collecting my tools to descend to my cottage down in the village below, where it is already dark, when I raise my eyes, and see coming over the hill six soldiers. In the midst of them is a tall man with his arms bound—tied to his sides—like this!"

With the aid of his indispensable cap, he represented a man with his elbows bound fast at his hips, with cords that were knotted behind him.

"I stand aside, messieurs, by my heap of stones, to see the soldiers and their prisoner pass (for it is a solitary road, that, where any spectacle is well worth looking at), and at first, as they approach, I see no more than that they are six soldiers with a tall man bound, and that they are almost black to my sight—except on the side of the sun going to bed, where they have a red edge, messieurs. Also, I see that their long shadows are on the hollow ridge on the opposite side of the road, and are on the hill above it, and are like the shadows of giants. Also, I see that they are covered with dust, and that the dust moves with them as they come, tramp, tramp! But when they advance quite near to me, I recognise the tall man, and he recognises me. Ah, but he would be well content to precipitate himself over the hillside once again, as on the evening when he and I first encountered, close to the same spot!"

He described it as if he were there, and it was evident that he saw it vividly; perhaps he had not seen much in his life.

"I do not show the soldiers that I recognise the tall man; he does not show the soldiers that he recognises me; we do it, and we know it, with our eyes. 'Come on!' says the chief of that company, pointing to the village, 'bring him fast to his tomb!' and they bring him faster. I follow. His arms are swelled because of being bound so tight, his wooden shoes are large and clumsy, and he is lame. Because he is lame, and consequently slow, they drive him with their guns—like this!"

He imitated the action of a man's being impelled forward by the butt-ends of muskets.

"As they descend the hill like madmen running a race, he falls. They laugh and pick him up again. His face is bleeding and covered with dust, but he cannot touch it; thereupon they laugh again. They bring him into the village; all the village runs to look; they take him past the mill, and up to the prison; all the village sees the prison gate open in the darkness of night, and swallow him—like this!"

He opened his mouth as wide as he could, and shut it with a sounding snap of his teeth. Observant of his unwillingness to mar the effect by opening it again, Defarge said, "Go on, Jacques."

"All the village," pursued the mender of roads, on tip-toe and in a low voice, "withdraws; all the village whispers by the fountain; all the village sleeps; all the village dreams of that unhappy one, within the locks and bars of the prison on the crag, and never to come out of it, except to perish. In the morning, with my tools upon my shoulder, eating my morsel of black bread as I go, I make a circuit by the prison, on my way to my work. There I see him, high up, behind the bars of a lofty iron cage, bloody and dusty as last night, looking through. He has no hand free, to wave to me; I dare not call to him; he regards me like a dead man."

Defarge and the three glanced darkly at one another. The looks of all of them were dark, repressed, and revengeful, as they listened to the countryman's story; the manner of all of them, while it was secret, was authoritative too. They had the air of a rough tribunal; Jacques One and Two sitting on the old pallet-bed, each with his chin resting on his hand, and his eyes intent on the road-mender;

Jacques Three, equally intent, on one knee behind them, with his agitated hand always gliding over the network of fine nerves about his mouth and nose; Defarge standing between them and the narrator, whom he had stationed in the light of the window, by turns looking from him to them, and from them to him.

"Go on, Jacques," said Defarge.

"He remains up there in his iron cage some days. The village looks at him by stealth, for it is afraid. But it always looks up, from a distance, at the prison on the crag; and in the evening, when the work of the day is achieved and it assembles to gossip at the fountain, all faces are turned towards the prison. Formerly, they were turned towards the posting-house; now, they are turned towards the prison. They whisper at the fountain, that although condemned to death he will not be executed; they say that petitions have been presented in Paris, showing that he was enraged and made mad by the death of his child; they say that a petition has been presented to the King himself. What do I know? It is possible. Perhaps yes, perhaps no."

"Listen then, Jacques," Number One of that name sternly interposed. "Know that a petition was presented to the King and Queen. All here, yourself excepted, saw the King take it, in his carriage in the street, sitting beside the Queen. It is Defarge whom you see here, who, at the hazard of his life, darted out before the horses, with the petition in his hand."

"And once again listen, Jacques!" said the kneeling Number Three: his fingers ever wandering over and over those fine nerves, with a strikingly greedy air, as if he hungered for something—that was neither food nor drink; "the guard, horse and foot, surrounded the petitioner, and struck him blows. You hear?"

"I hear, messieurs."

"Go on then," said Defarge.

"Again; on the other hand, they whisper at the fountain," resumed the countryman, "that he is brought down into our country to be executed on the spot, and that he will very certainly be executed. They even whisper that because he has slain Monseigneur, and because Monseigneur was the father of his tenants—serfs—what you will—he will be executed as a parricide. One old man says at the fountain, that his right hand, armed with the knife, will be burnt off before his face; that, into wounds which will be made in his arms, his breast, and his legs, there will be poured boiling oil, melted lead, hot resin, wax, and sulphur; finally, that he will be torn limb from limb by four strong horses. That old man says, all this was actually done to a prisoner who made an attempt on the life of the late King, Louis Fifteen. But how do I know if he lies? I am not a scholar."

"Listen once again then, Jacques!" said the man with the restless hand and the craving air. "The name of that prisoner was Damiens, and it was all done in open day, in the open streets of this city of Paris; and nothing was more noticed in the vast concourse that saw it done, than the crowd of ladies of quality and fashion, who were full of eager attention to the last—to the last, Jacques, prolonged until nightfall, when he had lost two legs and an arm, and still breathed! And it was done—why, how old are you?"

"Thirty-five," said the mender of roads, who looked sixty.

"It was done when you were more than ten years old; you might have seen it."

"Enough!" said Defarge, with grim impatience. "Long live the Devil! Go on."

"Well! Some whisper this, some whisper that; they speak of nothing else; even the fountain appears to fall to that tune. At length, on Sunday night when all the village is asleep, come soldiers, winding down from the prison, and their guns ring on the stones of the little street. Workmen dig, workmen hammer, soldiers laugh and sing; in the morning, by the fountain, there is raised a gallows forty feet high, poisoning the water."

The mender of roads looked *through* rather than *at* the low ceiling, and pointed as if he saw the gallows somewhere in the sky.

"All work is stopped, all assemble there, nobody leads the cows out, the cows are there with the rest. At midday, the roll of drums. Soldiers have marched into the prison in the night, and he is in the midst of many soldiers. He is bound as before, and in his mouth there is a gag—tied so, with a tight string, making him look almost as if he laughed." He suggested it, by creasing his face with his two thumbs, from the corners of his mouth to his ears. "On the top of the gallows is fixed the knife, blade upwards, with its point in the air. He is hanged there forty feet high—and is left hanging, poisoning the water."

They looked at one another, as he used his blue cap to wipe his face, on which the perspiration had started afresh while he recalled the spectacle.

"It is frightful, messieurs. How can the women and the children draw water! Who can gossip of an evening, under that shadow! Under it, have I said? When I left the village, Monday evening as   5 the sun was going to bed, and looked back from the hill, the shadow struck across the church, across the mill, across the prison—seemed to strike across the earth, messieurs, to where the sky rests upon it!"

The hungry man gnawed one of his fingers as he looked at the other three, and his finger quivered with the craving that was on him.

"That's all, messieurs. I left at sunset (as I had been warned to do), and I walked on, that night and half next day, until I met (as I was warned I should) this comrade. With him, I came on, now   15 riding and now walking, through the rest of yesterday and through last night. And here you see me!"

After a gloomy silence, the first Jacques said, "Good! You have acted and recounted faithfully. Will you wait for us a little, outside the door?"

"Very willingly," said the mender of roads. Whom Defarge escorted to the top of the stairs, and, leaving seated there, returned.

The three had risen, and their heads were together when he came back to the garret.

"How say you, Jacques?" demanded Number One. "To be regis-   25 tered?"

"To be registered, as doomed to destruction," returned Defarge.

"Magnificent!" croaked the man with the craving.

"The château and all the race?" inquired the first.

"The château and all the race," returned Defarge. "Extermination."

The hungry man repeated, in a rapturous croak, "Magnificent!" and began gnawing another finger.

"Are you sure," asked Jacques Two, of Defarge, "that no embarrassment can arise from our manner of keeping the register?   35 Without doubt it is safe, for no one beyond ourselves can decipher it; but shall we always be able to decipher it—or, I ought to say, will she?"

"Jacques," returned Defarge, drawing himself up, "if madame my wife undertook to keep the register in her memory alone, she would not lose a word of it—not a syllable of it. Knitted, in her own stitches and her own symbols, it will always be as plain to her as the sun. Confide in Madame Defarge. It would be easier for the weakest poltroon that lives, to erase himself from existence, than to erase one letter of his name or crimes from the knitted register of Madame Defarge."

There was a murmur of confidence and approval, and then the man who hungered asked: "Is this rustic to be sent back soon? I hope so. He is very simple; is he not a little dangerous?"

"He knows nothing," said Defarge; "at least nothing more than would easily elevate himself to a gallows of the same height. I charge myself with him; let him remain with me; I will take care of him, and set him on his road. He wishes to see the fine world—the King, the Queen, and Court; let him see them on Sunday."

"What?" exclaimed the hungry man, staring. "Is it a good sign, that he wishes to see royalty and nobility?"

"Jacques," said Defarge, "judiciously show a cat milk, if you wish her to thirst for it. Judiciously show a dog his natural prey, if you wish him to bring it down one day."

Nothing more was said, and the mender of roads, being found already dozing on the topmost stair, was advised to lay himself down on the pallet-bed and take some rest. He needed no persuasion, and was soon asleep.

Worse quarters than Defarge's wine-shop could easily have been found in Paris for a provincial slave of that degree. Saving for a mysterious dread of madame by which he was constantly haunted, his life was very new and agreeable. But, madame sat all day at her counter, so expressly unconscious of him, and so particularly determined not to perceive that his being there had any connection with anything below the surface, that he shook in his wooden shoes whenever his eye lighted on her. For, he contended with himself that it was impossible to foresee what that lady might pretend next; and he felt assured that if she should take it into her brightly ornamented head to pretend that she had seen him do a murder and afterwards flay the victim, she would infallibly go through with it until the play was played out.

Therefore, when Sunday came, the mender of roads was not enchanted (though he said he was) to find that madame was to accompany monsieur and himself to Versailles. It was additionally disconcerting to have madame knitting all the way there, in a public conveyance; it was additionally disconcerting yet, to have madame in the crowd in the afternoon, still with her knitting in her hands as the crowd waited to see the carriage of the King and   5 Queen.

"You work hard, madame," said a man near her.

"Yes," answered Madame Defarge; "I have a good deal to do."

"What do you make, madame?"

"Many things."

"For instance—"

"For instance," returned Madame Defarge, composedly, "shrouds."

The man moved a little further away, as soon as he could, and the mender of roads fanned himself with his blue cap: feeling it   15 mightily close and oppressive. If he needed a King and Queen to restore him, he was fortunate in having his remedy at hand; for, soon the large-faced King and the fair-faced Queen came in their golden coach, attended by the shining Bull's Eye of their Court, a glittering multitude of laughing ladies and fine lords, and in jewels and silks and powder and splendour and elegantly spurning figures, and handsomely disdainful faces of both sexes, the mender of roads bathed himself, so much to his temporary intoxication, that he cried Long live the King, Long live the Queen, Long live everybody and everything! as if he had never heard of ubiquitous Jacques in   25 his time. Then, there were gardens, courtyards, terraces, fountains, green banks, more King and Queen, more Bull's Eye, more lords and ladies, more Long live they all! until he absolutely wept with sentiment. During the whole of this scene, which lasted some three hours, he had plenty of shouting and weeping and sentimental company, and throughout Defarge held him by the collar, as if to restrain him from flying at the objects of his brief devotion and tearing them to pieces.

"Bravo!" said Defarge, clapping him on the back when it was over, like a patron; "you are a good boy!"   35

The mender of roads was now coming to himself, and was mistrustful of having made a mistake in his late demonstrations; but no.

"You are the fellow we want," said Defarge, in his ear; "you make these fools believe that it will last for ever. Then, they are the more insolent, and it is nearer ended."

"Hey!" cried the mender of roads, reflectively; "that's true."

"These fools know nothing. While they despise your breath, and would stop it for ever and ever, in you or in a hundred like you rather than in one of their own horses or dogs, they only know what your breath tells them. Let it deceive them, then, a little longer; it cannot deceive them too much."

Madame Defarge looked superciliously at the client, and nodded in confirmation.

"As to you," said she, "you would shout and shed tears for anything, if it made a show and a noise. Say! Would you not?"

"Truly, madame, I think so. For the moment."

"If you were shown a great heap of dolls, and were set upon them to pluck them to pieces and despoil them for your own advantage, you would pick out the richest and gayest. Say! Would you not?"

"Truly yes, madame."

"Yes. And if you were shown a flock of birds, unable to fly, and were set upon them to strip them of their feathers for your own advantage, you would set upon the birds of the finest feathers; would you not?"

"It is true, madame."

"You have seen both dolls and birds to-day," said Madame Defarge, with a wave of her hand towards the place where they had last been apparent; "now, go home!"

Chapter 16. Still Knitting

Madame Defarge and monsieur her husband returned amicably to the bosom of Saint Antoine, while a speck in a blue cap toiled through the darkness, and through the dust, and down the weary miles of avenues by the wayside, slowly tending towards that point of the compass where the château of Monsieur the Marquis, now in his grave, listened to the whispering trees. Such ample leisure had the stone faces, now, for listening to the trees and to the fountain, that the few village scarecrows who, in their quest for herbs to eat and fragments of dead stick to burn, strayed within sight of the great stone courtyard and terrace staircase, had it borne in upon their starved fancy that the expression of the faces was altered. A rumour just lived in the village—had a faint and bare existence there, as its people had—that when the knife struck home, the faces changed, from faces of pride to faces of anger and pain; also, that when that dangling figure was hauled up forty feet above the fountain, they changed again, and bore a cruel look of being avenged, which they would henceforth bear for ever. In the stone face over the great window of the bed-chamber where the murder was done, two fine dints were pointed out in the sculptured nose, which everybody recognised, and which nobody had seen of old; and on the scarce occasions when two or three ragged peasants emerged from the crowd to take a hurried peep at Monsieur the Marquis petrified, a skinny finger would not have pointed to it for a minute, before they all started away among the moss and leaves, like the more fortunate hares who could find a living there.

Château and hut, stone face and dangling figure, the red stain on the stone floor, and the pure water in the village well—thousands of acres of land—a whole province of France—all France itself—lay under the night sky, concentrated into a faint hair-breadth line. So does a whole world, with all its greatnesses and littlenesses, lie in a twinkling star. And as mere human knowledge can split a ray of light and analyse the manner of its composition, so, sublimer intelligences may read in the feeble shining of this earth of ours every thought and act, every vice and virtue, of every responsible creature on it.

The Defarges, husband and wife, came lumbering under the starlight, in their public vehicle, to that gate of Paris whereunto their journey naturally tended. There was the usual stoppage at the barrier guard-house, and the usual lanterns came glancing forth for the usual examination and inquiry. Monsieur Defarge alighted; knowing one or two of the soldiery there, and one of the police. The latter he was intimate with, and affectionately embraced.

When Saint Antoine had again enfolded the Defarges in his dusky wings, and they, having finally alighted near the Saint's boundaries, were picking their way on foot through the black mud and offal of his streets, Madame Defarge spoke to her husband:

"Say then, my friend; what did Jacques of the police tell thee?"

"Very little to-night, but all he knows. There is another spy commissioned for our quarter. There may be many more, for all that he can say, but he knows of one."

"Eh well!" said Madame Defarge, raising her eyebrows with a cool business air. "It is necessary to register him. How do they call that man?"

"He is English."

"So much the better. His name?"

"Barsad," said Defarge, making it French by pronunciation. But, he had been so careful to get it accurately, that he then spelt it with perfect correctness.

"Barsad," repeated madame. "Good. Christian name?"

"John."

"John Barsad," repeated madame, after murmuring it once to herself. "Good. His appearance; is it known?"

"Age, about forty years; height, about five feet nine; black hair; complexion dark; generally, rather handsome visage; eyes dark, face thin, long, and sallow; nose aquiline, but not straight, having a peculiar inclination towards the left cheek; expression, therefore, sinister!"

"Eh my faith. It is a portrait!" said madame, laughing. "He shall be registered to-morrow."

They turned into the wine-shop, which was closed (for it was midnight) and where Madame Defarge immediately took her post at her desk, counted the small moneys that had been taken during her absence, examined the stock, went through the entries in the book, made other entries of her own, checked the serving man in every possible way, and finally dismissed him to bed. Then she turned out the contents of the bowl of money for the second time, and began knotting them up in her handkerchief, in a chain of separate knots, for safe keeping through the night. All this while, Defarge, with his pipe in his mouth, walked up and down, complacently admiring, but never interfering; in which condition, indeed, as to the business and his domestic affairs, he walked up and down through life.

The night was hot, and the shop, close shut and surrounded by so foul a neighbourhood, was ill-smelling. Monsieur Defarge's olfactory sense was by no means delicate, but the stock of wine smelt much stronger than it ever tasted, and so did the stock of rum and brandy and aniseed. He whiffed the compound of scents away, as he put down his smoked-out pipe.

"You are fatigued," said madame, raising her glance as she   5
knotted the money. "There are only the usual odours."

"I am a little tired," her husband acknowledged.

"You are a little depressed, too," said madame, whose quick eyes had never been so intent on the accounts, but they had had a ray or two for him. "Oh, the men, the men!"

"But my dear!" began Defarge.

"But my dear!" repeated madame, nodding firmly; "but my dear! You are faint of heart to-night, my dear!"

"Well, then," said Defarge, as if a thought were wrung out of his breast, "it *is* a long time."   15

"It is a long time," repeated his wife; "and when is it not a long time? Vengeance and retribution require a long time; it is the rule."

"It does not take a long time to strike a man with lightning," said Defarge.

"How long," demanded madame, composedly, "does it take to make and store the lightning? Tell me."

Defarge raised his head thoughtfully, as if there were something in that too.

"It does not take a long time," said madame, "for an earthquake to swallow a town. Eh well! Tell me how long it takes to prepare   25
the earthquake?"

"A long time, I suppose," said Defarge.

"But when it is ready, it takes place, and grinds to pieces everything before it. In the meantime, it is always preparing, though it is not seen or heard. That is your consolation. Keep it."

She tied a knot with flashing eyes, as if it throttled a foe.

"I tell thee," said madame, extending her right hand for emphasis, "that although it is a long time on the road, it is on the road and coming. I tell thee it never retreats, and never stops. I tell thee it is always advancing. Look around and consider the lives of   35
all the world that we know, consider the faces of all the world that we know, consider the rage and discontent to which the Jacquerie addresses itself with more and more of certainty every hour. Can such things last? Bah! I mock you."

"My brave wife," returned Defarge, standing before her with his head a little bent, and his hands clasped at his back, like a docile and attentive pupil before his catechist, "I do not question all this. But it has lasted a long time, and it is possible—you know well, my wife, it is possible—that it may not come, during our lives."

"Eh well! How then?" demanded madame, tying another knot, as if there were another enemy strangled.

"Well!" said Defarge, with a half-complaining and half-apologetic shrug. "We shall not see the triumph."

"We shall have helped it," returned madame, with her extended hand in strong action. "Nothing that we do is done in vain. I believe, with all my soul, that we shall see the triumph. But even if not, even if I knew certainly not, show me the neck of an aristocrat and tyrant, and still I would—"

Then madame, with her teeth set, tied a very terrible knot indeed.

"Hold!" cried Defarge, reddening a little as if he felt charged with cowardice; "I too, my dear, will stop at nothing."

"Yes! But it is your weakness that you sometimes need to see your victim and your opportunity, to sustain you. Sustain yourself without that. When the time comes, let loose a tiger and a devil; but wait for the time with the tiger and the devil chained—not shown—yet always ready."

Madame enforced the conclusion of this piece of advice by striking her little counter with her chain of money as if she knocked its brains out, and then gathering the heavy handkerchief under her arm in a serene manner, and observing that it was time to go to bed.

Next noontide saw the admirable woman in her usual place in the wine-shop, knitting away assiduously. A rose lay beside her, and if she now and then glanced at the flower, it was with no infraction of her usual preoccupied air. There were a few customers, drinking or not drinking, standing or seated, sprinkled about. The day was very hot, and heaps of flies, who were extending their inquisitive and adventurous perquisitions into all the glutinous little glasses near madame, fell dead at the bottom. Their decease made no impression on the other flies out promenading, who looked at them in the coolest manner (as if they themselves were elephants, or something as far removed), until they met the same fate.

Curious to consider how heedless flies are!—perhaps they thought as much at Court that sunny summer day.

A figure entering at the door threw a shadow on Madame Defarge which she felt to be a new one. She laid down her knitting, and began to pin the rose in her headdress, before she looked at the figure. 5

It was curious. The moment Madame Defarge took up the rose, the customers ceased talking, and began gradually to drop out of the wine-shop.

"Good day, madame," said the new-comer.

"Good day, monsieur."

She said it aloud, but added to herself, as she resumed her knitting: "Hah! Good day, age about forty, height about five feet nine, black hair, generally rather handsome visage, complexion dark, eyes dark, thin long and sallow face, aquiline nose but not straight, having a peculiar inclination towards the left cheek which 15 imparts a sinister expression! Good day, one and all!"

"Have the goodness to give me a little glass of old cognac, and a mouthful of cool fresh water, madame."

Madame complied with a polite air.

"Marvelous cognac this, madame!"

It was the first time it had ever been so complimented, and Madame Defarge knew enough of its antecedents to know better. She said, however, that the cognac was flattered, and took up her knitting. The visitor watched her fingers for a few moments, and took the opportunity of observing the place in general. 25

"You knit with great skill, madame."

"I am accustomed to it."

"A pretty pattern too!"

"You think so?" said madame, looking at him with a smile.

"Decidedly. May one ask what it is for?"

"Pastime," said madame, looking at him with a smile, while her fingers moved nimbly.

"Not for use?"

"That depends. I may find a use for it one day. If I do—well," said madame, drawing a breath and nodding her head with a stern 35 kind of coquetry, "I'll use it!"

It was remarkable: but the taste of Saint Antoine seemed to be decidedly opposed to a rose on the headdress of Madame Defarge.

Two men had entered separately and had been about to order drinks, when, catching sight of that novelty, they faltered, made a pretence of looking about as if for some friend who was not there, and went away. Nor, of those who had been there when this visitor
5   entered, was there one left. They had all dropped off. The spy had kept his eyes open, but had been able to detect no sign. They had lounged away in a poverty-stricken, purposeless, accidental manner, quite natural and unimpeachable.

"JOHN," thought madame, checking off her work as her fingers knitted, and her eyes looked at the stranger. "Stay long enough, and I shall knit 'BARSAD' before you go."

"You have a husband, madame?"

"I have."

"Children?"

15   "No children."

"Business seems bad?"

"Business is very bad; the people are so poor."

"Ah, the unfortunate, miserable people! So oppressed, too—as you say."

"As *you* say," madame retorted, correcting him, and deftly knitting an extra something into his name that boded him no good.

"Pardon me: certainly it was I who said so, but you naturally think so. Of course."

"*I* think?" returned madame, in a high voice. "I and my husband
25   have enough to do to keep this wine-shop open, without thinking. All we think, here, is how to live. That is the subject *we* think of, and it gives us, from morning to night, enough to think about, without embarrassing our heads concerning others. *I* think for others? No, no."

The spy, who was there to pick up any crumbs he could find, or make, did not allow his baffled state to express itself in his sinister face; but, stood with an air of gossiping gallantry, leaning his elbow on Madame Defarge's little counter, and occasionally sipping his cognac.

35   "A bad business this, madame, of Gaspard's execution. Ah! the poor Gaspard!" With a sigh of great compassion.

"My faith!" returned madame, coolly and lightly, "if people use knives for such purposes, they have to pay for it. He knew beforehand what the price of his luxury was; he has paid the price."

"I believe," said the spy, dropping his soft voice to a tone that invited confidence, and expressing an injured revolutionary susceptibility in every muscle of his wicked face: "I believe there is much compassion and anger in this neighbourhood, touching the poor fellow? Between ourselves."

"Is there?" asked madame, vacantly.   5

"Is there not?"

"—Here is my husband!" said Madame Defarge.

As the keeper of the wine-shop entered at the door, the spy saluted him by touching his hat, and saying, with an engaging smile, "Good day, Jacques!" Defarge stopped short, and stared at him.

"Good day, Jacques!" the spy repeated; with not quite so much confidence, or quite so easy a smile under the stare.

"You deceive yourself, monsieur," returned the keeper of the   15
wine-shop. "You mistake me for another. That is not my name. I am Ernest Defarge."

"It is all the same," said the spy, airily, but discomfited too; "good day!"

"Good day!" answered Defarge, drily.

"I was saying to madame, with whom I had the pleasure of chatting when you entered, that they tell me there is—and no wonder!—much sympathy and anger in Saint Antoine, touching the unhappy fate of poor Gaspard."

"No one has told me so," said Defarge, shaking his head. "I   25
know nothing of it."

Having said it, he passed behind the little counter, and stood with his hand on the back of his wife's chair, looking over that barrier at the person to whom they were both opposed, and whom either of them would have shot with the greatest satisfaction.

The spy, well used to his business, did not change his unconscious attitude, but drained his little glass of cognac, took a sip of fresh water, and asked for another glass of cognac. Madame Defarge poured it out for him, took to her knitting again, and hummed a little song over it.   35

"You seem to know this quarter well; that is to say, better than I do?" observed Defarge.

"Not at all, but I hope to know it better. I am so profoundly interested in its miserable inhabitants."

"Hah!" muttered Defarge.

"The pleasure of conversing with you, Monsieur Defarge, recalls to me, " pursued the spy, "that I have the honour of cherishing some interesting associations with your name."

"Indeed!" said Defarge, with much indifference.

"Yes, indeed. When Doctor Manette was released, you, his old domestic, had the charge of him, I know. He was delivered to you. You see I am informed of the circumstances?"

"Such is the fact, certainly," said Defarge. He had had it conveyed to him, in an accidental touch of his wife's elbow as she knitted and warbled, that he would do best to answer, but always with brevity.

"It was to you," said the spy, "that his daughter came; and it was from your care that his daughter took him, accompanied by a neat brown monsieur; how is he called?—in a little wig—Lorry—of the bank of Tellson and Company—over to England."

"Such is the fact," repeated Defarge.

"Very interesting remembrances!" said the spy. "I have known Doctor Manette and his daughter, in England."

"Yes?" said Defarge.

"You don't hear much about them now?" said the spy.

"No," said Defarge.

"In effect," madame struck in, looking up from her work and her little song, "we never hear about them. We received the news of their safe arrival, and perhaps another letter, or perhaps two; but, since then, they have gradually taken their road in life—we, ours—and we have held no correspondence."

"Perfectly so, madame," replied the spy. "She is going to be married."

"Going?" echoed madame. "She was pretty enough to have been married long ago. You English are cold, it seems to me."

"Oh! You know I am English."

"'I perceive your tongue is," returned madame; "and what the tongue is, I suppose the man is."

He did not take the identification as a compliment; but he made the best of it, and turned it off with a laugh. After sipping his cognac to the end, he added:

"Yes, Miss Manette is going to be married. But not to an Englishman; to one who, like herself, is French by birth. And speaking of Gaspard (ah, poor Gaspard! It was cruel, cruel!), it is a curious thing that she is going to marry the nephew of Monsieur the Marquis, for whom Gaspard was exalted to that height of so many feet; in other words, the present Marquis. But he lives unknown in England, he is no Marquis there; he is Mr. Charles   5 Darnay. D'Aulnais is the name of his mother's family."

Madame Defarge knitted steadily, but the intelligence had a palpable effect upon her husband. Do what he would, behind the little counter, as to the striking of a light and the lighting of his pipe, he was troubled, and his hand was not trustworthy. The spy would have been no spy if he had failed to see it, or to record it in his mind.

Having made, at least, this one hit, whatever it might prove to be worth, and no customers coming in to help him to any other, Mr. Barsad paid for what he had drunk, and took his leave: taking   15 occasion to say, in a genteel manner, before he departed, that he looked forward to the pleasure of seeing Monsieur and Madame Defarge again. For some minutes after he had emerged into the outer presence of Saint Antoine, the husband and wife remained exactly as he had left them, lest he should come back.

"Can it be true," said Defarge, in a low voice, looking down at his wife as he stood smoking with his hand on the back of her chair, "what he has said of Ma'amselle Manette?"

"As he has said it," returned madame, lifting her eyebrows a little, "it is probably false. But it may be true."   25

"If it is—" Defarge began, and stopped.

"If it is?" repeated his wife.

"—And if it does come, while we live to see it triumph—I hope, for her sake, Destiny will keep her husband out of France."

"Her husband's destiny," said Madame Defarge, with her usual composure, "will take him where he is to go, and will lead him to the end that is to end him. That is all I know."

"But it is very strange—now, at least, is it not very strange"— said Defarge, rather pleading with his wife to induce her to admit it, "that, after all our sympathy for Monsieur her father, and her-   35 self, her husband's name should be proscribed under your hand at this moment, by the side of that infernal dog's who has just left us?"

"Stranger things than that will happen when it does come,"

answered madame. "I have them both here, of a certainty; and they are both here for their merits; that is enough."

She rolled up her knitting when she had said those words, and presently took the rose out of the handkerchief that was wound about her head. Either Saint Antoine had an instinctive sense that the objectionable decoration was gone, or Saint Antoine was on the watch for its disappearance; howbeit, the Saint took courage to lounge in, very shortly afterwards, and the wine-shop recovered its habitual aspect.

In the evening, at which season of all others Saint Antoine turned himself inside out, and sat on door-steps and window-ledges, and came to the corners of vile streets and courts, for a breath of air, Madame Defarge with her work in her hand was accustomed to pass from place to place and from group to group: a missionary—there were many like her—such as the world will do well never to breed again. All the women knitted. They knitted worthless things; but, the mechanical work was a mechanical sub-stitute for eating and drinking: the hands moved for the jaws and the digestive apparatus: if the bony fingers had been still, the stomachs would have been more famine-pinched.

But, as the fingers went, the eyes went, and the thoughts. And as Madame Defarge moved on from group to group, all three went quicker and fiercer among every little knot of women that she had spoken with, and left behind.

Her husband smoked at his door, looking after her with admira-tion. "A great woman," said he, "strong woman, a grand woman, a frightfully grand woman!"

Darkness closed around, and then came the ringing of church bells and the distant beating of the military drums in the Palace Courtyard, as the women sat knitting, knitting. Darkness encom-passed them. Another darkness was closing in as surely, when the church bells, then ringing pleasantly in many an airy steeple over France, should be melted into thunder cannon; when the military drums should be beating to drown a wretched voice, that night all-potent as the voice of Power and Plenty, Freedom and Life. So much was closing in about the women who sat knitting, knitting, that they their very selves were closing in round a structure yet unbuilt, where they were to sit knitting, knitting, counting drop-ping heads.

Chapter 17. One Night

Never did the sun go down with a brighter glory on the quiet corner of Soho, than one memorable evening when the Doctor and his daughter sat under the plane-tree together. Never did the moon rise with a milder radiance over great London, than on that night when it found them still seated under the tree, and shone upon their faces through its leaves.

Lucie was to be married to-morrow. She had reserved this last evening for her father, and they sat alone under the plane-tree.

"You are happy, my dear father?"

"Quite, my child."

They had said little, though they had been there a long time. When it was yet light enough to work and read, she had neither engaged herself in her usual work, nor had she read to him. She had employed herself in both ways, at his side under the tree, many and many a time; but this time was not quite like any other, and nothing could make it so.

"And I am very happy to-night, dear father. I am deeply happy in the love that Heaven has so blessed—my love for Charles, and Charles's love for me. But, if my life were not to be still consecrated to you, or if my marriage were so arranged as that it would part us, even by the length of a few of these streets, I should be more unhappy and self-reproachful now than I can tell you. Even as it is—"

Even as it was, she could not command her voice.

In the sad moonlight, she clasped him by the neck, and laid her face upon his breast. In the moonlight which is always sad, as the light of the sun itself is—as the light called human life is—as its coming and its going.

"Dearest dear! Can you tell me, this last time, that you feel quite, quite sure, no new affections of mine, and no new duties of mine, will ever interpose between us? I know it well, but do you know it? In your own heart, do you feel quite certain?"

Her father answered, with a cheerful firmness of conviction he could scarcely have assumed. "Quite sure, my darling! More than

169

that," he added, as he tenderly kissed her: "my future is far brighter, Lucie, seen through your marriage, than it could have been—nay, than it ever was—without it."

"If I could hope *that*, my father!—"

"Believe it, love! Indeed it is so. Consider how natural and how plain it is, my dear, that it should be so. You, devoted and young, cannot fully appreciate the anxiety I have felt that your life should not be wasted—"

She moved her hand towards his lips, but he took it in his, and repeated the word.

"—wasted, my child—should not be wasted, struck aside from the natural order of things—for my sake. Your unselfishness cannot entirely comprehend how much my mind has gone on this; but, only ask yourself, how could my happiness be perfect, while yours was incomplete?"

"If I had never seen Charles, my father, I should have been quite happy with you."

He smiled at her unconscious admission that she would been unhappy without Charles, having seen him; and replied:

"My child, you did see him, and it is Charles. If it had not been Charles, it would have been another. Or, if it had been no other, I should have been the cause, and then the dark part of my life would have cast its shadow beyond myself, and would have fallen on you."

It was the first time, except at the trial, of her ever hearing him refer to the period of his suffering. It gave her a strange and new sensation while his words were in her ears; and she remembered it long afterwards.

"See!" said the Doctor of Beauvais, raising his hand towards the moon. "I have looked at her from my prison-window, when I could not bear her light. I have looked at her when it has been such torture to me to think of her shining upon what I had lost, that I have beaten my head against my prison-walls. I have looked at her, in a state so dull and lethargic, that I have thought of nothing but the number of horizontal lines I could draw across her at the full, and the number of perpendicular lines with which I could intersect them." He added in his inward and pondering manner, as he looked at the moon, "It was twenty either way, I remember, and the twentieth was difficult to squeeze in."

The strange thrill with which she heard him go back to that time deepened as he dwelt upon it; but, there was nothing to shock her in the manner of his reference. He only seemed to contrast his present cheerfulness and felicity with the dire endurance that was over.

"I have looked at her, speculating thousands of times upon the unborn child from whom I had been rent. Whether it was alive. Whether it had been born alive, or the poor mother's shock had killed it. Whether it was a son who would some day avenge his father. (There was a time in my imprisonment, when my desire for vengeance was unbearable.) Whether it was a son who would never know his father's story; who might even live to weigh the possibility of his father's having disappeared of his own will and act. Whether it was a daughter who would grow to be a woman."

She drew closer to him, and kissed his cheek and his hand.

"I have pictured my daughter, to myself, as perfectly forgetful of me—rather, altogether ignorant of me, and unconscious of me. I have cast up the years of her age, year after year. I have seen her married to a man who knew nothing of my fate. I have altogether perished from the remembrance of the living, and in the next generation my place was a blank."

"My father! Even to hear that you had such thoughts of a daughter who never existed strikes to my heart as if I had been that child."

"You, Lucie? It is out of the consolation and restoration you have brought to me that these remembrances arise, and pass between us and the moon on this last night.—What did I say just now?"

"She knew nothing of you. She cared nothing for you."

"So! But on other moonlight nights, when the sadness and the silence have touched me in a different way—have affected me with something as like a sorrowful sense of peace, as any emotion that had pain for its foundations could—I have imagined her as coming to me in my cell, and leading me out into the freedom beyond the fortress. I have seen her image in the moonlight often, as I now see you; except that I never held her in my arms: it stood between the little grated window and the door. But, you understand that that was not the child I am speaking of?"

"The figure was not; the—the—image; the fancy?"

"No. That was another thing. It stood before my disturbed sense of sight, but it never moved. The phantom that my mind pursued was another and more real child. Of her outward appearance I know no more than that she was like her mother. The other had that likeness too—as you have—but was not the same. Can you follow me, Lucie? Hardly, I think? I doubt you must have been a solitary prisoner to understand these perplexed distinctions."

His collected and calm manner could not prevent her blood from running cold, as he thus tried to anatomise his old condition.

"In that more peaceful state, I have imagined her, in the moonlight, coming to me and taking me out to show me that the home of her married life was full of her loving remembrance of her lost father. My picture was in her room, and I was in her prayers. Her life was active, cheerful, useful; but my poor history pervaded it all."

"I was that child, my father. I was not half so good, but in my love that was I."

"And she showed me her children," said the Doctor of Beauvais, "and they had heard of me, and had been taught to pity me. When they passed a prison of the State, they kept far from its frowning walls, and looked up at its bars, and spoke in whispers. She could never deliver me; I imagined that she always brought me back after showing me such things. But then, blessed with the relief of tears, I fell upon my knees, and blessed her."

"I am that child, I hope, my father. O my dear, my dear, will you bless me as fervently to-morrow?"

"Lucie, I recall these old troubles in the reason that I have to-night for loving you better than words can tell, and thanking God for my great happiness. My thoughts, when they were wildest, never rose near the happiness that I have known with you, and that we have before us."

He embraced her, solemnly commended her to Heaven, and humbly thanked Heaven for having bestowed her on him. By and by, they went into the house.

There was no one bidden to the marriage but Mr. Lorry; there was even to be no bridesmaid but the gaunt Miss Pross. The marriage was to make no change in their place of residence; they had been able to extend it, by taking to themselves the upper rooms formerly belonging to the apocryphal invisible lodger, and they desired nothing more.

Doctor Manette was very cheerful at the little supper. They were only three at table, and Miss Pross made the third. He regretted that Charles was not there; was more than half disposed to object to the loving little plot that kept him away; and drank to him affectionately.

So, the time came for him to bid Lucie good night, and they separated. But, in the stillness of the third hour of the morning, Lucie came downstairs again, and stole into his room; not free from unshaped fears, beforehand.

All things, however, were in their places; all was quiet; and he lay asleep, his white hair picturesque on the untroubled pillow, and his hands lying quiet on the coverlet. She put her needless candle in the shadow at a distance, crept up to his bed, and put her lips to his; then, leaned over him, and looked at him.

Into his handsome face the bitter waters of captivity had worn; but, he covered up their tracks with a determination so strong, that he held the mastery of them even in his sleep. A more remarkable face in its quiet, resolute, and guarded struggle with an unseen assailant was not to be beheld in all the wide dominions of sleep, that night.

She timidly laid her hand on his dear breast, and put up a prayer that she might ever be as true to him as her love aspired to be, and as his sorrows deserved. Then, she withdrew her hand, and kissed his lips once more, and went away. So the sunrise came, and the shadows of the leaves of the plane-tree moved upon his face, as softly as her lips had moved in praying for him.

Chapter 18. Nine Days

The marriage-day was shining brightly, and they were ready outside the closed door of the Doctor's room, where he was speaking with Charles Darnay. They were ready to go to church; the beautiful bride, Mr. Lorry, and Miss Pross—to whom the event through a gradual process of reconcilement to the inevitable, would have been one of absolute bliss, but for the yet lingering consideration that her brother Solomon should have been the bridegroom.

"And so," said Mr. Lorry, who could not sufficiently admire the bride, and who had been moving round her to take in every point of her quiet, pretty dress; "and so it was for this, my sweet Lucie, that I brought you across the Channel, such a baby! Lord bless me! How little I thought what I was doing! How lightly I valued the 5 obligation I was conferring on my friend Mr. Charles!"

"You didn't mean it," remarked the matter-of-fact Miss Pross, "and therefore how could you know it? Nonsense!"

"Really? Well; but don't cry," said the gentle Mr. Lorry.

"I am not crying," said Miss Pross; "*you* are."

"I, my Pross?" (By this time, Mr. Lorry dared to be pleasant with her; on occasion.)

"You were, just now; I saw you do it, and I don't wonder at it. Such a present of plate as you have made 'em is enough to bring tears into anybody's eyes. There's not a fork or a spoon in the 15 collection," said Miss Pross, "that I didn't cry over, last night after the box came, till I couldn't see it."

"I am highly gratified," said Mr. Lorry, "though upon my honour, I had no intention of rendering those trifling articles of remembrance invisible to any one. Dear me! This is an occasion that makes a man speculate on all he has lost. Dear, dear, dear! To think that there might have been a Mrs. Lorry, any time these fifty years almost!"

"Not at all!" From Miss Pross.

"You think there never might have been a Mrs. Lorry?" asked 25 the gentleman of that name.

"Pooh!" rejoined Miss Pross; "you were a bachelor in your cradle."

"Well!" observed Mr. Lorry, beamingly adjusting his little wig, "that seems probable, too."

"And you were cut out for a bachelor," pursued Miss Pross, "before you were put in your cradle."

"Then, I think," said Mr. Lorry, "that I was very unhandsomely dealt with, and that I ought to have had a voice in the selection of my pattern. Enough! Now, my dear Lucie," drawing his arm 35 soothingly round her waist, "I hear them moving in the next room, and Miss Pross and I, as two formal folks of business, are anxious not to lose the final opportunity of saying something to you that you wish to hear. You leave your good father, my dear, in hands as earnest and as loving as your own; he shall be taken every conceivable care of: during the next fortnight, while you are in War-wickshire and thereabouts, even Tellson's shall go to the wall (comparatively speaking) before him. And when, at the fortnight's end, he comes to join you and your beloved husband, on your other fortnight's trip in Wales, you shall say that we have sent him to you in the best health and in the happiest frame. Now I hear Somebody's step coming to the door. Let me kiss my dear girl with an old-fashioned bachelor blessing, before Somebody comes to claim his own."

For a moment, he held the fair face from him to look at the well-remembered expression on the forehead, and then laid the bright golden hair against his little brown wig, with a genuine tenderness and delicacy which, if such things be old-fashioned, were as old as Adam.

The door of the Doctor's room opened, and he came out with Charles Darnay. He was so deadly pale—which had not been the case when they went in together—that no vestige of colour was to be seen in his face. But, in the composure of his manner he was unaltered, except that to the shrewd glance of Mr. Lorry it dis-closed some shadowy indication that the old air of avoidance and dread had lately passed over him, like a cold wind.

He gave his arm to his daughter, and took her downstairs to the chariot which Mr. Lorry had hired in honour of the day. The rest followed in another carriage, and soon, in a neighbouring church, where no strange eyes looked on, Charles Darnay and Lucie Manette were happily married.

Besides the glancing tears that shone among the smiles of the little group when it was done, some diamonds, very bright and sparkling, glanced on the bride's hand, which were newly released from the dark obscurity of one of Mr. Lorry's pockets. They returned home to breakfast, and all went well, and in due course the golden hair that had mingled with the poor shoemaker's white locks in the Paris garret were mingled with them again in the morning sunlight, on the threshold of the door at parting.

It was a hard parting, though it was not for long. But her father cheered her, and said at last, gently disengaging himself from her enfolding arms, "Take her, Charles! She is yours!"

And her agitated hand waved to them from a chaise window, and she was gone.

The corner being out of the way of the idle and curious, and the preparations having been very simple and few, the Doctor, Mr. Lorry, and Miss Pross were left quite alone. It was when they turned into the welcome shade of the cool old hall, that Mr. Lorry
5 observed a great change to have come over the Doctor; as if the golden arm uplifted there had struck him a poisoned blow.

He had naturally repressed much, and some revulsion might have been expected in him when the occasion for repression was gone. But, it was the old scared lost look that troubled Mr. Lorry; and through his absent manner of clasping his head and drearily wandering away into his own room when they got upstairs, Mr. Lorry was reminded of Defarge the wine-shop keeper, and the starlight ride.

"I think," he whispered to Miss Pross, after anxious considera-
15 tion, "I think we had best not speak to him just now, or at all disturb him. I must look in at Tellson's; so I will go there at once and come back presently. Then, we will take him for a ride into the country, and dine there, and all will be well."

It was easier for Mr. Lorry to look in at Tellson's, than to look out of Tellson's. He was detained two hours. When he came back, he ascended the old staircase alone, having asked no question of the servant; going thus into the Doctor's rooms, he was stopped by a low sound of knocking.

"Good God!" he said, with a start. "What's that?"
25 Miss Pross, with a terrified face, was at his ear. "O me, O me! All is lost!" cried she, wringing her hands. "What is to be told to Ladybird? He doesn't know me, and is making shoes!"

Mr. Lorry said what he could to calm her, and went himself into the Doctor's room. The bench was turned towards the light, as it had been when he had seen the shoemaker at his work before, and his head was bent down, and he was very busy.

"Doctor Manette. My dear friend, Doctor Manette!"

The Doctor looked at him for a moment—half inquiringly, half as if he were angry at being spoken to—and bent over his work
35 again.

He had laid aside his coat and waistcoat; his shirt was open at the throat, as it used to be when he did that work; and even the old haggard, faded surface of face had come back to him. He worked hard—impatiently—as if in some sense of having been interrupted.

Mr. Lorry glanced at the work in his hand, and observed that it was a shoe of the old size and shape. He took up another that was lying by him, and asked what it was?

"A young lady's walking shoe," he muttered, without looking up. "It ought to have been finished long ago. Let it be."   5

"But, Doctor Manette. Look at me!"

He obeyed, in the old mechanically submissive manner, without pausing in his work.

"You know me, my dear friend? Think again. This is not your proper occupation. Think, dear friend!"

Nothing would induce him to speak more. He looked up, for an instant at a time, when he was requested to do so; but, no persuasion would extract a word from him. He worked, and worked, and worked, in silence, and words fell on him as they would have fallen on an echoless wall, or on the air. The only ray of hope that   15 Mr. Lorry could discover, was, that he sometimes furtively looked up without being asked. In that, there seemed a faint expression of curiosity or perplexity—as though he were trying to reconcile some doubts in his mind.

Two things at once impressed themselves on Mr. Lorry, as important above all others; the first, that this must be kept secret from Lucie; the second that it must be kept secret from all who knew him. In conjunction with Miss Pross, he took immediate steps towards the latter precaution, by giving out that the Doctor was not well, and required a few days of complete rest. In aid of the   25 kind deception to be practised on his daughter, Miss Pross was to write, describing his having been called away professionally, and referring to an imaginary letter of two or three hurried lines in his own hand, represented to have been addressed to her by the same post.

These measures, advisable to be taken in any case, Mr. Lorry took in the hope of his coming to himself. If that should happen soon, he kept another course in reserve; which was, to have a certain opinion that he thought the best, on the Doctor's case.

In the hope of his recovery, and of resort to this third course   35 being thereby rendered practicable, Mr. Lorry resolved to watch him attentively, with as little appearance as possible of doing so. He therefore made arrangements to absent himself from Tellson's for the first time in his life, and took his post by the window in the same room.

He was not long in discovering that it was worse than useless to speak to him, since, on being pressed, he became worried. He abandoned that attempt in the first day, and resolved merely to keep himself always before him, as a silent protest against the delusion into which he had fallen, or was falling. He remained, therefore, in his seat near the window, reading and writing, and expressing in as many pleasant and natural ways as he could think of, that it was a free place.

Doctor Manette took what was given him to eat and drink, and worked on, that first day, until it was too dark to see—worked on, half an hour after Mr. Lorry could not have seen, for his life, to read or write. When he put his tools aside as useless, until morning, Mr. Lorry rose and said to him:

"Will you go out?"

He looked down at the floor on either side of him in the old manner, looked up in the old manner, and repeated in the old low voice:

"Out?"

"Yes; for a walk with me. Why not?"

He made no effort to say why not, and said not a word more. But, Mr. Lorry thought he saw, as he leaned forward on his bench in the dusk, with his elbows on his knees and his head in his hands, that he was in some misty way asking himself, "Why not?" The sagacity of the man of business perceived an advantage here, and determined to hold it.

Miss Pross and he divided the night into two watches, and observed him at intervals from the adjoining room. He paced up and down for a long time before he lay down; but, when he did finally lay himself down, he fell asleep. In the morning, he was up betimes, and went straight to his bench and to work.

On the second day, Mr. Lorry saluted him cheerfully by his name, and spoke to him on topics that had been of late familiar to them. He returned no reply, but it was evident that he heard what was said, and that he thought about it, however confusedly. This encouraged Mr. Lorry to have Miss Pross in with her work, several times during the day; at those times, they quietly spoke of Lucie, and of her father then present, precisely in the usual manner, and as if there were nothing amiss. This was done without any demonstrative accompaniment, not long enough or often enough to harass him; and it lightened Mr. Lorry's friendly heart to believe that he looked up oftener, and that he appeared to be stirred by some perception of inconsistencies surrounding him.

When it fell dark again, Mr. Lorry asked him as before: "Dear Doctor, will you go out?"

As before, he repeated, "Out?"

"Yes; for a walk with me. Why not?"

This time, Mr. Lorry feigned to go out when he could extract no answer from him, and, after remaining absent for an hour, returned. In the meanwhile, the Doctor had removed to the seat in the window, and had sat there looking down at the plane-tree; but, on Mr. Lorry's return, he slipped away to his bench.

The time went very slowly on, and Mr. Lorry's hope darkened, and his heart grew heavier again, and grew yet heavier and heavier every day. The third day came and went, the fourth, the fifth. Five days, six days, seven days, eight days, nine days.

With a hope ever darkening, and with a heart always growing heavier and heavier, Mr. Lorry passed through this anxious time. The secret was well kept, and Lucie was unconscious and happy; but he could not fail to observe that the shoemaker, whose hand had been a little out at first, was growing dreadfully skilful, and that he had never been so intent on his work, and that his hands had never been so nimble and expert, as in the dusk of the ninth evening.

Chapter 19. An Opinion

Worn out by anxious watching, Mr. Lorry fell asleep at his post. On the tenth morning of his suspense, he was startled by the shining of the sun into the room where a heavy slumber had overtaken him when it was dark night.

He rubbed his eyes and roused himself; but he doubted, when he had done so, whether he was not still asleep. For, going to the door of the Doctor's room and looking in, he perceived that the shoemaker's bench and tools were put aside again, and that the Doctor himself sat reading at the window. He was in his usual morning dress, and his face (which Mr. Lorry could distinctly see), though still very pale, was calmly studious and attentive.

Even when he had satisfied himself that he was awake, Mr. Lorry felt giddily uncertain for some few moments whether the late shoemaking might not be a disturbed dream of his own; for, did not his eyes show him his friend before him in his accustomed clothing and aspect, and employed as usual; and was there any sign within their range, that the change of which he had so strong an impression had actually happened?

It was but the inquiry of his first confusion and astonishment, the answer being obvious. If the impression were not produced by a real corresponding and sufficient cause, how came he, Jarvis Lorry, there? How came he to have fallen asleep, in his clothes, on the sofa in Doctor Manette's consulting-room, and to be debating these points outside the Doctor's bedroom door in the early morning?

Within a few minutes, Miss Pross stood whispering at his side. If he had had any particle of doubt left, her talk would of necessity have resolved it; but he was by that time clear-headed, and had none. He advised that they should let the time go by until the regular breakfast-hour, and should then meet the Doctor as if nothing unusual had occurred. If he appeared to be in his customary state of mind, Mr. Lorry would then cautiously proceed to seek direction and guidance from the opinion he had been, in his anxiety, so anxious to obtain.

Miss Pross submitting herself to his judgment, the scheme was worked out with care. Having abundance of time for his usual methodical toilette, Mr. Lorry presented himself at the breakfast-hour in his usual white linen, and with his usual neat leg. The Doctor was summoned in the usual way, and came to breakfast.

So far as it was possible to comprehend him without overstepping those delicate and gradual approaches which Mr. Lorry felt to be the only safe advance, he at first supposed that his daughter's marriage had taken place yesterday. An incidental allusion, purposely thrown out, to the day of the week, and the day of the month, set him thinking and counting, and evidently made him uneasy. In all other respects, however, he was so composedly himself, that Mr. Lorry determined to have the aid he sought. And that aid was his own.

Therefore, when the breakfast was done and cleared away, and he and the Doctor were left together, Mr. Lorry said, feelingly:

"My dear Manette, I am anxious to have your opinion, in confidence, on a very curious case in which I am deeply interested; that is to say, it is very curious to me; perhaps, to your better information it may be less so."   5

Glancing at his hands, which were discoloured by his late work, the Doctor looked troubled, and listened attentively. He had already glanced at his hands more than once.

"Doctor Manette," said Mr. Lorry touching him affectionately on the arm, "the case is the case of a particularly dear friend of mine. Pray give your mind to it, and advise me well for his sake— and above all, for his daughter's—his daughter's, my dear Manette."

"If I understand," said the Doctor, in a subdued tone, "some mental shock—?"

"Yes!"

"Be explicit," said the Doctor. "Spare no detail."   15

Mr. Lorry saw that they understood one another, and proceeded.

"My dear Manette, it is the case of an old and a prolonged shock, of great acuteness and severity to the affections, the feelings, the—the—as you express it—the mind. The mind. It is the case of a shock under which the sufferer was borne down, one cannot say for how long, because I believe he cannot calculate the time himself, and there are no other means of getting at it. It is the case of a shock from which the sufferer recovered, by a process that he cannot trace himself—as I once heard him publicly relate in a   25 striking manner. It is the case of a shock from which he has recovered, so completely, as to be a highly intelligent man, capable of close application of mind, and great exertion of body, and of constantly making fresh additions to his stock of knowledge, which was already very large. But, unfortunately, there has been"—he paused and took a deep breath—"a slight relapse."

The Doctor, in a low voice, asked, "Of how long duration?"

"Nine days and nights."

"How did it show itself? I infer," glancing at his hands again, "in the resumption of some old pursuit connected with the shock?"   35

"That is the fact."

"Now, did you ever see him," asked the Doctor, distinctly and collectedly, though in the same low voice, "engaged in that pursuit originally?"

"Once."

"And when the relapse fell on him, was he in most respects—or in all respects—as he was then?"

"I think in all respects."

"You spoke of his daughter. Does his daughter know of the relapse?"

"No. It has been kept from her, and I hope will always be kept from her. It is known only to myself, and to one other who may be trusted."

The Doctor grasped his hand, and murmured, "That was very kind. That was very thoughtful!" Mr. Lorry grasped his hand in return, and neither of the two spoke for a little while.

"Now, my dear Manette," said Mr. Lorry, at length, in his most considerate and most affectionate way, "I am a mere man of business, and unfit to cope with such intricate and difficult matters. I do not possess the kind of information necessary; I do not possess the kind of intelligence; I want guiding. There is no man in this world on whom I could so rely for right guidance, as on you. Tell me, how does this relapse come about? Is there danger of another? Could a repetition of it be prevented? How should a repetition of it be treated? How does it come about at all? What can I do for my friend? No man ever can have been more desirous in his heart to serve a friend, than I am to serve mine, if I knew how. But I don't know how to originate in such a case. If your sagacity, knowledge, and experience could put me on the right track, I might be able to do so much; unenlightened and undirected, I can do so little. Pray discuss it with me; pray enable me to see it a little more clearly, and teach me how to be a little more useful."

Doctor Manette sat meditating after these earnest words were spoken, and Mr. Lorry did not press him.

"I think it probable," said the Doctor, breaking silence with an effort, "that the relapse you have described, my dear friend, was not quite unforeseen by its subject."

"Was it dreaded by him?" Mr. Lorry ventured to ask.

"Very much." He said it with an involuntary shudder.

"You have no idea how such an apprehension weighs on the sufferer's mind, and how difficult—how almost impossible—it is, for him to force himself to utter a word upon the topic that oppresses him."

"Would he," asked Mr. Lorry, "be sensibly relieved if he could prevail upon himself to impart that secret brooding to any one, when it is on him?"

"I think so. But it is, as I have told you, next to impossible. I even believe it—in some cases—to be quite impossible."   5

"Now," said Mr. Lorry, gently laying his hand on the Doctor's arm again, after a short silence on both sides, "to what would you refer this attack?"

"I believe," returned Doctor Manette, "that there had been a strong and extraordinary revival of the train of thought and remembrance that was the first cause of the malady. Some intense associations of a most distressing nature were vividly recalled, I think. It is probable that there had long been a dread lurking in his mind, that those associations would be recalled—say, under certain circumstances—say, on a particular occasion. He tried to prepare   15 himself in vain; perhaps the effort to prepare himself made him less able to bear it."

"Would he remember what took place in the relapse?"asked Mr. Lorry, with natural hesitation.

The Doctor looked desolately round the room, shook his head, and answered, in a low voice, "Not at all."

"Now, as to the future," hinted Mr. Lorry.

"As to the future," said the Doctor, recovering firmness, "I should have great hope. As it pleased Heaven in its mercy to restore him so soon, I should have great hope. He, yielding under the   25 pressure of a complicated something, long dreaded and long vaguely foreseen and contended against, and recovering after the cloud had burst and passed, I should hope that the worst was over."

"Well, well! That's good comfort. I am thankful!" said Mr. Lorry.

"I am thankful!" repeated the Doctor, bending his head with reverence.

"There are two other points," said Mr. Lorry, "on which I am anxious to be instructed. I may go on?"

"You cannot do your friend a better service." The Doctor gave   35 him his hand.

"To the first, then. He is of a studious habit, and unusually energetic; he applies himself with great ardour to the acquisition of professional knowledge, to the conducting of experiments, to many things. Now, does he do too much?"

"I think not. It may be the character of his mind, to be always in singular need of occupation. That may be, in part, natural to it; in part, the result of affliction. The less it was occupied with healthy things, the more it would be in danger of turning in the unhealthy direction. He may have observed himself, and made the discovery."

"You are sure that he is not under too great a strain?"

"I think I am quite sure of it."

"My dear Manette, if he were overworked now—"

"My dear Lorry, I doubt if that could easily be. There has been a violent stress in one direction, and it needs a counter-weight."

"Excuse me, as a persistent man of business. Assuming for a moment that he *was* overworked; it would show itself in some renewal of this disorder?"

"I do not think so. I do not think," said Doctor Manette with the firmness of self-conviction, "that anything but the one train of association would renew it. I think that, henceforth, nothing but some extraordinary jarring of that chord could renew it. After what has happened, and after his recovery, I find it difficult to imagine any such violent sounding of that string again. I trust, and I almost believe, that the circumstances likely to renew it are exhausted."

He spoke with the diffidence of a man who knew how slight a thing would overset the delicate organisation of the mind, and yet with the confidence of a man who had slowly won his assurance out of personal endurance and distress. It was not for his friend to abate that confidence. He professed himself more relieved and encouraged than he really was, and approached his second and last point. He felt it to be the most difficult of all; but, remembering his old Sunday-morning conversation with Miss Pross, and remembering what he had seen in the last nine days, he knew that he must face it.

"The occupation resumed under the influence of this passing affliction so happily recovered from," said Mr. Lorry, clearing his throat, "we will call—Blacksmith's work, Blacksmith's work. We will say, to put a case and for the sake of illustration, that he had been used, in his bad time, to work at a little forge. We will say that he was unexpectedly found at his forge again. Is it not a pity that he should keep it by him?"

The Doctor shaded his forehead with his hand, and beat his foot nervously on the ground.

"He has always kept it by him," said Mr. Lorry, with an anxious look at his friend. "Now, would it not be better that he should let it go?"

Still, the Doctor, with shaded forehead, beat his foot nervously on the ground.

"You do not find it easy to advise me?" said Mr. Lorry. "I quite understand it to be a nice question. And yet I think—" And there he shook his head, and stopped.

"You see," said Doctor Manette, turning to him after an uneasy pause, "it is very hard to explain, consistently, the innermost workings of this poor man's mind. He once yearned so frightfully for that occupation, and it was so welcome when it came; no doubt it relieved his pain so much, by substituting the perplexity of the fingers for the perplexity of the brain, and by substituting, as he became more practised, the ingenuity of the hands for the ingenuity of the mental torture; that he has never been able to bear the thought of putting it quite out of his reach. Even now, when I believe he is more hopeful of himself than he has ever been, and even speaks of himself with a kind of confidence, the idea that he might need that old employment, and not find it, gives him a sudden sense of terror, like that which one may fancy strikes to the heart of a lost child."

He looked like his illustration, as he raised his eyes to Mr. Lorry's face.

"But may not—mind! I ask for information, as a plodding man of business who only deals with such material objects as guineas, shillings, and bank-notes—may not the retention of the thing involve the retention of the idea? If the thing were gone, my dear Manette, might not the fear go with it? In short, is it not a concession to the misgiving, to keep the forge?"

There was another silence.

"You see, too," said the Doctor, tremulously, "it is such an old companion."

"I would not keep it," said Mr. Lorry, shaking his head, for he gained in firmness as he saw the Doctor disquieted. "I would recommend him to sacrifice it. I only want your authority. I am sure it does no good. Come! Give me your authority, like a dear good man. For his daughter's sake, my dear Manette!"

Very strange to see what a struggle there was within him.

"In her name, then, let it be done; I sanction it. But, I would not take it away while he was present. Let it be removed when he is not there; let him miss his old companion after an absence."

Mr. Lorry readily engaged for that, and the conference was
5   ended. They passed the day in the country, and the Doctor was quite restored. On the three following days he remained perfectly well, and on the fourteenth day he went away to join Lucie and her husband. The precaution that had been taken to account for his silence, Mr. Lorry had previously explained to him, and he had written to Lucie in accordance with it, and she had no suspicions.

On the night of the day on which he had left the house, Mr. Lorry went into his room with a chopper, saw, chisel, and hammer, attended by Miss Pross carrying a light. There, with closed doors,
and in a mysterious and guilty manner, Mr. Lorry hacked the
15   shoemaker's bench to pieces, while Miss Pross held the candle as if she were assisting at a murder—for which, indeed, in her grimness, she was no unsuitable figure. The burning of the body (previously reduced to pieces convenient for the purpose) was commenced without delay in the kitchen fire; and the tools, shoes, and leather were buried in the garden. So wicked do destruction and secrecy appear to honest minds, that Mr. Lorry and Miss Pross, while engaged in the commission of their deed and in the removal of its traces, almost felt, and almost looked, like accomplices in a horrible crime.

Chapter 20. A Plea

25   When the newly-married pair came home, the first person who appeared, to offer his congratulations, was Sydney Carton. They had not been at home many hours when he presented himself. He was not improved in habits, or in looks, or in manner; but there was a certain rugged air of fidelity about him, which was new to the observation of Charles Darnay.

He watched his opportunity of taking Darnay aside into a window, and of speaking to him when no one overheard.

"Mr. Darnay," said Carton, "I wish we might be friends."

"We are already friends, I hope."

"You are good enough to say so, as a fashion of speech; but, I don't mean any fashion of speech. Indeed, when I say I wish we might be friends, I scarcely mean quite that, either."

Charles Darnay—as was natural—asked him, in all good-humour and good-fellowship, what he did mean?

"Upon my life," said Carton, smiling, "I find that easier to comprehend in my own mind, than to convey to yours. However, let me try. You remember a certain famous occasion when I was more drunk than—than usual?"

"I remember a certain famous occasion when you forced me to confess that you had been drinking."

"I remember it too. The curse of those occasions is heavy upon me, for I always remember them. I hope it may be taken into account one day, when all days are at an end for me! Don't be alarmed; I am not going to preach."

"I am not at all alarmed. Earnestness in you is anything but alarming to me."

"Ah!" said Carton, with a careless wave of his hand, as if he waved that away. "On the drunken occasion in question (one of a large number, as you know), I was insufferable about liking you, and not liking you. I wish you would forget it."

"I forgot it long ago."

"Fashion of speech again! But, Mr. Darnay, oblivion is not so easy to me, as you represent it to be to you. I have by no means forgotten it, and a light answer does not help me to forget it."

"If it was a light answer," returned Darnay, "I beg your forgiveness for it. I had no other object than to turn a slight thing, which, to my surprise, seems to trouble you too much, aside. I declare to you on the faith of a gentleman, that I have long dismissed it from my mind. Good Heaven, what was there to dismiss! Have I had nothing more important to remember, in the great service you rendered me that day?"

"As to the great service," said Carton, "I am bound to avow to you, when you speak of it in that way, that it was mere professional claptrap. I don't know that I cared what became of you, when I rendered it.—Mind! I say when I rendered it; I am speaking of the past."

"You make light of the obligation," returned Darnay, "but I will not quarrel with *your* light answer."

"Genuine truth, Mr. Darnay, trust me! I have gone aside from my purpose; I was speaking about our being friends. Now, you know me; you know I am incapable of all the higher and better flights of men. If you doubt it, ask Stryver, and he'll tell you so."

"I prefer to form my own opinion, without the aid of his."

"Well! At any rate you know me as a dissolute dog, who has never done any good, and never will."

"I don't know that you 'never will.'"

"But I do, and you must take my word for it. Well! If you could endure to have such a worthless fellow, and a fellow of such indifferent reputation, coming and going at odd times, I should ask that I might be permitted to come and go as a privileged person here; that I might be regarded as an useless (and I would add, if it were not for the resemblance I detected between you and me), an unornamental, piece of furniture, tolerated for its old service, and taken no notice of. I doubt if I should abuse the permission. It is a hundred to one if I should avail myself of it four times in a year. It would satisfy me, I dare say, to know that I had it."

"Will you try?"

"That is another way of saying that I am placed on the footing I have indicated. I thank you, Darnay. I may use that freedom with your name?"

"I think so, Carton, by this time."

They shook hands upon it, and Sydney turned away. Within a minute afterwards, he was, to all outward appearance, as unsubstantial as ever.

When he was gone, and in the course of an evening passed with Miss Pross, the Doctor, and Mr. Lorry, Charles Darnay made some mention of this conversation in general terms, and spoke of Sydney Carton as a problem of carelessness and recklessness. He spoke of him, in short, not bitterly or meaning to bear hard upon him, but as anybody might who saw him as he showed himself.

He had no idea that this could dwell in the thoughts of his fair young wife; but, when he afterwards joined her in their own room, he found her waiting for him with the old pretty lifting of the forehead strongly marked.

"We are thoughtful to-night!" said Darnay, drawing his arm about her.

"Yes, dearest Charles," with her hand on his breast, and the inquiring and attentive expression fixed upon him; "we are rather thoughtful to-night, for we have something on our mind to-night."

"What is it, my Lucie?"

"Will you promise not to press one question on me, if I beg you not to ask it?"

"Will I promise? What will I not promise to my Love?"

What, indeed, with his hand putting aside the golden hair from the cheek, and his other hand against the heart that beat for him!

"I think, Charles, poor Mr. Carton deserves more consideration and respect than you expressed for him to-night."

"Indeed, my own? Why so?"

"That is what you are not to ask me! But I think—I know—he does."

"If you know it, it is enough. What would you have me do, my Life?"

"I would ask you, dearest, to be very generous with him always, and very lenient on his faults when he is not by. I would ask you to believe that he has a heart he very, very seldom reveals, and that there are deep wounds in it. My dear, I have seen it bleeding."

"It is a painful reflection to me," said Charles Darnay, quite astounded, "that I should have done him any wrong. I never thought this of him."

"My husband, it is so. I fear he is not to be reclaimed; there is scarcely a hope that anything in his character or fortunes is reparable now. But, I am sure that he is capable of good things, gentle things, even magnanimous things."

She looked so beautiful in the purity of her faith in this lost man, that her husband could have looked at her as she was for hours.

"And, O my dearest Love!" she urged, clinging nearer to him, laying her head upon his breast, and raising her eyes to his, "remember how strong we are in our happiness, and how weak he is in his misery!"

The supplication touched him home. "I will always remember it, dear Heart! I will remember it as long as I live."

He bent over the golden head, and put the rosy lips to his, and folded her in his arms. If one forlorn wanderer then pacing the dark streets could have heard her innocent disclosure, and could have seen the drops of pity kissed away by her husband from the soft blue eyes so loving of that husband, he might have cried to the night—and the words would not have parted from his lips for the first time—

"God bless her for her sweet compassion!"

Chapter 21. Echoing Footsteps

A wonderful corner for echoes, it has been remarked, that corner where the Doctor lived. Ever busily winding the golden thread which bound her husband, and her father, and herself, and her old directress and companion, in a life of quiet bliss, Lucie sat in the still house in the tranquilly resounding corner, listening to the echoing footsteps of years.

At first, there were times, though she was a perfectly happy young wife, when her work would slowly fall from her hands, and her eyes would be dimmed. For there was something coming in the echoes, something light, afar off, and scarcely audible yet, that stirred her heart too much. Fluttering hopes and doubts—hope, of a love as yet unknown to her: doubts, of her remaining upon earth, to enjoy that new delight—divided her breast. Among the echoes then, there would arise the sound of footsteps at her own early grave; and thoughts of the husband who would be left so desolate, and who would mourn for her so much, swelled to her eyes, and broke like waves.

That time passed, and her little Lucie lay on her bosom. Then, among the advancing echoes, there was the tread of her tiny feet and the sound of her prattling words. Let greater echoes resound as they would, the young mother at the cradle side could always hear those coming. They came, and the shady house was sunny with a child's laugh, and the Divine friend of children, to whom in her trouble she had confided hers, seemed to take her child in His arms, as He took the child of old, and made it a sacred joy to her.

Ever busily winding the golden thread that bound them all together, weaving the service of her happy influence through the tissue of all their lives, and making it predominate nowhere, Lucie heard in the echoes of years none but friendly and soothing sounds. Her husband's step was strong and prosperous among them; her father's firm and equal. Lo, Miss Pross, in harness of string, awakening the echoes, as an unruly charger, whip-corrected, snorting and pawing the earth under the plane-tree in the garden!

Even when there were sounds of sorrow among the rest, they were not harsh nor cruel. Even when golden hair, like her own, lay in a halo on a pillow round the worn face of a little boy, and he said, with a radiant smile, "Dear papa and mamma, I am very sorry to leave you both, and to leave my pretty sister; but I am called, and I must go!" those were not tears all of agony that wetted his young mother's cheek, as the spirit departed from her embrace that had been entrusted to it. Suffer them and forbid them not. They see my Father's face. O Father, blessed words!

Thus, the rustling of an Angel's wings got blended with the other echoes, and they were not wholly of earth, but had in them that breath of Heaven. Sighs of the winds that blew over a little garden-tomb were mingled with them also, and both were audible to Lucie, in a hushed murmur—like the breathing of a summer sea asleep upon a sandy shore—as the little Lucie, comically studious at the task of the morning, or dressing a doll at her mother's footstool, chattered in the tongues of the Two Cities that were blended in her life.

The echoes rarely answered to the actual tread of Sydney Carton. Some half-dozen times a year, at most, he claimed his privilege of coming in uninvited, and would sit among them through the evening, as he had once done often. He never came there heated with wine. And one other thing regarding him was whispered in the echoes, which has been whispered by all true echoes for ages and ages.

No man ever really loved a woman, lost her, and knew her with a blameless though an unchanged mind, when she was a wife and a mother, but her children had a strange sympathy with him—an instinctive delicacy of pity for him. What fine hidden sensibilities are touched in such a case, no echoes tell; but it is so, and it was so here. Carton was the first stranger to whom little Lucie held out her chubby arms, and he kept his place with her as she grew. The little boy had spoken of him, almost at the last. "Poor Carton! Kiss him for me!"

Mr. Stryver shouldered his way through the law, like some great engine forcing itself through turbid water, and dragged his useful friend in his wake, like a boat towed astern. As the boat so favoured is usually in a rough plight, and mostly under water, so, Sydney had a swamped life of it. But, easy and strong custom, unhappily so much easier and stronger in him than any stimulating sense of desert or disgrace, made it the life he was to lead; and he no more thought of emerging from his state of lion's jackal, than any real jackal may be supposed to think of rising to be a lion. Stryver was rich; had married a florid widow with property and three boys, who had nothing particularly shining about them but the straight hair of their dumpling heads.

These three young gentlemen, Mr. Stryver, exuding patronage of the most offensive quality from every pore, had walked before him like three sheep to the quiet corner in Soho, and had offered as pupils to Lucie's husband: delicately saying, "Halloa! here are three lumps of bread-and-cheese towards your matrimonial picnic, Darnay!" The polite rejection of the three lumps of bread-and-cheese had quite bloated Mr. Stryver with indignation, which he afterwards turned to account in the training of the young gentlemen, by directing them to beware of the pride of beggars, like that tutor-fellow. He was also in the habit of declaiming to Mrs. Stryver, over his full-bodied wine, on the arts Mrs. Darnay had once put in practice to "catch" him, and on the diamond-cut-diamond arts in himself, madam, which had rendered him "not to be caught." Some of his King's Bench familiars, who were occasionally parties to the full-bodied wine and the lie, excused him for the latter by saying that he had told it so often, that he believed it himself— which is surely such an incorrigible aggravation of an originally bad offence, as to justify any such offender's being carried off to some suitably retired spot, and there hanged out of the way.

These were among the echoes to which Lucie, sometimes pensive, sometimes amused and laughing, listened in the echoing corner, until her little daughter was six years old. How near to her heart the echoes of her child's tread came, and those of her own dear father's, always active and self-possessed, and those of her dear husband's, need not be told. Nor, how the slightest echo of their united home, directed by herself with such a wise and elegant thrift that it was more abundant than any waste, was music to her. Nor, how there were echoes all about her, sweet in her ears, of the many times her father had told her that he found her more devoted to him married (if that could be) than single, and of the many times her husband had said to her that no cares and duties seemed to divide her love for him or her help to him, and asked her "What is the magic secret, my darling, of your being everything to all of us, as if there were only one of us, yet never seeming to be hurried, or to have too much to do?"

But, there were other echoes, from a distance, that rumbled menacingly in the corner all through this space of time. And it was now, about little Lucie's sixth birthday, that they began to have an awful sound, as of a great storm in France with a dreadful sea rising.

On a night in mid-July, one thousand seven hundred and eighty-nine, Mr. Lorry came in late, from Tellson's, and sat himself down by Lucie and her husband in the dark window. It was a hot, wild night, and they were all three reminded of the old Sunday night when they had looked at the lightning from the same place.

"I began to think," said Mr. Lorry, pushing his brown wig back, "that I should have to pass the night at Tellson's. We have been so full of business all day, that we have not known what to do first, or which way to turn. There is such an uneasiness in Paris, that we have actually a run of confidence upon us! Our customers over there seem not to be able to confide their property to us fast enough. There is positively a mania among some of them for sending it to England."

"That has a bad look," said Darnay.

"A bad look, you say, my dear Darnay? Yes, but we don't know what reason there is in it. People are so unreasonable! Some of us at Tellson's are getting old, and we really can't be troubled out of the ordinary course without due occasion."

"Still," said Darnay, "you know how gloomy and threatening the sky is."

"I know that, to be sure," assented Mr. Lorry, trying to persuade himself that his sweet temper was soured, and that he grumbled, "but I am determined to be peevish after my long day's botheration. Where is Manette?"

"Here he is," said the Doctor, entering the dark room at the moment.

"I am quite glad you are at home; for these hurries and forebodings, by which I have been surrounded all day long, have made me nervous without reason. You are not going out, I hope?"

"No; I am going to play backgammon with you, if you like," said the Doctor.

"I don't think I do like, if I may speak my mind. I am not fit to be pitted against you to-night. Is the tea-board still there, Lucie? I can't see."

"Of course, it has been kept for you."

"Thank ye, my dear. The precious child is safe in bed?"

"And sleeping soundly."

"That's right; all safe and well! I don't know why anything should be otherwise than safe and well here, thank God; but I have been so put out all day, and I am not as young as I was! My tea, my dear! Thank ye. Now, come and take your place in the circle, and let us sit quiet, and hear the echoes about which you have your theory."

"Not a theory; it was a fancy."

"A fancy, then, my wise pet," said Mr. Lorry, patting her hand. "They are very numerous and very loud, though, are they not? Only hear them!"

Headlong, mad, and dangerous footsteps to force their way into anybody's life, footsteps not easily made clean again if once stained red, the footsteps raging in Saint Antoine afar off, as the little circle sat in the dark London window.

Saint Antoine had been, that morning, a vast dusky mass of scarecrows heaving to and fro, with frequent gleams of light above the billowy heads, where steel blades and bayonets shone in the sun. A tremendous roar arose from the throat of Saint Antoine, and a forest of naked arms struggled in the air like shrivelled branches of trees in a winter wind: all the fingers convulsively clutching at every weapon or semblance of a weapon that was thrown up from the depths below, no matter how far off.

Who gave them out, whence they last came, where they began, through what agency they crookedly quivered and jerked, scores at a time, over the heads of the crowd, like a kind of lightning, no eye in the throng could have told; but, muskets were being distributed—so were cartridges, powder, and ball, bars of iron and wood, knives, axes, pikes, every weapon that distracted ingenuity could discover or devise. People who could lay hold of nothing else, set themselves with bleeding hands to force stones and bricks out of their places in walls. Every pulse and heart in Saint Antoine was on high-fever strain and at high-fever heat. Every living creature there held life as of no account, and was demented with a passionate readiness to sacrifice it.

As a whirlpool of boiling waters has a centre point, so all this raging circled round Defarge's wine-shop, and every human drop in the caldron had a tendency to be sucked towards the vortex where Defarge himself, already begrimed with gunpowder and sweat, issued orders, issued arms, thrust this man back, dragged this man forward, disarmed one to arm another, laboured and strove in the thickest of the uproar.

"Keep near to me, Jacques Three," cried Defarge; "and do you, Jacques One and Two, separate and put yourselves at the head of as many of these patriots as you can. Where is my wife?"

"Eh, well! Here you see me!" said madame, composed as ever, but not knitting to-day. Madame's resolute right hand was occupied with an axe, in place of the usual softer implements, and in her girdle were a pistol and a cruel knife.

"Where do you go, my wife?"

"I go," said madame, "with you at present. You shall see me at the head of women, by and by."

"Come, then!" cried Defarge, in a resounding voice. "Patriots and friends, we are ready! The Bastille!"

With a roar that sounded as if all the breath in France had been shaped into the detested word, the living sea rose, wave on wave, depth on depth, and overflowed the city to that point. Alarm-bells ringing, drums beating, the sea raging and thundering on its new beach, the attack began.

Deep ditches, double drawbridge, massive stone walls, eight great towers, cannon, muskets, fire and smoke. Through the fire and through the smoke—in the fire and in the smoke, for the sea cast him up against a cannon, and on the instant he became a cannonier—Defarge of the wine-shop worked like a manful soldier, two fierce hours.

Deep ditch, single drawbridge, massive stone walls, eight great towers, cannon, muskets, fire and smoke. One drawbridge down!

"Work, comrades all, work! Work, Jacques One, Jacques Two, Jacques One Thousand, Jacques Two Thousand, Jacques Five-and-Twenty Thousand; in the name of all the Angels or the Devils—which you prefer— work!" Thus Defarge of the wine-shop,
5 still at his gun, which had long grown hot.

"To me, women!" cried madame his wife. "What! We can kill as well as the men when the place is taken!" And to her, with a shrill thirsty cry, trooping women variously armed, but all armed alike in hunger and revenge.

Cannon, muskets, fire and smoke; but, still the deep ditch, the single drawbridge, the massive stone walls, and the eight great towers. Slight displacements of the raging sea, made by the falling wounded. Flashing weapons, blazing torches, smoking waggon-loads of wet straw, hard work at neighbouring barricades in all
15 directions, shrieks, volleys, execrations, bravery without stint, boom, smash and rattle, and the furious sounding of the living sea; but, still the deep ditch, and the single drawbridge, and the massive stone walls, and the eight great towers, and still Defarge of the wine-shop at his gun, grown doubly hot by the service of four fierce hours.

A white flag from within the fortress, and a parley—this dimly perceptible through the raging storm, nothing audible in it—suddenly the sea rose immeasurably wider and higher, and swept Defarge of the wine-shop over the lowered drawbridge, past
25 the massive stone outer walls, in among the eight great towers surrendered!

So resistless was the force of the ocean bearing him on, that even to draw his breath or turn his head was as impracticable as if he had been struggling in the surf at the South Sea, until he was landed in the outer courtyard of the Bastille. There, against an angle of a wall, he made a struggle to look about him. Jacques Three was nearly at his side; Madame Defarge, still heading some of her women, was visible in the inner distance, and her knife was in her hand. Everywhere was tumult, exultation, deafening and maniacal
35 bewilderment, astounding noise, yet furious dumb-show.

"The prisoners!"

"The records!"

"The secret cells!"

"The instruments of torture!"

"The prisoners!"

Of all these cries, and ten thousand incoherencies, "The prisoners!" was the cry most taken up by the sea that rushed in, as if there were an eternity of people, as well as of time and space. When the foremost billows rolled past, bearing the prison officers with them, and threatening them all with instant death if any secret nook remained undisclosed, Defarge laid his strong hand on the breast of one of these men—a man with a gray head, who had a lighted torch in his hand—separated him from the rest, and got him between himself and the wall.

"Show me the North Tower!" said Defarge. "Quick!"

"I will faithfully," replied the man, "if you will come with me. But there is no one there."

"What is the meaning of One Hundred and Five, North Tower?" asked Defarge. "Quick!"

"The meaning, monsieur?"

"Does it mean a captive, or a place of captivity? Or do you mean that I shall strike you dead?"

"Kill him!" croaked Jacques Three, who had come close up.

"Monsieur, it is a cell."

"Show it me!"

"Pass this way, then."

Jacques Three, with his usual craving on him, and evidently disappointed by the dialogue taking a turn that did not seem to promise bloodshed, held by Defarge's arm as he held the turnkey's. Their three heads had been close together during this brief discourse, and it had been as much as they could do to hear one another, even then: so tremendous was the noise of the living ocean, in its irruption into the fortress, and its inundation of the courts and passages and staircases. All around outside, too, it beat the walls with a deep, hoarse roar, from which occasionally, some partial shouts of tumult broke and leaped into the air like spray.

Through gloomy vaults where the light of day had never shone, past hideous doors of dark dens and cages, down cavernous flights of steps, and again up steep rugged ascents of stone and brick, more like dry waterfalls than staircases, Defarge, the turnkey, and Jacques Three, linked hand and arm, went with all the speed they could make. Here and there, especially at first, the inundation started on them and swept by; but when they had done descending, and were winding and climbing up a tower, they were alone. Hemmed in here by the massive thickness of walls and arches, the storm within the fortress and without was only audible to them in a dull, sub-dued way, as if the noise out of which they had come had almost destroyed their sense of hearing.

The turnkey stopped at a low door, put a key in a clashing lock, swung the door slowly open, and said, as they all bent their heads and passed in:

"One Hundred and Five, North Tower!"

There was a small, heavily-grated, unglazed window high in the wall, with a stone screen before it, so that the sky could be only seen by stooping low and looking up. There was a small chimney, heavily barred across, a few feet within. There was a heap of old feathery wood-ashes on the hearth. There was a stool, and table, and a straw bed. There were the four blackened walls, and a rusted iron ring in one of them.

"Pass that torch slowly along these walls, that I may see them," said Defarge to the turnkey.

The man obeyed, and Defarge followed the light closely with his eyes.

"Stop!—Look here, Jacques!"

"A. M.!" croaked Jacques Three, as he read greedily.

"Alexandre Manette," said Defarge in his ear, following the letters with his swart forefinger, deeply engrained with gunpowder. "And here he wrote 'a poor physician.' And it was he, without doubt, who scratched a calendar on this stone. What is that in your hand? A crowbar? Give it me!"

He had still the linstock of his gun in his own hand. He made a sudden exchange of the two instruments, and turning on the worm-eaten stool and table, beat them to pieces in a few blows.

"Hold the light higher!" he said, wrathfully, to the turnkey. "Look among those fragments with care, Jacques. And see! Here is my knife," throwing it to him; "rip open that bed, and search the straw. Hold the light higher, you!"

With a menacing look at the turnkey he crawled upon the hearth, and, peering up the chimney, struck and prised at its sides with the crowbar, and worked at the iron grating across it. In a few minutes, some mortar and dust came dropping down, which he averted his face to avoid; and in it, and in the old wood-ashes, and in a crevice in the chimney into which his weapon had slipped or wrought itself, he groped with a cautious touch.

"Nothing in the wood, and nothing in the straw, Jacques?"

"Nothing."

"Let us collect them together, in the middle of the cell. So! Light them, you!"

The turnkey fired the little pile, which blazed high and hot. Stooping again to come out at the low-arched door, they left it burning, and retraced their way to the courtyard; seeming to recover their sense of hearing as they came down, until they were in the raging flood once more.

They found it surging and tossing, in quest of Defarge himself. Saint Antoine was clamorous to have its wine-shop keeper foremost in the guard upon the governor who had defended the Bastille and shot the people. Otherwise, the governor would be marched to the Hôtel de Ville for judgment. Otherwise, the governor would escape, and the people's blood (suddenly of some value, after many years of worthlessness) be unavenged.

In the howling universe of passion and contention that seemed to encompass this grim old officer, conspicuous in his gray coat and red decoration, there was but one quite steady figure, and that was a woman's. "See, there is my husband!" she cried pointing him out. "See Defarge!" She stood immovable close to the grim old officer, and remained immovable close to him; remained immovable close to him through the streets, as Defarge and the rest bore him along; remained immovable close to him when he got near his destination, and began to be struck at from behind; remained immovable close to him when the long-gathering rain of stabs and blows fell heavy; was so close to him when he dropped dead under it, that, suddenly animated, she put her foot upon his neck, and with her cruel knife—long ready—hewed off his head.

The hour was come, when Saint Antoine was to execute his horrible idea of hoisting up men for lamps to show what he could be and do. Saint Antoine's blood was up, and the blood of tryanny and domination by the iron hand was down—down on the steps of the Hôtel de Ville where the governor's body lay—down on the sole of the shoe of Madame Defarge where she had trodden on the body to steady it for mutilation. "Lower the lamp yonder!" cried Saint Antoine, after glaring round for a new means of death; "here is one of his soldiers to be left on guard!" The swinging sentinel was posted, and the sea rushed on.

The sea of black and threatening waters, and of destructive upheaving of wave against wave, whose depths were yet unfath-omed and whose forces were yet unknown. The remorseless sea of turbulently swaying shapes, voices of vengeance, and faces hardened in the furnaces of suffering until the touch of pity could make no mark on them.

But, in the ocean of faces where every fierce and furious expression was in vivid life, there were two groups of faces—each seven in number—so fixedly contrasting with the rest, that never did sea roll which bore more memorable wrecks with it. Seven faces of prisoners, suddenly released by the storm that had burst their tomb, were carried high overhead: all scared, all lost, all wondering and amazed, as if the Last Day were come, and those who rejoiced around them were lost spirits. Other seven faces there were, carried higher, seven dead faces, whose drooping eyelids and half-seen eyes awaited the Last Day. Impassive faces, yet with a suspended—not an abolished— expression on them; faces, rather, in a fearful pause, as having yet to raise the drooped lids of the eyes, and bear witness with the bloodless lips, "THOU DIDST IT!"

Seven prisoners released, seven gory heads on pikes, the keys of the accursed fortress of the eight strong towers, some discovered letters and other memorials of prisoners of old time, long dead of broken hearts—such, and suchlike, the loudly echoing footsteps of Saint Antoine escort through the Paris streets in mid-July, one thousand seven hundred and eighty-nine. Now, Heaven defeat the fancy of Lucie Darnay, and keep these feet far out of her life! For, they are headlong, mad, and dangerous; and in the years so long after the breaking of the cask at Defarge's wine-shop door, they are not easily purified when once stained red.

Chapter 22. *The Sea Still Rises*

Haggard Saint Antoine had had only one exultant week in which to soften his modicum of hard and bitter bread to such extent as he could, with the relish of fraternal embraces and congratulations, when Madame Defarge sat at her counter, as usual, presiding over the customers. Madame Defarge wore no rose in her head, for the 5 great brotherhood of Spies had become, even in one short week, extremely chary of trusting themselves to the saint's mercies. The lamps across his streets had a portentously elastic swing with them.

Madame Defarge, with her arms folded, sat in the morning light and heat, contemplating the wine-shop and the street. In both, there were several knots of loungers, squalid and miserable, but now with a manifest sense of power enthroned on their distress. The raggedest night-cap, awry on the wretchedest head, had this crooked significance in it: "I know how hard it has grown for me, the wearer of this, to support life in myself; but do you know how 15 easy it has grown for me, the wearer of this, to destroy life in you?" Every lean bare arm, that had been without work before, had this work always ready for it now, that it could strike. The fingers of the knitting women were vicious, with the experience that they could tear. There was a change in the appearance of Saint Antoine; the image had been hammering into this for hundreds of years, and the last finishing blows had told mightily on the expression.

Madame Defarge sat observing it, with such suppressed approval as was to be desired in the leader of the Saint Antoine women. One 25 of her sisterhood knitted beside her. The short, rather plump wife of a starved grocer, and the mother of two children withal, this lieutenant had already earned the complimentary name of The Vengeance.

"Hark!" said The Vengeance. "Listen, then! Who comes?"

As if a train of powder laid from the outermost bound of the Saint Antoine Quarter to the wine-shop door, had been suddenly fired, a fast-spreading murmur came rushing along.

"It is Defarge," said madame. "Silence, patriots!"

Defarge came in breathless, pulled off a red cap he wore, and looked around him. "Listen, everywhere!" said madame again. "Listen to him!" Defarge stood, panting, against a background of eager eyes and open mouths, formed outside the door; all those within the wine-shop had sprung to their feet.

"Say then, my husband. What is it?"

"News from the other world!"

"How, then?" cried madame, contemptuously. "The other world?"

"Does everybody here recall old Foulon, who told the famished people that they might eat grass, and who died, and went to Hell?"

"Everybody!" from all throats.

"The news is of him. He is among us!"

"Among us!" from the universal throat again. "And dead?"

"Not dead! He feared us so much—and with reason—that he caused himself to be represented as dead, and had a grand mock-funeral. But they have found him alive, hiding in the country, and have brought him in. I have seen him but now, on his way to the Hôtel de Ville, a prisoner. I have said that he had reason to fear us. Say all! *Had* he reason?"

Wretched old sinner of more than threescore years and ten, if he had never known it yet, he would have known it in his heart of hearts if he could have heard the answering cry.

A moment of profound silence followed. Defarge and his wife looked steadfastly at one another. The Vengeance stooped, and the jar of a drum was heard as she moved it at her feet behind the counter.

"Patriots!" said Defarge, in a determined voice, "are we ready?"

Instantly Madame Defarge's knife was in her girdle; the drum was beating in the streets, as if it and a drummer had flown together by magic; and The Vengeance, uttering terrific shrieks, and flinging her arms about her head like all the forty Furies at once, was tearing from house to house, rousing the women.

The men were terrible, in the bloody-minded anger with which they looked from windows, caught up what arms they had, and came pouring down into the streets; but, the women were a sight to chill the boldest. From such household occupations as their bare poverty yielded, from their children, from their aged and their sick crouching on the bare ground famished and naked, they ran out with streaming hair, urging one another, and themselves, to mad-

ness with the wildest cries and actions. Villain Foulon taken, my
sister! Old Foulon taken, my mother! Miscreant Foulon taken, my
daughter! Then, a score of others ran into the midst of these,
beating their breasts, tearing their hair, and screaming, Foulon
alive! Foulon who told the starving people they might eat grass!   5
Foulon who told my old father that he might eat grass, when I had
no bread to give him! Foulon who told my baby it might suck
grass, when these breasts were dry with want! O mother of God,
this Foulon! O Heaven, our suffering! Hear me, my dead baby and
my withered father: I swear on my knees, on these stones, to
avenge you on Foulon! Husbands, and brothers, and young men,
Give us the blood of Foulon, Give us the head of Foulon, Give us
the heart of Foulon, Give us the body and soul of Foulon, Rend
Foulon to pieces, and dig him into the ground, that grass may grow
from him! With these cries, numbers of the women, lashed into   15
blind frenzy, whirled about, striking and tearing at their own
friends until they dropped into a passionate swoon, and were only
saved by the men belonging to them from being trampled under
foot.

Nevertheless, not a moment was lost; not a moment! This
Foulon was at the Hôtel de Ville, and might be loosed. Never, if
Saint Antoine knew his own sufferings, insults, and wrongs! Armed
men and women flocked out of the Quarter so fast, and drew even
these last dregs after them with such a force of suction, that within
a quarter of an hour there was not a human creature in Saint   25
Antoine's bosom but a few old crones and the wailing children.

No. They were all by that time choking the Hall of Examination
where this old man, ugly and wicked, was, and overflowing into the
adjacent open space and streets. The Defarges, husband and wife,
The Vengeance, and Jacques Three were in the first press, and at
no great distance from him in the Hall.

"See!" cried madame, pointing with her knife. "See the old
villain bound with ropes. That was well done to tie a bunch of grass
upon his back. Ha, ha! That was well done. Let him eat it now!"
Madame put her knife under her arm, and clapped her hands as at   35
a play.

The people immediately behind Madame Defarge, explaining
the cause of her satisfaction to those behind them, and those again
explaining to others, and those to others, the neighbouring streets
resounded with the clapping of hands. Similarly, during two or

three hours of drawl, and the winnowing of many bushels of words, Madame Defarge's frequent expressions of impatience were taken up, with marvelous quickness, at a distance: the more readily, because certain men who had by some wonderful exercise of agility climbed up the external architecture to look in from the windows, knew Madame Defarge well, and acted as a telegraph between her and the crowd outside the building.

At length the sun rose so high that it struck a kindly ray as of hope or protection, directly down upon the old prisoner's head. The favour was too much to bear; in an instant the barrier of dust and chaff, that had stood surprisingly long, went to the winds, and Saint Antoine got him!

It was known directly, to the furthest confines of the crowd. Defarge had but sprung over a railing and a table, and folded the miserable wretch in a deadly embrace—Madame Defarge had but followed and turned her hand in one of the ropes with which he was tied—The Vengeance and Jacques Three were not yet up with them, and the men at the windows had not yet swooped into the Hall, like birds of prey from their high perches—when the cry seemed to go up, all over the city, "Bring him out! Bring him to the lamp!"

Down, and up, and head foremost on the steps of the building; now, on his knees; now, on his feet; now, on his back; dragged, and struck at, and stifled by the bunches of grass and straw that were thrust into his face by hundreds of hands; torn, bruised, panting, bleeding, yet always entreating and beseeching for mercy; now full of vehement agony of action, with a small clear space about him as the people drew one another back that they might see; now, a log of dead wood drawn through a forest of legs; he was hauled to the nearest street corner where one of the fatal lamps swung, and there Madame Defarge let him go—as a cat might have done to a mouse—and silently and composedly looked at him while they made ready, and while he besought her: the women passionately screeching at him all the time, and the men sternly calling out to have him killed with grass in his mouth. Once, he went aloft, and the rope broke, and they caught him shrieking; then, the rope was merciful, and held him, and his head was soon upon a pike, with grass enough in the mouth for all Saint Antoine to dance at the sight of.

Nor was this the end of the day's bad work, for Saint Antoine so shouted and danced his angry blood up, that it boiled again, on hearing when the day closed in that the son-in-law of the despatched, another of the people's enemies and insulters, was coming into Paris under a guard five hundred strong, in cavalry alone. Saint Antoine wrote his crimes on flaring sheets of paper, seized him— would have torn him out of the breast of an army to bear Foulon company—set his head and heart on pikes, and carried the three spoils of the day, in wolf-procession, through the streets.

Not before dark night did the men and women come back to the children, wailing and breadless. Then, the miserable bakers' shops were beset by long files of them, patiently waiting to buy bad bread; and while they waited with stomachs faint and empty, they beguiled the time by embracing one another on the triumphs of the day, and achieving them again in gossip. Gradually, these strings of ragged people shortened and frayed away; and then poor lights began to shine in high windows, and slender fires were made in the streets, at which neighbours cooked in common, afterwards supping at their doors.

Scanty and insufficient suppers those, and innocent of meat, as of most other sauce to wretched bread. Yet, human fellowship infused some nourishment into the flinty viands, and struck some sparks of cheerfulness out of them. Fathers and mothers who had had their full share in the worst of the day played gently with their meagre children; and lovers, with such a world around them and before them, loved and hoped.

It was almost morning, when Defarge's wine-shop parted with its last knot of customers, and Monsieur Defarge said to madame his wife, in husky tones, while fastening the door:

"At last it is come, my dear!"

"Eh well!" returned madame. "Almost."

Saint Antoine slept, the Defarges slept: even The Vengeance slept with her starved grocer, and the drum was at rest. The drum's was the only voice in Saint Antoine that blood and hurry had not changed. The Vengeance, as custodian of the drum, could have wakened him up and had the same speech out of him as before the Bastille fell, or old Foulon was seized; not so with the hoarse tones of the men and women in Saint Antoine's bosom.

Chapter 23. Fire Rises

There was a change on the village where the fountain fell, and where the mender of roads went forth daily to hammer out of the stones on the highway such morsels of bread as might serve for patches to hold his poor ignorant soul and his poor reduced body together. The prison on the crag was not so dominant as of yore; there were soldiers to guard it, but not many; there were officers to guard the soldiers, but not one of them knew what his men would do—beyond this: that it would probably not be what he was ordered.

Far and wide lay a ruined country, yielding nothing but desolation. Every green leaf, every blade of grass and blade of grain, was as shrivelled and poor as the miserable people. Everything was bowed down, dejected, oppressed, and broken. Habitations, fences, domesticated animals, men, women, children, and the soil that bore them—all worn out.

Monseigneur (often a most worthy individual gentleman) was a national blessing, gave a chivalrous tone to things, was a polite example of luxurious and shining life, and a great deal more to equal purpose; nevertheless, Monseigneur as a class had, somehow or other, brought things to this. Strange that Creation, designed expressly for Monseigneur, should be so soon wrung dry and squeezed out! There must be something short-sighted in the eternal arrangements, surely! Thus it was, however; and the last drop of blood having been extracted from the flints, and the last screw of the rack having been turned so often that its purchase crumbled, and it now turned and turned with nothing to bite, Monseigneur began to run away from a phenomenon so low and unaccountable.

But, this was not the change on the village, and on many a village like it. For scores of years gone by, Monseigneur had squeezed it and wrung it, and had seldom graced it with his presence except for the pleasures of the chase—now, found in hunting the people; now, found in hunting the beasts, for whose preservation Monseigneur made edifying spaces of barbarous and barren wilderness. No. The change consisted in the appearance of strange faces of low caste, rather than in the disappearance of the high-caste, chiseled, and otherwise beatified and beatifying features of Monseigneur.

For, in these times, as the mender of roads worked, solitary, in the dust, not often troubling himself to reflect that dust he was and to dust he must return, being for the most part too much occupied in thinking how little he had for supper and how much more he would eat if he had it—in these times, as he raised his eyes from his lonely labour, and viewed the prospect, he would see some rough figure approaching on foot, the like of which was once a rarity in those parts, but was now a frequent presence. As it advanced, the mender of roads would discern without surprise that it was a shaggy-haired man, of almost barbarian aspect, tall, in wooden shoes that were clumsy even to the eyes of a mender of roads, grim, rough, swart, steeped in the mud and dust of many highways, dank with the marshy moisture of many low grounds, sprinkled with the thorns and leaves and moss of many byways through woods.

Such a man came upon him, like a ghost, at noon in the July weather, as he sat on his heap of stones under a bank, taking such shelter as he could get from a shower of hail.

The man looked at him, looked at the village in the hollow, at the mill, and at the prison on the crag. When he had identified these objects in what benighted mind he had, he said, in a dialect that was just intelligible:

"How goes it, Jacques?"

"All well, Jacques."

"Touch then!"

They joined hands, and the man sat down on the heap of stones.

"No dinner?"

"Nothing but supper now," said the mender of roads, with a hungry face.

"It is the fashion," growled the man. "I meet no dinner anywhere."

He took out a blackened pipe, filled it, lighted it with flint and steel, pulled at it until it was in a bright glow; then, suddenly held it from him and dropped something into it from between his finger and thumb, that blazed and went out in a puff of smoke.

"Touch then." It was the turn of the mender of roads to say it this time, after observing these operations. They again joined hands.

"To-night?" said the mender of roads.

5   "To-night," said the man, putting the pipe in his mouth.

"Where?"

"Here."

He and the mender of roads sat on the heap of stones looking silently at one another, with the hail driving in between them like a pigmy charge of bayonets, until the sky began to clear over the village.

"Show me!" said the traveller then, moving to the brow of the hill.

"See!" returned the mender of roads, with extended finger. "You 15 go down here, and straight through the street, and past the fountain—"

"To the Devil with all that!" interrupted the other, rolling his eyes over the landscape. "I go through no streets and past no fountains. Well?"

"Well! About two leagues beyond the summit of that hill above the village."

"Good. When do you cease to work?"

"At sunset."

"Will you wake me, before departing? I have walked two nights 25 without resting. Let me finish my pipe, and I shall sleep like a child. Will you wake me?"

"Surely."

The wayfarer smoked his pipe out, put it in his breast, slipped off his great wooden shoes, and lay down on his back on the heap of stones. He was fast asleep directly.

As the road-mender plied his dusty labour, and the hail-clouds, rolling away, revealed bright bars and streaks of sky which were responded to by silver gleams upon the landscape, the little man (who wore a red cap now, in place of his blue one) seemed 35 fascinated by the figure on the heap of stones. His eyes were so often turned towards it, that he used his tools mechanically, and, one would have said, to very poor account. The bronze face, the shaggy black hair and beard, the coarse woollen red cap, the rough medley dress of homespun stuff and hairy skins of beasts, the

powerful frame attenuated by spare living, and the sullen and
desperate compression of the lips in sleep, inspired the mender of
roads with awe. The traveller had travelled far, and his feet were
foot-sore, and his ankles chafed and bleeding; his great shoes,
stuffed with leaves and grass, had been heavy to drag over the
many long leagues, and his clothes were chafed into holes, as he
himself was into sores. Stooping down beside him, the road-mender
tried to get a peep at secret weapons in his breast or where not;
but, in vain, for he slept with his arms crossed upon him, and set
as resolutely as his lips. Fortified towns with their stockades, guardhouses, gates, trenches, and drawbridges seemed, to the mender of
roads, to be so much air as against this figure. And when he lifted
his eyes from it to the horizon and looked around, he saw in his
small fancy similar figures, stopped by no obstacle, tending to cen-
tres all over France.

The man slept on, indifferent to showers of hail and intervals of
brightness, to sunshine on his face and shadow, to the pattering
lumps of dull ice on his body and the diamonds into which the sun
changed them, until the sun was low in the west, and the sky was
glowing. Then, the mender of roads, having got his tools together
and all things ready to go down into the village, roused him.

"Good!" said the sleeper, rising on his elbow. "Two leagues
beyond the summit of the hill?"

"About."

"About. Good!"

The mender of roads went home, with the dust going on before
him according to the set of the wind, and was soon at the fountain,
squeezing himself in among the lean kine brought there to drink,
and appearing even to whisper to them in his whispering to all the
village. When the village had taken its poor supper, it did not
creep to bed, as it usually did, but came out of doors again, and
remained there.

A curious contagion of whispering was upon it, and also, when
it gathered together at the fountain in the dark, another curious
contagion of looking expectantly at the sky in one direction only.
Monsieur Gabelle, chief functionary of the place, became uneasy;
went out on his housetop alone, and looked in that direction too;
glanced down from behind his chimneys at the darkening faces by
the fountain below, and sent word to the sacristan who kept the

keys of the church, that there might be need to ring the tocsin by
and by.

The night deepened. The trees environing the old château,
keeping its solitary state apart, moved in a rising wind, as though
they threatened the pile of building massive and dark in the gloom.
Up the two terrace flights of steps the rain ran wildly, and beat at
the great door, like a swift messenger rousing those within; uneasy
rushes of wind went through the hall, among the old spears and
knives, and passed lamenting up the stairs, and shook the curtains
of the bed where the last Marquis had slept. East, west, north, and
south, through the woods, four heavy-treading, unkempt figures
crushed the high grass and cracked the branches, striding on cautiously to come together in the courtyard. Four lights broke out
there, and moved away in different directions, and all was black
again.

But, not for long. Presently, the château began to make itself
strangely visible by some light of its own, as though it were growing luminous. Then, a flickering streak played behind the architecture of the front, picking out transparent places, and showing
where balustrades, arches, and windows were. Then it soared
higher, and grew broader and brighter. Soon, from a score of the
great windows, flames burst forth, and the stone faces awakened,
stared out of fire.

A faint murmur arose about the house from the few people who
were left there, and there was a saddling of a horse and riding away.
There was spurring and splashing through the darkness, and bridle
was drawn in the space by the village fountain, and the horse in a
foam stood at Monsieur Gabelle's door. "Help, Gabelle! Help,
every one!" The tocsin rang impatiently, but other help (if that
were any) there was none. The mender of roads, and two hundred
and fifty particular friends, stood with folded arms at the fountain,
looking at the pillar of fire in the sky. "It must be forty feet high,"
said they, grimly; and never moved.

The rider from the château, and the horse in a foam, clattered
away through the village, and galloped up the stony steep, to the
prison on the crag. At the gate, a group of officers were looking at
the fire; removed from them, a group of soldiers. "Help, gen-
tlemen-officers! The château is on fire; valuable objects may be
saved from the flames by timely aid! Help, help!" The officers

looked towards the soldiers who looked at the fire; gave no orders; and answered, with shrugs and biting of lips, "It must burn."

As the rider rattled down the hill again and through the street, the village was illuminating. The mender of roads, and the two hundred and fifty particular friends, inspired as one man and woman by the idea of lighting up, had darted into their houses, and were putting candles in every dull little pane of glass. The general scarcity of everything occasioned candles to be borrowed in a rather peremptory manner of Monsieur Gabelle; and in a moment of reluctance and hesitation on that functionary's part, the mender of roads, once so submissive to authority, had remarked that carriages were good to make bonfires with, and that post-horses would roast.

The château was left to itself to flame and burn. In the roaring and raging of the conflagration, a red-hot wind, driving straight from the infernal regions, seemed to be blowing the edifice away. With the rising and falling of the blaze, the stone faces showed as if they were in torment. When the great masses of stone and timber fell, the face with the two dints in the nose became obscured: anon struggled out of the smoke again, as if it were the face of the cruel Marquis, burning at the stake and contending with the fire.

The château burned; the nearest trees, laid hold of by the fire, scorched and shrivelled; trees at a distance, fired by the four fierce figures, begirt the blazing edifice with a new forest of smoke. Molten lead and iron boiled in the marble basin of the fountain; the water ran dry; the extinguisher tops of the towers vanished like ice before the heat, and trickled down into four rugged wells of flame. Great rents and splits branched out in the solid walls, like crystallisation; stupefied birds wheeled about and dropped into the furnace; four fierce figures trudged away, east, west, north, and south, along the night-enshrouded roads, guided by the beacon they had lighted, towards their next destination. The illuminated village had seized hold of the tocsin, and, abolishing the lawful ringer, rang for joy.

Not only that; but the village, light-headed with famine, fire, and bell-ringing, and bethinking itself that Monsieur Gabelle had to do with the collection of rent and taxes—though it was but a small instalment of taxes, and no rent at all, that Gabelle had got in those latter days—became impatient for an interview with him, and, surrounding his house, summoned him to come forth for

personal conference. Whereupon, Monsieur Gabelle did heavily bar his door, and retire to hold counsel with himself. The result of that conference was that Gabelle again withdrew himself to his house-top behind his stack of chimneys; this time resolved, if his door
5   was broken in (he was a small Southern man of retaliative temperament), to pitch himself head foremost over the parapet, and crush a man or two below.

Probably, Monsieur Gabelle passed a long night up there, with the distant château for fire and candle, and the beating at his door, combined with the joy-ringing, for music; not to mention his having an ill-omened lamp slung across the road before his posting-house gate, which the village showed a lively inclination to displace in his favour. A trying suspense, to be passing a whole summer night on the brink of the black ocean, ready to take that plunge
15 into it upon which Monsieur Gabelle had resolved! But, the friendly dawn appearing at last, and the rush-candles of the village guttering out, the people happily dispersed, and Monsieur Gabelle came down bringing his life with him for that while.

Within a hundred miles, and in the light of other fires, there were other functionaries less fortunate, that night and other nights, whom the rising sun found hanging across once-peaceful streets, where they had been born and bred; also, there were other villages and townspeople less fortunate than the mender of roads and his fellows, upon whom the functionaries and soldiery turned with
25 success, and whom they strung up in their turn. But, the fierce figures were steadily wending east, west, north, and south, be that as it would; and whosoever hung, fire burned. The altitude of the gallows that would turn to water and quench it, no functionary, by any stretch of mathematics, was able to calculate successfully.

Chapter 24. Drawn to the Loadstone Rock

In such risings of fire and risings of sea—the firm earth shaken by the rushes of an angry ocean which had now no ebb, but was always on the flow, higher and higher, to the terror and wonder of the beholders on the shore—three years of tempest were consumed.

Three more birthdays of little Lucie had been woven by the golden thread into the peaceful tissue of the life of her home.

Many a night and many a day had its inmates listened to the echoes in the corner, with hearts that failed them when they heard the thronging feet. For, the footsteps had become to their minds as the footsteps of a people, tumultuous under a red flag and with their country declared in danger, changed into wild beasts, by terrible enchantment long persisted in.

Monseigneur, as a class, had dissociated himself from the phenomenon of his not being appreciated: of his being so little wanted in France, as to incur considerable danger of receiving his dismissal from it, and this life together. Like the fabled rustic who raised the Devil with infinite pains, and was so terrified at the sight of him that he could ask the Enemy no question, but immediately fled; so, Monseigneur, after boldly reading the Lord's Prayer backwards for a great number of years, and performing many other potent spells for compelling the Evil One, no sooner beheld him in his terrors than he took to his noble heels.

The shining Bull's Eye of the Court was gone, or it would have been the mark for a hurricane of national bullets. It had never been a good eye to see with—had long had the mote in it of Lucifer's pride, Sardanapalus's luxury, and a mole's blindness—but it had dropped out and was gone. The Court, from that exclusive inner circle to its outermost rotten ring of intrigue, corruption, and dissimulation, was all gone together. Royalty was gone; had been besieged in its Palace and "suspended," when the last tidings came over.

The August of the year one thousand seven hundred and ninety-two was come, and Monseigneur was by this time scattered far and wide.

As was natural, the headquarters and great gathering-place of Monseigneur, in London, was Tellson's Bank. Spirits are supposed to haunt the places where their bodies most resorted, and Monseigneur without a guinea haunted the spot where his guineas used to be. Moveover, it was the spot to which such French intelligence as was most to be relied upon came quickest. Again: Tellson's was a munificent house, and extended great liberality to old customers who had fallen from their high estate. Again: those nobles who had seen the coming storm in time, and anticipating plunder or confiscation, had made provident remittances to Tellson's, were always to be heard of there by their needy brethren. To which must be added that every new-comer from France reported himself and his tidings at Tellson's, almost as a matter of course. For such variety of reasons, Tellson's was at that time, as to French intelligence, a kind of High Exchange; and this was so well known to the public, and the inquiries made there were in consequence so numerous, that Tellson's sometimes wrote the latest news out in a line or so and posted it in the Bank windows, for all who ran through Temple Bar to read.

On a steaming, misty afternoon, Mr. Lorry sat at his desk, and Charles Darnay stood leaning on it, talking with him in a low voice. The penitential den once set apart for interviews with the House was now the news-exchange, and was filled to overflowing. It was within half an hour or so of the time of closing.

"But, although you are the youngest man that ever lived," said Charles Darnay, rather hesitating, "I must still suggest to you—"

"I understand. That I am too old?" said Mr. Lorry.

"Unsettled weather, a long journey, uncertain means of travelling, a disorganised country, a city that may not be even safe for you."

"My dear Charles," said Mr. Lorry, with cheerful confidence, "you touch some of the reasons for my going: not for my staying away. It is safe enough for me; nobody will care to interfere with an old fellow of hard upon fourscore when there are so many people there much better worth interfering with. As to its being a disorganised city, if it were not a disorganised city there would be no occasion to send somebody from our House here to our House there, who knows the city and the business, of old, and is in Tellson's confidence. As to the uncertain travelling, the long journey, and the winter weather, if I were not prepared to submit myself to a few inconveniences for the sake of Tellson's, after all these years, who ought to be?"

"I wish I were going myself," said Charles Darnay, somewhat restlessly, and like one thinking aloud.

"Indeed! You are a pretty fellow to object and advise!" exclaimed Mr. Lorry. "You wish you were going yourself? And you a Frenchman born? You are a wise counsellor."

"My dear Mr. Lorry, it is because I am a Frenchman born, that the thought (which I did not mean to utter here, however) has passed through my mind often. One cannot help thinking, having had some sympathy for the miserable people, and having abandoned something to them," he spoke here in his former thoughtful manner, "that one might be listened to, and might have 5 the power to persuade to some restraint. Only last night, after you had left us, when I was talking to Lucie—"

"When you were talking to Lucie," Mr. Lorry repeated. "Yes. I wonder you are not ashamed to mention the name of Lucie! Wishing you were going to France at this time of day!"

"However, I am not going," said Charles Darnay, with a smile. "It is more to the purpose that you say you are."

"And I am, in plain reality. The truth is, my dear Charles," Mr. Lorry glanced at the distant House, and lowered his voice, "you can have no conception of the difficulty with which our business is 15 transacted, and of the peril in which our books and papers over yonder are involved. The Lord above knows what the compromising consequence would be to numbers of people, if some of our documents were seized or destroyed; and they might be, at any time, you know, for who can say that Paris is not set afire to-day, or sacked to-morrow! Now, a judicious selection from these with the least possible delay, and the burying of them, or otherwise getting them out of harm's way, is within the power (without loss of precious time) of scarcely any one but myself, if any one. And shall I hang back, when Tellson's knows this and says this—Tell- 25 son's, whose bread I have eaten these sixty years—because I am a little stiff about the joints? Why, I am a boy, sir, to half a dozen old codgers here!"

"How I admire the gallantry of your youthful spirit, Mr. Lorry."

"Tut! Nonsense, sir!—And, my dear Charles," said Mr. Lorry, glancing at the House again, "you are to remember, that getting things out of Paris at this present time, no matter what things, is next to an impossibility. Papers and precious matters were this very day brought to us here (I speak in strict confidence; it is not business-like to whisper it, even to you), by the strangest bearers 35 you can imagine, every one of whom had his head hanging on by a single hair as he passed the Barriers. At another time, our parcels would come and go, as easily as in business-like Old England; but now, everything is stopped."

"And do you really go to-night?"

"I really go to-night, for the case has become too pressing to admit of delay."

"And do you take no one with you?"

"All sorts of people have been proposed to me, but I will have nothing to say to any of them. I intend to take Jerry. Jerry has been my body-guard on Sunday nights for a long time past, and I am used to him. Nobody will suspect Jerry of being anything but an English bull-dog, or of having any design in his head but to fly at somebody who touches his master."

"I must say again that I heartily admire your gallantry and youthfulness."

"I must say again, nonsense, nonsense! When I have executed this little commission, I shall, perhaps, accept Tellson's proposal to retire and live at my ease. Time enough, then, to think about growing old."

This dialogue had taken place at Mr. Lorry's usual desk, with Monseigneur swarming within a yard or two of it, boastful of what he would do to avenge himself on the rascal-people before long. It was too much the way of Monseigneur under his reverses as a refugee, and it was much too much the way of native British orthodoxy, to talk of this terrible Revolution as if it were the one only harvest ever known under the skies that had not been sown—as if nothing had ever been done, or omitted to be done, that had led to it—as if observers of the wretched millions in France, and of the misused and perverted resources that should have made them prosperous, had not seen it inevitably coming, years before, and had not in plain words recorded what they saw. Such vapouring, combined with the extravagant plots of Monseigneur for the restoration of a state of things that had utterly exhausted itself, and worn out Heaven and earth as well as itself, was hard to be endured without some remonstrance by any sane man who knew the truth. And it was such vapouring all about his ears, like a troublesome confusion of blood in his own head, added to a latent uneasiness in his mind, which had already made Charles Darnay restless, and which still kept him so.

Among the talkers was Stryver, of the King's Bench Bar, far on his way to state promotion, and, therefore, loud on the theme: broaching to Monseigneur his devices for blowing the people up and exterminating them from the face of the earth, and doing without them: and for accomplishing many similar objects akin in their nature to the abolition of eagles by sprinkling salt on the tails of the race. Him, Darnay heard with a particular feeling of objection; and Darnay stood divided between going away that he might hear no more, and remaining to interpose his word, when the thing that was to be went on to shape itself out.

The House approached Mr. Lorry, and laying a soiled and unopened letter before him, asked if he had yet discovered any traces of the person to whom it was addressed? The House laid the letter down so close to Darnay that he saw the direction—the more quickly because it was his own right name. The address, turned into English, ran:

"Very pressing. To Monsieur heretofore the Marquis St. Evrémonde, of France. Confided to the cares of Messrs. Tellson and Co., Bankers, London, England."

On the marriage morning, Doctor Manette had made it his one urgent and express request to Charles Darnay, that the secret of this name should be—unless he, the Doctor, dissolved the obligation—kept inviolate between them. Nobody else knew it to be his name; his own wife had no suspicion of the fact; Mr. Lorry could have none.

"No," said Mr. Lorry, in reply to the House; "I have referred it, I think, to everybody now here, and no one can tell me where this gentleman is to be found."

The hands of the clock verging upon the hour of closing the Bank, there was a general set of the current of talkers past Mr. Lorry's desk. He held the letter out inquiringly; and Monseigneur looked at it, in the person of this plotting and indignant refugee; and Monseigneur looked at it, in the person of that plotting and indignant refugee, and This, That, and The Other, all had something disparaging to say, in French or in English, concerning the Marquis who was not to be found.

"Nephew, I believe—but in any case degenerate successor—of the polished Marquis who was murdered," said one. "Happy to say, I never knew him."

"A craven who abandoned his post," said another—this Monseigneur had been got out of Paris, legs uppermost and half suffocated, in a load of hay—"some years ago."

"Infected with the new doctrines," said a third, eyeing the direction through his glass in passing; "set himself in opposition to the last Marquis, abandoned the estates when he inherited them, and left them to the ruffian herd. They will recompense him now, I hope, as he deserves."

"Hey?" cried the blatant Stryver. "Did he though? Is that the sort of fellow? Let us look at his infamous name. D—n the fellow!"

Darnay, unable to restrain himself any longer, touched Mr. Stryver on the shoulder, and said:

"I know the fellow."

"Do you, by Jupiter?" said Stryver. "I am sorry for it."

"Why?"

"Why, Mr. Darnay? D'ye hear what he did? Don't ask why, in these times."

"But I do ask why."

"Then I tell you again, Mr. Darnay, I am sorry for it. I am sorry to hear you putting any such extraordinary questions. Here is a fellow, who, infected by the most pestilent and blasphemous code of deviltry that ever was known, abandoned his property to the vilest scum of the earth that ever did murder by wholesale, and you ask me why I am sorry that a man who instructs youth knows him? Well, but I'll answer you. I am sorry because I believe there is contamination in such a scoundrel. That's why."

Mindful of the secret, Darnay with great difficulty checked himself, and said: "You may not understand the gentleman."

"I understand how to put you in a corner, Mr. Darnay," said Bully Stryver, "and I'll do it. If this fellow is a gentleman, I don't understand him. You may tell him so, with my compliments. You may also tell him, from me, that after abandoning his worldly goods and position to this butcherly mob, I wonder he is not at the head of them. But, no, gentlemen," said Stryver, looking all round, and snapping his fingers, "I know something of human nature, and I tell you that you'll never find a fellow like this fellow, trusting himself to the mercies of such precious protégés. No, gentlemen; he'll always show 'em a clean pair of heels very early in the scuffle, and sneak away."

With those words, and a final snap of his fingers, Mr. Stryver shouldered himself into Fleet Street, amidst the general approbation of his hearers. Mr. Lorry and Charles Darnay were left alone at the desk, in the general departure from the Bank.

"Will you take charge of the letter?" said Mr. Lorry. "You know where to deliver it?"

"I do."

"Will you undertake to explain that we suppose it to have been addressed here, on the chance of our knowing where to forward it, and that it has been here some time?"

"I will do so. Do you start for Paris from here?"

"From here, at eight."

"I will come back, to see you off."

Very ill at ease with himself, and with Stryver and most other men, Darnay made the best of his way into the quiet of the Temple, opened the letter, and read it. These were its contents:

Prison of the Abbaye, Paris.
June 21, 1792.

MONSIEUR HERETOFORE THE MARQUIS,

After having long been in danger of my life at the hands of the village, I have been seized, with great violence and indignity, and brought a long journey on foot to Paris. On the road I have suffered a great deal. Nor is that all; my house has been destroyed—razed to the ground.

The crime for which I am imprisoned, Monsieur heretofore the Marquis, and for which I shall be summoned before the tribunal, and shall lose my life (without your so generous help) is, they tell me, treason against the majesty of the people, in that I have acted against them for an emigrant. It is in vain I represent that I have acted for them, and not against, according to your commands. It is in vain I represent that, before the sequestration of emigrant property, I had remitted the imposts they had ceased to pay; that I had collected no rent; that I had had recourse to no process. The only response is, that I have acted for an emigrant, and where is that emigrant?

Ah! most gracious Monsieur heretofore the Marquis, where is that emigrant? I cry in my sleep where is he? I demand of Heaven, will he not come to deliver me? No answer. Ah! Monsieur heretofore the Marquis, I send my desolate cry across the sea, hoping it may perhaps reach your ears through the great bank of Tellson known at Paris!

For the love of Heaven, of justice, of generosity, of the honour of your noble name, I supplicate you, Monsieur heretofore the Marquis, to succour and release me. My fault is that I have been true to you. Oh! Monsieur heretofore the Marquis, I pray you be you true to me!

From this prison here of horror, whence I every hour tend nearer and nearer to destruction, I send you, Monsieur heretofore the Marquis, the assurance of my dolorous and unhappy service.

Your afflicted
GABELLE.

The latent uneasiness in Darnay's mind was roused to vigorous life by this letter. The peril of an old servant and a good one, whose only crime was fidelity to himself and his family, stared him so reproachfully in the face that, as he walked to and fro in the Temple considering what to do, he almost hid his face from the passers-by.

He knew very well that in his horror of the deed which had culminated the bad deeds and bad reputation of the old family house, in his resentful suspicions of his uncle, and in the aversion with which his conscience regarded the crumbling fabric that he was supposed to uphold, he had acted imperfectly. He knew very well that in his love for Lucie, his renunciation of his social place, though by no means new to his own mind, had been hurried and incomplete. He knew that he ought to have systematically worked it out and supervised it, and that he had meant to do it, and that it had never been done.

The happiness of his own chosen English home, the necessity of being always actively employed, the swift changes and troubles of the time which had followed on one another so fast, that the events of this week annihilated the immature plans of last week, and the events of the week following made all new again; he knew very well, that to the force of these circumstances he had yielded—not without disquiet, but still without continuous and accumulating resistance. That he had watched the times for a time of action, and that they had shifted and struggled until the time had gone by, and the nobility were trooping from France by every highway and byway, and their property was in course of confiscation and destruction, and their very names were blotting out, was as well known to himself as it could be to any new authority in France that might impeach him for it.

But, he had oppressed no man, he had imprisoned no man; he was so far from having harshly exacted payment of his dues, that he had relinquished them of his own will, thrown himself on a world with no favour in it, won his own private place there, and earned his own bread. Monsieur Gabelle had held the impoverished and involved estate on written instructions, to spare the people, to give them what little there was to give—such fuel as the heavy creditors would let them have in the winter, and such produce as could be saved from the same grip in the summer—and no doubt he had put the fact in plea and proof, for his own safety, so that it could not but appear now.

This favoured the desperate resolution Charles Darnay had begun to make, that he would go to Paris.

Yes. Like the mariner in the old story, the winds and streams had driven him within the influence of the Loadstone Rock, and it was drawing him to itself, and he must go. Everything that arose before his mind drifted him on, faster and faster, more and more steadily, to the terrible attraction. His latent uneasiness had been that bad aims were being worked out in his own unhappy land by bad instruments, and that he who could not fail to know that he was better than they, was not there, trying to do something to stay blood-shed, and assert the claims of mercy and humanity. With this uneasiness half stifled, and half reproaching him, he had been brought to the pointed comparison of himself with the brave old gentleman in whom duty was so strong; upon that comparison (injurious to himself) had instantly followed the sneers of Monseigneur, which had stung him bitterly, and those of Stryver, which above all were coarse and galling, for old reasons. Upon those had followed Gabelle's letter: the appeal of an innocent prisoner, in danger of death, to his justice, honour, and good name.

His resolution was made. He must go to Paris.

Yes. The Loadstone Rock was drawing him, and he must sail on, until he struck. He knew of no rock; he saw hardly any danger. The intention with which he had done what he had done, even although he had left it incompleted, presented it before him in an

aspect that would be gratefully acknowledged in France on his presenting himself to assert it. Then, that glorious vision of doing good, which is so often the sanguine mirage of so many good minds, arose before him, and he even saw himself in the illusion
5   with some influence to guide this raging Revolution that was running so fearfully wild.

As he walked to and fro with his resolution made, he considered that neither Lucie nor her father must know of it until he was gone. Lucie should be spared the pain of separation; and her father, always reluctant to turn his thoughts towards the dangerous ground of old, should come to the knowledge of the step, as a step taken, and not in the balance of suspense and doubt. How much of the incompleteness of his situation was referable to her father, through the painful anxiety to avoid reviving old associations of
15   France in his mind, he did not discuss with himself. But, that circumstance too had its influence in his course.

He walked to and fro, with thoughts very busy, until it was time to return to Tellson's and take leave of Mr. Lorry. As soon as he arrived in Paris he would present himself to this old friend, but he must say nothing of his intention now.

A carriage with post-horses was ready at the Bank door and Jerry was booted and equipped.

"I have delivered that letter," said Charles Darnay to Mr. Lorry. "I would not consent to your being charged with any written
25   answer, but perhaps you will take a verbal one?"

"That I will, and readily," said Mr. Lorry, "if it is not dangerous."

"Not at all. Though it is to a prisoner in the Abbaye."

"What is his name?" said Mr. Lorry, with his open pocket-book in his hand.

"Gabelle."

"Gabelle. And what is the message to the unfortunate Gabelle in prison?"

"Simply, 'that he has received the letter, and will come.' "
35   "Any time mentioned?"

"He will start upon his journey to-morrow night."

"Any person mentioned?"

"No."

He helped Mr. Lorry to wrap himself in a number of coats and

cloaks, and went out with him from the warm atmosphere of the
old Bank, into the misty air of Fleet Street. "My love to Lucie, and
to little Lucie," said Mr. Lorry at parting, "and take precious care
of them till I come back." Charles Darnay shook his head and
doubtfully smiled, as the carriage rolled away.   5

That night—it was the fourteenth of August—he sat up late,
and wrote two fervent letters; one was to Lucie, explaining the
strong obligation he was under to go to Paris, and showing her, at
length, the reasons that he had, for feeling confident that he could
become involved in no personal danger there; the other was to the
Doctor, confiding Lucie and their dear child to his care, and dwelling on the same topics with the strongest assurances. To both, he
wrote that he would despatch letters in proof of his safety immediately after his arrival.

It was a hard day, that day of being among them, with the first   15
reservation of their joint lives on his mind. It was a hard matter to
preserve the innocent deceit of which they were profoundly unsuspi-
cious. But, an affectionate glance at his wife, so happy and busy,
made him resolute not to tell her what impended (he had been
half moved to do it, so strange it was to him to act in anything
without her quiet aid), and the day passed quickly away. Early in
the evening he embraced her, and her scarcely less dear namesake,
pretending that he would return by and by (an imaginary engage-
ment took him out, and he had secreted a valise of clothes ready),
and so he emerged into the heavy mist of the heavy street, with a   25
heavier heart.

The unseen force was drawing him fast to itself, now, and all the
tides and winds were setting straight and strong towards it. He left
his two letters with a trusty porter, to be delivered half an hour
before midnight, and no sooner; took horse for Dover; and began
his journey. "For the love of Heaven, justice, of generosity, of the
honour of your noble name!" was the poor prisoner's cry with
which he strengthened his sinking heart, as he left all that was
dear on earth behind him, and floated away for the Loadstone
Rock.   35

BOOK THE THIRD: THE TRACK OF A STORM

Chapter 1. In Secret

The traveller fared slowly on his way, who fared towards Paris from England in the autumn of the year one thousand seven hundred and ninety-two. More than enough of bad roads, bad equipages, and bad horses he would have encountered to delay him,
5   though the fallen and unfortunate King of France had been upon his throne in all his glory; but, the changed times were fraught with other obstacles than these. Every town-gate and village taxing-house had its band of citizen-patriots, with their national muskets in a most explosive state of readiness, who stopped all comers and goers, cross-questioned them, inspected their papers, looked for their names in lists of their own, turned them back, or sent them on, or stopped them and laid them in hold, as their capricious judgment or fancy deemed best for the dawning Republic One and Indivisible, of Liberty, Equality, Fraternity, or Death.

15   A very few French leagues of his journey were accomplished, when Charles Darnay began to perceive that for him along these country roads there was no hope of return until he should have been declared a good citizen at Paris. Whatever might befall now, he must on to his journey's end. Not a mean village closed upon him, not a common barrier dropped across the road behind him, but he knew it to be another iron door in the series that was barred between him and England. The universal watchfulness so encompassed him, that if he had been taken in a net, or were being forwarded to his destination in a cage, he could not have felt his free-
35   dom more completely gone.

This universal watchfulness not only stopped him on the highway twenty times in a stage, but retarded his progress twenty times in a day, by riding after him and taking him back, riding before him and stopping him by anticipation, riding with him and keeping him in charge. He had been days upon his journey in France alone,   5
when he went to bed tired out, in a little town on the high road, still a long way from Paris.

Nothing but the production of the afflicted Gabelle's letter from his prison of the Abbaye would have got him on so far. His difficulty at the guard-house in this small place had been such that he felt his journey to have come to a crisis. And he was, therefore, as little surprised as a man could be, to find himself awakened at the small inn to which he had been remitted until morning, in the middle of the night.

Awakened by a timid local functionary and three armed patriots   15
in rough red caps and with pipes in their mouths, who sat down on the bed.

"Emigrant," said the functionary, "I am going to send you on to Paris, under an escort."

"Citizen, I desire nothing more than to get to Paris, though I could dispense with the escort."

"Silence!" growled a red-cap, striking at the coverlet with the butt-end of his musket. "Peace, aristocrat!"

"It is as the good patriot says," observed the timid functionary. "You are an aristocrat, and must have an escort—and must pay for   25
it."

"I have no choice," said Charles Darnay.

"Choice! Listen to him!" cried the same scowling red-cap. "As if it was not a favour to be protected from the lamp-iron!"

"It is always as the good patriot says," observed the functionary. "Rise and dress yourself, emigrant."

Darnay complied, and was taken back to the guard-house, where other patriots in rough red caps were smoking, drinking, and sleeping, by a watch-fire. Here he paid a heavy price for his escort, and hence he started with it on the wet, wet roads at three o'clock   35
in the morning.

The escort were two mounted patriots in red caps and tricoloured cockades, armed with national muskets and sabres, who rode one on either side of him. The escorted governed his own horse,

but a loose line was attached to his bridle, the end of which one of
the patriots kept girded round his wrist. In this state they set forth
with the sharp rain driving in their faces: clattering at a heavy
dragoon trot over the uneven town pavement, and out upon the
mire-deep roads. In this state they traversed without change, except
of horses and pace, all the mire-deep leagues that lay between them
and the capital.

They travelled in the night, halting an hour or two after
daybreak, and lying by until the twilight fell. The escort were so
wretchedly clothed, that they twisted straw round their bare legs,
and thatched their ragged shoulders to keep the wet off. Apart from
personal discomfort of being so attended, and apart from such
considerations of present danger as arose from one of the patriots
being chronically drunk, and carrying his musket very recklessly,
Charles Darnay did not allow the restraint that was laid upon him
to awaken any serious fears in his breast; for, he reasoned with
himself that it could have no reference to the merits of an
individual case that was not yet stated, and of representations,
confirmable by the prisoner in the Abbaye, that were not yet made.

But when they came to the town of Beauvais—which they did at
eventide, when the streets were filled with people—he could not
conceal from himself that the aspect of affairs was very alarming.
An ominous crowd gathered to see him dismount at the posting-
yard, and many voices called out loudly, "Down with the emigrant!"

He stopped in the act of swinging himself out of his saddle, and,
resuming it as his safest place, said:

"Emigrant, my friends! Do you not see me here, in France, of my
own will?"

"You are a cursed emigrant," cried a farrier, making at him in a
furious manner through the press, hammer in hand; "and you are a
cursed aristocrat!"

The postmaster interposed himself between this man and the
rider's bridle (at which he was evidently making), and soothingly
said, "Let him be; let him be! He will be judged at Paris."

"Judged!" repeated the farrier, swinging his hammer. "Ay! and
condemned as a traitor." At this the crowd roared approval.

Checking the postmaster, who was for turning his horse's head to
the yard (the drunken patriot sat composedly in his saddle looking

on, with the line round his wrist), Darnay said, as soon as he could make his voice heard:

"Friends, you deceive yourselves, or you are deceived. I am not a traitor."

"He lies!" cried the smith. "He is a traitor since the decree. His life is forfeit to the people. His cursed life is not his own!"

At the instant when Darnay saw a rush in the eyes of the crowd, which another instant would have brought upon him, the postmaster turned his horse into the yard, the escort rode in close upon his horse's flanks, and the postmaster shut and barred the crazy double gates. The farrier struck a blow upon them with his hammer, and the crowd groaned; but, no more was done.

"What is this decree that the smith spoke of?" Darnay asked the postmaster, when he had thanked him, and stood beside him in the yard.

"Truly, a decree for selling the property of emigrants."

"When passed?"

"On the fourteenth."

"The day I left England!"

"Everybody says it is but one of several, and that there will be others—if there are not already—banishing all emigrants, and condemning all to death who return. That is what he meant when he said your life was not your own."

"But there are no such decrees yet?"

"What do I know!" said the postmaster, shrugging his shoulders; "there may be, or there will be. It is all the same. What would you have?"

They rested on some straw in a loft until the middle of the night, and then rode forward again when all the town was asleep. Among the many wild changes observable on familiar things which made this wild ride unreal, not the least was the seeming rarity of sleep. After long and lonely spurring over dreary roads, they would come to a cluster of poor cottages, not steeped in darkness, but all glittering with lights, and would find the people, in a ghostly manner in the dead of the night, circling hand in hand round a shrivelled tree of Liberty, or all drawn up together singing a Liberty song. Happily, however, there was sleep in Beauvais that night to help them out of it, and they passed on once more into solitude and loneliness: jingling through the untimely cold and wet, among impoverished fields that had yielded no fruits of the earth that year, diversified by the blackened remains of burnt houses, and by the sudden emergence from ambuscade, and sharp reining up across their way, of patriot patrols on the watch on all the roads.

5 Daylight at last found them before the wall of Paris. The barrier was closed and strongly guarded when they rode up to it.

"Where are the papers of this prisoner?" demanded a resolute-looking man in authority, who was summoned out by the guard.

Naturally struck by the disagreeable word, Charles Darnay requested the speaker to take notice that he was a free traveller and French citizen, in charge of an escort which the disturbed state of the country had imposed upon him, and which he had paid for.

"Where," repeated the same personage, without taking any heed of him whatever, "are the papers of this prisoner?"

15 The drunken patriot had them in his cap, and produced them. Casting his eyes over Gabelle's letter, the same personage in authority showed some disorder and surprise, and looked at Darnay with a close attention.

He left escort and escorted without saying a word, however, and went into the guard-room; meanwhile, they sat upon their horses outside the gate. Looking about him while in this state of suspense, Charles Darnay observed that the gate was held by a mixed guard of soldiers and patriots, the latter far outnumbering the former; and that while ingress into the city for peasants' carts bringing in 25 supplies, and for similar traffic and traffickers, was easy enough, egress, even for the homeliest people, was very difficult. A numerous medley of men and women, not to mention beasts and vehicles of various sorts, was waiting to issue forth; but, the previous identification was so strict, that they filtered through the barrier very slowly. Some of these people knew their turn for examination to be so far off, that they lay down on the ground to sleep or smoke, while others talked together, or loitered about. The red cap and tricolour cockade were universal, both among men and women.

When he had sat in his saddle some half-hour, taking note of 35 these things, Darnay found himself confronted by the same man in authority, who directed the guard to open the barrier. Then he delivered to the escort, drunk and sober, a receipt for the escorted, and requested him to dismount. He did so, and the two patriots, leading his tired horse, turned and rode away without entering the city.

He accompanied his conductor into a guard-room, smelling of common wine and tobacco, where certain soldiers and patriots, asleep and awake, drunk and sober, and in various neutral states between sleeping and waking, drunkenness and sobriety, were standing and lying about. The light in the guard-house, half derived from the waning oil-lamps of the night, and half from the overcast day, was in a correspondingly uncertain condition. Some registers were lying open on a desk, and an officer of a coarse, dark aspect presided over these.

"Citizen Defarge," said he to Darnay's conductor, as he took a slip of paper to write on, "Is this the emigrant Evrémonde?"

"This is the man."

"Your age, Evrémonde?"

"Thirty-seven."

"Married, Evrémonde?"

"Yes."

"Where married?"

"In England."

"Without doubt. Where is your wife, Evrémonde?"

"In England."

"Without doubt. You are consigned, Evrémonde, to the prison of La Force."

"Just Heaven!" exclaimed Darnay. "Under what law, and for what offence?"

The officer looked up from his slip of paper for a moment.

"We have new laws, Evrémonde, and new offences, since you were here." He said it with a hard smile, and went on writing.

"I entreat you to observe that I have come here voluntarily, in response to that written appeal of a fellow-countryman which lies before you. I demand no more than the opportunity to do so without delay. Is not that my right?"

"Emigrants have no rights, Evrémonde," was the stolid reply. The officer wrote until he had finished, read over to himself what he had written, sanded it, and handed it to Defarge, with the words "In secret."

Defarge motioned with the paper to the prisoner that he must accompany him. The prisoner obeyed, and a guard of two armed patriots attended them.

"Is it you," said Defarge, in a low voice, as they went down the guard-house steps and turned into Paris, "who married the daughter of Doctor Manette, once a prisoner in the Bastille that is no more?"

"Yes," replied Darnay, looking at him with surprise.

"My name is Defarge, and I keep a wine-shop in the Quarter Saint Antoine. Possibly you have heard of me."

"My wife came to your house to reclaim her father? Yes!"

The word "wife" seemed to serve as a gloomy reminder to Defarge, to say with sudden impatience, "In the name of that sharp female newly born, and called La Guillotine, why did you come to France?"

"You heard me say why, a minute ago. Do you not believe it is the truth?"

"A bad truth for you," said Defarge, speaking with knitted brows, and looking straight before him.

"Indeed I am lost here. All here is so unprecedented, so changed, so sudden and unfair, that I am absolutely lost. Will you render me a little help?"

"None." Defarge spoke, always looking straight before him.

"Will you answer me a single question?"

"Perhaps. According to its nature. You can say what it is."

"In this prison that I am going to so unjustly, shall I have some free communication with the world outside?"

"You will see."

"I am not to be buried there, prejudged, and without any means of presenting my case?"

"You will see. But, what then? Other people have been similarly buried in worse prisons, before now."

"But never by me, Citizen Defarge."

Defarge glanced darkly at him for answer, and walked on in a steady and set silence. The deeper he sank into this silence, the fainter hope there was—or so Darnay thought—of his softening in any slight degree. He, therefore, made haste to say:

"It is of the utmost importance to me (you know, Citizen, even better than I, of how much importance) that I should be able to communicate to Mr. Lorry of Tellson's Bank, an English gentleman who is now in Paris, the simple fact, without comment, that I have been thrown into the prison of La Force. Will you cause that to be done for me?"

"I will do," Defarge doggedly rejoined, "nothing for you. My duty is to my country and the People. I am the sworn servant of both, against you. I will do nothing for you."

Charles Darnay felt it hopeless to entreat him further, and his pride was touched besides. As they walked on in silence, he could not but see how used the people were to the spectacle of prisoners passing along the streets. The very children scarcely noticed him. A few passers turned their heads, and a few shook their fingers at him as an aristocrat; otherwise, that a man in good clothes should be going to prison was no more remarkable than that a labourer in working clothes should be going to work. In one narrow, dark, and dirty street through which they passed, an excited orator, mounted on a stool, was addressing an excited audience on the crimes against the people, of the king and the royal family. The few words that he caught from this man's lips first made it known to Charles Darnay that the king was in prison, and that the foreign ambassadors had one and all left Paris. On the road (except at Beauvais) he had heard absolutely nothing. The escort and the universal watchfulness had completely isolated him.

That he had fallen among far greater dangers than those which had developed themselves when he left England, he of course knew now. That perils had thickened about him fast, and might thicken faster and faster yet, he of course knew now. He could not but admit to himself that he might not have made this journey, if he could have foreseen the events of a few days. And yet his misgivings were not so dark as, imagined by the light of this later time, they would appear. Troubled as the future was, it was the unknown future, and in its obscurity there was ignorant hope. The horrible massacre, days and nights long, which, within a few rounds of the clock, was to set a great mark of blood upon the blessed garnering time of harvest, was as far out of his knowledge as if it had been a hundred thousand years away. The "sharp female newly born, and called La Guillotine," was hardly known to him, or to the generality of people, by name. The frightful deeds that were to be soon done were probably unimagined at that time in the brains of the doers. How could they have a place in the shadowy conceptions of a gentle mind?

Of unjust treatment in detention and hardship, and in cruel separation from his wife and child, he foreshadowed the likelihood, or the uncertainty; but, beyond this, he dreaded nothing distinctly.

With this on his mind, which was enough to carry into a dreary prison courtyard, he arrived at the prison of La Force.

A man with a bloated face opened the strong wicket, to whom Defarge presented "The Emigrant Evrémonde."

"What the Devil! How many more of them!" exclaimed the man with the bloated face.

Defarge took his receipt without noticing the exclamation, and withdrew, with his two fellow-patriots.

"What the Devil, I say again!" exclaimed the gaoler, left with his wife. "How many more!"

The gaoler's wife, being provided with no answer to the question, merely replied, "One must have patience, my dear!" Three turn-keys who entered, responsive to a bell she rang, echoed the sentiment, and one added, "For the love of Liberty"; which sounded in that place like an inappropriate conclusion.

The prison of La Force was a gloomy prison, dark and filthy, and with a horrible smell of foul sleep in it. Extraordinary how soon the noisome flavour of imprisoned sleep becomes manifest in all such places that are ill cared for!

"In secret, too," grumbled the gaoler, looking at the written paper. "As if I was not already full to bursting!"

He stuck the paper on a file, in an ill-humour, and Charles Darnay awaited his further pleasure for half an hour: sometimes, pacing to and fro in the strong arched room; sometimes, resting on a stone seat; in either case detained to be imprinted on the memory of the chief and his subordinates.

"Come!" said the chief, at length taking up his keys, "come with me, emigrant."

Through the dismal prison twilight, his new charge accompanied him by corridor and staircase, many doors clanging and locking behind them, until they came into a large, low, vaulted chamber, crowded with prisoners of both sexes. The women were seated at a long table, reading and writing, knitting, sewing, and embroidering; the men were for the most part standing behind their chairs, or lingering up and down the room.

In the instinctive association of prisoners with shameful crime and disgrace, the new-comer recoiled from this company. But the crowning unreality of his long unreal ride was their all at once rising to receive him, with every refinement of manner known to the time, and with all the engaging graces and courtesies of life.

So strangely clouded were these refinements by the prison manners and gloom, so spectral did they become in the inappropriate squalor and misery through which they were seen, that Charles Darnay seemed to stand in a company of the dead. Ghosts all! The ghost of beauty, the ghost of stateliness, the ghost of elegance, the ghost of pride, the ghost of frivolity, the ghost of wit, the ghost of youth, the ghost of age, all waiting their dismissal from the desolate shore, all turning on him eyes that were changed by the death they had died in coming there.

It struck him motionless. The gaoler standing at his side, and the other gaolers moving about, who would have been well enough as to appearance in the ordinary exercise of their functions, looked so extravagantly coarse contrasted with sorrowing mothers and blooming daughters who were there—with the apparitions of the coquette, the young beauty, and the mature woman delicately bred—that the inversion of all experience and likelihood which the scene of shadows presented, was heightened to its utmost. Surely, ghosts all. Surely, the long unreal ride some progress of disease that had brought him to these gloomy shades!

"In the name of the assembled companions in misfortune," said a gentleman of courtly appearance and address, coming forward, "I have the honour of giving you welcome to La Force, and of condoling with you on the calamity that has brought you among us. May it soon terminate happily! It would be an impertinence elsewhere, but it is not so here, to ask your name and condition?"

Charles Darnay roused himself, and gave the required information, in words as suitable as he could find.

"But I hope," said the gentleman, following the chief gaoler with his eyes, who moved across the room, "that you are not in secret?"

"I do not understand the meaning of the term, but I have heard them say so."

"Ah, what a pity! We so much regret it! But take courage; several members of our society have been in secret, at first, and it has lasted but a short time." Then he added, raising his voice, "I grieve to inform the society—in secret."

There was a murmur of commiseration as Charles Darnay crossed the room to a grated door where the gaoler awaited him, and many voices—among which, the soft and compassionate voices of women were conspicuous—gave him good wishes and encouragement. He turned at the grated door, to render the thanks of his heart; it closed under the gaoler's hand; and the apparitions vanished from his sight for ever.

5   The wicket opened on a stone staircase, leading upward. When they had ascended forty steps (the prisoner of half an hour already counted them), the gaoler opened a low black door, and they passed into a solitary cell. It struck cold and damp, but it was not dark.

"Yours," said the gaoler.

"Why am I confined alone?"

"How do I know!"

"I can buy pen, ink, and paper?"

"Such are not my orders. You will be visited, and can ask then.
15   At present, you may buy your food, and nothing more."

There were, in the cell, a chair, a table, and a straw mattress. As the gaoler made a general inspection of these objects, and of the four walls, before going out, a wandering fancy wandered through the mind of the prisoner leaning against the wall opposite to him, that this gaoler was so unwholesomely bloated, both in face and person, as to look like a man who had been drowned and filled with water. When the gaoler was gone, he thought in the same wandering way, "Now am I left, as if I were dead." Stopping then, to look down at the mattress, he turned from it with a sick feeling, and
25   thought, "And here in these crawling creatures is the first condition of the body after death."

"Five paces by four and a half, five paces by four and half, five paces by four and a half." The prisoner walked to and fro in his cell, counting its measurement, and the roar of the city arose like muffled drums with a wild swell of voices added to them. "He made shoes, he made shoes, he made shoes." The prisoner counted the measurement again, and paced faster, to draw his mind with him from that latter repetition. "The ghosts that vanished when the wicket closed. There was one among them, the appearance of a lady
35   dressed in black, who was leaning in the embrasure of a window, and she had a light shining upon her golden hair, and she looked like . . . Let us ride on again, for God's sake, through the illuminated villages with the people all awake! . . . He made shoes, he made shoes, he made shoes. . . . Five paces by four and a half."

With such scraps tossing and rolling upward from the depths of his mind, the prisoner walked faster and faster, obstinately counting and counting; and the roar of the city changed to this extent—that it still rolled in like muffled drums, but with the wail of voices that he knew, in the swell that rose above them.

5

Chapter 2. The Grindstone

Tellson's bank, established in the Saint Germain Quarter of Paris, was in a wing of a large house, approached by a courtyard and shut off from the street by a high wall and a strong gate. The house belonged to a great nobleman who had lived in it until he made a flight from the troubles, in his own cook's dress, and got across the borders. A mere beast of the chase flying from hunters, he was still in his metempsychosis no other than the same Monseigneur, the preparation of whose chocolate for whose lips had once occupied three strong men besides the cook in question.

Monseigneur gone, and the three strong men absolving them- 15 selves from the sin of having drawn his high wages, by being more than ready and willing to cut his throat on the altar of the dawning Republic One and Indivisible of Liberty, Equality, Fraternity, or Death, Monseigneur's house had been first sequestrated, and then confiscated. For, all things moved so fast, and decree followed decree with that fierce precipitation, that now upon the third night of the autumn month of September, patriot emissaries of the law were in possession of Monseigneur's house, and had marked it with the tricolour, and were drinking brandy in its state apartments.

A place of business in London like Tellson's place of business in 25 Paris would soon have driven the House out of its mind and into the Gazette. For, what would staid British responsibility and respectability have said to orange-trees in boxes in a bank courtyard, and even to a Cupid over the counter? Yet such things were. Tellson's had whitewashed the Cupid, but he was still to be seen on the ceiling, in the coolest linen, aiming (as he very often does) at money from morning to night. Bankruptcy must inevitably have come of this young pagan, in Lombard Street, London, and also of

a curtained alcove in the rear of the immortal boy, and also of a
looking-glass let into the wall, and also of clerks not at all old, who
danced in public on the slightest provocation. Yet, a French
Tellson's could get on with these things exceedingly well, and, as
long as the times held together, no man had taken fright at them,
and drawn out his money.

What money would be drawn out of Tellson's henceforth, and
what would lie there, lost and forgotten; what plate and jewels
would tarnish in Tellson's hiding-places, while the depositors rusted
in prisons, and when they should have violently perished; how
many accounts with Tellson's, never to be balanced in this world,
must be carried over into the next; no man could have said, that
night, any more than Mr. Jarvis Lorry could, though he thought
heavily of these questions. He sat by a newly lighted wood fire (the
blighted and unfruitful year was prematurely cold), and on his
honest and courageous face there was a deeper shade than the
pendent lamp could throw, or any object in the room distortedly
reflect—a shade of horror.

He occupied rooms in the Bank, in his fidelity to the House of
which he had grown to be a part, like strong root-ivy. It chanced
that they derived a kind of security from the patriotic occupation of
the main building, but the true-hearted old gentleman never
calculated about that. All such circumstances were indifferent to
him, so that he did his duty. On the opposite side of the courtyard,
under a colonnade, was extensive standing for carriages—where,
indeed, some carriages of Monseigneur yet stood. Against two of
the pillars were fastened two great flaring flambeaux, and in the
light of these, standing out in the open air, was a large grindstone: a
roughly mounted thing which appeared to have hurriedly been
brought there from some neighbouring smithy, or other workshop.
Rising and looking out of window at these harmless objects, Mr.
Lorry shivered, and retired to his seat by the fire. He had opened
not only the glass window, but the lattice blind outside it, and he
had closed both again, and he shivered through his frame.

From the streets beyond the high wall and the strong gate there
came the usual night hum of the city, with now and then an
indescribable ring to it, weird and unearthly, as if some unwonted
sounds of a terrible nature were going up to Heaven.

"Thank God," said Mr. Lorry, clasping his hands, "that no one near and dear to me is in this dreadful town to-night. May He have mercy on all who are in danger!"

Soon afterwards, the bell at the great gate sounded, and he thought, "They have come back!" and sat listening. But, there was no loud irruption into the courtyard, as he had expected, and he heard the gate clash again, and all was quiet.

The nervousness and dread that were upon him inspired that vague uneasiness respecting the Bank which a great change would naturally awaken, with such feelings roused. It was well guarded, and he got up to go among the trusty people who were watching it, when his door suddenly opened, and two figures rushed in, at sight of which he fell back in amazement.

Lucie and her father! Lucie with her arms stretched out to him, and with that old look of earnestness so concentrated and intensified, that it seemed as though it had been stamped upon her face expressly to give force and power to it in this one passage of her life.

"What is this?" cried Mr. Lorry, breathless and confused. "What is the matter? Lucie! Manette! What has happened? What has brought you here? What is it?"

With the look fixed upon him, in her paleness and wildness, she panted out in his arms, imploringly, "O my dear friend! My husband!"

"Your husband, Lucie?"

"Charles."

"What of Charles?"

"Here."

"Here, in Paris?"

"Has been here some days—three or four—I don't know how many—I can't collect my thoughts. An errand of generosity brought him here unknown to us; he was stopped at the barrier, and sent to prison."

The old man uttered an irrepressible cry. Almost at the same moment, the bell of the great gate rang again, and a loud noise of feet and voices came pouring into the courtyard.

"What is that noise?" said the Doctor, turning towards the window.

"Don't look!" cried Mr. Lorry. "Don't look out! Manette, for your life, don't touch the blind!"

The Doctor turned, with his hand upon the fastening of the

window, and said, with a cool bold smile:

"My dear friend, I have a charmed life in this city. I have been a Bastille prisoner. There is no patriot in Paris—in Paris? in France —who, knowing me to have been a prisoner in the Bastille, would touch me, except to overwhelm me with embraces, or carry me in triumph. My old pain has given me a power that has brought us through the barrier, and gained us news of Charles there, and brought us here. I knew it would be so; I knew I could help Charles out of all danger; I told Lucie so.—What is that noise?" His hand was again upon the window.

"Don't look!" cried Mr. Lorry, absolutely desperate. "No, Lucie, my dear, nor you!" He got his arm round her, and held her. "Don't be so terrified, my love. I solemnly swear to you that I know of no harm having happened to Charles; that I had no suspicion even of his being in this fatal place. What prison is he in?"

"La Force!"

"La Force! Lucie, my child, if ever you were brave and service-able in your life—and you were always both—you will compose yourself now, to do exactly as I bid you; for more depends upon it than you can think, or I can say. There is no help for you in any action on your part to-night; you cannot possibly stir out. I say this, because what I must bid you to do for Charles's sake is the hardest thing to do of all. You must instantly be obedient, still, and quiet. You must let me put you in a room at the back here. You must leave your father and me alone for two minutes, and as there are Life and Death in the world you must not delay."

"I will be submissive to you. I see in your face that you know I can do nothing else than this. I know you are true."

The old man kissed her, and hurried her into his room, and turned the key; then, came hurrying back to the Doctor, and opened the window and partly opened the blind, and put his hand upon the Doctor's arm, and looked out with him into the court-yard.

Looked out upon a throng of men and women:not enough in number, or near enough, to fill the courtyard: not more than forty or fifty in all. The people in possession of the house had let them in at the gate, and they had rushed in to work at the grindstone; it had evidently been set up there for their purpose, as in a convenient and retired spot.

But, such awful workers, and such awful work!

The grindstone had a double handle, and turning at it madly were two men, whose faces, as their long hair flapped back when the whirlings of the grindstone brought their faces up, were more horrible and cruel than the visages of the wildest savages in their most barbarous disguise. False eyebrows and false moustaches were stuck upon them, and their hideous countenances were all bloody and sweaty, and all awry with howling, and all staring and glaring with beastly excitement and want of sleep. As these ruffians turned and turned, their matted locks now flung forward over their eyes, now flung backward over their necks, some women held wine to their mouths that they might drink; and what with dropping blood, and what with dropping wine, and what with the stream of sparks struck out of the stone, all their wicked atmosphere seemed gore and fire. The eye could not detect one creature in the group free from the smear of blood. Shouldering one another to get next at the sharpening-stone were men stripped to the waist, with the stain all over their limbs and bodies; men in all sorts of rags, with the stain upon those rags; men devilishly set off with spoils of women's lace and silk and ribbon, with the stain dyeing those trifles through and through. Hatchets, knives, bayonets, swords, all brought to be sharpened, were all red with it. Some of the hacked swords were tied to the wrists of those who carried them, with strips of linen and fragments of dress: ligatures various in kind, but all deep of the one colour. And as the frantic wielders of these weapons snatched them from the stream of sparks and tore away into the streets, the same red hue was red in their frenzied eyes—eyes which any unbrutalised beholder would have given twenty years of life to petrify with a well-directed gun.

All this was seen in a moment, as the vision of a drowning man, or of any human creature at any very great pass, could see a world if it were there. They drew back from the window, and the Doctor looked for explanation in his friend's ashy face.

"They are," Mr. Lorry whispered the words, glancing fearfully round at the locked room, "murdering the prisoners. If you are sure of what you say; if you really have the power you think you have —as I believe you have—make yourself known to these devils, and get taken to La Force. It may be too late, I don't know, but let it not be a minute later!"

Doctor Manette pressed his hand, hastened bareheaded out of the room, and was in the courtyard when Mr. Lorry regained the blind.

His streaming white hair, his remarkable face, and the impetuous confidence of his manner, as he put the weapons aside like water, carried him in an instant to the heart of the concourse at the stone. For a few moments there was a pause, and a hurry, and a murmur, and the unintelligible sound of his voice; and then Mr. Lorry saw him, surrounded by all, and in the midst of a line of twenty men long, all linked shoulder to shoulder, and hand to shoulder, hurried out with cries of—"Live the Bastille prisoner! Help for the Bastille prisoner's kindred in La Force! Room for the Bastille prisoner in front there! Save the prisoner Evrémonde at La Force!" and a thousand answering shouts.

He closed the lattice again with a fluttering heart, closed the window and the curtain, hastened to Lucie, and told her that her father was assisted by the people, and gone in search of her husband. He found her child and Miss Pross with her; but it never occurred to him to be surprised by their appearance until a long time afterwards, when he sat watching them in such quiet as the night knew.

Lucie had, by that time, fallen into a stupor on the floor at his feet, clinging to his hand. Miss Pross had laid the child down on his own bed, and her head had gradually fallen on the pillow beside her pretty charge. O the long, long night, with the moans of the poor wife! And O the long, long night, with no return of her father and no tidings!

Twice more in the darkness the bell at the great gate sounded, and the irruption was repeated, and the grindstone whirled and spluttered. "What is it?" cried Lucie, affrighted. "Hush! The soldiers' swords are sharpened there," said Mr. Lorry. "The place is national property now, and used as a kind of armoury, my love."

Twice more in all; but, the last spell of work was feeble and fitful. Soon afterwards the day began to dawn, and he softly detached himself from the clasping hand, and cautiously looked out again. A man, so besmeared that he might have been a sorely wounded soldier creeping back to consciousness on a field of slain, was rising from the pavement by the side of the grindstone, and looking about him with a vacant air. Shortly, this worn-out murderer descried in the imperfect light one of the carriages of Monseigneur, and, staggering to that gorgeous vehicle, climbed in at the door, and shut himself up to take his rest on its dainty cushions.

The great grindstone, Earth, had turned when Mr. Lorry looked out again, and the sun was red on the courtyard. But, the lesser grindstone stood alone there in the calm morning air, with a red upon it that the sun had never given, and would never take away.

Chapter 3. The Shadow

One of the first considerations which arose in the business mind of Mr. Lorry when business hours came round, was this—that he had no right to imperil Tellson's by sheltering the wife of an emigrant prisoner under the Bank roof. His own possessions, safety, life, he would have hazarded for Lucie and her child, without a moment's demur; but the great trust he held was not his own, and as to that business charge he was a strict man of business.

At first, his mind reverted to Defarge, and he thought of finding out the wine-shop again and taking counsel with its master in reference to the safest dwelling-place in the distracted state of the city. But, the same consideration that suggested him, repudiated him; he lived in the most violent Quarter, and doubtless was influential there, and deep in its dangerous workings.

Noon coming, and the Doctor not returning, and every minute's delay tending to compromise Tellson's, Mr. Lorry advised with Lucie. She said that her father had spoken of hiring a lodging for a short term, in that Quarter, near the banking-house. As there was no business objection to this, and as he foresaw that even if it were all well with Charles, and he were to be released, he could not hope to leave the city, Mr. Lorry went out in quest of such a lodging, and found a suitable one, high up in a removed by-street where the closed blinds in all the other windows of a high melancholy square of buildings marked deserted homes.

To this lodging he at once removed Lucie and her child, and Miss Pross: giving them what comfort he could, and much more than he had himself. He left Jerry with them, as a figure to fill a doorway that would bear considerable knocking on the head, and returned to his own occupations. A disturbed and doleful mind he brought to bear upon them, and slowly and heavily the day lagged on with him.

5   It wore itself out, and wore him out with it, until the Bank closed. He was again alone in his room of the previous night, considering what to do next, when he heard a foot upon the stair. In a few moments, a man stood in his presence, who, with a keenly observant look at him, addressed him by his name.

"Your servant," said Mr. Lorry. "Do you know me?"

He was a strongly made man with dark curling hair, from forty-five to fifty years of age. For answer he repeated, without any change of emphasis, the words:

"Do you know me?"

15   "I have seen you somewhere."

"Perhaps at my wine-shop?"

Much interested and agitated, Mr. Lorry said: "You come from Doctor Manette?"

"Yes. I come from Doctor Manette."

"And what says he? What does he send me?"

Defarge gave into his anxious hand an open scrap of paper. It bore the words in the Doctor's writing:

"Charles is safe, but I cannot safely leave this place yet. I have obtained the favour that the bearer has a short note from Charles
25   to his wife. Let the bearer see his wife."

It was dated from La Force, within an hour.

"Will you accompany me," said Mr. Lorry, joyfully relieved after reading this note aloud, "to where his wife resides?"

"Yes," returned Defarge.

Scarcely noticing, as yet, in what a curiously reserved and mechanical way Defarge spoke, Mr. Lorry put on his hat and they went down into the courtyard. There, they found two women, one knitting.

"Madame Defarge, surely!" said Mr. Lorry, who had left her in
35   exactly the same attitude some seventeen years ago.

"It is she," observed her husband.

"Does madame go with us?" inquired Mr. Lorry, seeing that she moved as they moved.

"Yes. That she may be able to recognise the faces and know the persons. It is for their safety."

Beginning to be struck by Defarge's manner, Mr. Lorry looked dubiously at him, and led the way. Both the women followed; the second woman being The Vengeance.

They passed through the intervening streets as quickly as they might, ascended the staircase of the new domicile, were admitted by Jerry, and found Lucie weeping, alone. She was thrown into a transport by the tidings Mr. Lorry gave her of her husband, and clasped the hand that delivered his note—little thinking what it had been doing near him in the night, and might, but for a chance, have done to him.

DEAREST—Take courage. I am well, and your father has influence around me. You cannot answer this. Kiss our child for me.

That was all the writing. It was so much, however, to her who received it, that she turned from Defarge to his wife, and kissed one of the hands that knitted. It was a passionate, loving, thankful, womanly action, but the hand made no response—dropped cold and heavy, and took to its knitting again.

There was something in its touch that gave Lucie a check. She stopped in the act of putting the note in her bosom, and, with her hands yet at her neck, looked terrified at Madame Defarge. Madame Defarge met the lifted eyebrows and forehead with a cold, impassive stare.

"My dear," said Mr. Lorry, striking in to explain; "there are frequent risings in the streets; and, although it is not likely they will ever trouble you, Madame Defarge wishes to see those whom she has the power to protect at such times, to the end that she may know them—that she may identify them. I believe," said Mr. Lorry, rather halting in his reassuring words, as the stony manner of all the three impressed itself upon him more and more, "I state the case, Citizen Defarge?"

Defarge looked gloomily at his wife, and gave no other answer than a gruff sound of acquiescence.

"You had better, Lucie," said Mr. Lorry, doing all he could to propitiate, by tone and manner, "have the dear child here, and our good Pross. Our good Pross, Defarge, is an English lady, and knows no French."

The lady in question, whose rooted conviction that she was more than a match for any foreigner was not to be shaken by distress and danger, appeared with folded arms, and observed in English to The Vengeance, whom her eyes first encountered, "Well, I am sure. Boldface! I hope *you* are pretty well!" She also bestowed a British cough on Madame Defarge; but, neither of the two took much heed of her.

"Is that his child?" said Madame Defarge, stopping in her work for the first time, and pointing her knitting-needle at little Lucie as if it were the finger of Fate.

"Yes, madame," answered Mr. Lorry; "this is our poor prisoner's darling daughter, and only child."

The shadow attendant on Madame Defarge and her party seemed to fall so threatening and dark on the child, that her mother instinctively kneeled on the ground beside her, and held her to her breast. The shadow attendant on Madame Defarge and her party seemed then to fall, threatening and dark, on both the mother and the child.

"It is enough, my husband," said Madame Defarge. "I have seen them. We may go."

But, the suppressed manner had enough of menace in it—not visible and presented, but indistinct and withheld—to alarm Lucie into saying, as she laid her appealing hand on Madame Defarge's dress:

"You will be good to my poor husband. You will do him no harm. You will help me to see him if you can?"

"Your husband is not my business here," returned Madame Defarge, looking down at her with perfect composure. "It is the daughter of your father who is my business here."

"For my sake, then, be merciful to my husband. For my child's sake! She will put her hands together and pray you to be merciful. We are more afraid of you than of these others."

Madame Defarge received it as a compliment, and looked at her husband. Defarge, who had been uneasily biting his thumb-nail and looking at her, collected his face into a sterner expression.

"What is it that your husband says in that little letter?" asked Madame Defarge, with a lowering smile. "Influence; he says something touching influence?"

"That my father," said Lucie, hurriedly taking the paper from her breast, but with her alarmed eyes on her questioner and not on it, "has much influence around him."

"Surely it will release him!" said Madame Defarge. "Let it do so." 5

"As a wife and mother," cried Lucie, most earnestly, "I implore you to have pity on me and not to exercise any power that you possess against my innocent husband, but to use it in his behalf. O sister-woman, think of me. As a wife and mother!"

Madame Defarge looked, coldly as ever, at the suppliant, and said, turning to her friend The Vengeance:

"The wives and mothers we have been used to see, since we were as little as this child, and much less, have not been greatly considered? We have known *their* husbands and fathers laid in prison 15 and kept from them, often enough? All our lives, we have seen our sister-women suffer, in themselves and in their children, poverty, nakedness, hunger, thirst, sickness, misery, oppression and neglect of all kinds?"

"We have seen nothing else," returned The Vengeance.

"We have borne this a long time," said Madame Defarge, turning her eyes again upon Lucie. "Judge you! Is it likely that the trouble of one wife and mother would be much to us now?"

She resumed her knitting and went out. The Vengeance followed. Defarge went last, and closed the door.

"Courage, my dear Lucie," said Mr. Lorry, as he raised her. 25 "Courage, courage! So far all goes well with us—much, much better than it has of late gone with many poor souls. Cheer up, and have a thankful heart."

"I am not thankless, I hope, but that dreadful woman seems to throw a shadow on me and on all my hopes."

"Tut, tut!" said Mr. Lorry; "what is this despondency in the brave little breast? A shadow indeed! No substance in it, Lucie."

But the shadow of the manner of these Defarges was dark upon himself, for all that, and in his secret mind it troubled him greatly. 35

Doctor Manette did not return until the morning of the fourth day of his absence. So much of what had happened in that dreadful time as could be kept from the knowledge of Lucie was so well concealed from her, that not until long afterwards, when France and she were far apart, did she know that eleven hundred defenceless prisoners of both sexes and all ages had been killed by the populace; that four days and nights had been darkened by this deed of horror; and that the air around her had been tainted by the slain. She only knew that there had been an attack upon the prisons, that all political prisoners had been in danger, and that some had been dragged out by the crowd and murdered.

To Mr. Lorry, the Doctor communicated under an injunction of secrecy on which he had no need to dwell, that the crowd had taken him through a scene of carnage to the prison of La Force. That in the prison he had found a self-appointed tribunal sitting, before which the prisoners were brought singly, and by which they were rapidly ordered to be put forth to be massacred, or to be released, or (in a few cases) to be sent back to their cells. That presented by his conductors to this tribunal, he had announced himself by name and profession as having been for eighteen years a secret and unaccused prisoner in the Bastille; that one of the body so sitting in judgment had risen and identified him, and that this man was Defarge.

That hereupon he had ascertained, through the registers on the table, that his son-in-law was among the living prisoners, and had pleaded hard to the tribunal—of whom some members were asleep and some awake, some dirty with murder and some clean, some sober and some not—for his life and liberty. That in the first frantic greetings lavished on himself as a notable sufferer under the overthrown system, it had been accorded to him to have Charles Darnay brought before the lawless court, and examined. That he seemed on the point of being at once released, when the tide in his favour met with some unexplained check (not intelligible to the Doctor), which led to a few words of secret conference. That the

246

man sitting as president had then informed Doctor Manette that the prisoner must remain in custody, but should, for his sake, be held inviolate in safe custody. That immediately, on a signal, the prisoner was removed to the interior of the prison again; but, that he, the Doctor, had then so strongly pleaded for permission to 5 remain and assure himself that his son-in-law was, through no malice or mischance, delivered to the concourse whose murderous yells outside the gate had often drowned the proceedings, that he had obtained the permission, and had remained in that Hall of Blood until the danger was over.

The sights he had seen there, with brief snatches of food and sleep by intervals, shall remain untold. The mad joy over the prisoners who were saved had astounded him scarcely less than the mad ferocity against those who were cut to pieces. One prisoner there was, he said, who had been discharged into the street free, 15 but at whom a mistaken savage had thrust a pike as he passed out. Being besought to go to him and dress the wound, the Doctor had passed out at the same gate, and had found him in the arms of a company of Samaritans, who were seated on the bodies of their victims. With an inconsistency as monstrous as anything in this awful nightmare, they had helped the healer, and tended the wounded man with the gentlest solicitude—had made a litter for him and escorted him carefully from the spot—had then caught up their weapons and plunged anew into a butchery so dreadful, that the Doctor had covered his eyes with his hands, and swooned 25 away in the midst of it.

As Mr. Lorry received these confidences, and as he watched the face of his friend, now sixty-two years of age, a misgiving arose within him that such dread experiences would revive the old danger. But, he had never seen his friend in his present aspect: he had never at all known him in his present character. For the first time the Doctor felt, now, that his suffering was strength and power. For the first time he felt that in that sharp fire he had slowly forged the iron which could break the prison door of his daughter's husband, and deliver him. "It all tended to a good end, my 35 friend; it was not mere waste and ruin. As my beloved child was helpful in restoring me to myself, I will be helpful now in restoring the dearest part of herself to her; by the aid of Heaven I will do it!" Thus, Doctor Manette. And when Jarvis Lorry saw the

kindled eyes, the resolute face, the calm strong look and bearing of
the man whose life always seemed to him to have been stopped,
like a clock, for so many years, and then set going again with an
energy which had lain dormant during the cessation of its useful-
5 ness, he believed.

Greater things than the Doctor had at that time to contend with
would have yielded before his persevering purpose. While he kept
himself in his place, as a physician, whose business was with all
degrees of mankind, bond and free, rich and poor, bad and good,
he used his personal influence so wisely, that he was soon the
inspecting physician of three prisons, and among them of La Force.
He could now assure Lucie that her husband was no longer
confined alone, but was mixed with the general body of prisoners;
he saw her husband weekly, and brought sweet messages to her,
15 straight from his lips; sometimes her husband himself sent a letter
to her (though never by the Doctor's hand), but she was not
permitted to write to him: for, among the many wild suspicions of
plots in the prisons, the wildest of all pointed at emigrants who
were known to have made friends or permanent connections
abroad.

This new life of the Doctor's was an anxious life, no doubt; still,
the sagacious Mr. Lorry saw that there was a new sustaining pride
in it. Nothing unbecoming tinged the pride; it was a natural and
worthy one; but he observed it as a curiosity. The Doctor knew,
25 that up to that time, his imprisonment had been associated, in the
minds of his daughter and his friend, with his personal affliction,
deprivation, and weakness. Now that this was changed, and he
knew himself to be invested through that old trial with forces to
which they both looked for Charles's ultimate safety and deliver-
ance, he became so far exalted by the change, that he took the lead
and direction, and required them as the weak, to trust to him as the
strong. The preceding relative positions of himself and Lucie were
reversed, yet only as the liveliest gratitude and affection could
reverse them, for he could have had no pride but in rendering some
35 service to her who had rendered so much to him. "All curious to
see," thought Mr. Lorry, in his amiably shrewd way, "but all
natural and right; so, take the lead, my dear friend, and keep it; it
couldn't be in better hands."

But, though the Doctor tried hard, and never ceased trying, to
get Charles Darnay set at liberty, or at least to get him brought to

trial, the public current of the time set too strong and fast for him. The new era began; the king was tried, doomed, and beheaded; the Republic of Liberty, Equality, Fraternity, or Death, declared for victory or death against the world in arms; the black flag waved night and day from the great towers of Notre Dame; three hundred thousand men, summoned to rise against the tyrants of the earth, rose from all the varying soils of France, as if the dragon's teeth had been sown broadcast, and had yielded fruit equally on hill and plain, on rock, in gravel, and alluvial mud, under the bright sky of the South and under the clouds of the North, in fell and forest, in the vineyards and the olive-grounds and among the cropped grass and the stubble of the corn, along the fruitful banks of the broad rivers, and in the sand of the sea-shore. What private solicitude could rear itself against the deluge of the Year One of Liberty—the deluge rising from below, not falling from above, and with the windows of Heaven shut, not opened!

There was no pause, no pity, no peace, no interval of relenting rest, no measurement of time. Though days and nights circled as regularly as when time was young, and the evening and morning were the first day, other count of time there was none. Hold of it was lost in the raging fever of a nation, as it is in the fever of one patient. Now, breaking the unnatural silence of a whole city, the executioner showed the people the head of the king—and now, it seemed almost in the same breath, the head of his fair wife which had had eight weary months of imprisoned widowhood and misery, to turn it gray.

And yet, observing the strange law of contradiction which obtains in all such cases, the time was long, while it flamed by so fast. A revolutionary tribunal in the capital, and forty or fifty thousand revolutionary committees all over the land; a law of the Suspected, which struck away all security for liberty or life, and delivered over any good and innocent person to any bad and guilty one; prisons gorged with people who had committed no offence, and could obtain no hearing; these things became the established order and nature of appointed things, and seemed to be ancient usage before they were many weeks old. Above all, one hideous figure grew as familiar as if it had been before the general gaze from the foundations of the world—the figure of the sharp female called La Guillotine.

It was the popular theme for jests; it was the best cure for headache, it infallibly prevented the hair from turning gray, it imparted a peculiar delicacy to the complexion, it was the National Razor which shaved close: who kissed La Guillotine looked through the little window and sneezed into the sack. It was the sign of the regeneration of the human race. It superseded the Cross. Models of it were worn on breasts from which the Cross was discarded, and it was bowed down to and believed in where the Cross was denied.

It sheared off heads so many, that it and the ground it most polluted were a rotten red. It was taken to pieces, like a toy-puzzle for a young Devil, and was put together again when the occasion wanted it. It hushed the eloquent, struck down the powerful, abolished the beautiful and good. Twenty-two friends of high public mark, twenty-one living and one dead, it had lopped the heads off, in one morning, in as many minutes. The name of the strong man of Old Scripture had descended to the chief functionary who worked it; but, so armed, he was stronger than his namesake, and blinder, and tore away the gates of God's own Temple every day.

Among these terrors, and the brood belonging to them, the Doctor walked with a steady head: confident in his power, cautiously persistent in his end, never doubting that he would save Lucie's husband at last. Yet the current of the time swept by, so strong and deep, and carried the time away so fiercely, that Charles had lain in prison one year and three months when the Doctor was thus steady and confident. So much more wicked and distracted had the Revolution grown in that December month, that the rivers of the South were encumbered with the bodies of the violently drowned by night, and prisoners were shot in lines and squares under the southern wintry sun. Still, the Doctor walked among the terrors with a steady hand. No man better known than he, in Paris at that day; no man in a stranger situation. Silent, humane, indispensable in hospital and prison, using his art equally among assassins and victims, he was a man apart. In the exercise of his skill, the appearance and the story of the Bastille Captive removed him from all other men. He was not suspected or brought in question, any more than if he had indeed been recalled to life some eighteen years before, or were a Spirit moving among mortals.

Chapter 5. The Wood-Sawyer

One year and three months. During all that time Lucie was never sure, from hour to hour, but that the Guillotine would strike off her husband's head next day. Every day, through the stony streets, the tumbrils now jolted heavily, filled with Condemned. Lovely girls; bright women, brown-haired, black-haired, and gray; youths; 5 stalwart men and old; gentle born and peasant born; all red wine for La Guillotine, all daily brought into light from the dark cellars of the loathsome prisons, and carried to her through the streets to slake her devouring thirst. Liberty, equality, fraternity, or death—the last, much the easiest to bestow, O Guillotine!

If the suddenness of her calamity, and the whirling wheels of the time, had stunned the Doctor's daughter into awaiting the result in idle despair, it would but have been with her as it was with many. But, from the hour when she had taken the white head to her fresh young bosom in the garret of Saint Antoine, she had been true to 15 her duties. She was truest to them in the season of trial, as all the quietly loyal and good will always be.

As soon as they were established in their new residence, and her father had entered on the routine of his avocations, she arranged the little household as exactly as if her husband had been there. Everything had its appointed place and its appointed time. Little Lucie she taught as regularly as if they had all been united in their English home. The slight devices with which she cheated herself in the show of a belief that they would soon be reunited—the little preparations for his speedy return, the setting aside of his chair and 25 his books—these, and the solemn prayer at night for one dear prisoner especially, among the many unhappy souls in prison and the shadow of death—were almost the only outspoken reliefs of her heavy mind.

She did not greatly alter in appearance. The plain dark dresses, akin to mourning dresses, which she and her child wore, were as neat and as well attended to as the brighter clothes of happy days. She lost her colour, and the old and intent expression was a constant, not an occasional, thing; otherwise, she remained very pretty

251

and comely. Sometimes, at night on kissing her father, she would burst into the grief she had repressed all day, and would say that her sole reliance, under Heaven, was on him. He always resolutely answered: "Nothing can happen to him without my knowledge, and I know that I can save him, Lucie."

They had not made the round of their changed life many weeks, when her father said to her, on coming home one evening:

"My dear, there is an upper window in the prison, to which Charles can sometimes gain access at three in the afternoon. When he can get to it—which depends on many uncertainties and incidents—he might see you in the street, he thinks, if you stood in a certain place that I can show you. But you will not be able to see him, my poor child, and even if you could, it would be unsafe for you to make a sign of recognition."

"O show me the place, my father, and I will go there every day."

From that time, in all weathers, she waited there two hours. As the clock struck two, she was there, and at four she turned resignedly away. When it was not too wet or inclement for her child to be with her, they went together; at other times she was alone; but she never missed a single day.

It was the dark and dirty corner of a small winding street. The hovel of a cutter of wood into lengths for burning was the only house at that end; all else was wall. On the third day of her being there, he noticed her.

"Good day, citizeness."

"Good day, citizen."

This mode of address was now prescribed by decree. It had been established voluntarily some time ago, among the more thorough patriots; but, was now law for everybody.

"Walking here again, citizeness?"

"You see me, citizen!"

The wood-sawyer, who was a little man with a redundancy of gesture (he had once been a mender of roads), cast a glance at the prison, pointed at the prison, and putting his ten fingers before his face to represent bars, peeped through them jocosely.

"But it's not my business," said he. And went on sawing his wood.

Next day he was looking out for her, and accosted her the moment she appeared.

"What? Walking here again, citizeness?"

"Yes, citizen."

"Ah! A child too! Your mother, is it not, my little citizeness?"

"Do I say yes, Mamma?" whispered little Lucie, drawing close to her.

"Yes, dearest."

"Yes, citizen."

"Ah! But it's not my business. My work is my business. See my saw! I call it my Little Guillotine. La, la, la; La, la, la! And off his head comes!"

The billet fell as he spoke, and he threw it into a basket.

"I call myself the Samson of the firewood guillotine. See here again! Loo, loo, loo; Loo, loo, loo! And off *her* head comes! Now, a child. Tickle, tickle; Pickle, pickle! And off *its* head comes. All the family!"

Lucie shuddered as he threw two more billets into his basket, but it was impossible to be there while the wood-sawyer was at work, and not be in his sight. Thenceforth, to secure his good will, she always spoke to him first, and often gave him drink-money, which he readily received.

He was an inquisitive fellow, and sometimes when she had quite forgotten him in gazing at the prison roof and grates, and in lifting her heart up to her husband, she would come to herself to find him looking at her, with his knee on his bench and his saw stopped in its work. "But it's not my business!" he would generally say at those times, and would briskly fall to his sawing again.

In all weathers, in the snow and frost of winter, in the bitter winds of spring, in the hot sunshine of summer, in the rains of autumn, again in the snow and frost of winter, Lucie passed two hours of every day at this place; and every day on leaving it, she kissed the prison wall. Her husband saw her (so she learned from her father) it might be once in five or six times: it might be twice or thrice running: it might be, not for a week or a fortnight together. It was enough, that he could and did see her when the chances served, and on that possibility she would have waited out the day, seven days a week.

These occupations brought her round to the December month, wherein her father walked among the terrors with a steady head. On a lightly-snowing afternoon she arrived at the usual corner. It was a day of some wild rejoicing, and a festival. She had seen the houses, as she came along, decorated with little pikes, and with little red caps stuck upon them; also, with tricoloured ribbons; also, with the standard inscription (tricoloured letters were the favourite), Republic One and Indivisible. Liberty, Equality, Fraternity, or Death!

The miserable shop of the wood-sawyer was so small, that its whole surface furnished very indifferent space for this legend. He had got somebody to scrawl it up for him, however, who had squeezed Death in with most inappropriate difficulty. On his house-top he displayed pike and cap, as a good citizen must, and in a window he had stationed his saw inscribed as his "Little Sainte Guillotine"—for the great sharp female was by that time popularly canonised. His shop was shut and he was not there, which was a relief to Lucie, and left her quite alone.

But, he was not far off, for presently she heard a troubled movement and a shouting coming along, which filled her with fear. A moment afterwards, and a throng of people came pouring round the corner by the prison wall, in the midst of whom was the wood-sawyer hand in hand with The Vengeance. There could not be fewer than five hundred people, and they were dancing like five thousand demons. There was no other music than their own singing. They danced to the popular Revolution song, keeping a ferocious time that was like a gnashing of teeth in unison. Men and women danced together, women danced together, men danced together, as hazard had brought them together. At first, they were a mere storm of coarse red caps and coarse woollen rags; but, as they filled the place, and stopped to dance about Lucie, some ghastly apparition of a dance-figure gone raving mad arose among them. They advanced, retreated, struck at one another's hands, clutched at one another's heads, spun round alone, caught one another and spun round in pairs, until many of them dropped. While those were down, the rest linked hand in hand, and all spun round together: then the ring broke, and in separate rings of two and four they turned and turned until they all stopped at once, began again, struck, clutched, and tore, and then reversed the spin, and all spun round another way. Suddenly they stopped again, paused, struck out the time afresh, formed into lines the width of the public way, and, with their heads low down and their hands high up, swooped screaming off. No fight could have been half so terrible as this dance. It was so emphatically a fallen sport—a something once innocent, delivered over to all devilry—a healthy pastime changed into a means of angering the blood, bewildering the senses, and steeling the heart. Such grace as was visible in it made it the uglier, showing how warped and perverted all things good by nature were become. The maidenly bosom bared to this, the pretty almost-child's head thus distracted, the delicate foot mincing in this slough of blood and dirt, were types of the disjointed time.

This was the Carmagnole. As it passed, leaving Lucie frightened and bewildered in the doorway of the wood-sawyer's house, the feathery snow fell as quietly and lay as white and soft, as if it had never been.

"O my father!" for he stood before her when she lifted up the eyes she had momentarily darkened with her hand; "such a cruel, bad sight."

"I know, my dear, I know. I have seen it many times. Don't be frightened! Not one of them would harm you."

"I am not frightened for myself, my father. But when I think of my husband, and the mercies of these people—"

"We will set him above their mercies very soon. I left him climbing to the window, and I came to tell you. There is no one here to see. You may kiss your hand towards that highest shelving roof."

"I do so, Father, and I send him my soul with it."

"You cannot see him, my poor dear?"

"No, Father," said Lucie, yearning and weeping as she kissed her hand, "no."

A footstep in the snow. Madame Defarge. "I salute you, citizeness," from the Doctor. "I salute you, citizen." This in passing. Nothing more. Madame Defarge gone, like a shadow over the white road.

"Give me your arm, my love. Pass from here with an air of cheerfulness and courage, for his sake. That was well done"; they had left the spot; "it shall not be in vain. Charles is summoned for to-morrow."

"For to-morrow!"

"There is no time to lose. I am well prepared, but there are precautions to be taken, that could not be taken until he was actually summoned before the Tribunal. He has not received the notice yet, but I know that he will presently be summoned for to-morrow, and removed to the Conciergerie; I have timely information. You are not afraid?"

She could scarcely answer, "I trust in you."

"Do so, implicitly. Your suspense is nearly ended, my darling; he shall be restored to you within a few hours; I have encompassed him with every protection. I must see Lorry."

He stopped. There was a heavy lumbering of wheels within hearing. They both knew too well what it meant. One. Two. Three. Three tumbrils faring away with their dread loads over the hushing snow.

"I must see Lorry," the Doctor repeated, turning her another way.

The staunch old gentleman was still in his trust; had never left it. He and his books were in frequent requisition as to property confiscated and made national. What he could save for the owners, he saved. No better man living to hold fast by what Tellson's had in keeping, and to hold his peace.

A murky red and yellow sky, and a rising mist from the Seine, denoted the approach of darkness. It was almost dark when they arrived at the Bank. The stately residence of Monseigneur was altogether blighted and deserted. Above a heap of dust and ashes in the court ran the letters: National Property. Republic One and Indivisible. Liberty, Equality, Fraternity, or Death!

Who could that be with Mr. Lorry—the owner of the riding-coat upon the chair—who must not be seen? From whom, newly arrived, did he come out, agitated and surprised, to take his favourite in his arms? To whom did he appear to repeat her faltering words, when, raising his voice and turning his head towards the door of the room from which he had issued, he said: "Removed to the Conciergerie and summoned for to-morrow"?

Chapter 6. Triumph

The dread Tribunal of five judges, public prosecutor, and determined jury, sat every day. Their lists went forth every evening, and were read out by the gaolers of the various prisons to their prisoners. The standard gaoler-joke was, "Come out and listen to the evening paper, you inside there!"

"Charles Evrémonde, called Darnay!"

So at last began the evening paper at La Force.

When a name was called, its owner stepped apart into a spot reserved for those who were announced as being thus fatally recorded. Charles Evrémonde, called Darnay, had reason to know the usage; he had seen hundreds pass away so.

His bloated gaoler, who wore spectacles to read with, glanced over them to assure himself that he had taken his place, and went through the list, making a similar short pause at each name. There were twenty-three names, but only twenty were responded to; for one of the prisoners so summoned had died in gaol and been forgotten, and two had already been guillotined and forgotten. The list was read, in the vaulted chamber where Darnay had seen the associated prisoners on the night of his arrival. Every one of those had perished in the massacre; every human creature he had since cared for and parted with had died on the scaffold.

There were hurried words of farewell and kindness, but the parting was soon over. It was the incident of every day, and the society of La Force were engaged in the preparation of some games of forfeits and a little concert, for that evening. They crowded to the grates and shed tears there; but, twenty places in the projected entertainments had to be refilled, and the time was, at best, short to the lock-up hour, when the common rooms and corridors would be delivered over to the great dogs who kept watch there through the night. The prisoners were far from insensible or unfeeling; their ways arose out of a condition of the time. Similarly, though with a subtle difference, a species of fervour or intoxication, known, without doubt, to have led some persons to brave the guillotine unnecessarily, and to die by it, was not mere boastfulness, but a

wild infection of the wildly shaken public mind. In seasons of
pestilence, some of us will have a secret attraction to the disease—a
terrible passing inclination to die of it. And all of us have like
wonders hidden in our breasts, only needing circumstances to evoke
them.

The passage to the Conciergerie was short and dark; the night in
its vermin-haunted cells was long and cold. Next day, fifteen
prisoners were put to the bar before Charles Darnay's name was
called. All the fifteen were condemned, and the trials of the whole
occupied an hour and a half.

"Charles Evrémonde, called Darnay," was at length arraigned.

His judges sat upon the bench in feathered hats; but the rough
red cap and tricoloured cockade was the headdress otherwise
prevailing. Looking at the jury and the turbulent audience, he
might have thought that the usual order of things was reversed, and
that the felons were trying the honest men. The lowest, cruelest,
and worst populace of a city, never without its quantity of low,
cruel, and bad, were the directing spirits of the scene: noisily
commenting, applauding, disapproving, anticipating, and precipi-
tating the result, without a check. Of the men, the greater part
were armed in various ways; of the women, some wore knives,
some daggers, some ate and drank as they looked on, many knitted.
Among these last was one with a spare piece of knitting under her
arm as she worked. She was in a front row, by the side of a man
whom he had never seen since his arrival at Barrier, but whom
he directly remembered as Defarge. He noticed that she once or
twice whispered in his ear, and that she seemed to be his wife; but,
what he most noticed in the two figures was, that although they
were posted as close to himself as they could be, they never looked
towards him. They seemed to be waiting for something with a
dogged determination, and they looked at the jury, but at nothing
else. Under the President sat Doctor Manette, in his usual quiet
dress. As well as the prisoner could see, he and Mr. Lorry were the
only men there, unconnected with the Tribunal, who wore their
usual clothes, and had not assumed the coarse garb of the
Carmagnole.

Charles Evrémonde, called Darnay, was accused by the public
prosecutor as an emigrant, whose life was forfeit to the Republic,
under the decree which banished all emigrants on pain of Death. It

was nothing that the decree bore date since his return to France. There he was, and there was the decree; he had been taken in France, and his head was demanded.

"Take off his head!" cried the audience. "An enemy to the Republic!"

The President rang his bell to silence those cries, and asked the prisoner whether it was not true that he had lived many years in England?

Undoubtedly it was.

Was he not an emigrant then? What did he call himself?

Not an emigrant, he hoped, within the sense and spirit of the law.

Why not? the President desired to know.

Because he had voluntarily relinquished a title that was distasteful to him, and a station that was distasteful to him, and had left his country—he submitted before the word emigrant in the present acceptation by the tribunal was in use—to live by his own industry in England, rather than on the industry of the overladen people of France.

What proof had he of this?

He handed in the names of two witnesses: Théophile Gabelle, and Alexandre Manette.

But he had married in England? the President reminded him.

True, but not an English woman.

A citizeness of France?

Yes. By birth.

Her name and family?

"Lucie Manette, only daughter of Doctor Manette, the good physician who sits there."

This answer had a happy effect upon the audience. Cries in exaltation of the well-known good physician rent the hall. So capriciously were the people moved, that tears immediately rolled down several ferocious countenances which had been glaring at the prisoner a moment before, as if with impatience to pluck him out into the streets and kill him.

On these few steps of his dangerous way, Charles Darnay had set his foot according to Doctor Manette's reiterated instructions. The same cautious counsel directed every step that lay before him, and had prepared every inch of his road.

The President asked, why had he returned to France when he did, and not sooner?

He had not returned sooner, he replied, simply because he had no means of living in France, save those he had resigned; whereas, in England, he lived by giving instruction in the French language and literature. He had returned when he did, on the pressing and written entreaty of a French citizen, who represented that his life was endangered by his absence. He had come back, to save a citizen's life, and to bear his testimony, at whatever personal hazard, to the truth. Was that criminal in the eyes of the Republic?

The populace cried enthusiastically, "No!" and the President rang his bell to quiet them. Which it did not, for they continued to cry "No!" until they left off, of their own will.

The President required the name of that citizen? The accused explained that the citizen was his first witness. He also referred with confidence to the citizen's letter, which had been taken from him at the Barrier, but which he did not doubt would be found among the papers then before the President.

The Doctor had taken care that it should be there—had assured him that it would be there—and at this stage of the proceedings it was produced and read. Citizen Gabelle was called to confirm it, and did so. Citizen Gabelle hinted, with infinite delicacy and politeness, that in the pressure of business imposed on the Tribunal by the multitudes of enemies of the Republic with which it had to deal, he had been slightly overlooked in his prison of the Abbaye—in fact, had rather passed out of the Tribunal's patriotic remembrance—until three days ago; when he had been summoned before it, and had been set at liberty on the jury's declaring themselves satisfied that the accusation against him was answered, as to himself, by the surrender of the citizen Evrémonde, called Darnay.

Doctor Manette was next questioned. His high personal popularity, and the clearness of his answers, made a great impression; but, as he proceeded, as he showed that the accused was his first friend on his release from his long imprisonment; that the accused had remained in England, always faithful and devoted to his daughter and himself in their exile; that, so far from being in favour with the aristocrat government there, he had actually been tried for his life by it, as the foe of England and friend of the United States—as he brought these circumstances into view, with the greatest discretion and with the straightforward force of truth and earnestness, the jury and the populace became one. At last, when he appealed by name to Monsieur Lorry, an English gentleman then and there present, who, like himself, had been a witness on that English trial and could corroborate his account of it, the jury declared that they had heard enough, and that they were ready with their votes if the President were content to receive them.

At every vote (the jurymen voted aloud and individually), the populace set up a shout of applause. All the voices were in the prisoner's favour, and the President declared him free.

Then began one of those extraordinary scenes with which the populace sometimes gratified their fickleness, or their better impulses towards generosity and mercy, or which they regarded as some set-off against their swollen account of cruel rage. No man can decide now to which of these motives such extraordinary scenes were referable; it is probable, to a blending of all the three, with the second predominating. No sooner was the acquittal pronounced, than tears were shed as freely as blood at another time, and such fraternal embraces were bestowed upon the prisoner by as many of both sexes as could rush at him, that after his long and unwholesome confinement, he was in danger of fainting from exhaustion; none the less he knew very well that the very same people, carried by another current, would have rushed at him with the very same intensity, to rend him to pieces and strew him over the streets.

His removal, to make way for other accused persons who were to be tried, rescued him from these caresses for the moment. Five were to be tried together, next, as enemies of the Republic, forasmuch as they had not assisted it by word or deed. So quick was the Tribunal to compensate itself and the nation for a chance lost, that these five came down to him before he left the place, condemned to die within twenty-four hours. The first of them told him so, with the customary prison sign of Death—a raised finger—and they all added in words, "Long live the Republic!"

The five had had, it is true, no audience to lengthen their proceedings, for when he and Doctor Manette emerged from the gate, there was a great crowd about it, in which there seemed to be every face he had seen in court—except two, for which he looked in vain. On his coming out, the concourse made at him anew, weeping, embracing, and shouting, all by turns and all together, until the very tide of the river on the bank of which the mad scene was acted, seemed to run mad, like the people on the shore.

They put him into a great chair they had among them, and which they had taken either out of the court itself, or one of its rooms or passages. Over the chair they had thrown a red flag, and to the back of it they had bound a pike with a red cap on its top. In this car of triumph, not even the Doctor's entreaties could prevent his being carried to his home on men's shoulders, with a confused sea of red caps heaving about him, and casting up to sight from the stormy deep such wrecks of faces, that he more than once misdoubted his mind being in confusion, and that he was in the tumbril on his way to the Guillotine.

In wild dreamlike procession, embracing whom they met and pointing him out, they carried him on. Reddening the snowy streets with the prevailing Republican colour, in winding and tramping through them, as they had reddened them below the snow with a deeper dye, they carried him thus into the courtyard of the building where he lived. Her father had gone on before, to prepare her, and when her husband stood upon his feet, she dropped insensible in his arms.

As he held her to his heart and turned her beautiful head between his face and the brawling crowd, so that his tears and her lips might come together unseen, a few of the people fell to dancing. Instantly, all the rest fell to dancing, and the courtyard overflowed with the Carmagnole. Then, they elevated into the vacant chair a young woman from the crowd to be carried as the Goddess of Liberty, and then swelling and overflowing out into the adjacent streets, and along the river's bank, and over the bridge, the Carmagnole absorbed them every one and whirled them away.

After grasping the Doctor's hand, as he stood victorious and proud before him; after grasping the hand of Mr. Lorry, who came panting in breathless from his struggle against the waterspout of the Carmagnole; after kissing little Lucie, who was lifted up to clasp her arms round his neck; and after embracing the everzealous and faithful Pross who lifted her; he took his wife in his arms, and carried her up to their rooms.

"Lucie! My own! I am safe."

"O dearest Charles, let me thank God for this on my knees as I have prayed to Him."

They all reverently bowed their heads and hearts. When she was again in his arms, he said to her:

"And now speak to your father, dearest. No other man in all this France could have done what he has done for me." 5

She laid her head upon her father's breast, as she had lain his poor head on her own breast, long, long ago. He was happy in the return he had made her, he was recompensed for his suffering, he was proud of his strength. "You must not be weak, my darling," he remonstrated; "don't tremble so. I have saved him."

Chapter 7. A Knock at the Door

"I have saved him." It was not another of the dreams in which he had often come back; he was really here. And yet his wife trembled, and a vague but heavy fear was upon her.

All the air around was so thick and dark, the people were so 15
passionately revengeful and fitful, the innocent were so constantly put to death on vague suspicion and black malice, it was so impossible to forget that many as blameless as her husband, and as dear to others as he was to her, every day shared the fate from which he had been clutched, that her heart could not be as lightened of its load as she felt it ought to be. The shadows of the wintry afternoon were beginning to fall, and even now the dreadful carts were rolling through the streets. Her mind pursued them, looking for him among the condemned; and then she clung to his real presence and trembled more.

Her father, cheering her, showed a compassionate superiority to 25
this woman's weakness, which was wonderful to see. No garret, no shoemaking, no One Hundred and Five, North Tower, now! He had accomplished the task he had set himself, his promise was redeemed, he had saved Charles. Let them all lean upon him.

Their housekeeping was of a very frugal kind: not only because that was the safest way of life, involving the least offence to the people, but because they were not rich, and Charles, throughout his

imprisonment, had had to pay heavily for his bad food, and for his guard, and towards the living of the poorer prisoners. Partly on this account, and partly to avoid a domestic spy, they kept no servant; the citizen and citizeness who acted as porters at the courtyard gate
5   rendered them occasional service; and Jerry (almost wholly transferred to them by Mr. Lorry) had become their daily retainer, and had his bed there every night.

It was an ordinance of the Republic One and Indivisible of Liberty, Equality, Fraternity, or Death, that on the door or doorpost of every house, the name of every inmate must be legibly inscribed in letters of a certain size, at a certain convenient height from the ground. Mr. Jerry Cruncher's name, therefore, duly embellished the doorpost down below; and, as the afternoon shadows deepened, the owner of that name himself appeared, from over-
15   looking a painter whom Doctor Manette had employed to add to the list the name of Charles Evrémonde, called Darnay.

In the universal fear and distrust that darkened the time, all the usual harmless ways of life were changed. In the Doctor's little household, as in very many others, the articles of daily consumption that were wanted were purchased every evening, in small quantities and at various small shops. To avoid attracting notice, and to give as little occasion as possible for talk and envy, was the general desire.

For some months past, Miss Pross and Mr. Cruncher had discharged the office of purveyors; the former carrying the money;
25   the latter, the basket. Every afternoon at about the time when the public lamps were lighted, they fared forth on this duty, and made and brought home such purchases as were needful. Although Miss Pross, through her long association with a French family, might have known as much of their language as of her own, if she had had a mind, she had no mind in that direction; consequently, she knew no more of that "nonsense" (as she was pleased to call it) than Mr. Cruncher did. So her manner of marketing was to plump a noun-substantive at the head of a shopkeeper without any introduction in the nature of an article, and, if it happened not to
35   be the name of the thing she wanted, to look round for that thing, lay hold of it, and hold on by it until the bargain was concluded. She always made a bargain for it, by holding up, as a statement of its just price, one finger less than the merchant held up, whatever his number might be.

"Now, Mr. Cruncher," said Miss Pross, whose eyes were red with felicity; "if you are ready, I am."

Jerry hoarsely professed himself at Miss Pross's service. He had worn all his rust off long ago, but nothing would file his spiky head down.

"There's all manner of things wanted," said Miss Pross, "and we shall have a precious time of it. We want wine, among the rest. Nice toasts these red heads will be drinking, wherever we buy it."

"It will be much the same to your knowledge, miss, I should think," retorted Jerry, "whether they drink your health or the Old Un's."

"Who's he?" said Miss Pross.

Mr. Cruncher, with some diffidence, explained himself as meaning "Old Nick's."

"Ha!" said Miss Pross, "it doesn't need an interpreter to explain the meaning of these creatures. They have but one, and it's Midnight Murder, and Mischief!"

"Hush, dear! Pray, pray, be cautious!" cried Lucie.

"Yes, yes, yes, I'll be cautious," said Miss Pross; "but I may say among ourselves, that I do hope there will be no oniony and tobaccoey smotherings in the form of embracings all round, going on in the streets. Now, Ladybird, never you stir from that fire till I come back! Take care of the dear husband you have recovered, and don't move your pretty head from his shoulders as you have it now, till you see me again! May I ask a question, Doctor Manette, before I go?"

"I think you may take that liberty," the Doctor answered, smiling.

"For gracious' sake, don't talk about liberty; we have quite enough of that," said Miss Pross.

"Hush, dear! Again?" Lucie remonstrated.

"Well, my sweet," said Miss Pross, nodding her head emphatically, "the short and the long of it is, that I am a subject of His Most Gracious Majesty King George the Third." Miss Pross curtsied at the name. "And as such, my maxim is, Confound their politics, Frustrate their knavish tricks, On him our hopes we fix, God save the King!"

Mr. Cruncher, in an access of loyalty, growlingly repeated the words after Miss Pross, like somebody at church.

"I am glad you have so much of the Englishman in you, though I wish you had never taken that cold in your voice," said Miss Pross, approvingly. "But the question, Doctor Manette. Is there"—it was the good creature's way to affect to make light of anything that was a great anxiety with them all, and to come at it in this chance manner—"is there any prospect, yet, of our getting out of this place?"

"I fear not yet. It would be dangerous for Charles yet."

"Heigh-ho-hum!" said Miss Pross, cheerfully repressing a sigh as she glanced at her darling's golden hair in the light of the fire, "then we must have patience and wait: that's all. We must hold up our heads and fight low, as my brother Solomon used to say. Now, Mr. Cruncher!—Don't you move, Ladybird!"

They went out, leaving Lucie, and her husband, her father, and the child, by a bright fire. Mr. Lorry was expected back presently from the banking house. Miss Pross had lighted the lamp, but had put it aside in a corner, that they might enjoy the firelight undisturbed. Little Lucie sat by her grandfather with her hands clasped through his arm: and he, in a tone not rising much above a whisper, began to tell her a story of a great and powerful fairy who had opened a prison-wall and let out a captive who had once done the fairy a service. All was subdued and quiet, and Lucie was more at ease than she had been.

"What is that?" she cried, all at once.

"My dear!" said her father, stopping in his story, and laying his hand on hers, "command yourself. What a disordered state you are in! The least thing—nothing—startles you! *You*, your father's daughter!"

"I thought, my father," said Lucie, excusing herself, with a pale face and in a faltering voice, "that I heard strange feet upon the stairs."

"My love, the staircase is as still as Death."

As he said the word, a blow was struck upon the door.

"Oh Father, Father. What can this be! Hide Charles. Save him!"

"My child," said the Doctor, rising, and laying his hand upon her shoulder, "I *have* saved him. What weakness is this, my dear! Let me go to the door."

He took the lamp in his hand, crossed the two intervening outer rooms, and opened it. A rude clattering of feet over the floor, and four rough men in red caps, armed with sabres and pistols, entered the room.

"The Citizen Evrémonde, called Darnay," said the first.

"Who seeks him?" answered Darnay.

"I seek him. We seek him. I know you, Evrémonde; I saw you before the Tribunal to-day. You are again the prisoner of the Republic."

The four surrounded him, where he stood with his wife and child clinging to him.

"Tell me how and why am I again a prisoner?"

"It is enough that you return straight to the Conciergerie, and will know to-morrow. You are summoned for to-morrow."

Doctor Manette, whom this visitation had so turned into stone, that he stood with the lamp in his hand, as if he were a statue made to hold it, moved after these words were spoken, put the lamp down, and confronting the speaker, and taking him, not ungently, by the loose front of his red woollen shirt, said:

"You know him, you have said. Do you know me?"

"Yes, I know you, Citizen Doctor."

"We all know you, Citizen Doctor," said the other three.

He looked abstractedly from one to another, and said, in a lower voice, after a pause:

"Will you answer his question to me then? How does this happen?"

"Citizen Doctor," said the first, reluctantly, "he has been denounced to the section of Saint Antoine. This citizen," pointing out the second who had entered, "is from Saint Antoine."

"He is accused by Saint Antoine."

"Of what?" asked the Doctor.

"Citizen Doctor," said the first, with his former reluctance, "ask no more. If the Republic demands sacrifices from you, without doubt you as a good patriot will be happy to make them. The Republic goes before all. The People is supreme. Evrémonde, we are pressed."

"One word," the Doctor entreated. "Will you tell me who denounced him?"

"It is against rule," answered the first; "but you can ask him of Saint Antoine here."

The Doctor turned his eyes upon that man, who moved uneasily on his feet, rubbed his beard a little, and at length said:

"Well! Truly it is against rule. But he is denounced—and gravely—by the Citizen and Citizeness Defarge. And by one other."

"What other?"

5   "Do *you* ask, Citizen Doctor?"

"Yes."

"Then," said he of Saint Antoine, with a strange look, "you will be answered to-morrow. Now, I am dumb!"

Chapter 8. A Hand at Cards

Happily unconscious of the new calamity at home, Miss Pross threaded her way along the narrow streets and crossed the river by the bridge of the Pont-Neuf, reckoning in her mind the number of indispensable purchases she had to make. Mr. Cruncher, with the basket, walked at her side. They both looked to the right and to the left into most of the shops they passed, had a wary eye for

15   all gregarious assemblages of people, and turned out of their road to avoid any very excited groups of talkers. It was a raw evening, and the misty river, blurred to the eye with blazing lights and to the ear with harsh noises, showed where the barges were stationed in which the smiths worked, making guns for the Army of the Republic. Woe to the man who played tricks with *that* Army, or got undeserved promotion in it! Better for him that his beard had never grown, for the National Razor shaved him close.

Having purchased a few small articles of grocery, and a measure of oil for the lamp, Miss Pross bethought herself of the wine they

25   wanted. After peeping into several wine-shops, she stopped at the sign of The Good Republican Brutus of Antiquity, not far from the National Palace, once (and twice) the Tuileries, where the aspect of things rather took her fancy. It had a quieter look than any other place of the same description they had passed, and, though red with patriotic caps, was not so red as the rest. Sounding Mr. Cruncher, and finding him of her opinion, Miss Pross resorted to The Good Republican Brutus of Antiquity, attended by her cavalier.

Slightly observant of the smoky lights; of the people, pipe in mouth, playing with limp cards and yellow dominoes; of the one bare-breasted, bare-armed, soot-begrimed workman reading a journal aloud, and of the others listening to him; of the weapons worn, or laid aside to be resumed; of the two or three customers fallen forward asleep, who in the popular high-shouldered shaggy black spencer looked, in that attitude, like slumbering bears or dogs; the two outlandish customers approached the counter, and showed what they wanted.

As their wine was measuring out, a man parted from another man in a corner, and rose to depart. In going, he had to face Miss Pross. No sooner did he face her, than Miss Pross uttered a scream, and clapped her hands.

In a moment, the whole company were on their feet. That somebody was assassinated by somebody vindicating a difference of opinion was the likeliest occurrence. Everybody looked to see somebody fall, but only saw a man and a woman standing staring at each other; the man with all the outward aspect of a Frenchman and a thorough Republican; the woman, evidently English.

What was said in this disappointing anti-climax, by the disciples of The Good Republican Brutus of Antiquity, except that it was something very voluble and loud, would have been as so much Hebrew or Chaldean to Miss Pross and her protector, though they had been all ears. But, they had no ears for anything in their surprise. For, it must be recorded, that not only was Miss Pross lost in amazement and agitation, but, Mr. Cruncher—though it seemed on his own separate and individual account—was in a state of the greatest wonder.

"What is the matter?" said the man who had caused Miss Pross to scream; speaking in a vexed, abrupt voice (though in a low tone), and in English.

"Oh, Solomon, dear Solomon!" cried Miss Pross, clapping her hands again. "After not setting eyes upon you or hearing of you for so long a time, do I find you here!"

"Don't call me Solomon. Do you want to be the death of me?" asked the man, in a furtive, frightened way.

"Brother, brother!" cried Miss Pross, bursting into tears. "Have I ever been so hard with you that you ask me such a cruel question?"

"Then hold your meddlesome tongue," said Solomon, "and

come out, if you want to speak to me. Pay for your wine, and come out. Who's this man?"

Miss Pross, shaking her loving and dejected head at her by no means affectionate brother, said through her tears, "Mr. Cruncher."

5 "Let him come out too," said Solomon. "Does he think me a ghost?"

Apparently, Mr. Cruncher did, to judge from his looks. He said not a word, however, and Miss Pross, exploring the depths of her reticule through her tears with great difficulty, paid for her wine. As she did so, Solomon turned to the followers of The Good Republican Brutus of Antiquity, and offered a few words of explanation in the French language, which caused them all to relapse into their former places and pursuits.

"Now," said Solomon, stopping at the dark street corner, "what 15 do you want?"

"How dreadfully unkind in a brother nothing has ever turned my love away from!" cried Miss Pross, "to give me such a greeting, and show me no affection."

"There. Con-found it! There," said Solomon, making a dab at Miss Pross's lips with his own. "Now are you content?"

Miss Pross only shook her head and wept in silence.

"If you expect me to be surprised," said her brother Solomon, "I am not surprised; I knew you were here; I know of most people who are here. If you really don't want to endanger my existence— 25 which I half believe you do—go your ways as soon as possible, and let me go mine. I am busy. I am an official."

"My English brother Solomon," mourned Miss Pross, casting up her tear-fraught eyes, "that had the makings in him of one of the best and greatest of men in his native country, an official among foreigners, and such foreigners! I would almost sooner have seen the dear boy lying in his—"

"I said so!" cried her brother, interrupting. "I knew it. You want to be the death of me. I shall be rendered Suspected by my own sister. Just as I am getting on!"

35 "The gracious and merciful Heavens forbid!" cried Miss Pross. "Far rather would I never see you again, dear Solomon, though I have ever loved you truly, and ever shall. Say but one affectionate word to me, and tell me there is nothing angry or estranged between us, and I will detain you no longer."

Good Miss Pross! As if the estrangement between them had come of any culpability of hers. As if Mr. Lorry had not known it for a fact, years ago, in the quiet corner in Soho, that this precious brother had spent her money and left her!

He was saying the affectionate word, however, with a far more grudging condescension and patronage than he could have shown if their relative merits and positions had been reversed (which is invariably the case, all the world over), when Mr. Cruncher, touching him on the shoulder, hoarsely and unexpectedly interposed with the following singular question:

"I say! Might I ask the favour? As to whether your name is John Solomon, or Solomon John?"

The official turned towards him with sudden distrust. He had not previously uttered a word.

"Come!" said Mr. Cruncher. "Speak out, you know." (Which, by the way, was more than he could do himself.) "John Solomon, or Solomon John? She calls you Solomon, and she must know, being your sister. And I know you're John, you know. Which of the two goes first? And regarding that name of Pross, likewise. That warn't your name over the water."

"What do you mean?"

"Well, I don't know all I mean, for I can't call to mind what your name was, over the water."

"No?"

"No. But I'll swear it was a name of two syllables."

"Indeed?"

"Yes. T'other one's was one syllable. I know you. You was a spy-witness at the Bailey. What, in the name of the Father of Lies, own father to yourself, was you called at that time?"

"Barsad," said another voice, striking in.

"That's the name for a thousand pound!" cried Jerry.

The speaker who struck in was Sydney Carton. He had his hands behind him under the skirts of his riding-coat, and he stood at Mr. Cruncher's elbow as negligently as he might have stood at the Old Bailey itself.

"Don't be alarmed, my dear Miss Pross. I arrived at Mr. Lorry's, to his surprise, yesterday evening; we agreed that I would not present myself elsewhere until all was well, or unless I could be useful; I present myself here, to beg a little talk with your brother. I wish you had a better employed brother than Mr. Barsad. I wish for your sake Mr. Barsad was not a sheep of the prisons."

Sheep was a cant word of the time for a spy, under the gaolers. The spy, who was pale, turned paler, and asked him how he dared—

"I'll tell you," said Sydney. "I lighted on you, Mr. Barsad, coming out of the prison of the Conciergerie while I was contemplating the walls, an hour or more ago. You have a face to be remembered, and I remember faces well. Made curious by seeing you in that connection, and having a reason, to which you are no stranger, for associating you with the misfortunes of a friend now very unfortunate, I walked in your direction. I walked into the wine-shop here, close after you, and sat near you. I had no difficulty in deducing from your unreserved conversation, and the rumour openly going about among your admirers, the nature of your calling. And gradually, what I had done at random seemed to shape itself into a purpose, Mr. Barsad."

"What purpose?" the spy asked.

"It would be troublesome, and might be dangerous, to explain in the street. Could you favour me, in confidence, with some minutes of your company—at the office of Tellson's Bank, for instance?"

"Under a threat?"

"Oh! Did I say that?"

"Then, why should I go there?"

"Really, Mr. Barsad, I can't say, if you can't."

"Do you mean that you won't say, sir?" the spy irresolutely asked.

"You apprehend me very clearly, Mr. Barsad. I won't."

Carton's negligent recklessness of manner came powerfully in aid of his quickness and skill, in such a business as he had in his secret mind, and with such a man as he had to do with. His practiced eye saw it, and made the most of it.

"Now, I told you so," said the spy, casting a reproachful look at his sister; "if any trouble comes of this, it's your doing."

"Come, come, Mr. Barsad!" exclaimed Sydney. "Don't be ungrateful. But for my great respect for your sister, I might not have led up so pleasantly to a little proposal that I wish to make for our mutual satisfaction. Do you go with me to the Bank?"

"I'll hear what you have got to say. Yes, I'll go with you."

"I propose that we first conduct your sister safely to the corner of her own street. Let me take your arm, Miss Pross. This is not a good city, at this time, for you to be out in, unprotected; and as your escort knows Mr. Barsad, I will invite him to Mr. Lorry's with us. Are we ready? Come then!"

Miss Pross recalled soon afterwards, and to the end of her life remembered, that as she pressed her hands on Sydney's arm and looked up in his face, imploring him to do no hurt to Solomon, there was a braced purpose in the arm and a kind of inspiration in the eyes, which not only contradicted his light manner, but changed and raised the man. She was too much occupied then with fears for the brother who so little deserved her affection, and with Sydney's friendly reassurances, adequately to heed what she observed.

They left her at the corner of the street, and Carton led the way to Mr. Lorry's, which was within a few minutes' walk. John Barsad, or Solomon Pross, walked at his side.

Mr. Lorry had just finished his dinner, and was sitting before a cheery little log or two of fire—perhaps looking into their blaze for the picture of that younger elderly gentleman from Tellson's, who had looked into the red coals at the Royal George at Dover, now a good many years ago. He turned his head as they entered, and showed the surprise with which he saw a stranger.

"Miss Pross's brother, sir," said Sydney. "Mr. Barsad."

"Barsad?" repeated the old gentleman. "Barsad? I have an association with the name—and with the face."

"I told you you had a remarkable face, Mr. Barsad," observed Carton, coolly. "Pray sit down."

As he took a chair himself, he supplied the link that Mr. Lorry wanted, by saying to him with a frown, "Witness at that trial." Mr. Lorry immediately remembered, and regarded his new visitor with an undisguised look of abhorrence.

"Mr. Barsad has been recognized by Miss Pross as the affectionate brother you have heard of," said Sydney, "and has acknowledged the relationship. I pass to worse news. Darnay has been arrested again."

Struck with consternation, the old gentleman exclaimed, "What do you tell me! I left him safe and free within these two hours, and am about to return to him!"

"Arrested for all that. When was it done, Mr. Barsad?"

"Just now, if at all."

"Mr. Barsad is the best authority possible, sir," said Sydney, "and
I have it from Mr. Barsad's communication to a friend and brother
sheep over a bottle of wine, that the arrest has taken place. He left
the messengers at the gate, and saw them admitted by the porter.
There is no earthly doubt that he is retaken."

Mr. Lorry's business eye read in the speaker's face that it was loss
of time to dwell upon the point. Confused, but sensible that
something might depend upon his presence of mind, he commanded himself, and was silently attentive.

"Now, I trust," said Sydney to him, "that the name and
influence of Doctor Manette may stand him in as good stead
to-morrow—you said he would be before the Tribunal to-morrow,
Mr. Barsad?—"

"Yes; I believe so."

"—In as good stead to-morrow as to-day. But it may not be so. I
own to you, I am shaken, Mr. Lorry, by Doctor Manette's not
having the power to prevent his arrest."

"He may not have known of it beforehand," said Mr. Lorry.

"But that very circumstance would be alarming, when we remember how identified he is with his son-in-law."

"That's true," Mr. Lorry acknowledged, with his troubled hand
at his chin, and his troubled eyes on Carton.

"In short," said Sydney, "this is a desperate time, when desperate
games are played for desperate stakes. Let the Doctor play the
winning game; I will play the losing one. No man's life here is
worth purchase. Any one carried home by the people to-day may be
condemned to-morrow. Now, the stake I have resolved to play for,
in case of the worst, is a friend in the Conciergerie. And the friend
I purpose to myself to win is Mr. Barsad."

"You need have good cards, sir," said the spy.

"I'll run them over. I'll see what I hold.—Mr. Lorry, you know
what a brute I am; I wish you'd give me a little brandy."

It was put before him, and he drank off a glassful—drank off
another glassful—pushed the bottle thoughtfully away.

"Mr. Barsad," he went on, in the tone of one who really was
looking over a hand at cards: "Sheep of the prisons, emissary of
Republican committees, now turnkey, now prisoner, always spy and
secret informer, so much the more valuable here for being English

that an Englishman is less open to suspicion of subornation in those characters than a Frenchman, represents himself to his employers under a false name. That's a very good card. Mr. Barsad, now in the employ of the republican French government, was formerly in the employ of the aristocratic English government, the enemy of France and freedom. That's an excellent card. Inference clear as day in this region of suspicion, that Mr. Barsad, still in the pay of the aristocratic English government, is the spy of Pitt, the treacherous foe of the Republic crouching in its bosom, the English traitor and agent of all mischief so much spoken of and so difficult to find. That's a card not to be beaten. Have you followed my hand, Mr. Barsad?"

"Not to understand your play," returned the spy, somewhat uneasily.

"I play my ace, denunciation of Mr. Barsad to the nearest Section Committee. Look over your hand, Mr. Barsad, and see what you have. Don't hurry."

He drew the bottle near, poured out another glassful of brandy, and drank it off. He saw that the spy was fearful of his drinking himself into a fit state for the immediate denunciation of him. Seeing it, he poured out and drank another glassful.

"Look over your hand carefully, Mr. Barsad. Take time."

It was a poorer hand than he suspected. Mr. Barsad saw losing cards in it that Sydney Carton knew nothing of. Thrown out of his honourable employment in England, through too much unsuccessful hard swearing there—not because he was wanted there: our English reasons for vaunting our superiority to secrecy and spies are of very modern date—he knew that he had crossed the Channel, and accepted service in France: first, as a tempter and an eavesdropper among his own countrymen there: gradually, as a tempter and an eavesdropper among the natives. He knew that under the overthrown government he had been a spy upon Saint Antoine and Defarge's wine-shop; had received from the watchful police such heads of information concerning Doctor Manette's imprisonment, release, and history, as should serve him for an introduction to familiar conversation with the Defarges; and tried them on Madame Defarge, and had broken down with them signally. He always remembered with fear and trembling that that terrible woman had knitted when he talked with her, and had looked ominously at him as her fingers moved. He had since seen her, in the Section of Saint Antoine, over and over again produce her knitted registers, and denounce people whose lives the guillotine then surely swallowed up. He knew, as every one employed as he was did, that he was never safe; that flight was impossible; that he was tied fast under the shadow of the axe; and that in spite of his utmost tergiversation and treachery in furtherance of the reigning terror, a word might bring it down upon him. Once denounced, and on such grave grounds as had just now been suggested to his mind, he foresaw that the dreadful woman of whose unrelenting character he had seen many proofs, would produce against him that fatal register, and would quash his last chance of life. Besides that all secret men are men soon terrified, here were surely cards enough of one black suit to justify the holder in growing rather livid as he turned them over.

"You scarcely seem to like your hand," said Sydney, with the greatest composure. "Do you play?"

"I think, sir," said the spy, in the meanest manner, as he turned to Mr. Lorry, "I may appeal to a gentleman of your years and benevolence to put it to this other gentleman, so much your junior, whether he can under any circumstances reconcile it to his station to play that ace of which he has spoken. I admit that I am a spy, and that it is considered a discreditable station—though it must be filled by somebody; but this gentleman is no spy, and why should he so demean himself as to make himself one?"

"I play my ace, Mr. Barsad," said Carton, taking the answer on himself, and looking at his watch, "without any scruple, in a very few minutes."

"I should have hoped, gentlemen both," said the spy, always striving to hook Mr. Lorry into the discussion, "that your respect for my sister—"

"I could not better testify my respect for your sister than by finally relieving her of her brother," said Sydney Carton.

"You think not, sir?"

"I have thoroughly made up my mind about it."

The smooth manner of the spy, curiously in dissonance with his ostentatiously rough dress, and probably with his usual demeanour, received such a check from the inscrutability of Carton—who was a mystery to wiser and honester men than he—that it faltered here and failed him. While he was at a loss, Carton said, resuming his former air of contemplating cards:

"And indeed, now I think again, I have a strong impression that I have another good card here, not yet enumerated. That friend and fellow-sheep, who spoke of himself as pasturing in the country prisons; who was he?"

"French. You don't know him," said the spy, quickly.

"French, eh?" repeated Carton, musing, and not appearing to notice him at all, though he echoed the word. "Well; he may be."

"Is, I assure you," said the spy; "though it's not important."

"Though it's not important," repeated Carton in the same mechanical way—"though it's not important—No, it's not important. No. Yet I know the face."

"I think not. I am sure not. It can't be," said the spy.

"It—can't—be," muttered Sydney Carton, retrospectively, and filling his glass (which fortunately was a small one) again. "Can't—be. Spoke good French. Yet like a foreigner, I thought?"

"Provincial," said the spy.

"No. Foreign!" cried Carton, striking his open hand on the table, as a light broke clearly on his mind. "Cly! Disguised, but the same man. We had that man before us at the Old Bailey."

"Now, there you are hasty, sir," said Barsad, with a smile that gave his aquiline nose an extra inclination to one side; "there you really give me an advantage over you. Cly (who I will unreservedly admit, at this distance of time, was a partner of mine) has been dead several years. I attended him in his last illness. He was buried in London, at the church of Saint Pancras-in-the-Fields. His unpopularity with the blackguard multitude at the moment prevented my following his remains, but I helped to lay him in his coffin."

Here Mr. Lorry became aware, from where he sat, of a most remarkable goblin shadow on the wall. Tracing it to its source, he discovered it to be caused by a sudden extraordinary rising and stiffening of all the risen and stiff hair on Mr. Cruncher's head.

"Let us be reasonable," said the spy, "and let us be fair. To show you how mistaken you are, and what an unfounded assumption yours is, I will lay before you a certificate of Cly's burial, which I happen to have carried in my pocket-book," with a hurried hand he produced and opened it, "ever since. There it is. Oh, look at it, look at it! You may take it in your hand; it's no forgery."

Here Mr. Lorry perceived the reflection on the wall to elongate, and Mr. Cruncher rose and stepped forward. His hair could not have been more violently on end, if it had been that moment dressed by the cow with the crumpled horn in the house that Jack built.

Unseen by the spy, Mr. Cruncher stood at his side, and touched him on the shoulder like a ghostly bailiff.

"That there Roger Cly, master," said Mr. Cruncher, with a taciturn and iron-bound visage. "So *you* put him in his coffin?"

"I did."

"Who took him out of it?"

Barsad leaned back in his chair, and stammered, "What do you mean?"

"I mean," said Mr. Cruncher, "that he warn't never in it. No! Not he! I'll have my head took off, if he was ever in it."

The spy looked round at the two gentlemen; they both looked in unspeakable astonishment at Jerry.

"I tell you," said Jerry, "that you buried paving-stones and earth in that there coffin. Don't go and tell *me* that you buried Cly. It was a take-in. Me and two more knows it."

"How do you know it?"

"What's that to you? Ecod!" growled Mr. Cruncher, "it's you I have got an old grudge agin, is it, with your shameful impositions upon tradesmen! I'd catch hold of your throat and choke you for half a guinea."

Sydney Carton, who, with Mr. Lorry, had been lost in amazement at this turn of the business, here requested Mr. Cruncher to moderate and explain himself.

"At another time, sir," he returned, evasively, "the present time is ill-conwenient for explainin'. What I stand to is, that he knows well wot that there Cly was never in that there coffin. Let him say he was, in so much as a word of one syllable, and I'll either catch hold of his throat and choke him for half a guinea"—Mr. Cruncher dwelt upon this as quite a liberal offer—"or I'll out and announce him."

"Humph! I see one thing," said Carton. "I hold another card, Mr. Barsad. Impossible, here in raging Paris, with Suspicion filling the air, for you to outlive denunciation, when you are in communication with another aristocratic spy of the same antecedents as yourself, who, moreover, has the mystery about him of having feigned death and come to life again! A plot in the prisons, of the foreigner against the Republic. A strong card—a certain Guillotine card! Do you play?"

"No!" returned the spy. "I throw up. I confess that we were so unpopular with the outrageous mob, that I only got away from England at the risk of being ducked to death, and that Cly was so ferreted up and down that he never would have got away at all but for that sham. Though how this man knows it was a sham is a wonder of wonders to me."

"Never you trouble your head about this man," retorted the contentious Mr. Cruncher; "you'll have trouble enough with giving your attention to that gentleman. And look here! Once more"—Mr. Cruncher could not be restrained from making rather an ostentatious parade of his liberality—"I'd catch hold of your throat and choke you for half a guinea."

The sheep of the prisons turned from him to Sydney Carton, and said, with more decision, "It has come to a point. I go on duty soon, and can't overstay my time. You told me you had a proposal; what is it? Now, it is of no use asking too much of me. Ask me to do anything in my office, putting my head in great extra danger, and I had better trust my life to the chances of a refusal than the chances of consent. In short, I should make that choice. You talk of desperation. We are all desperate here. Remember! I may denounce you if I think proper, and I can swear my way through stone walls, and so can others. Now, what do you want with me?"

"Not very much. You are a turnkey at the Conciergerie?"

"I tell you once for all, there is no such thing as an escape possible," said the spy, firmly.

"Why need you tell me what I have not asked? You are a turnkey at the Conciergerie?"

"I am sometimes."

"You can be when you choose?"

"I can pass in and out when I choose."

Sydney Carton filled another glass with brandy, poured it slowly out upon the hearth, and watched it as it dropped. It being all spent, he said, rising:

"So far, we have spoken before these two, because it was as well that the merits of the cards should not rest solely between you and me. Come into the dark room here, and let us have one final word alone."

Chapter 9. The Game Made

While Sydney Carton and the sheep of the prisons were in the adjoining dark room, speaking so low that not a sound was heard, Mr. Lorry looked at Jerry in considerable doubt and mistrust. That honest tradesman's manner of receiving the look did not inspire confidence; he changed the leg on which he rested, as often as if he had fifty of those limbs, and were trying them all; he examined his finger-nails with a very questionable closeness of attention; and whenever Mr. Lorry's eye caught his, he was taken with that peculiar kind of short cough requiring the hollow of a hand before it, which is seldom, if ever, known to be an infirmity attendant on perfect openness of character.

"Jerry," said Mr. Lorry. "Come here."

Mr. Cruncher came forward sideways, with one of his shoulders in advance of him.

"What have you been, besides a messenger?"

After some cogitation, accompanied with an intent look at his patron, Mr. Cruncher conceived the luminous idea of replying, "Agricultooral character."

"My mind misgives me much," said Mr. Lorry, angrily, shaking his forefinger at him, "that you have used the respectable and great house of Tellson's as a blind, and that you have had an unlawful occupation of an infamous description. If you have, don't expect me to befriend you when you get back to England. If you have, don't expect me to keep your secret. Tellson's shall not be imposed upon."

"I hope, sir," pleaded the abashed Mr. Cruncher, "that a gentleman like yourself wot I've had the honour of odd jobbing till I'm gray at it, would think twice about harming of me, even if it wos so—I don't say it is, but even if it wos. And which it is to be took into account that if it wos, it wouldn't, even then, be all o' one side. There'd be two sides to it. There might be medical doctors at the present hour, a picking up their guineas where a honest tradesman don't pick up his fardens—fardens! no, nor yet his half

280

fardens—half fardens! no, nor yet his quarter—a banking away like
smoke at Tellson's and a cocking their medical eyes at that
tradesman on the sly, a going in and going out to their own
carriages—ah! equally like smoke, if not more so. Well, that 'ud be
imposing, too, on Tellson's. For you cannot sarse the goose and not   5
the gander. And here's Mrs. Cruncher, or leastways wos in the Old
England times, and would be to-morrow, if cause given, a floppin'
again the business to that degree as is ruinating—stark ruinating!
Whereas them medical doctors' wives don't flop—catch 'em at it!
Or, if they flop, their floppings goes in favour of more patients, and
how can you rightly have one without t'other? Then, wot with
undertakers, and wot with parish clerks, and wot with sextons, and
wot with private watchmen (all awaricious and all in it), a man
wouldn't get much by it, even if it wos so. And wot little a man did
get, would never prosper with him, Mr. Lorry. He'd never have no   15
good of it; he'd want all along to be out of the line, if he could see
his way out, being once in—even if it wos so."

"Ugh!" cried Mr. Lorry, rather relenting, nevertheless. "I am
shocked at the sight of you."

"Now, what I would humbly offer to you, sir," pursued Mr.
Cruncher, "even if it wos so, which I don't say it is—"

"Don't prevaricate," said Mr. Lorry.

"No, I will *not*, sir," returned Mr. Cruncher, as if nothing were
further from his thought or practice—"which I don't say it is—wot
I would humbly offer to you, sir, would be this. Upon that there   25
stool, at that there bar, sets that there boy of mine, brought up and
growed up to be a man, wot will errand you, message you,
general-light-job you, till your heels is where your head is, if such
should be your wishes. If it wos so, which I still don't say it is (for I
will not prewaricate to you, sir), let that there boy keep his father's
place, and take care of his mother; don't blow upon that boy's
father—do not do it, sir—and let that father go into the line of the
reg'lar diggin', and make amends for what he would have un-dug—
if it wos so—by diggin' of 'em in with a will, and with conwictions
respectin' the futur' keepin' of 'em safe. That, Mr. Lorry," said Mr.   35
Cruncher, wiping his forehead with his arm, as an announcement
that he had arrived at the peroration of his discourse, "is wot I
would respectfully offer to you, sir. A man don't see all this here
goin' on dreadful round him, in the way of subjects without heads,

dear me, plentiful enough fur to bring the price down to porterage and hardly that, without havin' his serious thoughts of things. And these here would be mine, if it wos so, entreatin' of you fur to bear in mind that wot I said just now, I up and said in the good cause
5 when I might have kep' it back."

"That at least is true," said Mr. Lorry. "Say no more now. It may be that I shall yet stand your friend, if you deserve it, and repent in action—not in words. I want no more words."

Mr. Cruncher knuckled his forehead, as Sydney Carton and the spy returned from the dark room. "Adieu, Mr. Barsad," said the former; "our arrangement thus made, you have nothing to fear from me."

He sat down in a chair on the hearth, over against Mr. Lorry. When they were alone, Mr. Lorry asked him what he had done?
15 "Not much. If it should go ill with the prisoner, I have ensured access to him, once."

Mr. Lorry's countenance fell.

"It is all I could do," said Carton. "To propose too much would be to put this man's head under the axe, and, as he himself said, nothing worse could happen to him if he were denounced. It was obviously the weakness of the position. There is no help for it."

"But access to him," said Mr. Lorry, "if it should go ill before the Tribunal, will not save him."

"I never said it would."

25 Mr. Lorry's eyes gradually sought the fire; his sympathy with his darling, and the heavy disappointment of this second arrest, gradually weakened them; he was an old man now, overborne with anxiety of late, and his tears fell.

"You are a good man and a true friend," said Carton, in an altered voice. "Forgive me if I notice that you are affected. I could not see my father weep, and sit by, careless. And I could not respect your sorrow more, if you were my father. You are free from that misfortune, however."

Though he said the last words, with a slip into his usual manner,
35 there was a true feeling and respect both in his tone and in his touch, that Mr. Lorry, who had never seen the better side of him, was wholly unprepared for. He gave him his hand, and Carton gently pressed it.

"To return to poor Darnay," said Carton. "Don't tell *her* of this interview, or this arrangement. It would not enable *her* to go to see him. She might think it was contrived, in case of the worst, to convey to him the means of anticipating the sentence."

Mr. Lorry had not thought of that, and he looked quickly at Carton to see if it were in his mind. It seemed to be; he returned the look, and evidently understood it.

"She might think a thousand things," Carton said, "and any of them would only add to her trouble. Don't speak of me to her. As I said to you when I first came, I had better not see her. I can put my hand out, to do any little helpful work for her that my hand can find to do, without that. You are going to her, I hope? She must be very desolate to-night."

"I am going now, directly."

"I am glad of that. She has such a strong attachment to you and reliance on you. How does she look?"

"Anxious and unhappy, but very beautiful."

"Ah!"

It was a long, grieving sound, like a sigh—almost like a sob. It attracted Mr. Lorry's eyes to Carton's face, which was turned to the fire. A light, or a shade (the old gentleman could not have said which), passed from it as swiftly as a change would sweep over a hillside on a wild bright day, and he lifted his foot to put back one of the little flaming logs, which was tumbling forward. He wore the white riding-coat and top-boots then in vogue, and the light of the fire touching their light surfaces made him look very pale, with his long brown hair, all untrimmed, hanging loose about him. His indifference to fire was sufficiently remarkable to elicit a word of remonstrance from Mr. Lorry; his boot was still upon the hot embers of the flaming log, when it had broken under the weight of his foot.

"I forgot it," he said.

Mr. Lorry's eyes were again attracted to his face. Taking note of the wasted air which clouded the naturally handsome features, and having the expression of prisoners' faces fresh in his mind, he was strongly reminded of that expression.

"And your duties here have drawn to an end, sir?" said Carton, turning to him.

"Yes. As I was telling you last night when Lucie came in so unexpectedly, I have at length done all that I can do here. I hoped to have left them in perfect safety, and then to have quitted Paris. I have my Leave to Pass. I was ready to go."

They were both silent.

"Yours is a long life to look back upon, sir?" said Carton, wistfully.

"I am in my seventy-eighth year."

"You have been useful all your life; steadily and constantly occupied; trusted, respected, and looked up to?"

"I have been a man of business, ever since I have been a man. Indeed, I may say that I was a man of business when a boy."

"See what a place you fill at seventy-eight. How many people will miss you when you leave it empty!"

"A solitary old bachelor," answered Mr. Lorry, shaking his head. "There is nobody to weep for me."

"How can you say that? Wouldn't *she* weep for you? Wouldn't her child?"

"Yes, yes, thank God. I didn't quite mean what I said."

"It *is* a thing to thank God for; is it not?"

"Surely, surely."

"If you could say, with truth, to your own solitary heart, to-night, 'I have secured to myself the love and attachment, the gratitude or respect, of no human creature; I have won myself a tender place in no regard; I have done nothing good or serviceable to be remembered by'; your seventy-eight years would be seventy-eight heavy curses; would they not?"

"You say truly, Mr. Carton; I think they would be."

Sydney turned his eyes again upon the fire, and, after a silence of a few moments, said:

"I should like to ask you: Does your childhood seem far off? Do the days when you sat at your mother's knee seem days of very long ago?"

Responding to his softened manner, Mr. Lorry answered:

"Twenty years back, yes; at this time of my life, no. For, as I draw closer and closer to the end, I travel in the circle, nearer and nearer to the beginning. It seems to be one of the kind smoothings and preparings of the way. My heart is touched now, by many remembrances that had long fallen asleep, of my pretty young mother (and I so old!), and by many associations of the days when what we call the World was not so real with me, and my faults were not confirmed in me."

"I understand the feeling!" exclaimed Carton, with a bright flush. "And you are the better for it?"

"I hope so."

Carton terminated the conversation here, by rising to help him on with his outer coat. "But you," said Mr. Lorry, reverting to the theme, "you are young."

"Yes," said Carton. "I am not old, but my young way was never the way to age. Enough of me."

"And of me, I am sure," said Mr. Lorry. "Are you going out?"

"I'll walk with you to her gate. You know my vagabond and restless habits. If I should prowl about the streets a long time, don't be uneasy; I shall reappear in the morning. You go to the Court tomorrow?"

"Yes, unhappily."

"I shall be there, but only as one of the crowd. My spy will find a place for me. Take my arm, sir."

Mr. Lorry did so, and they went downstairs and out in the streets. A few minutes brought them to Mr. Lorry's destination. Carton left him there; but lingered at a little distance, and turned back to the gate again when it was shut, and touched it. He had heard of her going to the prison every day. "She came out here," he said, looking about him, "turned this way, must have trod on these stones often. Let me follow in her steps."

It was ten o'clock at night when he stood before the prison of La Force, where she had stood hundreds of times. A little wood-sawyer, having closed his shop, was smoking his pipe at his shop-door.

"Good night, citizen," said Sydney Carton, pausing in going by; for the man eyed him inquisitively.

"Good night, citizen."

"How goes the Republic?"

"You mean the Guillotine. Not ill. Sixty-three to-day. We shall mount to a hundred soon. Samson and his men complain sometimes, of being exhausted. Ha, ha, ha! He is so droll, that Samson. Such a barber!"

"Do you often go to see him—"

"Shave? Always. Every day. What a barber! You have seen him at work?"

"Never."

"Go and see him when he has a good batch. Figure this to yourself, citizen; he shaved the sixty-three to-day, in less than two pipes! Less than two pipes. Word of honour!"

As the grinning little man held out the pipe he was smoking, to explain how he timed the executioner, Carton was so sensible of a rising desire to strike the life out of him, that he turned away.

"But you are not English," said the wood-sawyer, "though you wear English dress?"

"Yes," said Carton, pausing again, and answering over his shoulder.

"You speak like a Frenchman."

"I am an old student here."

"Aha, a perfect Frenchman! Good night, Englishman."

"Good night, citizen."

15 "But go and see that droll dog," the little man persisted, calling after him. "And take a pipe with you!"

Sydney had not gone far out of sight, when he stopped in the middle of the street under a glimmering lamp, and wrote with his pencil on a scrap of paper. Then, traversing, with the decided step of one who remembered the way well, several dark and dirty streets—much dirtier than usual, for the best public thoroughfares remained uncleansed in those times of terror—he stopped at a chemist's shop, which the owner was closing with his own hands. A small, dim, crooked shop, kept in a tortuous, up-hill thoroughfare,

25 by a small, dim, crooked man.

Giving this citizen, too, good night, as he confronted him at his counter, he laid the scrap of paper before him. "Whew!" the chemist whistled softly, as he read it. "Hi! hi! hi!"

Sydney Carton took no heed, and the chemist said:

"For you, citizen?"

"For me."

"You will be careful to keep them separate, citizen? You know the consequences of mixing them?"

"Perfectly."

35 Certain small packets were made and given to him. He put them, one by one, in the breast of his inner coat, counted out the money for them, and deliberately left the shop. "There is nothing more to do," said he, glancing upward at the moon, "until to-morrow. I can't sleep."

It was not a reckless manner, the manner in which he said these words aloud under the fast-sailing clouds, nor was it more expressive of negligence than defiance. It was the settled manner of a tired man, who had wandered and struggled and got lost, but who at length struck into his road and saw its end.

Long ago, when he had been famous among his earliest competitors as a youth of great promise, he had followed his father to the grave. His mother had died, years before. These solemn words, which had been read at his father's grave, arose in his mind as he went down the dark streets, among the heavy shadows, with the moon and the clouds sailing on high above him. "I am the resurrection and the life, saith the Lord: he that believeth in me, though he were dead, yet shall he live: and whosoever liveth and believeth in me, shall never die."

In a city dominated by the axe, alone at night, with natural sorrow rising in him for the sixty-three who had been that day put to death, and for to-morrow's victims then awaiting their doom in the prisons, and still of to-morrow's and to-morrow's, the chain of association that brought the words home, like a rusty old ship's anchor from the deep, might have been easily found. He did not seek it, but repeated them and went on.

With a solemn interest in the lighted windows where the people were going to rest, forgetful through a few calm hours of the horrors surrounding them; in the towers of the churches, where no prayers were said, for the popular revulsion had even travelled that length of self-destruction from years of priestly impostors, plunderers, and profligates; in the distant burial-places, reserved, as they wrote upon the gates, for Eternal Sleep; in the abounding gaols; and in the streets along which the sixties rolled to a death which had become so common and material, that no sorrowful story of a haunting Spirit ever arose among the people out of all the working of the Guillotine; with a solemn interest in the whole life and death of the city settling down to its short nightly pause in fury; Sydney Carton crossed the Seine again for the lighted streets.

Few coaches were abroad, for riders in coaches were liable to be suspected, and gentility hid its head in red nightcaps, and put on heavy shoes, and trudged. But, the theatres were all well filled, and the people poured cheerfully out as he passed, and went chatting home. At one of the theatre doors, there was a little girl with a mother, looking for a way across the street through the mud. He carried the child over, and before the timid arm was loosed from his neck asked her for a kiss.

"I am the resurrection and the life, saith the Lord: he that believeth in me, though he were dead, yet shall he live: and whosoever liveth and believeth in me, shall never die."

Now that the streets were quiet, and the night wore on, the words were in the echoes of his feet, and were in the air. Perfectly calm and steady, he sometimes repeated them to himself as he walked; but he heard them always.

The night wore out, and, as he stood upon the bridge listening to the water as it splashed the river-walls of the Island of Paris, where the picturesque confusion of houses and cathedral shone bright in the light of the moon, the day came coldly, looking like a dead face out of the sky. Then, the night, with the moon and the stars, turned pale and died, and for a little while it seemed as if Creation were delivered over to Death's dominion.

But the glorious sun, rising, seemed to strike those words, that burden of the night, straight and warm to his heart in its long bright rays. And looking along them, with reverently shaded eyes, a bridge of light appeared to span the air between him and the sun, while the river sparkled under it.

The strong tide, so swift, so deep, and certain, was like a congenial friend in the morning stillness. He walked by the stream, far from the houses, and in the light and warmth of the sun fell asleep on the bank. When he awoke and was afoot again, he lingered there yet a little longer, watching an eddy that turned and turned purposeless, until the stream absorbed it, and carried it on to the sea.—"Like me!"

A trading-boat, with a sail of the softened colour of a dead leaf, then glided into his view, floated by him, and died away. As its silent track in the water disappeared, the prayer that had broken up out of his heart for a merciful consideration of all his poor blindness and errors, ended in the words, "I am the resurrection and the life."

Mr. Lorry was already out when he got back, and it was easy to surmise where the good old man was gone. Sydney Carton drank nothing but a little coffee, ate some bread, and, having washed and changed to refresh himself, went out to the place of trial.

The court was all astir and a-buzz, when the black sheep—whom many fell away from in dread—pressed him into an obscure corner among the crowd. Mr. Lorry was there, and Doctor Manette was there. She was there, sitting beside her father.

When her husband was brought in, she turned a look upon him, so sustaining, so encouraging, so full of admiring love and pitying tenderness, yet so courageous for his sake, that it called the healthy blood into his face, brightened his glance, and animated his heart. If there had been any eyes to notice the influence of her look on Sydney Carton, it would have been seen to be the same influence exactly.

Before that unjust Tribunal, there was little or no order of procedure, ensuring to any accused person any reasonable hearing. There could have been no such Revolution, if all laws, forms, and ceremonies had not first been so monstrously abused that the suicidal vengeance of the Revolution was to scatter them all to the winds.

Every eye was turned to the jury. The same determined patriots and good republicans as yesterday and the day before, and to-morrow and the day after. Eager and prominent among them, one man with a craving face, and his fingers perpetually hovering about his lips, whose appearance gave great satisfaction to the spectators. A life-thirsting, cannibal-looking, bloody-minded juryman, the Jacques Three of Saint Antoine. The whole jury, as a jury of dogs empanelled to try the deer.

Every eye then turned to the five judges and the public prosecutor. No favourable leaning in that quarter to-day. A fell uncompromising, murderous business-meaning there. Every eye then sought some other eye in the crowd, and gleamed at it approvingly; and heads nodded at one another, before bending forward with a strained attention.

Charles Evrémonde, called Darnay. Released yesterday. Re-accused and retaken yesterday. Indictment delivered to him last night. Suspected and denounced enemy of the Republic, aristocrat, one of a family of tyrants, one of a race proscribed, for that they had used their abolished privileges to the infamous oppression of the people. Charles Evrémonde, called Darnay, in right of such proscription absolutely dead in law.

To this effect, in as few or fewer words, the public prosecutor.

The President asked, was the accused openly denounced or secretly?

"Openly, President."

"By whom?"

"Three voices. Ernest Defarge, wine-vendor of Saint Antoine."

"Good."

"Thérèse Defarge, his wife."

"Good."

"Alexandre Manette, physician."

A great uproar took place in the court, and in the midst of it, Doctor Manette was seen, pale and trembling, standing where he had been seated.

"President, I indignantly protest to you that this is a forgery and a fraud. You know the accused to be the husband of my daughter. My daughter, and those dear to her, are far dearer to me than my life. Who and where is the false conspirator who says that I denounce the husband of my child!"

"Citizen Manette, be tranquil. To fail in submission to the authority of the Tribunal would be to put yourself out of law. As to what is dearer to you than life, nothing can be so dear to a good citizen as the Republic."

Loud acclamations hailed this rebuke. The President rang his bell, and with warmth resumed.

"If the Republic should demand of you the sacrifice of your child herself, you would have no duty but to sacrifice her. Listen to what is to follow. In the meanwhile, be silent!"

Frantic acclamations were again raised. Doctor Manette sat down, with his eyes looking around, and his lips trembling; his daughter drew closer to him. The craving man on the jury rubbed his hands together, and restored the usual hand to his mouth.

Defarge was produced, when the court was quiet enough to admit of his being heard, and rapidly expounded the story of the imprisonment, and of his having been a mere boy in the Doctor's service, and of the release, and of the state of the prisoner when released and delivered to him. This short examination followed, for the court was quick with its work.

"You did good service at the taking of the Bastille, citizen?"

"I believe so."

Here, an excited woman screeched from the crowd: "You were

one of the best patriots there. Why not say so? You were a cannonier that day there, and you were among the first to enter the accursed fortress when it fell. Patriots, I speak the truth!"

It was The Vengeance who, amidst the warm commendations of the audience, thus assisted the proceedings. The President rang his bell; but The Vengeance, warming with encouragement, shrieked, "I defy that bell!" wherein she was likewise much commended.

"Inform the Tribunal of what you did that day within the Bastille, citizen."

"I knew," said Defarge, looking down at his wife, who stood at the bottom of the steps on which he was raised, looking steadily up at him; "I knew that this prisoner, of whom I speak, had been confined in a cell known as One Hundred and Five, North Tower. I knew it from himself. He knew himself by no other name than One Hundred and Five, North Tower, when he made shoes under my care. As I serve my gun that day, I resolve, when the place shall fall, to examine that cell. It falls. I mount to the cell, with a fellow-citizen who is one of the jury, directed by a gaoler. I examine it, very closely. In a hole in the chimney, where a stone has been worked out and replaced, I find a written paper. This is that written paper. I have made it my business to examine some specimens of the writing of Doctor Manette. This is the writing of Doctor Manette. I confide this paper, in the writing of Doctor Manette, to the hands of the President."

"Let it be read."

In a dead silence and stillness—the prisoner under trial looked lovingly at his wife, his wife only looking from him to look with solicitude at her father, Doctor Manette keeping his eyes fixed on the reader, Madame Defarge never taking hers from the prisoner, Defarge never taking his from his feasting wife, and all the other eyes there intent upon the Doctor, who saw none of them—the paper was read, as follows.

Chapter 10. *The Substance of the Shadow*

"I, Alexandre Manette, unfortunate physician, native of Beauvais, and afterwards resident in Paris, write this melancholy paper in my doleful cell in the Bastille, during the last month of the year 1767. I write it at stolen intervals, under every difficulty. I design to secrete
5   it in the wall of the chimney, where I have slowly and laboriously made a place of concealment for it. Some pitying hand may find it there, when I and my sorrows are dust.

"These words are formed by the rusty iron point with which I write with difficulty in scrapings of soot and charcoal from the chimney, mixed with blood, in the last month of the tenth year of my captivity. Hope has quite departed from my breast. I know from terrible warnings I have noted in myself that my reason will not long remain unimpaired, but I solemnly declare that I am at this time in the possession of my right mind—that my memory is
15   exact and circumstantial—and that I write the truth as I shall answer for these my last recorded words, whether they be ever read by men or not, at the Eternal Judgment-seat.

"One cloudy moonlight night, in the third week of December (I think the twenty-second of the month) in the year 1757, I was walking on a retired part of the quay by the Seine for the refreshment of the frosty air, at an hour's distance from my place of residence in the Street of the School of Medicine, when a carriage came along behind me, driven very fast. As I stood aside to let that carriage pass, apprehensive that it might otherwise run me down, a
25   head was put out at the window, and a voice called to the driver to stop.

"The carriage stopped as soon as the driver could rein in his horse, and the same voice called to me by my name. I answered. The carriage was then so far in advance of me that the two gentlemen had time to open the door and alight before I came up with it. I observed that they were both wrapped in cloaks, and appeared to conceal themselves. As they stood side by side near the carriage door, I also observed that they both looked of about my own age, or rather younger, and that they were greatly alike, in stature, manner, voice, and (as far as I could see) face too.

"'You are Doctor Manette?' said one.

"'I am.'

"'Doctor Manette, formerly of Beauvais,' said the other; 'the young physician, originally an expert surgeon, who within the last year or two has made a rising reputation in Paris?'

"'Gentlemen,' I returned, 'I am that Doctor Manette of whom you speak so graciously.'

"'We have been to your residence,' said the first, 'and not being so fortunate as to find you there, and being informed that you were probably walking in this direction, we followed, in the hope of overtaking you. Will you please to enter the carriage?'

"The manner of both was imperious, and they both moved, as these words were spoken, so as to place me between themselves and the carriage door. They were armed. I was not.

"'Gentlemen,' said I, 'pardon me; but I usually inquire who does me the honour to seek my assistance, and what is the nature of the case to which I am summoned.'

"The reply to this was made by him who had spoken second. 'Doctor, your clients are people of condition. As to the nature of the case, our confidence in your skill assures us that you will ascertain it for yourself better than we can describe it. Enough. Will you please to enter the carriage?'

"I could do nothing but comply, and I entered it in silence. They both entered after me—the last springing in, after putting up the steps. The carriage turned about, and drove on at its former speed.

"I repeat this conversation exactly as it occurred. I have no doubt that it is, word for word, the same. I describe everything exactly as it took place, constraining my mind not to wander from the task. Where I make the broken marks that follow here, I leave off for the time, and put my paper in its hiding-place. . . .

"The carriage left the streets behind, passed the North Barrier, and emerged upon the country road. At two-thirds of a league from the Barrier—I did not estimate the distance at that time, but afterwards when I traversed it—it struck out of the main avenue, and presently stopped at a solitary house. We all three alighted, and walked, by a damp soft footpath in a garden where a neglected fountain had overflowed, to the door of the house. It was not opened immediately, in answer to the ringing of the bell, and one of my two conductors struck the man who opened it, with his heavy riding-glove, across the face.

"There was nothing in this action to attract my particular attention, for I had seen common people struck more commonly than dogs. But, the other of the two, being angry likewise, struck the man in like manner with his arm; the look and bearing of the brothers were then so exactly alike, that I then first perceived them to be twin brothers.

"From the time of our alighting at the outer gate (which we found locked, and which one of the brothers had opened to admit us, and had relocked), I had heard cries proceeding from an upper chamber. I was conducted to this chamber straight, the cries growing louder as we ascended the stairs, and I found a patient in a high fever of the brain, lying on a bed.

"The patient was a woman of great beauty, and young; assuredly not much past twenty. Her hair was torn and ragged, and her arms were bound to her sides with sashes and handkerchiefs. I noticed that these bonds were all portions of a gentleman's dress. On one of them, which was a fringed scarf for a dress of ceremony, I saw the armorial bearings of a noble, and the letter E.

"I saw this, within the first minute of my contemplation of the patient; for, in her restless strivings she had turned over on her face on the edge of the bed, had drawn the end of the scarf into her mouth, and was in danger of suffocation. My first act was to put out my hand to relieve her breathing; and in moving the scarf aside, the embroidery in the corner caught my sight.

"I turned her gently over, placed my hands upon her breast to calm her and keep her down, and looked into her face. Her eyes were dilated and wild, and she constantly uttered piercing shrieks, and repeated the words, 'My husband, my father, and my brother!' and then counted up to twelve, and said, 'Hush!' For an instant, and no more, she would pause to listen, and then the piercing shrieks would begin again, and she would repeat the cry, 'My husband, my father, and my brother!' and would count up to twelve, and say 'Hush!' There was no variation in the order, or the manner. There was no cessation, but the regular moment's pause, in the utterance of these sounds.

" 'How long,' I asked, 'has this lasted?'

"To distinguish the brothers, I will call them the elder and the

younger; by the elder, I mean him who exercised the most
authority. It was the elder who replied, 'Since about this hour last
night.'

" 'She has a husband, a father, and a brother?'

" 'A brother.'   5

" 'I do not address her brother?'

"He answered with great contempt, 'No.'

" 'She has some recent association with the number twelve?'

"The younger brother impatiently rejoined, 'With twelve
o'clock.'

" 'See, gentlemen,' said I, still keeping my hands upon her breast,
'how useless I am, as you have brought me! If I had known what I
was coming to see, I could have come provided. As it is, time must
be lost. There are no medicines to be obtained in this lonely place.'

"The elder brother looked to the younger, who said haughtily,   15
'There is a case of medicines here'; and brought it from a closet,
and put it on the table. . . .

"I opened some of the bottles, smelt them, and put the stoppers
to my lips. If I had wanted to use anything save narcotic medicines
that were poisons in themselves, I would not have administered any
of those.

" 'Do you doubt them?' asked the younger brother.

" 'You see, monsieur, I am going to use them,' I replied, and said
no more.

"I made the patient swallow, with great difficulty, and after many   25
efforts, the dose that I desired to give. As I intended to repeat it
after a while, and as it was necessary to watch its influence, I then
sat down by the side of the bed. There was a timid and suppressed
woman in attendance (wife of the man downstairs), who had
retreated into a corner. The house was damp and decayed,
indifferently furnished—evidently, recently occupied and tem-
porarily used. Some thick old hangings had been nailed up before
the windows, to deaden the sound of the shrieks. They continued
to be uttered in their regular succession, with the cry, 'My husband,
my father, and my brother!' the counting up to twelve, and 'Hush!'   35
The frenzy was so violent, that I had not unfastened the bandages
restraining the arms, but, I had looked to them, to see that they
were not painful. The only spark of encouragement in the case was,
that my hand upon the sufferer's breast had this much soothing

influence, that for minutes at a time it tranquillised the figure. It had no effect upon the cries: no pendulum could be more regular.

"For the reason that my hand had this effect (I assume), I had sat by the side of the bed for half an hour, with the two brothers looking on, before the elder said:

"'There is another patient.'

"I was startled and asked, 'Is it a pressing case?'

"'You had better see,' he carelessly answered; and took up a light. . . .

"The other patient lay in a back room across a second staircase, which was a species of loft over a stable. There was a low plastered ceiling to a part of it; the rest was open, to the ridge of the tiled roof, and there were beams across. Hay and straw were stored in that portion of the place, fagots for firing, and a heap of apples in sand. I had to pass through that part, to get at the other. My memory is circumstantial and unshaken. I try it with these details, and I see them all, in this my cell in the Bastille, near the close of the tenth year of my captivity, as I saw them all that night.

"On some hay on the ground, with a cushion thrown under his head, lay a handsome peasant boy—a boy of not more than seventeen at the most. He lay on his back, with his teeth set, his right hand clenched on his breast, and his glaring eyes looking straight upward. I could not see where his wound was, as I kneeled on one knee over him; but, I could see that he was dying of a wound from a sharp point.

"'I am a doctor, my poor fellow,' said I. 'Let me examine it.'

"'I do not want it examined,' he answered; 'let it be.'

"It was under his hand, and I soothed him to let me move his hand away. The wound was a sword-thrust, received from twenty to twenty-four hours before, but no skill could have saved him if it had been looked to without delay. He was then dying fast. As I turned my eyes to the elder brother, I saw him looking down at this handsome boy whose life was ebbing out, as if he were a wounded bird, or hare, or rabbit; not at all as if he were a fellow-creature.

"'How has this been done, monsieur?' said I.

"'A crazed young common dog! A serf! Forced my brother to draw upon him, and has fallen by my brother's sword—like a gentleman.'

"There was no touch of pity, sorrow, or kindred humanity in this answer. The speaker seemed to acknowledge that it was inconvenient to have that different order of creature dying there, and that it would have been better if he had died in the usual obscure routine of his vermin kind. He was quite incapable of any compassionate feeling about the boy, or about his fate.

"The boy's eyes had slowly moved to him as he had spoken, and they now slowly moved to me.

" 'Doctor, they are very proud, these nobles; but we common dogs are proud too, sometimes. They plunder us, outrage us, beat us, kill us; but we have a little pride left, sometimes. She—have you seen her, Doctor?'

"The shrieks and the cries were audible there, though subdued by the distance. He referred to them, as if she were lying in our presence.

"I said, 'I have seen her.'

" 'She is my sister, Doctor. They have had their shameful rights, these nobles, in the modesty and virtue of our sisters, many years, but we have had good girls among us. I know it, and have heard my father say so. She was a good girl. She was betrothed to a good young man, too; a tenant of his. We were all tenants of his—that man's who stands there. The other is his brother, the worst of a bad race.

"It was with the greatest difficulty that the boy gathered bodily force to speak; but, his spirit spoke with a dreadful emphasis.

" 'We were so robbed by that man who stands there, as all we common dogs are by those superior beings—taxed by him without mercy, obliged to work for him without pay, obliged to grind our corn at his mill, obliged to feed scores of his tame birds on our wretched crops, and forbidden for our lives to keep a single tame bird of our own, pillaged and plundered to that degree that when we chanced to have a bit of meat, we ate it in fear, with the door barred and the shutters closed, that his people should not see it and take it from us—I say, we were so robbed, and hunted, and were made so poor, that our father told us it was a dreadful thing to bring a child into the world, and that what we should most pray for was that our women might be barren and our miserable race die out!'

"I had never before seen the sense of being oppressed, bursting forth like a fire. I had supposed that it must be latent in the people

somewhere; but, I had never seen it break out, until I saw it in the
dying boy.

" 'Nevertheless, Doctor, my sister married. He was ailing at that
time, poor fellow, and she married her lover, that she might tend
5   and comfort him in our cottage—our dog-hut, as that man would
call it. She had not been married many weeks, when that man's
brother saw her and admired her, and asked that man to lend her to
him—for what are husbands among us! He was willing enough, but
my sister was good and virtuous, and hated his brother with a
hatred as strong as mine. What did the two then, to persuade her
husband to use his influence with her, to make her willing?'

"The boy's eyes, which had been fixed on mine, slowly turned to
the looker-on, and I saw in the two faces that all he said was true.
The two opposing kinds of pride confronting one another, I can
15   see, even in this Bastille; the gentleman's all negligent indifference;
the peasant's, all trodden-down sentiment, and passionate revenge.

" 'You know, Doctor, that it is among the rights of these nobles
to harness us common dogs to carts, and drive us. They so
harnessed him and drove him. You know that it is among their
rights to keep us in their grounds all night, quieting the frogs, in
order that their noble sleep may not be disturbed. They kept him
out in the unwholesome mists at night, and ordered him back into
his harness in the day. But he was not persuaded. No! Taken out of
harness one day at noon, to feed—if he could find food—he sobbed
25   twelve times, once for every stroke of the bell, and died on her
bosom.'

"Nothing human could have held life in the boy but his
determination to tell all his wrong. He forced back the gathering
shadows of death, as he forced his clenched right hand to remain
clenched, and to cover his wound.

" 'Then, with that man's permission and even with his aid, his
brother took her away; in spite of what I know she must have told
his brother—and what that is, will not be long unknown to you,
Doctor, if it is now—his brother took her away—for his pleasure
35   and diversion, for a little while. I saw her pass me on the road.
When I took the tidings home, our father's heart burst; he never
spoke one of the words that filled it. I took my young sister (for I
have another) to a place beyond the reach of this man, and where,
at least, she will never be *his* vassal. Then, I tracked the brother

here, and last night climbed in—a common dog, but sword in hand.—Where is the loft window? It was somewhere here?'

"The room was darkening to his sight; the world was narrowing around him. I glanced about me, and saw that the hay and straw were trampled over the floor, as if there had been a struggle.

" 'She heard me, and ran in. I told her not to come near us till he was dead. He came in and first tossed me some pieces of money; then struck at me with a whip. But I, though a common dog, so struck at him as to make him draw. Let him break into as many pieces as he will the sword that he stained with my common blood; he drew to defend himself—thrust at me with all his skill for his life.'

"My glance had fallen, but a few moments before, on the fragments of a broken sword, lying among the hay. That weapon was a gentleman's. In another place lay an old sword that seemed to have been a soldier's.

" 'Now, lift me up, Doctor; lift me up. Where is he?'

" 'He is not here,' I said, supporting the boy, and thinking that he referred to the brother.

" 'He! Proud as these nobles are, he is afraid to see me. Where is the man who was here? Turn my face to him.'

"I did so, raising the boy's head against my knee. But, invested for the moment with extraordinary power, he raised himself completely: obliging me to rise too, or I could not have still supported him.

" 'Marquis,' said the boy, turned to him with his eyes opened wide, and his right hand raised, 'in the days when all these things are to be answered for, I summon you and yours, to the last of your bad race, to answer for them. I mark this cross of blood upon you, as a sign that I do it. In the days when all these things are to be answered for, I summon your brother, the worst of the bad race, to answer for them separately. I mark this cross of blood upon him, as a sign that I do it.'

"Twice, he put his hand to the wound in his breast, and with his forefinger drew a cross in the air. He stood for an instant with the finger yet raised, and, as it dropped, he dropped with it, and I laid him down dead. . . .

"When I returned to the bedside of the young woman, I found her raving in precisely the same order and continuity. I knew that this might last for many hours, and that it would probably end in the silence of the grave.

"I repeated the medicines I had given her, and I sat at the side of the bed until the night was far advanced. She never abated the piercing quality of her shrieks, never stumbled in the distinctness or the order of her words. They were always 'My husband, my father, and my brother! One, two, three, four, five, six, seven, eight, nine, ten, eleven, twelve. Hush!'

"This lasted twenty-six hours from the time when I first saw her. I had come and gone twice, and was again sitting by her, when she began to falter. I did what little could be done to assist that opportunity, and by and by she sank into a lethargy, and lay like the dead.

"It was as if the wind and rain had lulled at last, after a long and fearful storm. I released her arms, and called the woman to assist me to compose her figure and the dress she had torn. It was then that I knew her condition to be that of one in whom the first expectations of being a mother have arisen; and it was then that I lost the little hope I had had of her.

" 'Is she dead?' asked the Marquis, whom I will still describe as the elder brother, coming booted into the room from his horse.

" 'Not dead,' said I; 'but like to die.'

" 'What strength there is in these common bodies!' he said, looking down at her with some curiosity.

" 'There is prodigious strength,' I answered him, 'in sorrow and despair.'

"He first laughed at my words, and then frowned at them. He moved a chair with his foot near to mine, ordered the woman away, and said in a subdued voice:

" 'Doctor, finding my brother in this difficulty with these hinds, I recommended that your aid should be invited. Your reputation is high, and, as a young man with your fortune to make, you are probably mindful of your interest. The things that you see here are things to be seen, and not spoken of.'

"I listened to the patient's breathing, and avoided answering.

" 'Do you honour me with your attention, Doctor?'

" 'Monsieur,' said I, 'in my profession, the communications of patients are always received in confidence.' I was guarded in my answer, for I was troubled in my mind with what I had heard and seen.

"Her breathing was so difficult to trace, that I carefully tried the pulse and the heart. There was life, and no more. Looking round as I resumed my seat, I found both the brothers intent upon me. . . .

"I write so with much difficulty, the cold is so severe, I am so fearful of being detected and consigned to an underground cell and total darkness, that I must abridge this narrative. There is no confusion or failure in my memory; it can recall, and could detail, every word that was ever spoken between me and those brothers.

"She lingered for a week. Towards the last, I could understand some few syllables that she said to me, by placing my ear close to her lips. She asked me where she was, and I told her; who I was, and I told her. It was in vain that I asked her for her family name. She faintly shook her head upon the pillow, and kept her secret, as the boy had done.

"I had no opportunity of asking her any question, until I had told the brothers she was sinking fast, and could not live another day. Until then, though no one was ever presented to her consciousness save the woman and myself, one or other of them had always jealously sat behind the curtain at the head of the bed when I was there. But when it came to that, they seemed careless what communication I might hold with her; as if—the thought passed through my mind—I were dying too.

"I always observed that their pride bitterly resented the younger brother's (as I call him) having crossed swords with a peasant, and that peasant a boy. The only consideration that appeared to affect the mind of either of them was the consideration that this was highly degrading to the family, and was ridiculous. As often as I caught the younger brother's eyes, their expression reminded me that he disliked me deeply, for knowing what I knew from the boy. He was smoother and more polite to me than the elder; but I saw this. I also saw that I was an encumbrance in the mind of the elder, too.

"My patient died, two hours before midnight—at a time, by my watch, answering almost to the minute when I had first seen her. I was alone with her, when her forlorn young head drooped gently on one side, and all her earthly wrongs and sorrows ended.

"The brothers were waiting in a room downstairs, impatient to ride away. I had heard them, alone at the bedside, striking their boots with their riding-whips, and loitering up and down.

" 'At last she is dead?' said the elder, when I went in.

" 'She is dead,' said I.

" 'I congratulate you, my brother,' were his words as he turned round.

"He had before offered me money, which I had postponed taking. He now gave me a rouleau of gold. I took it from his hand, but laid it on the table. I had considered the question, and had resolved to accept nothing.

" 'Pray excuse me,' said I. 'Under the circumstances, no.'

"They exchanged looks, but bent their heads to me as I bent mine to them, and we parted without another word on either side. . . .

"I am weary, weary, weary—worn down by misery. I cannot read what I have written with this gaunt hand.

"Early in the morning, the rouleau of gold was left at my door in a little box, with my name on the outside. From the first, I had anxiously considered what I ought to do. I decided, that day, to write privately to the Minister, stating the nature of the two cases to which I had been summoned, and the place to which I had gone: in effect, stating all the circumstances. I knew what Court influence was, and what the immunities of the nobles were, and I expected that the matter would never be heard of; but I wished to relieve my own mind. I had kept the matter a profound secret, even from my wife; and this, too, I resolved to state in my letter. I had no apprehension whatever of my real danger; but I was conscious that there might be danger for others, if others were compromised by possessing the knowledge that I possessed.

"I was much engaged that day, and could not complete my letter that night. I rose long before my usual time next morning to finish it. It was the last day of the year. The letter was lying before me just completed, when I was told that a lady waited, who wished to see me. . . .

"I am growing more and more unequal to the task I have set myself. It is so cold, so dark, my senses are so benumbed, and the gloom upon me is so dreadful.

"The lady was young, engaging, and handsome, but not marked for long life. She was in great agitation. She presented herself to me as the wife of the Marquis St. Evrémonde. I connected the title by which the boy had addressed the elder brother, with the initial letter embroidered on the scarf, and had no difficulty in arriving at the conclusion that I had seen that nobleman very lately.

"My memory is still accurate, but I cannot write the words of our conversation. I suspect that I am watched more closely than I was, and I know not at what times I may be watched. She had in part suspected, and in part discovered, the main facts of the cruel story, of her husband's share in it, and my being resorted to. She did not know that the girl was dead. Her hope had been, she said in great distress, to show her, in secret, a woman's sympathy. Her hope had been to avert the wrath of Heaven from a house that had long been hateful to the suffering many.

"She had reasons for believing that there was a young sister living, and her greatest desire was to help that sister. I could tell her nothing but that there was such a sister; beyond that, I knew nothing. Her inducement to come to me, relying on my confidence, had been the hope that I could tell her the name and place of abode. Whereas, to this wretched hour I am ignorant of both. . . .

"These scraps of paper fail me. One was taken from me, with a warning, yesterday. I must finish my record to-day.

"She was a good, compassionate lady, and not happy in her marriage. How could she be! The brother distrusted and disliked her, and his influence was all opposed to her; she stood in dread of him, and in dread of her husband too. When I handed her down to the door, there was a child, a pretty boy from two to three years old, in her carriage.

" 'For his sake, Doctor,' she said, pointing to him in tears, 'I would do all I can to make what poor amends I can. He will never prosper in his inheritance otherwise. I have a presentiment that if no other innocent atonement is made for this, it will one day be required of him. What I have left to call my own—it is little beyond the worth of a few jewels—I will make it the first charge of his life to bestow, with the compassion and lamenting of his dead mother, on this injured family, if the sister can be discovered.'

"She kissed the boy, and said, caressing him, 'It is for thine own dear sake. Thou wilt be faithful, little Charles?' The child answered her bravely, 'Yes!' I kissed her hand, and she took him in her arms, and went away caressing him. I never saw her more.

"As she had mentioned her husband's name in the faith that I knew it, I added no mention of it to my letter. I sealed my letter, and, not trusting it out of my own hands, delivered it myself that day.

"That night, the last night of the year, towards nine o'clock, a

man in a black dress rang at my gate, demanded to see me, and
softly followed my servant, Ernest Defarge, a youth upstairs. When
my servant came into the room where I sat with my wife—O my
wife, beloved of my heart! My fair young English wife!—we saw
the man, who was supposed to be at the gate, standing silent
behind him.

"An urgent case in the Rue St. Honoré, he said. It would not
detain me, he had a coach in waiting.

"It brought me here, it brought me to my grave. When I was
clear of the house, a black muffler was drawn tightly over my
mouth from behind, and my arms were pinioned. The two brothers
crossed the road from a dark corner, and identified me with a single
gesture. The Marquis took from his pocket the letter I had written,
showed it me, burnt it in the light of a lantern that was held, and
extinguished the ashes with his foot. Not a word was spoken. I was
brought here, I was brought to my living grave.

"If it had pleased God to put it in the hard heart of either of the
brothers, in all these frightful years, to grant me any tidings of my
dearest wife—so much as to let me know by a word whether alive
or dead—I might have thought that He had not quite abandoned
them. But, now I believe that the mark of the red cross is fatal to
them, and that they have no part in His mercies. And them and
their descendants, to the last of their race, I, Alexandre Manette,
unhappy prisoner, do this last night of the year 1767, in my
unbearable agony, denounce to the times when all these things
shall be answered for. I denounce them to Heaven and to earth."

A terrible sound arose when the reading of this document was
done. A sound of craving and eagerness that had nothing articulate
in it but blood. The narrative called up the most revengeful
passions of the time, and there was not a head in the nation but
must have dropped before it.

Little need, in presence of that tribunal and that auditory, to
show how the Defarges had not made the paper public, with the
other captured Bastille memorials borne in procession, and had
kept it, biding their time. Little need to show that this detested
family name had long been anathematised by Saint Antoine, and
was wrought into the fatal register. The man never trod ground
whose virtues and services would have sustained him in that place
that day, against such denunciation.

And all the worse for the doomed man, that the denouncer was a well-known citizen, his own attached friend, the father of his wife. One of the frenzied aspirations of the populace was for imitations of the questionable public virtues of antiquity, and for sacrifices and self-immolations on the people's altar. Therefore when the President said (else had his own head quivered on his shoulders) that the good physician of the Republic would deserve better still of the Republic by rooting out an obnoxious family of aristocrats, and would doubtless feel a sacred glow and joy in making his daughter a widow and her child an orphan, there was wild excitement, patriotic fervour, not a touch of human sympathy.

"Much influence around him, has that Doctor?" murmured Madame Defarge, smiling to The Vengeance. "Save him now, my Doctor, save him!"

At every juryman's vote, there was a roar. Another and another. Roar and roar.

Unanimously voted. At heart and by descent an aristocrat, an enemy of the Republic, a notorious oppressor of the People. Back to the Conciergerie, and Death within four-and-twenty hours!

Chapter 11. Dusk

The wretched wife of the innocent man thus doomed to die fell under the sentence, as if she had been mortally stricken. But, she uttered no sound; and so strong was the voice within her, representing that it was she of all the world who must uphold him in his misery and not augment it, that it quickly raised her, even from that shock.

The judges having to take part in a public demonstration out of doors, the Tribunal adjourned. The quick noise and movement of the court's emptying itself by many passages had not ceased, when Lucie stood stretching out her arms towards her husband, with nothing in her face but love and consolation.

"If I might touch him! If I might embrace him once! O, good citizens, if you would have so much compassion for us!"

There was but a gaoler left, along with two of the four men who

had taken him last night, and Barsad. The people had all poured
out to the show in the streets. Barsad proposed to the rest, "Let her
embrace him then; it is but a moment." It was silently acquiesced
in, and they passed her over the seats in the hall to a raised place,
5   where he, by leaning over the dock, could hold her in his arms.

"Farewell, dear darling of my soul. My parting blessing on my
love. We shall meet again, where the weary are at rest!"

They were her husband's words, as he held her to his bosom.

"I can bear it, dear Charles. I am supported from above: don't
suffer for me. A parting blessing for our child."

"I send it to her by you. I kiss her by you. I say farewell to her by
you."

"My husband. No! A moment!" He was tearing himself apart
from her. "We shall not be separated long. I feel that this will
15   break my heart by and by; but I will do my duty while I can, and
when I leave her, God will raise up friends for her, as He did for
me."

Her father had followed her, and would have fallen on his knees
to both of them, but that Darnay put out a hand and seized him,
crying:

"No, no! What have you done, what have you done, that you
should kneel to us! We know now what a struggle you made of old.
We know now what you underwent when you suspected my
descent, and when you knew it. We know now the natural
25   antipathy you strove against, and conquered, for her dear sake. We
thank you with all our hearts, and all our love and duty. Heaven be
with you!"

Her father's only answer was to draw his hands through his white
hair, and wring them with a shriek of anguish.

"It could not be otherwise," said the prisoner. "All things have
worked together as they have fallen out. It was the always-vain
endeavour to discharge my poor mother's trust that first brought
my fatal presence near you. Good could never come of such evil, a
happier end was not in nature to so unhappy a beginning. Be
35   comforted, and forgive me. Heaven bless you!"

As he was drawn away, his wife released him, and stood looking
after him with her hands touching one another in the attitude of
prayer, and with a radiant look upon her face, in which there was
even a comforting smile. As he went out at the prisoners' door, she

turned, laid her head lovingly on her father's breast, tried to speak to him, and fell at his feet.

Then, issuing from the obscure corner from which he had never moved, Sydney Carton came and took her up. Only her father and Mr. Lorry were with her. His arm trembled as it raised her, and supported her head. Yet, there was an air about him that was not all of pity—that had a flush of pride in it.

"Shall I take her to a coach? I shall never feel her weight."

He carried her lightly to the door, and laid her tenderly down in a coach. Her father and their old friend got into it, and he took his seat beside the driver.

When they arrived at the gateway where he had paused in the dark not many hours before, to picture to himself on which of the rough stones of the street her feet had trodden, he lifted her again, and carried her up the staircase to their rooms. There, he laid her down on a couch, where her child and Miss Pross wept over her.

"Don't recall her to herself," he said, softly, to the latter, "she is better so. Don't revive her to consciousness, while she only faints."

"Oh, Carton, Carton, dear Carton!" cried little Lucie, springing up and throwing her arms passionately round him, in a burst of grief. "Now that you have come, I think you will do something to help mamma, something to save papa! Oh, look at her, dear Carton! Can you, of all the people who love her, bear to see her so?"

He bent over the child, and laid her blooming cheek against his face. He put her gently from him, and looked at her unconscious mother.

"Before I go," he said, and paused—"I may kiss her?"

It was remembered afterwards that when he bent down and touched her face with his lips, he murmured some words. The child, who was nearest to him, told them afterwards, and told her grandchildren when she was a handsome old lady, that she heard him say, "A life you love."

When he had gone out into the next room, he turned suddenly on Mr. Lorry and her father, who were following, and said to the latter:

"You had great influence but yesterday, Doctor Manette; let it at least be tried. These judges, and all the men in power, are very friendly to you, and very recognisant of your services; are they not?"

"Nothing connected with Charles was concealed from me. I had the strongest assurances that I should save him; and I did." He returned the answer in great trouble, and very slowly.

"Try them again. The hours between this and to-morrow after-
5   noon are few and short, but try."

"I intend to try. I will not rest a moment."

"That's well. I have known such energy as yours do great things before now—though never," he added, with a smile and a sigh together, "such great things as this. But try! Of little worth as life is when we misuse it, it is worth that effort. It would cost nothing to lay down if it were not."

"I will go," said Doctor Manette, "to the Prosecutor and the President straight, and I will go to others whom it is better not to name. I will write too, and—But stay! There is a celebration in the
15   streets, and no one will be accessible until dark."

"That's true. Well! It is a forlorn hope at the best, and not much the forlorner for being delayed till dark. I should like to know how you speed; though, mind! I expect nothing! When are you likely to have seen these dread powers, Doctor Manette?"

"Immediately after dark, I should hope. Within an hour or two from this."

"It will be dark soon after four. Let us stretch the hour or two. If I go to Mr. Lorry's at nine, shall I hear what you have done, either from our friend or from yourself?"

25   "Yes."

"May you prosper!"

Mr. Lorry followed Sydney to the outer door, and, touching him on the shoulder as he was going away, caused him to turn.

"I have no hope," said Mr. Lorry, in a sorrowful whisper.

"Nor have I."

"If any one of these men, or all of these men, were disposed to spare him—which is a large supposition; for what is his life, or any man's to them!—I doubt if they durst spare him after the demonstration in the court."

35   "And so do I. I heard the fall of the axe in that sound."

Mr. Lorry leaned his arm upon the doorpost, and bowed his face upon it.

"Don't despond," said Carton, very gently; "don't grieve. I encouraged Doctor Manette in this idea, because I felt that it might one day be consolatory to her. Otherwise, she might think 'his life was wantonly thrown away or wasted,' and that might trouble her."

"Yes, yes, yes," returned Mr. Lorry, drying his eyes, "you are right. But he will perish; there is no real hope."

"Yes. He will perish; there is no real hope," echoed Carton. And walked with a settled step, downstairs.

Chapter 12. Darkness

Sydney Carton paused in the street, not quite decided where to go. "At Tellson's banking-house at nine," he said, with a musing face. "Shall I do well, in the meantime, to show myself? I think so. It is best that these people should know there is such a man as I here; it is a sound precaution, and may be a necessary preparation. But care, care, care! Let me think it out!"

Checking his steps, which had begun to tend towards an object, he took a turn or two in the already darkening street, and traced the thought in his mind to its possible consequences. His first impression was confirmed. "It is best," he said, finally resolved, "that these people should know there is such a man as I here." And he turned his face towards Saint Antoine.

Defarge had described himself, that day, as the keeper of a wine-shop in the Saint Antoine suburb. It was not difficult, for one who knew the city well, to find his house without asking any question. Having ascertained its situation, Carton came out of those closer streets again, and dined at a place of refreshment and fell sound asleep after dinner. For the first time in many years, he had no strong drink. Since last night he had taken nothing but a little light thin wine, and last night he had dropped the brandy slowly down on Mr. Lorry's hearth like a man who had done with it.

It was as late as seven o'clock when he awoke refreshed, and went out into the streets again. As he passed along towards Saint Antoine, he stopped at a shop-window where there was a mirror, and slightly altered the disordered arrangement of his loose cravat,

and his coat-collar, and his wild hair. This done he went on direct
to Defarge's, and went in.

There happened to be no customer in the shop but Jacques
Three, of the restless fingers and the croaking voice. This man,
5 whom he had seen upon the jury, stood drinking at the little
counter, in conversation with the Defarges, man and wife. The
Vengeance assisted in the conversation, like a regular member of
the establishment.

As Carton walked in, took his seat and asked (in very indifferent
French) for a small measure of wine, Madame Defarge cast a
careless glance at him, and then a keener, and then a keener, and
then advanced to him herself, and asked him what it was he had
ordered.

He repeated what he had already said.

15 "English?" asked Madame Defarge, inquisitively raising her dark
eyebrows.

After looking at her, as if the sound of even a single French word
were slow to express itself to him, he answered, in his former strong
foreign accent, "Yes, madame, yes. I am English!"

Madame Defarge returned to her counter to get the wine, and, as
he took up a Jacobin journal and feigned to pore over it puzzling
out its meaning, he heard her say, "I swear to you, like
Evrémonde!"

Defarge brought him the wine, and gave him good evening.

25 "How?"

"Good evening."

"Oh! Good evening, citizen," filling his glass. "Ah! and good
wine. I drink to the Republic."

Defarge went back to the counter, and said, "Certainly, a little
like." Madame sternly retorted, "I tell you a good deal like."
Jacques Three pacifically remarked, "He is so much in your mind,
see you, madame." The amiable Vengeance added, with a laugh,
"Yes, my faith! And you are looking forward with so much pleasure
to seeing him once more to-morrow!"

35 Carton followed the lines and words of his paper with a slow
forefinger, and with a studious and absorbed face. They were all
leaning their arms on the counter close together, speaking low.
After a silence of a few moments, during which they all looked
towards him without disturbing his outward attention from the

Jacobin editor, they resumed their conversation.

"It is true what madame says," observed Jacques Three. "Why stop? There is great force in that. Why stop?"

"Well, well," reasoned Defarge, "but one must stop somewhere. After all, the question is still where?"

"At extermination," said madame.

"Magnificent!" croaked Jacques Three. The Vengeance, also, highly approved.

"Extermination is good doctrine, my wife," said Defarge, rather troubled; "in general, I say nothing against it. But this Doctor has suffered much; you have seen him to-day; you have observed his face when the paper was read."

"I have observed his face!" repeated madame, contemptuously and angrily. "Yes. I have observed his face. I have observed his face to be not the face of a true friend of the Republic. Let him take care of his face!"

"And you have observed, my wife," said Defarge, in a deprecatory manner, "the anguish of his daughter, which must be a dreadful anguish to him!"

"I have observed his daughter," repeated madame; "yes, I have observed his daughter, more times than one. I have observed her to-day, and I have observed her other days. I have observed her in the court, and I have observed her in the street by the prison. Let me but lift my finger—!" She seemed to raise it (the listener's eyes were always on his paper), and to let it fall with a rattle on the ledge before her, as if the axe had dropped.

"The citizeness is superb!" croaked the juryman.

"She is an angel!" said The Vengeance, and embraced her.

"As to thee," pursued madame, implacably, addressing her husband, "if it depended on thee—which, happily, it does not—thou wouldst rescue this man even now."

"No!" protested Defarge. "Not if to lift this glass would do it! But I would leave the matter there. I say, stop there."

"See you then, Jacques," said Madame Defarge, wrathfully; "and see you, too, my little Vengeance; see you both! Listen! For other crimes as tyrants and oppressors, I have this race a long time on my register, doomed to destruction and extermination. Ask my husband, is that so."

"It is so," asserted Defarge, without being asked.

"In the beginning of the great days, when the Bastille falls, he finds this paper of to-day, and he brings it home, and in the middle of the night when this place is clear and shut, we read it, here on this spot, by the light of this lamp. Ask him, is that so."

5 "It is so," assented Defarge.

"That night, I tell him, when the paper is read through, and the lamp is burnt out, and the day is gleaming in above those shutters and between those iron bars, that I have now a secret to communicate. Ask him, is that so."

"It is so," assented Defarge again.

"I communicate to him that secret. I smite this bosom with these two hands as I smite it now, and I tell him, 'Defarge, I was brought up among the fishermen of the seashore, and that peasant family so injured by the two Evrémonde brothers, as that Bastille 15 paper describes, is my family. Defarge, that sister of the mortally wounded boy upon the ground was my sister, that husband was my sister's husband, that unborn child was their child, that brother was my brother, that father was my father, those dead are my dead, and that summons to answer for those things descends to me!' Ask him, is that so."

"It is so," assented Defarge once more.

"Then tell wind and fire where to stop," returned madame; "but don't tell me."

Both her hearers derived a horrible enjoyment from the deadly 25 nature of her wrath—the listener could feel how white she was, without seeing her—and both highly commended it. Defarge, a weak minority, interposed a few words for the memory of the compassionate wife of the Marquis; but only elicited from his own wife a repetition of her last reply. "Tell the wind and the fire where to stop; not me!"

Customers entered, and the group was broken up. The English customer paid for what he had had, perplexedly counted his change, and asked, as a stranger, to be directed towards the National Palace. Madame Defarge took him to the door, and put 35 her arm on his, in pointing out the road. The English customer was not without his reflections then, that it might be a good deed to seize that arm, lift it, and strike under it sharp and deep.

But, he went his way, and was soon swallowed up in the shadow of the prison wall. At the appointed hour, he emerged from it to present himself in Mr. Lorry's room again, where he found the old gentleman walking to and fro in restless anxiety. He said he had been with Lucie until just now, and had only left her for a few minutes, to come and keep his appointment. Her father had not been seen, since he quitted the banking-house towards four o'clock. She had some faint hopes that his mediation might save Charles, but they were very slight. He had been more than five hours gone: where could he be?

Mr. Lorry waited until ten; but, Doctor Manette not returning, and he being unwilling to leave Lucie any longer, it was arranged that he should go back to her, and come to the banking-house again at midnight. In the meanwhile, Carton could wait alone by the fire for the Doctor.

He waited and waited, and the clock struck twelve; but Doctor Manette did not come back. Mr. Lorry returned, and found no tidings of him, and brought none. Where could he be?

They were discussing this question, and were almost building up some weak structure of hope on his prolonged absence, when they heard him on the stairs. The instant he entered the room, it was plain that all was lost.

Whether he had really been to any one, or whether he had been all that time traversing the streets, was never known. As he stood staring at them, they asked him no question, for his face told them everything.

"I cannot find it," said he, "and I must have it. Where is it?"

His head and throat were bare, and, as he spoke with a helpless look straying all around, he took his coat off, and let it drop on the floor.

"Where is my bench? I have been looking everywhere for my bench, and I can't find it. What have they done with my work? Time presses: I must finish those shoes."

They looked at one another, and their hearts died within them.

"Come, come!" said he, in a whimpering miserable way; "let me get to work. Give me my work."

Receiving no answer, he tore his hair, and beat his feet upon the ground, like a distracted child.

"Don't torture a poor forlorn wretch," he implored them, with a dreadful cry, "but give me my work! What is to become of us, if those shoes are not done to-night?"

Lost, utterly lost!

It was so clearly beyond hope to reason with him, or try to restore him, that—as if by agreement—they each put a hand upon his shoulder, and soothed him to sit down before the fire, with a promise that he should have his work presently. He sank into the chair, and brooded over the embers, and shed tears. As if all that had happened since the garret time were a momentary fancy, or a dream, Mr. Lorry saw him shrink into the exact figure that Defarge had had in keeping.

Affected, and impressed with terror as they both were, by this spectacle of ruin, it was not a time to yield to such emotions. His lonely daughter, bereft of her final hope and reliance, appealed to them both too strongly. Again, as if by agreement, they looked at one another with one meaning in their faces. Carton was the first to speak:

"The last chance is gone: it was not much. Yes; he had better be taken to her. But, before you go, will you, for a moment, steadily attend to me? Don't ask me why I make the stipulations I am going to make, and exact the promise I am going to exact; I have a reason—a good one."

"I do not doubt it," answered Mr. Lorry. "Say on."

The figure in the chair between them was all the time monotonously rocking itself to and fro, and moaning. They spoke in such a tone as they would have used if they had been watching by a sick-bed in the night.

Carton stooped to pick up the coat, which lay almost entangling his feet. As he did so, a small case in which the Doctor was accustomed to carry the list of his day's duties fell lightly on the floor. Carton took it up, and there was a folded paper in it. "We should look at this!" he said. Mr. Lorry nodded his consent. He opened it, and exclaimed, "Thank God!"

"What is it?" asked Mr. Lorry, eagerly.

"A moment! Let me speak of it in its place. First," he put his hand in his coat, and took another paper from it, "that is the certificate which enables me to pass out of this city. Look at it. You see—Sydney Carton, an Englishman?"

Mr. Lorry held it open in his hand, gazing in his earnest face.

"Keep it for me until to-morrow. I shall see him to-morrow, you remember, and I had better not take it into the prison."

"Why not?"

"I don't know; I prefer not to do so. Now, take this paper that Doctor Manette has carried about him. It is a similar certificate, enabling him and his daughter and her child, at any time, to pass the barrier and the frontier. You see?"

"Yes!"

"Perhaps he obtained it as his last and utmost precaution against evil, yesterday. When is it dated? But no matter; don't stay to look; put it up carefully with mine and your own. Now, observe! I never doubted until within this hour or two, that he had or could have such a paper. It is good, until recalled. But it may be soon recalled, and, I have reason to think, will be."

"They are not in danger?"

"They are in great danger. They are in danger of denunciation by Madame Defarge. I know it from her own lips. I have overheard words of that woman's, to-night, which have presented their danger to me in strong colours. I have lost no time, and since then, I have seen the spy. He confirms me. He knows that a wood-sawyer, living by the prison-wall, is under the control of the Defarges, and has been rehearsed by Madame Defarge as to his having seen *her*"—he never mentioned Lucie's name—"making signs and signals to prisoners. It is easy to foresee that the pretence will be the common one, a prison plot, and that it will involve her life—and perhaps her child's—and perhaps her father's—for both have been seen with her at that place. Don't look so horrified. You will save them all."

"Heaven grant I may, Carton! But how?"

"I am going to tell you how. It will depend on you, and it could depend on no better man. This new denunciation will certainly not take place until after to-morrow; probably not until two or three days afterwards; more probably a week afterwards. You know it is a capital crime, to mourn for, or sympathise with, a victim of the Guillotine. She and her father would unquestionably be guilty of this crime, and this woman (the inveteracy of whose pursuit cannot be described) would wait to add that strength to her case, and make herself doubly sure. You follow me?"

"So attentively, and with so much confidence in what you say, that for the moment I lose sight," touching the back of the Doctor's chair, "even of this distress."

"You have money, and can buy the means of travelling to the

sea-coast as quickly as the journey can be made. Your preparations
have been completed for some days, to return to England. Early
to-morrow have your horses ready, so that they may be in starting
trim at two o'clock in the afternoon."

5   "It shall be done!"

His manner was so fervent and inspiring, that Mr. Lorry caught
the flame, and was as quick as youth.

"You are a noble heart. Did I say we could depend upon no
better man? Tell her, to-night, what you know of her danger as
involving her child and her father. Dwell upon that, for she would
lay her own fair head beside her husband's cheerfully." He faltered
for an instant; then went on as before. "For the sake of her child
and her father, press upon her the necessity of leaving Paris, with
them and you, at that hour. Tell her that it was her husband's last

15   arrangement. Tell her that more depends upon it than she dare
believe, or hope. You think that her father, even in this sad state,
will submit himself to her; do you not?"

"I am sure of it."

"I thought so. Quietly and steadily have all these arrangements
made in the courtyard here, even to the taking of your own seat in
the carriage. The moment I come to you, take me in, and drive
away."

"I understand that I wait for you under all circumstances?"

"You have my certificate in your hand with the rest, you know,

25   and will reserve my place. Wait for nothing but to have my place
occupied, and then for England!"

"Why, then," said Mr. Lorry, grasping his eager but so firm and
steady hand, "it does not all depend on one old man, but I shall
have a young and ardent man at my side."

"By the help of Heaven you shall! Promise me solemnly that
nothing will influence you to alter the course on which we now
stand pledged to one another."

"Nothing, Carton."

"Remember these words to-morrow: change the course, or delay

35   in it—for any reason—and no life can possibly be saved, and many
lives must inevitably be sacrificed."

"I will remember them. I hope to do my part faithfully."

"And I hope to do mine. Now, good-bye!"

Though he said it with a grave smile of earnestness, and though

he even put the old man's hand to his lips, he did not part from
him then. He helped him so far to arouse the rocking figure before
the dying embers, as to get a cloak and hat put upon it, and to
tempt it forth to find where the bench and work were hidden that
it still moaningly besought to have. He walked on the other side of   5
it and protected it to the courtyard of the house where the afflicted
heart—so happy in the memorable time when he had revealed his
own desolate heart to it—outwatched the awful night. He entered
the courtyard and remained there for a few moments alone, looking
up at the light in the window of her room. Before he went away, he
breathed a blessing towards it, and a farewell.

Chapter 13. Fifty-two

In the black prison of the Conciergerie, the doomed of the day
awaited their fate. They were in number as the weeks of the year.
Fifty-two were to roll that afternoon on the life-tide of the city to
the boundless everlasting sea. Before their cells were quit of them,
new occupants were appointed; before their blood ran into the
blood spilled yesterday, the blood that was to mingle with theirs   15
to-morrow was already set apart.

Two score and twelve were told off. From the farmer-general of
seventy, whose riches could not buy his life, to the seamstress of
twenty, whose poverty and obscurity could not save her. Physical
diseases, engendered in the vices and neglects of men, will seize on
victims of all degrees; and the frightful moral disorder, born of
unspeakable suffering, intolerable oppression, and heartless
indifference, smote equally without distinction.

Charles Darnay, alone in a cell, had sustained himself with no
flattering delusion since he came to it from the Tribunal. In every   25
line of the narrative he had heard, he had heard his condemnation.
He had fully comprehended that no personal influence could
possibly save him, that he was virtually sentenced by the millions,
and that units could avail him nothing.

Nevertheless, it was not easy, with the face of his beloved wife
fresh before him, to compose his mind to what it must bear. His

hold on life was strong, and it was very, very hard to loosen; by gradual efforts and degrees unclosed a little here, it clenched the tighter there; and when he brought his strength to bear on that hand and it yielded, this was closed again. There was a hurry, too, in all his thoughts, a turbulent and heated working of his heart, that contended against resignation. If, for a moment, he did feel resigned, then his wife and child, who had to live after him, seemed to protest and to make it a selfish thing.

But, all this was at first. Before long the consideration that there was no disgrace in the fate he must meet, and that numbers went the same road wrongfully, and trod it firmly every day, sprang up to stimulate him. Next followed the thought that much of the future peace of mind enjoyable by the dear ones depended on his quiet fortitude. So, by degrees he calmed into the better state, when he could raise his thoughts much higher, and draw comfort down.

Before it had set in dark on the night of his condemnation, he had travelled thus far on his last way. Being allowed to purchase the means of writing, and a light, he sat down to write until such time as the prison lamps should be extinguished.

He wrote a long letter to Lucie, showing her that he had known nothing of her father's imprisonment, until he had heard of it from herself, and that he had been as ignorant as she of his father's and uncle's responsibility for that misery, until the paper had been read. He had already explained to her that his concealment from herself of the name he had relinquished was the one condition—fully intelligible now—that her father had attached to their betrothal, and was the one promise he had still exacted on the morning of their marriage. He entreated her, for her father's sake, never to seek to know whether her father had become oblivious of the existence of the paper, or had had it recalled to him (for the moment, or for good), by the story of the Tower, on that old Sunday under the dear old plane-tree in the garden. If he had preserved any definite remembrance of it, there could be no doubt that he had supposed it destroyed with the Bastille, when he had found no mention of it among the relics of prisoners which the populace had discovered there, and which had been described to all the world. He besought her—though he added that he knew it was needless—to console her father, by impressing him through every tender means she could think of, with the truth that he had done nothing for which he could justly reproach himself, but had uniformly forgotten himself for their joint sakes. Next to her preservation of his own last grateful love and blessing, and her overcoming of her sorrow, to devote herself to their dear child, he adjured her, as they would meet in Heaven, to comfort her father.

To her father himself, he wrote in the same strain; but, he told her father that he expressly confided his wife and child to his care. And he told him this, very strongly, with the hope of rousing him from any despondency or dangerous retrospect towards which he foresaw he might be tending.

To Mr. Lorry, he commended them all, and explained his worldly affairs. That done, with many added sentences of grateful friendship and warm attachment, all was done. He never thought of Carton. His mind was so full of the others, that he never once thought of him.

He had time to finish these letters before the lights were put out. When he lay down on his straw bed, he thought he had done with this world.

But, it beckoned him back in his sleep, and showed itself in shining forms. Free and happy, back in the old house in Soho (though it had nothing in it like the real house), unaccountably released and light of heart, he was with Lucie again, and she told him it was all a dream, and he had never gone away. A pause of forgetfulness, and then he had even suffered, and had come back to her, dead and at peace, and yet there was no difference in him. Another pause of oblivion, and he awoke in the sombre morning, unconscious where he was or what had happened, until it flashed upon his mind, "this is the day of my death!"

Thus had he come through the hours, to the day when the fifty-two heads were to fall. And now, while he was composed, and hoped that he could meet the end with quiet heroism, a new action began in his waking thoughts, which was very difficult to master.

He had never seen the instrument that was to terminate his life. How high it was from the ground, how many steps it had, where he would be stood, how he would be touched, whether the touching hands would be dyed red, which way his face would be turned, whether he would be the first, or might be the last: these and many similar questions, in no wise directed by his will, obtruded themselves over and over again, countless times. Neither were they connected with fear: he was conscious of no fear. Rather, they originated in a strange besetting desire to know what to do when the time came; a desire gigantically disproportionate to the few split moments to which it referred; a wondering that was more like the wondering of some other spirit within him, than his own.

The hours went on as he walked to and fro, and the clocks struck the numbers he would never hear again. Nine gone for ever, ten gone for ever, eleven gone for ever, twelve coming on to pass away. After a hard contest with that eccentric action of thought which had last perplexed him, he had got the better of it. He walked up and down, softly repeating their names to himself. The worst of the strife was over. He could walk up and down, free from distracting fancies, praying for himself and for them.

Twelve gone for ever.

He had been apprised that the final hour was three, and he knew he would be summoned some time earlier, inasmuch as the tumbrils jolted heavily and slowly through the streets. Therefore, he resolved to keep two before his mind, as the hour, and so to strengthen himself in the interval that he might be able, after that time, to strengthen others.

Walking regularly to and fro with his arms folded on his breast, a very different man from the prisoner who had walked to and fro at La Force, he heard one struck away from him, without surprise. The hour had measured like most other hours. Devoutly thankful to Heaven for his recovered self-possession, he thought, "There is but another now," and turned to walk again.

Footsteps in the stone passage outside the door. He stopped.

The key was put in the lock, and turned. Before the door was opened, or as it opened, a man said in a low voice, in English: "He has never seen me here; I have kept out of his way. Go you in alone; I wait near. Lose no time!"

The door was quickly opened and closed, and there stood before him face to face, quiet, intent upon him, with the light of a smile on his features, and a cautionary finger on his lip, Sydney Carton.

There was something so bright and remarkable in his look, that, for the first moment, the prisoner misdoubted him to be an apparition of his own imagining. But, he spoke, and it was his voice; he took the prisoner's hand, and it was his real grasp.

"Of all the people upon earth, you least expected to see me?" he said.

"I could not believe it to be you. I can scarcely believe it now. You are not"—the apprehension came suddenly into his mind—"a prisoner?"

"No. I am accidentally possessed of a power over one of the keepers here, and in virtue of it I stand before you. I come from her—your wife, dear Darnay."

The prisoner wrung his hand.

"I bring you a request from her."

"What is it?"

"A most earnest, pressing, and emphatic entreaty, addressed to you in the most pathetic tones of the voice so dear to you, that you well remember."

The prisoner turned his face partly aside.

"You have no time to ask me why I bring it, or what it means; I have no time to tell you. You must comply with it—take off those boots you wear, and draw on these of mine."

There was a chair against the wall of the cell, behind the prisoner. Carton, pressing forward, had already, with the speed of lightning, got him down into it, and stood over him, barefoot.

"Draw on those boots of mine. Put your hands to them; put your will to them. Quick!"

"Carton, there is no escaping from this place; it never can be done. You will only die with me. It is madness."

"It would be madness if I asked you to escape; but do I? When I ask you to pass out at that door, tell me it is madness and remain here. Change that cravat for this of mine, that coat for this of mine. While you do it, let me take this ribbon from your hair, and shake out your hair like this of mine!"

With wonderful quickness, and with a strength both of will and action, that appeared quite supernatural, he forced all these changes upon him. The prisoner was like a young child in his hands.

"Carton! Dear Carton! It is madness. It cannot be accomplished, it never can be done, it has been attempted, and has always failed. I implore you not to add your death to the bitterness of mine."

"Do I ask you, my dear Darnay, to pass the door? When I ask that, refuse. There are pen and ink and paper on this table. Is your hand steady enough to write?"

"It was when you came in."

"Steady it again, and write what I shall dictate. Quick, friend, quick!"

Pressing his hand to his bewildered head, Darnay sat down at the table. Carton, with his right hand in his breast, stood close beside him.

"Write exactly as I speak."

5 "To whom do I address it?"

"To no one." Carton still had his hand in his breast.

"Do I date it?"

"No."

The prisoner looked up at each question. Carton, standing over him with his hand in his breast, looked down.

" 'If you remember,' " said Carton, dictating, " 'the words that passed between us, long ago, you will readily comprehend this when you see it. You do remember them, I know. It is not in your nature to forget them.' "

15 He was drawing his hand from his breast; the prisoner chancing to look up in his hurried wonder as he wrote, the hand stopped, closing upon something.

"Have you written 'forget them'?" Carton asked.

"I have. Is that a weapon in your hand?"

"No; I am not armed."

"What is it in your hand?"

"You shall know directly. Write on; there are but a few words more." He dictated again. " 'I am thankful that the time has come, when I can prove them. That I do so is no subject for regret or 25 grief.' " As he said these words with his eyes fixed on the writer, his hand slowly and softly moved down close to the writer's face.

The pen dropped from Darnay's fingers on the table, and he looked about him vacantly.

"What vapour is that?" he asked.

"Vapour?"

"Something that crossed me?"

"I am conscious of nothing; there can be nothing here. Take up the pen and finish. Hurry, hurry!"

As if his memory were impaired, or his faculties disordered, the 35 prisoner made an effort to rally his attention. As he looked at Carton with clouded eyes and with an altered manner of breathing, Carton—his hand again in his breast—looked steadily at him.

"Hurry, hurry!"

The prisoner bent over the paper once more.

" 'If it had been otherwise' "—Carton's hand was again watchfully and softly stealing down—" 'I never should have used the longer opportunity. If it had been otherwise' "—the hand was at the prisoner's face—" 'I should but have had so much the more to answer for. If it had been otherwise—' " Carton looked at the pen and saw it was trailing off into unintelligible signs.

Carton's hand moved back to his breast no more. The prisoner sprang up with a reproachful look, but Carton's hand was close and firm at his nostrils, and Carton's left arm caught him round the waist. For a few seconds he faintly struggled with the man who had come to lay down his life for him; but, within a minute or so, he was stretched insensible on the ground.

Quickly, but with hands as true to the purpose as his heart was, Carton dressed himself in the clothes the prisoner had laid aside, combed back his hair, and tied it with the ribbon the prisoner had worn. Then, he softly called, "Enter there! Come in!" and the spy presented himself.

"You see?" said Carton, looking up, as he kneeled on one knee beside the insensible figure, putting the paper in the breast: "is your hazard very great?"

"Mr. Carton," the spy answered, with a timid snap of his fingers, "my hazard is not *that*, in the thick of business here, if you are true to the whole of your bargain."

"Don't fear me. I will be true to the death."

"You must be, Mr. Carton, if the tale of fifty-two is to be right. Being made right by you in that dress, I shall have no fear."

"Have no fear! I shall soon be out of the way of harming you, and the rest will soon be far from here, please God! Now, get assistance and take me to the coach."

"You?" said the spy nervously.

"Him, man, with whom I have exchanged. You go out at the gate by which you brought me in?"

"Of course."

"I was weak and faint when you brought me in, and I am fainter now you take me out. The parting interview has overpowered me. Such a thing has happened here, often, and too often. Your life is in your own hands. Quick! Call assistance!"

"You swear not to betray me?" said the trembling spy, as he paused for a last moment.

"Man, man!" returned Carton, stamping his foot; "have I sworn by no solemn vow already, to go through with this, that you waste the precious moments now? Take him yourself to the courtyard you know of, place him yourself in the carriage, show him yourself to Mr. Lorry, tell him yourself to give him no restorative but air, and to remember my words of last night, and his promise of last night, and drive away!"

The spy withdrew, and Carton seated himself at the table, resting his forehead on his hands. The spy returned immediately, with two men.

"How, then?" said one of them, contemplating the fallen figure. "So afflicted to find that his friend has drawn a prize in the lottery of Sainte Guillotine?"

"A good patriot," said the other, "could hardly have been more afflicted if the aristocrat had drawn a blank."

They raised the unconscious figure, placed it on a litter they had brought to the door, and bent to carry it away.

"The time is short, Evrémonde," said the spy, in a warning voice.

"I know it well," answered Carton. "Be careful of my friend, I entreat you, and leave me."

"Come, then, my children," said Barsad. "Lift him, and come away!"

The door closed, and Carton was left alone. Straining his powers of listening to the utmost, he listened for any sound that might denote suspicion or alarm. There was none. Keys turned, doors clashed, footsteps passed along distant passages: no cry was raised, or hurry made, that seemed unusual. Breathing more freely in a little while, he sat down at the table, and listened again until the clock struck two.

Sounds that he was not afraid of, for he divined their meaning, then began to be audible. Several doors were opened in succession, and finally his own. A gaoler, with a list in his hand, looked in, merely saying, "Follow me, Evrémonde!" and he followed into a large dark room, at a distance. It was a dark winter day, and what with the shadows within, and what with the shadows without, he could but dimly discern the others who were brought there to have their arms bound. Some were standing; some seated. Some were lamenting, and in restless motion; but, these were few. The great majority were silent and still, looking fixedly at the ground.

As he stood by the wall in a dim corner, while some of the fifty-two were brought in after him, one man stopped in passing, to embrace him, as having a knowledge of him. It thrilled him with a great dread of discovery; but the man went on. A very few moments after that, a young woman, with a slight girlish form, a sweet spare face in which there was no vestige of colour, and large widely opened patient eyes, rose from the seat where he had observed her sitting, and came to speak to him.

"Citizen Evrémonde," she said, touching him with her cold hand, "I am a poor little seamstress, who was with you in La Force."

He murmured for answer: "True. I forget what you were accused of?"

"Plots. Though the just Heaven knows I am innocent of any. Is it likely? Who would think of plotting with a poor little weak creature like me?"

The forlorn smile with which she said it so touched him, that tears started from his eyes.

"I am not afraid to die, Citizen Evrémonde, but I have done nothing. I am not unwilling to die, if the Republic which is to do so much good for us poor, will profit by my death; but I do not know how that can be, Citizen Evrémonde. Such a poor weak little creature!"

As the last thing on earth that his heart was to warm and soften to, it warmed and softened to this pitiable girl.

"I heard you were released, Citizen Evrémonde. I hoped it was true?"

"It was. But, I was again taken and condemned."

"If I may ride with you, Citizen Evrémonde, will you let me hold your hand? I am not afraid, but I am little and weak, and it will give me more courage."

As the patient eyes were lifted to his face, he saw a sudden doubt in them, and then astonishment. He pressed the work-worn, hunger-worn young fingers, and touched his lips.

"Are you dying for him?" she whispered.

"And his wife and child. Hush! Yes."

"Oh, you will let me hold your brave hand, stranger?"

"Hush! Yes, my poor sister; to the last."

The same shadows that are falling on the prison are falling, in that same hour of the early afternoon, on the Barrier with the crowd about it, when a coach going out of Paris drives up to be examined.

"Who goes here? Whom have we within? Papers!"

The papers are handed out, and read.

"Alexandre Manette. Physician. French. Which is he?"

This is he; this helpless, inarticulately murmuring, wandering old man pointed out.

"Apparently the Citizen-Doctor is not in his right mind? The Revolution-fever will have been too much for him?"

Greatly too much for him.

"Hah! Many suffer with it. Lucie. His daughter. French. Which is she?"

This is she.

"Apparently it must be. Lucie, the wife of Evrémonde; is it not?"

It is.

"Hah! Evrémonde has an assignation elsewhere. Lucie, her child. English. This is she?"

She and no other.

"Kiss me, child of Evrémonde. Now, thou hast kissed a good Republican; something new in thy family; remember it! Sydney Carton. Advocate. English. Which is he?"

He lies here, in this corner of the carriage. He, too, is pointed out.

"Apparently the English advocate is in a swoon?"

It is hoped he will recover in the fresher air. It is represented that he is not in strong health, and has separated sadly from a friend who is under the displeasure of the Republic.

"Is that all? It is not a great deal, that! Many are under the displeasure of the Republic, and must look out at the little window. Jarvis Lorry. Banker. English. Which is he?"

"I am he. Necessarily, being the last."

It is Jarvis Lorry who has replied to all the previous questions. It is Jarvis Lorry who has alighted and stands with his hands on the coach door, replying to a group of officials. They leisurely walk round the carriage and leisurely mount the box, to look at what little luggage it carries on the roof; the country-people hanging about press nearer to the coach doors and greedily stare in; a little child, carried by its mother, has its short arm held out for it, that it may touch the wife of an aristocrat who has gone to the Guillotine.

"Behold your papers, Jarvis Lorry, countersigned."

"One can depart, citizen?"

"One can depart. Forward, my postilions! A good journey!"

"I salute you, citizens.—And the first danger passed!"

These are again the words of Jarvis Lorry, as he clasps his hands, and looks upward. There is terror in the carriage, there is weeping, there is the heavy breathing of the insensible traveller.

"Are we not going too slowly? Can they not be induced to go faster?" asks Lucie, clinging to the old man.

"It would seem like flight, my darling. I must not urge them too much; it would rouse suspicion."

"Look back, look back, and see if we are pursued!"

"The road is clear, my dearest. So far, we are not pursued."

Houses in twos and threes pass by us, solitary farms, ruinous buildings, dye-works, tanneries, and the like, open country, avenues of leafless trees. The hard uneven pavement is under us, the soft deep mud is on either side. Sometimes, we strike into the skirting mud, to avoid the stones that clatter us and shake us; sometimes we stick in ruts and sloughs there. The agony of our impatience is then so great, that in our wild alarm and hurry we are for getting out and running—hiding—doing anything but stopping.

Out of the open country, in again among ruinous buildings, solitary farms, dye-works, tanneries, and the like, cottages in twos and threes, avenues of leafless trees. Have these men deceived us, and taken us back by another road? Is not this the same place twice over? Thank Heaven, no. A village. Look back, look back, and see if we are pursued! Hush! the posting-house.

Leisurely, our four horses are taken out; leisurely, the coach stands in the little street, bereft of horses, and with no likelihood upon it of ever moving again; leisurely, the new horses come into visible existence, one by one; leisurely, the new postilions follow, sucking and plaiting the lashes of their whips; leisurely, the old postilions count their money, make wrong additions, and arrive at dissatisfied results. All the time, our overfraught hearts are beating at a rate that would far outstrip the fastest gallop of the fastest horses ever foaled.

At length the new postilions are in their saddles, and the old are left behind. We are through the village, up the hill, and down the hill, and on the low watery grounds. Suddenly, the postilions exchange speech with animated gesticulation, and the horses are
5   pulled up, almost on their haunches. We are pursued?

"Ho! Within the carriage there. Speak then!"

"What is it?" asks Mr. Lorry, looking out at window.

"How many did they say?"

"I do not understand you."

"—At the last post. How many to the Guillotine to-day?"

"Fifty-two."

"I said so! A brave number! My fellow-citizen here would have it forty-two; ten more heads are worth having. The Guillotine goes handsomely. I love it. Hi forward. Whoop!"

15   The night comes on dark. He moves more; he is beginning to revive, and to speak intelligibly; he thinks they are still together; he asks him, by his name, what he has in his hand. O pity us, kind Heaven, and help us! Look out, look out, and see if we are pursued.

The wind is rushing after us, and the clouds are flying after us, and the moon is plunging after us, and the whole wild night is in pursuit of us; but, so far, we are pursued by nothing else.

Chapter 14. The Knitting Done

In that same juncture of time when the fifty-two awaited their fate, Madame Defarge held darkly ominous council with The Vengeance and Jacques Three of the Revolutionary Jury. Not in
25   the wine-shop did Madame Defarge confer with these ministers, but in the shed of the wood-sawyer, erst a mender of roads. The sawyer himself did not participate in the conference, but abided at a little distance, like an outer satellite who was not to speak until required, or to offer an opinion until invited.

"But our Defarge," said Jacques Three, "is undoubtedly a good Republican? Eh?"

"There is no better," the voluble Vengeance protested in her shrill notes, "in France."

"Peace, little Vengeance," said Madame Defarge, laying her hand with a slight frown on her lieutenant's lips, "hear me speak. My husband, fellow-citizen, is a good Republican and a bold man; he has deserved well of the Republic, and possesses its confidence. But my husband has his weaknesses, and he is so weak as to relent towards this Doctor." 5

"It is a great pity," croaked Jacques Three, dubiously shaking his head, with his cruel fingers at his hungry mouth; "it is not quite like a good citizen; it is a thing to regret."

"See you," said madame, "I care nothing for this Doctor, I. He may wear his head or lose it, for any interest I have in him; it is all one to me. But, the Evrémonde people are to be exterminated, and the wife and child must follow the husband and father."

"She has a fine head for it," croaked Jacques Three. "I have seen blue eyes and golden hair there, and they looked charming when 15 Samson held them up." Ogre that he was, he spoke like an epicure.

Madame Defarge cast down her eyes, and reflected a little.

"The child also," observed Jacques Three, with a meditative enjoyment of his words, "has golden hair and blue eyes. And we seldom have a child there. It is a pretty sight!"

"In a word," said Madame Defarge, coming out of her short abstraction, "I cannot trust my husband in this matter. Not only do I feel, since last night, that I dare not confide to him the details of my projects; but also I feel that if I delay, there is danger of his giving warning, and then they might escape." 25

"That must never be," croaked Jacques Three; "no one must escape. We have not half enough as it is. We ought to have six score a day."

"In a word," Madame Defarge went on, "my husband has not my reason for pursuing this family to annihilation, and I have not his reason for regarding this Doctor with any sensibility. I must act for myself, therefore. Come hither, little citizen."

The wood-sawyer, who held her in the respect, and himself in the submission, of mortal fear, advanced with his hand to his red cap.

"Touching those signals, little citizen," said Madame Defarge, 35 sternly, "that she made to the prisoners; you are ready to bear witness to them this very day?"

"Ay, ay, why not!" cried the sawyer. "Every day, in all weathers, from two to four, always signalling, sometimes with the little one, sometimes without. I know what I know. I have seen with my eyes."

He made all manner of gestures while he spoke, as if in incidental imitation of some few of the great diversity of signals that he had never seen.

"Clearly plots," said Jacques Three. "Transparently!"

"There is no doubt of the jury?" inquired Madame Defarge, letting her eyes turn to him with a gloomy smile.

"Rely upon the patriotic jury, dear citizeness. I answer for my fellow-jurymen."

"Now, let me see," said Madame Defarge, pondering again. "Yet once more! Can I spare this Doctor to my husband? I have no feeling either way. Can I spare him?"

"He would count as one head," observed Jacques Three, in a low voice. "We really have not heads enough; it would be a pity, I think."

"He was signalling with her when I saw her," argued Madame Defarge; "I cannot speak of one without the other; and I must not be silent, and trust the case wholly to him, this little citizen here. For I am not a bad witness."

The Vengeance and Jacques Three vied with each other in their fervent protestations that she was the most admirable and marvellous of witnesses. The little citizen, not to be outdone, declared her to be a celestial witness.

"He must take his chance," said Madame Defarge. "No, I cannot spare him! You are engaged at three o'clock; you are going to see the batch of to-day executed.—You?"

The question was addressed to the wood-sawyer, who hurriedly replied in the affirmative: seizing the occasion to add that he was the most ardent of Republicans, and that he would be in effect the most desolate of Republicans, if anything prevented him from enjoying the pleasure of smoking his afternoon pipe in the contemplation of the droll national barber. He was so very demonstrative herein, that he might have been suspected (perhaps was, by the dark eyes that looked contemptuously at him out of Madame Defarge's head) of having his small individual fears for his own personal safety, every hour in the day.

"I," said madame, "am equally engaged at the same place. After it is over—say at eight to-night—come you to me, in Saint

Antoine, and we will give information against these people at my Section."

The wood-sawyer said he would be proud and flattered to attend the citizeness. The citizeness looking at him, he became embarrassed, evaded her glance as a small dog would have done, retreated among his wood, and hid his confusion over the handle of the saw.

Madame Defarge beckoned the juryman and The Vengeance a little nearer to the door, and there expounded her further views of them thus:

"She will now be at home, awaiting the moment of his death. She will be mourning and grieving. She will be in a state of mind to impeach the justice of the Republic. She will be full of sympathy with its enemies. I will go to her."

"What an admirable woman; what an adorable woman!" exclaimed Jacques Three, rapturously. "Ah, my cherished!" cried The Vengeance; and embraced her.

"Take you my knitting," said Madame Defarge, placing it in her lieutenant's hands, "and have it ready for me in my usual seat. Keep me my usual chair. Go you there, straight, for there will probably be a greater concourse than usual, to-day."

"I willingly obey the orders of my chief," said The Vengeance with alacrity, and kissing her cheek. "You will not be late?"

"I shall be there before the commencement."

"And before the tumbrils arrive. Be sure you are there, my soul," said The Vengeance, calling after her, for she had already turned into the street, "before the tumbrils arrive!"

Madame Defarge slightly waved her hand, to imply that she heard, and might be relied upon to arrive in good time, and so went through the mud and round the corner of the prison wall. The Vengeance and the juryman, looking after her as she walked away, were highly appreciative of her fine figure, and her superb moral endowments.

There were many women at that time, upon whom the time laid a dreadfully disfiguring hand; but, there was not one among them more to be dreaded than this ruthless woman, now taking her way along the streets. Of a strong and fearless character, and shrewd sense and readiness, of great determination, of that kind of beauty which not only seems to impart to its possessor firmness and animosity, but to strike into others an instinctive recognition of those qualities; the troubled time would have heaved her up, under any circumstances. But, imbued from her childhood with a brooding sense of wrong, and an inveterate hatred of a class, opportunity had developed her into a tigress. She was absolutely without pity. If she had ever had the virtue in her, it had quite gone out of her.

It was nothing to her, that an innocent man was to die for the sins of his forefathers; she saw, not him, but them. It was nothing to her, that his wife was to be made a widow and his daughter an orphan; that was insufficient punishment, because they were her natural enemies and her prey, and as such had no right to live. To appeal to her, was made hopeless by her having no sense of pity, even for herself. If she had been laid low in the streets, in any of the many encounters in which she had been engaged, she would not have pitied herself: nor, if she had been ordered to the axe to-morrow, would she have gone to it with any softer feeling than a fierce desire to change places with the man who sent her there.

Such a heart Madame Defarge carried under her rough robe. Carelessly worn, it was a becoming robe enough, in a certain weird way, and her dark hair looked rich under her coarse red cap. Lying hidden in her bosom was a loaded pistol. Lying hidden at her waist was a sharpened dagger. Thus accoutred, and walking with the confident tread of such a character, and with the supple freedom of a woman who had habitually walked in her girlhood, barefoot and bare-legged, on the brown sea-sand, Madame Defarge took her way along the streets.

Now, when the journey of the travelling coach, at that very moment waiting for the completion of its load, had been planned out last night, the difficulty of taking Miss Pross in it had much engaged Mr. Lorry's attention. It was not merely desirable to avoid overloading the coach, but it was of the highest importance that the time occupied in examining it and its passengers, should be reduced to the utmost; since their escape might depend on the saving of only a few seconds here and there. Finally, he had proposed, after anxious consideration, that Miss Pross and Jerry, who were at liberty to leave the city, would leave it at three o'clock in the lightest-wheeled conveyance known to that period. Unencumbered with luggage, they would soon overtake the coach, and, passing it and preceding it on the road, would order its horses in advance, and greatly facilitate its progress during the precious hours of the night, when delay was the most to be dreaded.

Seeing in this arrangement the hope of rendering real service in that pressing emergency, Miss Pross hailed it with joy. She and Jerry had beheld the coach start, had known who it was that Solomon brought, had passed some ten minutes in tortures of suspense, and were now concluding their arrangements to follow the coach, even as Madame Defarge, taking her way through the streets, now drew nearer and nearer to the else-deserted lodging in which they held their consultation.

"Now what do you think, Mr. Cruncher," said Miss Pross, whose agitation was so great that she could hardly speak, or stand, or move, or live: "what do you think of our not starting from this courtyard? Another carriage having already gone from here to-day, it might awaken suspicion."

"My opinion, miss," returned Mr. Cruncher, "is as you're right. Likewise wot I'll stand by you, right or wrong."

"I am so distracted with fear and hope for our precious creatures," said Miss Pross, wildly crying, "that I am incapable of forming any plan. Are *you* capable of forming any plan, my dear good Mr. Cruncher?"

"Respectin' a future spear o' life, miss," returned Mr. Cruncher, "I hope so. Respectin' any present use o' this here blessed old head o' mine, I think not. Would you do me the favour, miss, to take notice o' two promises and wows wot it is my wishes fur to record in this here crisis?"

"Oh, for gracious' sake!" cried Miss Pross, still wildly crying, "record them at once, and get them out of the way, like an excellent man."

"First," said Mr. Cruncher, who was all in a tremble, and who spoke with an ashy and solemn visage, "them poor things well out o' this, never no more will I do it, never no more!"

"I am quite sure, Mr. Cruncher," returned Miss Pross, "that you never will do it again, whatever it is, and I beg you not to think it necessary to mention more particularly what it is."

"No, miss," returned Jerry, "it shall not be named to you. Second: them poor things well out o' this, and never no more will I interfere with Mrs. Cruncher's flopping, never no more!"

"Whatever housekeeping arrangement that may be," said Miss Pross, striving to dry her eyes and compose herself, "I have no doubt it is best that Mrs. Cruncher should have it entirely under her own superintendence.—O my poor darlings!"

"I go so far as to say, miss, morehover," proceeded Mr. Cruncher, with a most alarming tendency to hold forth as from a pulpit—"and let my words be took down and took to Mrs. Cruncher through yourself—that wot my opinions respectin' flopping has undergone a change, and that wot I only hope with all my heart as Mrs. Cruncher may be a flopping at the present time."

"There, there, there! I hope she is, my dear man," cried the distracted Miss Pross, "and I hope she finds it answering her expectations."

"Forbid it," proceeded Mr. Cruncher, with additional solemnity, additional slowness, and additional tendency to hold forth and hold out, "as anything wot I have ever said or done should be wisited on my earnest wishes for them poor creeturs now! Forbid it as we shouldn't all flop (if it was anyways conwenient) to get 'em out o' this here dismal risk! Forbid it, miss! Wot I say, for-*bid* it!" This was Mr. Cruncher's conclusion after a protracted but vain endeavour to find a better one.

And still Madame Defarge, pursuing her way along the streets, came nearer and nearer.

"If we ever get back to our native land," said Miss Pross, "you may rely upon my telling Mrs. Cruncher as much as I may be able to remember and understand of what you have so impressively said; and at all events you may be sure that I shall bear witness to your being thoroughly in earnest at this dreadful time. Now, pray let us think! My esteemed Mr. Cruncher, let us think!"

Still, Madame Defarge, pursuing her way along the streets, came nearer and nearer.

"If you were to go before," said Miss Pross, "and stop the vehicle and horses from coming here, and were to wait somewhere for me, wouldn't that be best?"

Mr. Cruncher thought it might be best.

"Where could you wait for me?" asked Miss Pross.

Mr. Cruncher was so bewildered that he could think of no locality but Temple Bar. Alas! Temple Bar was hundreds of miles away, and Madame Defarge was drawing very near indeed.

"By the cathedral door," said Miss Pross. "Would it be much out of the way, to take me in, near the great cathedral door between the two towers?"

"No, miss," answered Mr. Cruncher.

"Then, like the best of men," said Miss Pross, "go to the posting-house straight, and make that change."

"I am doubtful," said Mr. Cruncher, hesitating and shaking his head, "'bout leaving of you, you see. We don't know what may happen."

"Heaven knows we don't," returned Miss Pross, "but have no fear of me. Take me in at the cathedral, at three o'clock, or as near it as you can, and I am sure it will be better than our going from here. I feel certain of it. There! Bless you, Mr. Cruncher! Think—not of me, but of the lives that may depend on both of us!"

This exordium, and Miss Pross's two hands in quite agonised entreaty clasping his, decided Mr. Cruncher. With an encouraging nod or two, he immediately went out to alter the arrangements, and left her by herself to follow as she had proposed.

The having originated a precaution which was already in course of execution was a great relief to Miss Pross. The necessity of composing her appearance so that it should attract no special notice in the streets was another relief. She looked at her watch, and it was twenty minutes past two. She had no time to lose, but must get ready at once.

Afraid, in her extreme perturbation, of the loneliness of the deserted rooms, and of half-imagined faces peeping from behind every open door in them, Miss Pross got a basin of cold water and began laving her eyes, which were swollen and red. Haunted by her feverish apprehensions, she could not bear to have her sight obscured for a minute at a time by the dripping water, but constantly paused and looked around to see that there was no one watching her. In one of those pauses she recoiled and cried out, for she saw a figure standing in the room.

The basin fell to the ground broken, and the water flowed to the feet of Madame Defarge. By strange stern ways, and through much staining blood, those feet had come to meet that water.

Madame Defarge looked coldly at her, and said, "The wife of Evrémonde; where is she?"

It flashed upon Miss Pross's mind that the doors were all standing open, and would suggest the flight. Her first act was to shut them. There were four in the room, and she shut them all. She then placed herself before the door of the chamber which Lucie had occupied.

Madame Defarge's dark eyes followed her through this rapid movement, and rested on her when it was finished. Miss Pross had nothing beautiful about her; years had not tamed the wildness, or softened the grimness, of her appearance; but, she too, was a determined woman in her different way, and she measured Madame Defarge with her eyes, every inch.

"You might, from your appearance, be the wife of Lucifer," said Miss Pross, in her breathing. "Nevertheless, you shall not get the better of me. I am an Englishwoman."

Madame Defarge looked at her scornfully, but still with something of Miss Pross's own perception that they two were at bay. She saw a tight, hard, wiry woman before her, as Mr. Lorry had seen in the same figure a woman with a strong hand, in the years gone by. She knew full well that Miss Pross was the family's devoted friend; Miss Pross knew full well that Madame Defarge was the family's malevolent enemy.

"On my way yonder," said Madame Defarge, with a slight movement of her hand towards the fatal spot, "where they reserve my chair and my knitting for me, I am come to make my compliments to her in passing. I wish to see her."

"I know that your intentions are evil," said Miss Pross, "and you may depend upon it, I'll hold my own against them."

Each spoke in her own language; neither understood the other's words; both were very watchful, and intent to deduce, from look and manner, what the unintelligible words meant.

"It will do her no good to keep herself concealed from me at this moment," said Madame Defarge. "Good patriots will know what that means. Let me see her. Go tell her that I wish to see her. Do you hear?"

"If those eyes of yours were bed-winches," returned Miss Pross, "and I was an English four-poster, they shouldn't loose a splinter of me. No, you wicked foreign woman; I am your match."

Madame Defarge was not likely to follow these idiomatic remarks in detail; but, she so far understood them as to perceive that she was set at naught.

"Woman imbecile and pig-like!" said Madame Defarge, frowning. "I take no answer from you. I demand to see her. Either tell her that I demand to see her, or stand out of the way of the door and let me go to her!" This, with an angry explanatory wave of her right arm.

"I little thought," said Miss Pross, "that I should ever want to understand your nonsensical language; but I would give all I have, except the clothes I wear, to know whether you suspect the truth, or any part of it."

Neither of them for a single moment released the other's eyes. Madame Defarge had not moved from the spot where she stood when Miss Pross first became aware of her; but she now advanced one step.

"I am a Briton," said Miss Pross, "I am desperate. I don't care an English twopence for myself. I know that the longer I keep you here, the greater hope there is for my Ladybird. I'll not leave a handful of that dark hair upon your head, if you lay a finger on me!"

Thus Miss Pross, with a shake of her head and a flash of her eyes between every rapid sentence, and every rapid sentence a whole breath. Thus Miss Pross who had never struck a blow in her life.

But, her courage was of that emotional nature that it brought the irrepressible tears into her eyes. This was a courage that Madame Defarge so little comprehended as to mistake for weakness. "Ha, ha!" she laughed, "you poor wretch! What are you worth! I address myself to that Doctor." Then she raised her voice and called out, "Citizen Doctor! Wife of Evrémonde! Child of Evrémonde! Any person but this miserable fool, answer the Citizeness Defarge!"

Perhaps the following silence, perhaps some latent disclosure in the expression of Miss Pross's face, perhaps a sudden misgiving apart from either suggestion, whispered to Madame Defarge that they were gone. Three of the doors she opened swiftly, and looked in.

"Those rooms are all in disorder, there has been hurried packing, there are odds and ends upon the ground. There is no one in that room behind you! Let me look."

"Never!" said Miss Pross, who understood the request as perfectly as Madame Defarge understood the answer.

"If they are not in that room, they are gone, and can be pursued and brought back," said Madame Defarge to herself.

"As long as you don't know whether they are in that room or not, you are uncertain what to do," said Miss Pross to *herself*; "and you shall not know that, if I can prevent your knowing it; and know

5   that, or not know that, you shall not leave here while I can hold you."

"I have been in the streets from the first, nothing has stopped me, I will tear you to pieces, but I will have you from that door," said Madame Defarge.

"We are alone at the top of a high house in a solitary courtyard, we are not likely to be heard, and I pray for bodily strength to keep you here, while every minute you are here is worth a hundred thousand guineas to my darling," said Miss Pross.

Madame Defarge made at the door. Miss Pross, on the instinct of

15   the moment, seized her round the waist in both her arms, and held her tight. It was in vain for Madame Defarge to struggle and to strike; Miss Pross, with the vigorous tenacity of love, always so much stronger than hate, clasped her tight, and even lifted her from the floor in the struggle that they had. The two hands of Madame Defarge buffeted and tore her face; but, Miss Pross, with her head down, held her round the waist, and clung to her with more than the hold of a drowning woman.

Soon, Madame Defarge's hands ceased to strike, and felt at her encircled waist. "It is under my arm," said Miss Pross, in smothered

25   tones, "you shall not draw it. I am stronger than you, I bless Heaven for it. I'll hold you till one or other of us faints or dies!"

Madame Defarge's hands were at her bosom. Miss Pross looked up, saw what it was, struck at it, struck out a flash and a crash, and stood alone—blinded with smoke.

All this was in a second. As the smoke cleared, leaving an awful stillness, it passed out on the air, like the soul of the furious woman whose body lay lifeless on the ground.

In the first fright and horror of her situation, Miss Pross passed the body as far from it as she could, and ran down the stairs to call

35   for fruitless help. Happily, she bethought herself of the consequences of what she did, in time to check herself and go back. It was dreadful to go in at the door again; but she did go in, and even went near it, to get the bonnet and other things that she must wear. These she put on, out on the staircase, first shutting and

locking the door and taking away the key. She then sat down on the stairs a few moments to breathe and to cry, and then got up and hurried away.

By good fortune she had a veil on her bonnet, or she could hardly have gone along the streets without being stopped. By good fortune, too, she was naturally so peculiar in appearance as not to show disfigurement like any other woman. She needed both advantages, for the marks of gripping fingers were deep in her face, and her hair was torn, and her dress (hastily composed with unsteady hands) was clutched and dragged a hundred ways.

In crossing the bridge, she dropped the door key in the river. Arriving at the cathedral some few minutes before her escort, and waiting there, she thought, what if the key were already taken in a net, what if it were identified, what if the door were opened and the remains discovered, what if she were stopped at the gate, sent to prison, and charged with murder! In the midst of these fluttering thoughts, the escort appeared, took her in, and took her away.

"Is there any noise in the streets?" she asked him.

"The usual noises," Mr. Cruncher replied; and looked surprised by the question and by her aspect.

"I don't hear you," said Miss Pross. "What do you say?"

It was in vain for Mr. Cruncher to repeat what he said; Miss Pross could not hear him. "So I'll nod my head," thought Mr. Cruncher, amazed, "at all events she'll see that." And she did.

"Is there any noise in the streets now?" asked Miss Pross again, presently.

Again Mr. Cruncher nodded his head.

"I don't hear it."

"Gone deaf in a hour?" said Mr. Cruncher, ruminating, with his mind much disturbed; "wot's come to her?"

"I feel," said Miss Pross, "as if there had been a flash and a crash, and that crash was the last thing I should ever hear in this life."

"Blest if she ain't in a queer condition!" said Mr. Cruncher, more and more disturbed. "Wot can she have been a takin', to keep her courage up? Hark! There's the roll of them dreadful carts! You can hear that, miss?"

"I can hear," said Miss Pross, seeing that he spoke to her, "nothing. O, my good man, there was first a great crash, and then a great stillness, and that stillness seems to be fixed and unchangeable, never to be broken any more as long as my life lasts."

"If she don't hear the roll of those dreadful carts, now very nigh their journey's end," said Mr. Cruncher, glancing over his shoulder, "it's my opinion that indeed she never will hear anything else in
5   this world."

And indeed she never did.

Chapter 15. *The Footsteps Die Out For Ever*

Along the Paris streets, the death-carts rumble, hollow and harsh. Six tumbrils carry the day's wine to La Guillotine. All the devouring and insatiate monsters imagined since imagination could record itself, are fused in the one realisation, Guillotine. And yet there is not in France, with its rich variety of soil and climate, a blade, a leaf, a root, a sprig, a peppercorn, which will grow to maturity under conditions more certain than those that have produced this horror. Crush humanity out of shape once more, under similar
15   hammers, and it will twist itself into the same tortured forms. Sow the same seed of rapacious license and oppression over again, and it will surely yield the same fruit according to its kind.

Six tumbrils roll along the streets. Change these back again to what they were, thou powerful enchanter, Time, and they shall be seen to be the carriages of absolute monarchs, the equipages of feudal nobles, the toilettes of flaring Jezebels, the churches that are not my Father's house but dens of thieves, the huts of millions of starving peasants! No; the great magician who majestically works out the appointed order of the Creator never reverses his transfor-
25   mations. "If thou be changed into this shape by the will of God," say the seers to the enchanted, in the wise Arabian stories, "then remain so! But, if thou wear this form through mere passing conjuration, then resume thy former aspect!" Changeless and hopeless, the tumbrils roll along.

As the sombre wheels of the six carts go round, they seem to plough up a long crooked furrow among the populace in the streets. Ridges of faces are thrown to this side and to that, and the ploughs go steadily onward. So used are the regular inhabitants of the houses to the spectacle, that in many windows there are no people, and in some the occupation of the hands is not so much as suspended, while the eyes survey the faces in the tumbrils. Here and there, the inmate has visitors to see the sight; then he points his finger, with something of the complacency of a curator or authorised exponent, to this cart and to this, and seems to tell who sat here yesterday, and who there the day before.

Of the riders in the tumbrils, some observe these things, and all things on their last roadside, with an impassive stare; others, with a lingering interest in the ways of life and men. Some, seated with drooping heads, are sunk in silent despair; again, there are some so heedful of their looks that they cast upon the multitude such glances as they have seen in theatres, and in pictures. Several close their eyes, and think, or try to get their straying thoughts together. Only one, and he a miserable creature, of a crazed aspect, is so shattered and made drunk by horror, that he sings, and tries to dance. Not one of the whole number appeals, by look or gesture, to the pity of the people.

There is a guard of sundry horsemen riding abreast of the tumbrils, and faces are often turned up to some of them, and they are asked some questions. It would seem to be always the same question, for, it is always followed by a press of people towards the third cart. The horsemen abreast of that cart frequently point out one man in it with their swords. The leading curiosity is to know which is he; he stands at the back of the tumbril with his head bent down, to converse with a mere girl who sits on the side of the cart, and holds his hand. He has no curiosity or care for the scene about him, and always speaks to the girl. Here and there in the long street of St. Honoré, cries are raised against him. If they move him at all, it is only to a quiet smile, as he shakes his hair a little more loosely about his face. He cannot easily touch his face, his arms being bound.

On the steps of a church, awaiting the coming-up of the tumbrils, stands the spy and prison-sheep. He looks into the first of them: not there. He looks into the second: not there. He already asks himself, "Has he sacrificed me?" when his face clears, as he looks into the third.

"Which is Evrémonde?" says a man behind him.

"That. At the back there."

"With his hand in the girl's?"

"Yes."

The man cries, "Down, Evrémonde! To the Guillotine all aristocrats; Down, Evrémonde!"

5 "Hush, hush!" the spy entreats him, timidly.

"And why not, citizen?"

"He is going to pay the forfeit: it will be paid in five minutes more. Let him be at peace."

But the man continuing to exclaim, "Down, Evrémonde!" the face of Evrémonde is for a moment turned towards him. Evrémonde then sees the spy, and looks attentively at him, and goes his way.

The clocks are on the stroke of three, and the furrow ploughed among the populace is turning round, to come on into the place of 15 execution, and end. The ridges thrown to this side and to that, now crumble in and close behind the last plough as it passes on, for all are following to the Guillotine. In front of it, seated in chairs, as in a garden of public diversion, are a number of women, busily knitting. On one of the foremost chairs stands The Vengeance, looking about for her friend.

"Thérèse!" she cries, in her shrill tones. "Who has seen her? Thérèse Defarge!"

"She never missed before," says a knitting-woman of the sisterhood.

25 "No; nor will she miss now," cries The Vengeance, petulantly. "Thérèse!"

"Louder," the woman recommends.

Ay! Louder, Vengeance, much louder, and still she will scarcely hear thee. Louder yet, Vengeance, with a little oath or so added, and yet it will hardly bring her. Send other women up and down to seek her, lingering somewhere; and yet, although the messengers have done dread deeds, it is questionable whether of their own will they will go far enough to find her!

"Bad Fortune!" cries The Vengeance, stamping her foot in the 35 chair, "and here are the tumbrils! And Evrémonde will be despatched in a wink, and she not here! See her knitting in my hand, and her empty chair ready for her. I cry with vexation and disappointment!"

As The Vengeance descends from her elevation to do it, the

tumbrils begin to discharge their loads. The ministers of Sainte
Guillotine are robed and ready. Crash!—A head is held up, and the
knitting-women who scarcely lifted their eyes to look at it a
moment ago when it could think and speak, count One.

The second tumbril empties and moves on; the third comes up.   5
Crash!—And the knitting-women, never faltering or pausing in
their work, count Two.

The supposed Evrémonde descends, and the seamstress is lifted
out next after him. He has not relinquished her patient hand in
getting out, but still holds it as he promised. He gently places her
with her back to the crashing engine that constantly whirrs up and
falls, and she looks into his face and thanks him.

"But for you, dear stranger, I should not be so composed, for I
am naturally a poor little thing, faint of heart; nor should I have
been able to raise my thoughts to Him who was put to death, that   15
we might have hope and comfort here to-day. I think you were sent
to me by Heaven."

"Or you to me," says Sydney Carton. "Keep your eyes upon me,
dear child, and mind no other object."

"I mind nothing while I hold your hand. I shall mind nothing
when I let it go, if they are rapid."

"They will be rapid. Fear not!"

The two stand in the fast-thinning throng of victims, but they
speak as if they were alone. Eye to eye, voice to voice, hand to
hand, heart to heart, these two children of the Universal Mother,   25
else so wide apart and differing, have come together on the dark
highway, to repair home together, and to rest in her bosom.

"Brave and generous friend, will you let me ask you one last
question? I am very ignorant, and it troubles me—just a little."

"Tell me what it is."

"I have a cousin, an only relative and an orphan, like myself,
whom I love very dearly. She is five years younger than I, and she
lives in a farmer's house in the south country. Poverty parted us,
and she knows nothing of my fate—for I cannot write—and if I
could, how should I tell her! It is better as it is."   35

"Yes, yes; better as it is."

"What I have been thinking as we came along, and what I am
still thinking now, as I look into your kind strong face which gives
me much support, is this: If the Republic really does good to the

poor, and they come to be less hungry, and in all ways to suffer less, she may live a long time: she may even live to be old."

"What then, my gentle sister?"

"Do you think"—the uncomplaining eyes, in which there is so 5 much endurance, fill with tears, and the lips part a little more and tremble—"that it will seem long to me, while I wait for her in the better land where I trust both you and I will be mercifully sheltered?"

"It cannot be, my child; there is no time there, and no trouble there."

"You comfort me so much! I am so ignorant. Am I to kiss you now? Is the moment come?"

"Yes."

She kisses his lips; he kisses hers; they solemnly bless each other. 15 The spare hand does not tremble as he releases it; nothing worse than a sweet, bright constancy is in the patient face. She goes next before him—is gone; the knitting-women count Twenty-two.

"I am the Resurrection and the Life, saith the Lord: he that believeth in me, though he were dead, yet shall he live: and whosoever liveth and believeth in me shall never die."

The murmuring of many voices, the upturning of many faces, the pressing on of many footsteps in the outskirts of the crowd, so that it swells forward in a mass, like one great heave of water, all flashes away. Twenty-three.

25 They said of him, about the city that night, that it was the peacefullest man's face ever beheld there. Many added that he looked sublime and prophetic.

One of the most remarkable sufferers by the same axe—a woman—had asked at the foot of the same scaffold, not long before, to be allowed to write down the thoughts that were inspiring her. If he had given an utterance to his, and they were prophetic, they would have been these:

"I see Barsad, and Cly, Defarge, The Vengeance, the Juryman, the Judge, long ranks of the new oppressors who have risen on the 35 destruction of the old, perishing by this retributive instrument, before it shall cease out of its present use. I see a beautiful city and a brilliant people rising from this abyss, and, in their struggles to be truly free, in their triumphs and defeats, through long long years to come, I see the evil of this time and of the previous time of which this is the natural birth, gradually making expiation for itself and wearing out.

"I see the lives for which I lay down my life, peaceful, useful, prosperous and happy, in that England which I shall see no more. I see *her* with a child upon her bosom, who bears my name. I see her father, aged and bent, but otherwise restored, and faithful to all men in his healing office, and at peace. I see the good old man, so long their friend, in ten years' time enriching them with all he has, and passing tranquilly to his reward.

"I see that I hold a sanctuary in their hearts, and in the hearts of their descendants, generations hence. I see her, an old woman, weeping for me on the anniversary of this day. I see her and her husband, their course done, lying side by side in their last earthly bed, and I know that each was not more honoured and held sacred in the other's soul, than I was in the souls of both.

"I see that child who lay upon her bosom and who bore my name, a man winning his way up in that path of life which once was mine. I see him winning it so well, that my name is made illustrious there by the light of his. I see the blots I threw upon it faded away. I see him, foremost of the just judges and honoured men, bringing a boy of my name, with a forehead that I know and golden hair, to this place—then fair to look upon, with not a trace of this day's disfigurement—and I hear him tell the child my story, with a tender and faltering voice.

"It is a far, far better thing that I do, than I have ever done; it is a far, far better rest that I go to than I have ever known."

READER'S GUIDE

Henry I. Christ

READER'S GUIDE CONTENTS

INTRODUCTION

The centennial of Charles Dickens's death in 1970 was the occasion for the expression of the universal appreciation of this great novelist's talents. Memorial programs were held. Postage stamps were issued by various countries around the world. Movies made from the great Dickens novels were revived and enjoyed by millions. After a hundred years, characters like Sydney Carton, David Copperfield, Oliver Twist, and Mr. Micawber showed undiminished appeal.

Steven Marcus, in the *New York Times Book Review* for June 7, 1970, wrote, "Dickens was the most popular, the most beloved, the most adulated novelist the world has ever known. His fame was unexampled in his own time; nothing remotely resembling it has ever befallen another writer since. . . . Along with Shakespeare, Dickens is one of the two English writers who have attained what is now an unquestioned world standing." Dickens is read as enthusiastically today as he was read a century ago.

A Tale of Two Cities, like many Dickens novels, speaks directly to our times. The setting of social upheaval and radical change is one that we can identify with. The courage of people under stress holds lessons for us all.

A Tale of Two Cities is, however, much more than a social document. It is a fascinating tale of motivation and countermotivation, of fate and accident. It is a richly plotted novel with constant surprises to keep interest high. The two cities, London and Paris, are compared and contrasted. Characters from both cities begin to touch each others' lives, until they are inextricably bound together. The characters themselves are colorful and memorable.

For purposes of study through the *Reader's Guide,* the book has been divided into fourteen units. The units have been set up to correspond to a number of larger divisions in the story. Only two units, 1 and 7, consist of one chapter each. The first unit provides the background. Unit 7 provides a breather in the middle of the book, a kind of comic interlude that lets the reader relax while the forces build toward the climax of Unit 14. The units in the Guide are organized in five major strands:

Fitting the Jigsaw Together
The Characters and Their Motives
The Social and Historical Setting
Reading in Depth
Words in Their Contexts

Before beginning your reading of the book and your work with the *Reader's Guide,* read the following explanatory comments.

FITTING THE JIGSAW TOGETHER

Contemporary fiction sometimes subordinates plot, but readers a century ago liked a good story and expected writers to fit story elements neatly together. In *A Tale of Two Cities,* Dickens carefully plots his tale from the opening of the story on the lonely Dover road to its ending in Paris.

Nearly all characters, even minor ones, have important roles to play in *A Tale of Two Cities.* No one is introduced just for show. When a character wanders into the story and out again, you may be sure to hear of him again, perhaps at a crucial moment later in the story.

There is a major plot in the story centering around Dr. Manette and Lucie, which, in turn, is interlaced with minor plots. The Defarges, for example, represent a story thread that seems unimportant at first but that later becomes closely woven with the main thread of the story. The career of Jerry Cruncher, unimportant though it at first seems to the story, later plays a key part in the unwinding of the plot.

The manner in which Dickens presents the bits and pieces of his story may very well be compared to a jigsaw puzzle. In the course of working out a jigsaw puzzle, one may find bits and pieces that don't seem to belong anywhere. Finally, however, every piece falls neatly into place to form a perfect, whole design. There may be puzzlement and even frustration along the way, but the final fitting together is then all the more enjoyable. So it is with reading *A Tale of Two Cities.* The questions in this section will help you to see all the pieces clearly and to fit together, finally, the whole exciting design.

THE CHARACTERS AND THEIR MOTIVES

Dickens is deeply interested in people, and his novels reflect that interest. He wonders what makes people tick as he analyzes for us such complicated personalities as Madame Defarge and Sydney

Carton, perhaps the two major antagonists in the novel. Dickens is not just interested in telling us what happens. He also probes *why* and *how*.

The questions appraise the various characters, major and minor. Why does Dr. Manette act as he does? Is there hope for a person like Carton? In the ultimate crucible of character, which is stronger, love or hate? Questions like these explore some of the mainsprings of human emotion and motivation.

The minor characters, endlessly fascinating in Dickens, come in for an important share of the questions. John Barsad, Jerry Cruncher, Miss Pross, Jacques Three, The Vengeance—Dickens portrays a gallery of vivid people. Even the unnamed characters, like the wood-sawyer and the Attorney-General, come to life in Dickens's hand.

Does Dickens portray certain types of characters more success-fully than others? Is Carton more believable when he is with Lucie or with Stryver? Questions like these can stir up discussion and deepen understanding of the novelist's art.

THE SOCIAL AND HISTORICAL SETTING

From the opening description of "the best of times" and "the worst of times," we are caught up in the turbulent years at the end of the eighteenth century. Conditions in England and France are depicted with a journalist's eye and an artist's insight. The origins of the French Revolution are powerfully portrayed in the picture of conditions in France.

Questions in each unit emphasize and explore descriptive touches that reveal an era for us. We learn what it was like to travel in 1775 and how a noble treated the peasants in his village. We learn about legal procedures in an English court in 1780 and in a French court in 1792. The events are played out against a backdrop of history. The questions put these events into proper perspective.

READING IN DEPTH

Dickens has much to offer those readers who look beneath the surface, who appreciate his mastery of the novelist's technique. Dickens often uses humor to help build a character. He uses irony to highlight an event. He uses language skillfully, philosophizes about life in general, and in other ways invites the reader to linger a while and appreciate his insights.

Questions in each unit dig beneath the surface. These questions sometimes use certain terms that may need an explanatory note.

Symbolism. A symbol stands for something else. The stone faces on the château of the Marquis symbolize the cold, inflexible, bitter cruelty of the Marquis himself. Madame Defarge's knitting symbolizes the inevitable unhappy fate of those aristocrats whose names she has inscribed.

Foreshadowing. Dickens likes to give a hint of things to come. In Soho, Lucie and her visitors hear hundreds of footsteps echoing all around them. These footsteps foreshadow the vast crowds that will one day come into their lives. Note that foreshadowing may also be symbolic, as here. Dickens's emphasis upon the footsteps makes the reader a little uneasy—and that is the effect that Dickens wants.

Irony. There is often a great difference between what things appear to be and what they really are. Irony suggests the difference. Jerry Cruncher's description of himself as "an honest tradesman" is ironic, for what Jerry appears to be ("honest") and what he really is (engaged in an illegal enterprise) are quite different. The irony is sharpened by Jerry's unawareness of the contrast.

Simile and Metaphor. Both simile and metaphor compare apparently unlike objects. Simile makes the comparison direct and obvious by using *like* or *as* (page 4 of the text, lines 18–20). Metaphor makes the comparison without *like* or *as* (page 25, lines 36–37). These are both examples of *figurative language,* as is personification.

Personification. A writer may give human attributes to inanimate objects and other nonhuman things and qualities. This process is called personification, as when Dickens personifies the poverty-stricken district of Saint Antoine.

Paradox is a statement that seems self-contradictory, as in this one:

> "The heated argument with his fiancée cooled his affection toward her."

Here *heated* and *cool* seem to contradict each other. The famous statement about generalizations is paradoxical:

> "Every generalization is false—including this one."

If the statement is false, how can the generalization itself be false? Dickens likes to play with paradox.

QUESTIONS

Unit 1: A Time in History
Book the First, Chapter 1

FITTING THE JIGSAW TOGETHER

1. The story proper does not begin in Chapter 1. Rather, Dickens uses this chapter to express himself about the social and historical setting against which the story takes place. However, what suggestion concerning the characters and events of the story is made in the last paragraph of Chapter 1? What does the chapter suggest as a dominant mood of the story?

THE SOCIAL AND HISTORICAL SETTING

2. How does Dickens describe conditions in England in 1775?

3. What event does Dickens refer to in messages from "a congress of British subjects in America"?

4. How does he describe conditions in France in 1775?

5. Were there any resemblances between conditions in England and in France in 1775?

6. Who were the rulers of England and France at this time?

7. What comment does Dickens make about his own time, the time of writing?

8. What conditions resemble those of our own time?

READING IN DEPTH

9. How does Dickens use paradox in this chapter?

10. What does Dickens refer to by "a certain movable framework with a sack and a knife in it"? (page 2, line 16) What is the effect of this manner of description?

11. Why does Dickens make use of personification in talking about the Woodman, Fate, and the Farmer, Death?

12. How does Dickens use irony in describing the execution today "of an atrocious murderer" and tomorrow "of a wretched pilferer who had robbed a farmer's boy of sixpence"? Give another example of irony that conveys Dickens's passionate objection to evils of the period.

WORDS IN THEIR CONTEXTS

Each of the following five words is given in two contexts: (A) from the book and (B) in another sentence that provides a clue to its meaning. Select the best definition of the word as it appears in the two sentences.

1. *epoch* (page 1, line 2)

A. ". . . It was the *epoch* of belief. . . ."

B. The years of the Italian Renaissance were an *epoch* of great creativity and progress in both the arts and sciences.

   a. period of time   *c.* failure

   b. opposite   *d.* good example

2. *incredulity* (page 1, line 3)

A. ". . . It was the epoch of *incredulity*. . . ."

B. The theories of Columbus were looked on by many with *incredulity*, but he was finally proved right.

   a. confidence   *c.* disbelief

   b. unusual happenings   *d.* previous inexperience

3. *humane* (page 2, line 8)

A. ". . . She entertained herself, besides, with such *humane* achievements as sentencing a youth to have his hands cut off, his tongue torn out with pincers, and his body burned alive. . . ."

B. Nursing is a *humane* profession, dedicated to attending to the care and comfort of people in need of such attention.

   a. merciful   *c.* common

   b. technical   *d.* well-paid

4. *rustic* (page 2, line 20)

A. ". . . There were sheltered from the weather that very day, rude carts, bespattered with *rustic* mire. . . ."

B. Many of the Dutch artists preferred to paint country land-scapes, with *rustic* cottages and majestic windmills.

   a. sophisticated   *c.* lowly but dignified

   b. belonging to the   *d.* poorly cared for
      country

5. *myriads* (page 3, line 25)

A. "Thus did the year one thousand seven hundred and seventy-five conduct their Greatnesses, and *myriads* of small crea-tures—the creatures of this chronicle among the rest—along the roads that lay before them."

B. *Myriads* of black flies buzzed around us as we trudged through the wet woods.

   a. excellent examples   *c.* great numbers

   b. miracles   *d.* relatives

Unit 2: The Rescued Prisoner
Book the First, Chapters 2–6

FITTING THE JIGSAW TOGETHER

1. Why is Mr. Lorry traveling to Paris? Why does he plan to take Lucie with him?

2. Jerry Cruncher refers to himself as an "honest tradesman" (page 10, line 15) and suggests that "recalling to life" (page 9, line 2) would be disastrous for him. Keep these comments in mind. What is Jerry's connection with Tellson's Bank and Mr. Lorry?

3. Mr. Lorry says, " 'It is fifteen years since we—since I—came last from France.' " (page 15, lines 12–13) Why does he change *we* to *I*? Who might the other person have been? What is significant about the number of years he mentions? When Lucie mentions her father's story (page 19, line 27), what connection between Mr. Lorry and Lucie becomes apparent?

4. How else does Mr. Lorry try to prepare Lucie gently for the shock of the knowledge of her father's imprisonment?

5. How does the lock of hair saved by Dr. Manette serve to make the connection between past events and the present?

6. How does Lucie have roots in both France and England?

7. How do the Defarges cross the paths of Mr. Lorry and Lucie? What is their attitude, at this time, toward Dr. Manette?

THE CHARACTERS AND THEIR MOTIVES

8. Mr. Lorry is a study in appearances. His outward manner contrasts with his feelings and impulses.

    a. What clues to Mr. Lorry's character are provided when we meet him at the inn? What other clues to his character do we get in his meeting with Lucie?

  b. Mr. Lorry says, " 'I have no feelings. I am a mere machine.' " (page 19, line 26) Is this statement true or false? Why does Mr. Lorry so describe himself? Later he says, " 'That's business, and if business is to be done I had better do it.' " (page 41, lines 37–39) Why does he hide behind "business" to mask his real feelings?

  c. Mr. Lorry is quite overcome by the appearance of "the wild-looking woman," whose name, as you will learn, is Miss Pross. How does he react to her blunt and overpowering actions and comments?

  d. What does the "repeated blowings of his nose" add to our interpretation of Mr. Lorry's character?

9. At this point in the story Lucie Manette is about seventeen years old—possibly close to your age.

  a. How is she described?

  b. How does her conversation with Mr. Lorry reveal her character?

  c. How does Miss Pross's protective attitude toward Lucie help reveal Lucie's character?

  d. How does Lucie's behavior toward her father further reveal her character?

10. The two Defarges are a source of mystery and a challenge to the reader. Their characters are developed for us by little touches and subtle hints.

  a. When we first meet Monsieur Defarge at the wine incident, he says, " 'It's not my affair.' " (page 27, line 19) Why does he say this? Why does he scold the "tall joker" for writing the word "BLOOD"? (The joker's name is Gaspard, page 27, line 24. Remember the name.)

  b. In the wine shop Defarge seems to be extremely cautious in what he says and whom he talks to. What does this tell us about his character—and about the times he lives in?

  c. "Monsieur Defarge bent down on one knee to the child of his old master, and put her hand to his lips. It was a gentle action, but not at all gently done; a very remarkable transformation had come over him in a few seconds. He had no good-humor in his face, nor any openness of aspect left, but had become a secret, angry, dangerous man." What does this quotation mean? How does this description arouse our curiosity about Defarge?

d. What is Defarge's attitude toward Dr. Manette throughout the scene in the garret?

e. Defarge admits that he took Dr. Manette under protection at some danger to himself. What does this information tell us about Defarge? Defarge says, " 'Monsieur Manette is . . . best out of France.' " (page 41, lines 35–36) How does this statement arouse our curiosity about the situation revolving around Dr. Manette?

f. Madame Defarge says very little in these early pages, but we are very much aware of her presence. We get a vivid conception of her character from the descriptions and the little she does say. How does Madame Defarge appear to you at this point in the story?

11. The phrase "Recalled to Life" applies, of course, to Dr. Manette. Note how these early chapters emphasize the horror of his being "buried alive."

a. Early in these pages we are prepared for the appearance of Dr. Manette. How do Mr. Lorry's daydreams give us an inkling of the first actual appearance of Dr. Manette?

b. How is Dr. Manette actually described, in the garret?

c. How does Defarge try to prepare Mr. Lorry and Lucie for the interview with Dr. Manette?

d. Just before meeting her father, Lucie says, " 'I am afraid of it.' " (page 33, line 28) What does her use of the pronoun *it* tell us about her fears?

e. How does Defarge try to prepare Dr. Manette for the interview with Mr. Lorry and Lucie?

f. What does Dr. Manette himself tell us about his background?

g. How does Dr. Manette react in his meeting with Lucie?

h. Why does Mr. Lorry continue to wonder whether Dr. Manette is glad to be "recalled to life"?

12. The two minor characters, Jerry Cruncher and Miss Pross, appear briefly to prepare us for more important roles later on.

a. We first meet Jerry Cruncher as the messenger to the Dover mail. Why do the passengers distrust him?

b. How is Jerry first described when he stops the mail?

c. Miss Pross is first introduced as the "wild-looking woman" with red hair. How else is she described? How does her devotion to Lucie make clear her own character?

d. Miss Pross tends to be emotional rather than logical. How does her explanation for not going to France show a complete lack of logic?

THE SOCIAL AND HISTORICAL SETTING

13. We read a lot today about the difficulties and problems of transportation in automobiles, trains, subways, and airplanes. For one reason or another, throughout history travel has presented hardships. While the modes of travel have changed drastically, problems and inconveniences have always existed. The time of A Tale of Two Cities was no exception. Riding the Dover mail was an adventure.

a. Why did travelers feel insecure on the roads?

b. Why did travelers tend to distrust each other?

c. Are there any parallels between the situation described and the situation in parts of America today? Explain.

14. The word highwayman comes down to us from the seventeenth and eighteenth centuries to refer to a robber who pursued his "trade" on the lonely roads of England. The swaggering robber, often referred to as "Captain," would be hanged if caught, but catching him was not so easy. John Gay's comic The Beggar's Opera tells the tale of the highwayman Captain Macheath—and his unexpected fate.

a. What is meant by this comment: "Every posting-house and ale-house could produce somebody in 'the Captain's' pay"? (page 4, lines 35–37)

b. Who was responsible for protecting the Dover mail?

15. The episode of the spilled wine is dramatic, startling, and informative.

a. How do the people react to the spilled wine? What does this reaction tell us about their lot?

b. The scene is filled with a number of references and descriptions that convey a feeling of menace, of terrible violence to come. Give three or four such references or descriptions.

16. The Defarges seem able to see the horror of the time in perspective and to comment upon it subtly from time to time.

    a. Why does Defarge say, " 'A bitter taste it is that such poor cattle always have in their mouths, and hard lives they live' "? (page 29, lines 26–27) Why does he refer to the people as "cattle"?

    b. Monsieur Defarge admits that he shows poor Monsieur Manette to those "to whom the sight is likely to do good." (page 33, line 10) Why would the sight do somebody good?

    c. Monsieur Defarge allows himself an outcry against the injustice of the time. Why does he say, " 'Long live the Devil' "? (page 32, line 17)

17. In 1358 in France, the peasants rose up in revolt against the nobility. The name *Jacquerie* was applied to them, for the nickname *Jacques* had long been applied to the downtrodden French peasant. The name comes to life again in *A Tale of Two Cities.*

    a. Why should so many people seem to have the same name, *Jacques*?

    b. What does the existence of a secret group tell about the ruling establishment of the day and about the times themselves?

18. The *lettre-de-cachet* was one of the serious abuses of the French monarchy that led to the Revolution. Through its use, the king or a powerful nobleman could have a person suddenly and secretly thrown into prison for life without a trial or even a statement of charges. (See Mr. Lorry's explanation to Lucie, page 20, lines 23–34.)

    a. What is Mr. Lorry hinting to Lucie concerning what had happened to Dr. Manette? Specifically, what are the "blank forms"? From your knowledge of French history can you guess what the "dreadful place" was?

    b. This information helps put part of the jigsaw together. What important questions are raised in the mind of the reader concerning those past events in Dr. Manette's life?

READING IN DEPTH

19. Dickens often makes a word do two jobs. The word may have a simple meaning and a more profound one. When Dr. Manette, for example, is "recalled to life," Dickens wants us to draw parallels between Dr. Manette's nightmarish existence and death itself. The cell becomes a symbol of the death-in-life that Dr. Manette had to endure.

    a. Mr. Lorry thinks that he is going to "dig some one out of a grave." (page 11, line 19) How does this expression apply to Dr. Manette and his imprisonment?

    b. Chapter 3 is called "The Night Shadows." How does the title both describe the time of day and also symbolize Mr. Lorry's misgivings? What does Dickens suggest by the sunrise at the end of the chapter?

    c. Dickens sometimes makes the symbol obvious. For example, when the wine spills, someone writes "BLOOD" on a wall. How does the bursting of the wine cask resemble the outbreak of a revolution?

20. By the use of foreshadowing, Dickens prepares us for events to come. Sometimes these hints are symbolic, as well.

    a. How does the behavior of the people at the spilled-wine episode foreshadow their behavior when revolution comes?

    b. In the ominous description of Madame Defarge, there is additional foreshadowing of events to come. What is the effect of the phrase "saw nothing"? Do you think she saw nothing? Why or why not?

    c. Sometimes the foreshadowing is very subtle. It tantalizes us with just a hint, nothing more. Jerry Cruncher says, " 'You'd be in a Blazing bad way, if recalling to life was to come into fashion, Jerry!' " (page 9, lines 2–3) This foreshadows important events to come. What do you think might be the explanation for Jerry's comment?

21. Charles Dickens is a master of irony. He often uses irony to comment on the great differences between appearances and reality.

    a. The guard on the Dover mail could, if the light were blown out, "shut himself up inside, keep the flint and steel sparks well off the straw, and get a light with tolerable safety and ease (if he were lucky) in five minutes." (page 8, lines 19–21) What does Dickens really think of the guard's ability to get a coach-lamp lit in a hurry?

b. Mr. Lorry calls himself a "man of business," unfeeling and mechanical in his approach to life's problems. Why is his description of himself ironic?

22. Dickens is considered one of the world's great humorists in his creation of unusual characters and situations.

a. In his description of the Dover mail, how does Dickens show his flair for humor in the guard's arsenal of weapons, the passengers' attitude, and the coachman's opinion of his horses?

b. When the mail reaches Dover and the passengers get into the inn, there is a remarkable change in the appearance of those passengers. What does Dickens mean when he says, "But one kind of man was seen to go into it"?

23. Figurative language extends the possibilities of expression. Through simile and metaphor the author can make his statements more vivid and memorable.

a. What things are being compared in each of the following similes? How effective are they?

"There was a steaming mist in all the hollows, and it had roamed in its forlornness up the hill, like an evil spirit, seeking rest and finding none." (page 4, lines 18–20)

"The mildewy inside of the coach, with its damp and dirty straw, its disagreeable smell, and its obscurity, was rather like a larger dog-kennel." (page 13, lines 14–16)

"The coach (in a confused way, like the presence of pain under an opiate) was always with him." (page 11, lines 16–17)

b. What things are being compared in each of the following metaphors? How effective do you consider them?

"A people [of Saint Antoine] that had undergone a terrible grinding and re-grinding in the mill" (page 25, lines 35–37)

"The gaunt scarecrows of that region [the people of Saint Antoine]" (page 27, lines 9–10)

24a. Dickens says that "every human creature is constituted to be that profound secret and mystery to every other." (page 9, lines 4–5) Do you agree? Is it possible truly to know anyone else? Is it possible truly to know oneself? What do you think?

b. In his description of the old building in Saint Antoine, Dickens suggests that physical pollution can bring on spiritual pollution as well. Do you agree? In our own day, has man's continuing pollution of his natural environment affected his spiritual health as well?

25. For Dickens the end of a chapter can be a summarizing statement, a hint of something to come, or an unfinished comment that entices us to read on.

a. How does each chapter in this unit end?

b. Do you consider the chapter endings effective? Why or why not?

WORDS IN THEIR CONTEXTS

Each of the following ten words is given in two contexts: (A) from the book and (B) in another sentence that provides a clue to its meaning. Select the best definition of the word as it appears in the two sentences.

1. tremulous (page 4, line 9)

A. "With dropping heads and tremulous tails, they mashed their way through the thick mud, floundering and stumbling between whiles, as if they were falling to pieces at the larger joints."

B. Fearing a stern rebuke, Anne told her father, in a tremulous voice, about the dent in the car fender.

    a. strong   c. thin
    b. trembling   d. light

2. cessation (page 6, line 13)

A. "The stillness consequent on the cessation of the rumbling and labouring of the coach, added to the stillness of the night, made it very quiet indeed."

B. After the cessation of hostilities against Japan, the American government undertook to assist with the rebuilding of the country.

    a. build-up   c. repetition
    b. publication   d. stopping

3. *submerged* (page 9, line 15)

A. "I have had glimpses of buried treasure and other things *submerged.*"

B. The stricken submarine was lying on the bottom, *submerged* at a depth of eighty feet.

a. under water   c. moving about
b. discovered   d. announced

4. *sinister* (page 10, line 8)

A. "They had a *sinister* expression, under an old cocked-hat. . . ."

B. To the true believers in democracy, the dictator's words had a *sinister* ring as he urged his people to give up freedom for national glory.

a. pleasant   c. evil
b. profound   d. uncertain

5. *disconcerted* (page 23, line 27)

A. "Mr. Lorry was so exceedingly *disconcerted* by a question so hard to answer, that he could only look on, at a distance, with much feeble sympathy and humility. . . ."

B. The actress was momentarily *disconcerted* by the missed cue, but she quickly recovered her poise and repeated her line.

a. disturbed   c. challenged
b. attracted   d. cheered

6. *mutilated* (page 24, line 20)

A. "Others, men and women, dipped in the puddles with little mugs of *mutilated* earthenware. . . ."

B. The senator felt that his speech had been *mutilated* by the report, for a number of important points had been omitted.

a. stimulated   c. improved
b. accepted   d. damaged

7. *prevalent* (page 26, line 5)

A. "It [hunger] was *prevalent* everywhere."

B. Researchers discovered that malaria was *prevalent* in areas infested by mosquitoes.

a. conquered
b. commonly occurring
c. easily rejected
d. unseen

8. *homage* (page 29, line 36)

A. "She acknowledged their *homage* by bending her head, and giving them a quick look."

B. The singer's fans paid *homage* to her by turning out in great numbers for her concert in Central Park despite the rainy weather.

a. show of loyalty
b. homesickness
c. noisy disagreement
d. lukewarm appraisal

9. *transformation* (page 30, line 29)

A. "A very remarkable *transformation* had come over him in a few seconds."

B. When the interior decorator had completed the job, the owner of the house was amazed at the *transformation*.

a. upset
b. change
c. sight
d. stillness

10. *coercion* (page 42, line 35)

A. "In the submissive way of one long accustomed to obey under *coercion*, he ate and drank what they gave him to eat and drink. . . ."

B. The prisoner insisted that *coercion* had been used in extracting a confession from him.

a. encouragement
b. force
c. quiet
d. observer

Unit 3: The Trial

Book the Second, Chapters 1–3

FITTING THE JIGSAW TOGETHER

1. Five years have passed and the story is renewed on the occasion of a dramatic trial for treason.

    a. Who is being tried, what are the specific charges, and what is the penalty if the accused is found guilty?

    b. Why are Mr. Lorry, Dr. Manette, and Lucie present at the trial? What is their attitude toward Darnay? Why is Jerry Cruncher present?

    c. Over the period of five years, how have Dr. Manette and Lucie fared?

2. Identify John Barsad, Roger Cly, Stryver, and Carton and explain their roles at the trial.

3. What is the outcome of the trial? Whose activities seem to be chiefly responsible for the verdict?

4. What questions are raised in these chapters concerning certain puzzling aspects of the life and activities of Jerry Cruncher?

THE CHARACTERS AND THEIR MOTIVES

5. Charles Darnay takes the center of the stage because of his trial. Throughout the novel he and Sydney Carton are balanced against each other.

    a. How is Darnay described?

    b. How does Darnay show his courage in awaiting the verdict?

    c. How does Darnay show consideration in his reaction to Lucie's fainting?

6. Sydney Carton, we are shown, is everything that Darnay is not; yet we soon come to respect him.

    a. When we first meet Carton, he is described as a "wigged gentleman with his hands in his pockets, whose whole attention, when Mr. Cruncher looked at him then or afterwards, seemed to be concentrated on the ceiling of the court." (page 53, lines 37–39) Shortly afterward he is called "the one wigged gentleman who looked at the ceiling." (page 54, lines 15–16) What clues to Carton's character do these seem to present? Why do we suspect later that Carton's apparent inattentiveness is a pose?

b. As Jerry Cruncher looks at Carton, he comments to a neighbor, " 'I'd hold half a guinea that *he* don't get no law work to do. Don't look like the sort of one to get any, do he?' " (page 67, lines 25–26) How does Cruncher's evaluation suggest how Carton is looked upon by others? How accurate is Cruncher's appraisal?

c. Why does Sydney Carton volunteer to speak to Darnay?

7. John Barsad and Roger Cly are introduced in these chapters and then disappear for a while, to return later.

a. Why do the government lawyers so obviously overstate the meager virtues of Barsad and Cly? What do these "virtues" actually seem to consist of?

b. How is Barsad's true personality revealed for us on page 59, lines 14–38?

8. What picture do you get of the Cruncher family—Jerry, his wife, his son, and the relationship among them?

THE SOCIAL AND HISTORICAL SETTING

9. What is the chief characteristic of Tellson's Bank as conveyed by Dickens through his description? What analogy does Dickens make to the country as a whole?

10. What impressions does Dickens give of the whole system of English law and justice?

READING IN DEPTH

11. Who are the "blue-flies"? Why are they so called?

12. Though these chapters deal principally with a rather grim situation, there is also humor in them.

a. How does Jerry Cruncher confuse the words *Anno Domini,* the "year of our Lord"? (page 47, lines 25–29) What word does he intend by "Aggerawayter"?

b. How does young Jerry, "a grisly urchin of twelve" (page 47, line 15), resemble his father (page 50, lines 25–39)?

c. Why does Dickens use the invented-word combination "evil-adverbiously"? (page 55, line 20)

d. How does Dickens poke fun at the absurd eulogy of Roger Cly by the Attorney-General? (page 58) At the character of John Barsad? (pages 57, 59)

13. How will a modern reader be affected by Lucie's testimony on Darnay's remarks about George Washington, and the judge's reaction? (page 64)

14. Dickens enjoys showing us weaknesses in presenting the evidence against Darnay.

a. The Attorney-General concedes that the lists may not be in the prisoner's handwriting. (page 58, lines 19–22) Why might "You can't win" be applied to this kind of reasoning?

b. What is unreasonable about the Attorney-General's arguments that Darnay might have been on the Dover Mail?

c. What is unreasonable about the Attorney-General's assumption that the men Darnay met with in the boat were spies? (page 63, lines 2–19)

15. What does Dickens think of the statement "Whatever is, is right"? (page 53, line 1)

16. Why does Dickens use the expression "unconscious inconsistency" about Jerry Cruncher's thought processes? (page 48, line 31)

17. How does each of the three chapters end? Do you consider the endings effective?

WORDS IN THEIR CONTEXTS

1. eminence (page 45, line 7)

A. "They were even boastful of its eminence in those particulars, and were fired by an express conviction that, if it were not less objectionable, it would be less respectable."

B. Mickey Mantle owes his eminence among baseball heroes to his home-run record.

    a. adaptability   c. award
    b. place of honor   d. quiet reputation

2. *dismal* (page 46, line 6)

   A. ". . . You could hardly blink at it in the *dismal* twilight."

   B. It was a *dismal* day of gray skies and a chill rain.

     a. cheerful   *c.* gloomy

     b. irritating   *d.* fading

3. *animosity* (page 49, line 33)

   A. "He resented Mrs. Cruncher's saying grace with particular *animosity*."

   B. The audience showed *animosity* toward the speaker because of his backward, dangerous ideas.

     a. liveliness   *c.* neutral feeling

     b. appreciation   *d.* hatred

4. *demur* (page 53, line 14)

   A. "After some delay and *demur,* the door grudgingly turned on its hinges a very little way, and allowed Mr. Jerry Cruncher to squeeze himself into court."

   B. Since there was no *demur,* the chairman went ahead to the next item on the agenda.

     a. objection   *c.* cry of approval

     b. noise   *d.* vigorous action

5. *conspicuous* (page 54, line 23)

   A. "*Conspicuous* among these latter, like an animated bit of the spiked wall of Newgate, Jerry stood."

   B. At the Woodstock Festival there was a *conspicuous* emphasis upon youth.

     a. clearly visible   *c.* long-standing

     b. somewhat concealed *d.* optimistic

6. *flinched* (page 55, line 31)

   A. "The accused . . . neither *flinched* from the situation, nor assumed any theatrical air in it."

   B. Ed *flinched* involuntarily as he saw the car come to a screeching halt within inches of a stalled truck.

     a. stood still   *c.* shrank back

     b. relaxed   *d.* moved about

7. *immaculate* (page 58, line 4)

  A. ". . . . The lofty example of this *immaculate* and unimpeach-able witness for the Crown . . . had communicated itself to the prisoner's servant. . . ."

  B. The once-*immaculate* table cloth now had a large brown stain on it.

     a. spotless   *c.* rough

     b. new   *d.* noble

8. *insinuation* (page 59, line 15)

  A. "No, he scorned the base *insinuation*."

  B. By *insinuation,* rather than by direct statement, Iago poisoned the mind of Othello.

     a. comment   *c.* repetition

     b. retort   *d.* sly hint

9. *faculties* (page 65, line 2)

  A. "She had become familiar to me, when a gracious God restored my *faculties*."

  B. The attorney argued that his client could not be held re-sponsible because he was mentally ill and not in full com-mand of his *faculties.*

     a. college teachers   *c.* wealth and fame

     b. thinking abilities   *d.* situations

10. *audibly* (page 67, line 30)

  A. "He was the first to see it, and to say *audibly:* 'Officer! look to that young lady.' "

  B. Unless you speak *audibly,* you will lose your listeners.

     a. sharply   *c.* slowly enough to hold interest

     b. loud enough to be heard   *d.* logically enough to be under-stood

Unit 4: After the Trial
Book the Second, Chapters 4–6

FITTING THE JIGSAW TOGETHER

1. How does Darnay feel about Lucie?

2. After the acquittal, Dr. Manette has a surprising reaction to Darnay.

> "His face had become frozen, as it were, in a very curious look at Darnay: an intent look, deepening into a frown of dislike and distrust, not even unmixed with fear. With this strange expression on him his thoughts had wandered away." (page 71, lines 19–22)

What might account for this strange behavior on the part of Dr. Manette?

3. How does Carton suggest his own feelings toward Lucie as he talks with Darnay? As he talks with Stryver?

4. What information would Mr. Lorry like to have about Dr. Manette? How does Miss Pross feel about the uncovering of Dr. Manette's past?

5. What seizures is Dr. Manette subject to? How does he react to Darnay's story about the prisoner in the Tower?

6. Why does Darnay visit the house near Soho Square? Why does Carton come?

THE CHARACTERS AND THEIR MOTIVES

7. Stryver is obviously successful, largely because of his friendship with Carton.

    a. How is Stryver described on page 70, lines 26–31? What is Dickens's opinion of the man?

    b. What does the following statement tell us about Stryver?

> "It had once been noted at the Bar, that while Mr. Stryver was a glib man, and an unscrupulous, and a ready, and a bold, he had not that faculty of extracting the essence from

a heap of statements, which is among the most striking and necessary of the advocate's accomplishments." (page 76, lines 13–17)

Evidently, who had this faculty?

c. Twice on page 71 Stryver is mentioned as having "shouldered" his way into a group. The word is mentioned again at the top of page 76 and of 80. What does Dickens's use of this word tell us about Stryver?

d. How does Stryver show his lack of sensitivity in dealing with Carton?

e. According to old beliefs, jackals hunted the prey that the lion then consumed, the jackal being called the "lion-provider." Why is Stryver called the *lion* and Carton the *jackal*?

f. Dickens sometimes chooses names for specific reasons. Does the name *Stryver* suggest any quality?

8. Darnay is like Carton—and unlike him.

a. How does Darnay react to Carton's question, "Do you think I particularly like you?" How does Darnay show his good manners and essential decency?

b. How does Darnay show his gratitude to Stryver for being acquitted?

c. Why did Darnay let it be thought he would not be released from prison on the night of the acquittal?

9. The character of Sydney Carton begins to come to light—in what he says, what he does, how he reacts to others.

a. When we meet Carton after the trial he is "leaning against the wall where its shadow was darkest." (page 71, line 39) What does this phrase tell us about Carton's character?

b. " 'So, Mr. Lorry! Men of business may speak to Mr. Darnay now?' " (page 72, line 4) Why is Carton chiding Mr. Lorry here? How does Lorry look upon him?

c. Everyone congratulates Stryver. "Nobody had made any acknowledgment of Mr. Carton's part in the day's proceedings; nobody had known of it. He was unrobed, and was none the better for it in appearance." (page 72, lines 5–7) How does this neglect of Carton tell us something about him as well as about the others?

d. Why does Carton seem so bitter toward Darnay? (page 75, lines 13–21)

e. How does Carton, in speaking with Stryver and Darnay, refer to Lucie Manette? What do these references tell us about his attitude toward her? (Note that he goes to visit her in Soho.)

f. Carton constantly reveals his inner turmoil, but few people listen to him. He calls himself a "disappointed drudge" on page 75 and adds, " 'I care for no man on earth, and no man on earth cares for me.' " What does Carton seem to be seeking?

g. What explanation can you offer for the fact that a man with the obvious talents of Carton should have become so cynical and disillusioned?

h. Stryver holds himself up to Carton as an example to follow (page 79). Why is this so ironic?

i. Stryver asks Carton (page 79, line 1), " 'What has roughened your temper?' " How would you answer that question?

j. Carton is aware of his imperfections and is inclined toward self-pity. Can people like Carton be helped? How?

10. What additional information about Dr. Manette's present condition do we get on page 70, lines 4–24?

11. What additional information about Lucie Manette is provided in the description of her home? (page 83, lines 9–23)

12. What kind of person is Miss Pross's brother Solomon? What is Miss Pross's attitude toward him? How does Miss Pross show that she is not only protective of Lucie, but also possessive?

13. What opinion does Mr. Lorry have of Miss Pross?

THE SOCIAL AND HISTORICAL SETTING

14. How does Darnay's description of a dungeon in the Tower of London resemble conditions in the Bastille before the French Revolution?

READING IN DEPTH

15. Dickens's choice of the right word brightens many descriptions throughout the book.

a. What is the "human stew" that "had been boiling" in the court? (page 69, line 32)

b. When Carton asks Darnay, " 'You think I am drunk?' " Darnay replies, " 'I think you have been drinking.' " (page 74, lines 38–39) What is the distinction between the two statements? Which statement is a judgment and which a statement of fact?

c. Mr. Stryver's face is seen daily "bursting out of the bed of wigs, like a great sunflower pushing its way at the sun from among a rank garden full of flaring companions." (page 76, lines 10–12) What two things are being compared? What does this description tell us of Stryver?

16. Two important elements in foreshadowing are emphasized in these chapters: the resemblance of Darnay and Carton and the possible consequences for the future; and the great many people who would some day enter the lives of our characters.

a. Carton tells Darnay, " 'Don't let your sober face elate you, however; you don't know what it may come to.' " (page 75, lines 7–8) What does Carton mean here? (See also page 77, lines 26–31.)

b. Miss Pross says, " 'We shall have hundreds of people pretty soon!' " (page 87, lines 35–36) Carton says, " 'It comes surely.' " (page 91, line 14) Lucie says, " 'I have made the echoes out to be the echoes of all the footsteps that are coming by and by into our lives.' " (page 91, lines 31–33) The author says, "Perhaps, see the great crowd of people with its rush and roar, bearing down upon them, too." (page 92, lines 34–35) What do these quotations lead the reader to expect in later pages?

17. Dickens uses the symbol of "the golden thread" (page 70, line 18) to refer to Lucie. Do you consider this a good symbol? Why or why not?

18. We must read between the lines in a statement like this:

"The more business he [Stryver] got, the greater his power seemed to grow of getting at its pith and marrow; and however late at night he sat carousing with Sydney Carton, he always had his points at his fingers' ends in the morning." (page 76, lines 18–21)

Why was Stryver able to do so good a job? What did these late-night sessions do for him?

WORDS IN THEIR CONTEXTS

1. *beneficial* (page 70, line 21)
   A. ". . . The sound of her voice, the light of her face, the touch of her hand, had a strong *beneficial* influence with him almost always."
   B. If you find a low-sugar diet *beneficial,* it makes sense to continue with it.
      a. controlling
      b. powerful
      c. helpful
      d. negative

2. *fervently* (page 70, line 25)
   A. "Mr. Darnay had kissed her hand *fervently* and gratefully. . . ."
   B. The scientist talked *fervently* of the need to control pollution if life is to survive on earth.
      a. monotonously
      b. warmly
      c. hesitantly
      d. foolishly

3. *dispersed* (page 71, line 27)
   A. "The friends of the acquitted prisoner had *dispersed*. . . ."
   B. When the police arrived, the crowd *dispersed* and the streets were soon empty.
      a. shouted
      b. gathered together
      c. wept
      d. scattered

4. *terrestrial* (page 73, line 19)
   A. " 'Do you feel, yet, that you belong to this *terrestrial* scheme again, Mr. Darnay?' "
   B. The mystic was more concerned with affairs and concerns of the spirit world than the *terrestrial* one.
      a. pertaining to the earth
      b. carefully planned
      c. fully developed
      d. navigational

5. *lucrative* (page 76, line 1)
   A. "[Stryver was] shouldering his way to a large and *lucrative* practice. . . ."
   B. Teaching may not be a *lucrative* profession, but it provides satisfactions not dependent on money.
      a. imposing
      b. yielding wealth
      c. famous
      d. complicated

6. *adjoining* (page 77, line 35)

   A. ". . . The jackal . . . went into an *adjoining* room. . . ."

   B. The young couple went into an *adjoining* state for a marriage license because they could not get one in the state in which they resided.

      a. large   *c.* legal
      b. bordering   *d.* pleasant

7. *complied* (page 78, line 36)

   A. "The jackal . . . shook himself, yawned, shivered, and com-plied."

   B. As an alien, Jan was requested to register periodically, and he *complied*, reporting twice a year to the registry office.

      a. disagreed   *c.* resisted
      b. seemed indifferent   *d.* cooperated

8. *congenial* (page 81, line 33)

   A. "[The] street . . . had a *congenial* air of retirement on it."

   B. *Congenial* companions, pleasant surroundings, and good food always make our college reunions enjoyable.

      a. strange   *c.* obvious
      b. agreeable   *d.* forceful

9. *traversed* (page 82, line 27)

   A. "Occasionally, a stray workman, putting his coat on, trav-ersed the hall. . . ."

   B. Where once camels *traversed* the desert in lonely majesty, jeeps and trucks now cross the sandy terrain.

      a. observed   *c.* crossed
      b. made a noise   *d.* measured

10. *compunction* (page 85, line 35)

   A. "Solomon was a heartless scoundrel who had stripped her of everything she possessed . . . with no touch of *compunc-tion*. . . ."

   B. Edie seems to have no *compunction* about breaking a date at the last minute.

      a. courage   *c.* cheerfulness
      b. sense of guilt   *d.* heroism

Unit 5: Rumblings of Revolution
Book the Second, Chapters 7–9

FITTING THE JIGSAW TOGETHER

1. Why did the Marquis come to town?
2. What accident occurs on the Marquis's trip back to his home?
3. When the road mender says (page 103, line 4), " 'I looked at the man,' " what man is he referring to?
4. The Marquis is expecting someone named Charles. Who, in the story, is named Charles? What is the family relationship between the Marquis and Charles?
5. What episode in his life is Charles Darnay referring to when he says, " 'It carried me into great and unexpected peril' "? (page 108, line 29)
6. Charles suggests that the Marquis is in some disgrace at Court. (page 109, line 21) If the Marquis had still been powerful, what might have happened to Charles?
7. Darnay says (page 110, lines 14–15) that his family name is one of the most hated in France. How does the Marquis look upon that hatred?
8. What did Darnay's mother ask of him on her deathbed?
9. What declaration does Darnay make to his uncle?
10. In talking of England, the Marquis mentions a doctor and his daughter. (page 113, lines 6–8) About whom is he probably speaking? How does the Marquis's manner suggest that he knows something about that doctor and his daughter?
11. What happens to the Marquis? What clues to his murderer are given?

THE CHARACTERS AND THEIR MOTIVES

12. The person and character of the Marquis are carefully drawn.
    a. How is the Marquis described? (page 97, line 29–page 98, line 3)

   b. How does the Marquis show his personality in these episodes: the reception, the accident, listening to the road mender's story, listening to the widow's request, talking to Charles Darnay?

   c. Why does the Marquis feel so secure in his wealth, his rank, and his cruelty?

13. The two Defarges appear on the scene briefly after the death of the child, but their appearance is memorable.

   a. How does Monsieur Defarge comfort the father of the child?

   b. How does Madame Defarge show her courage before the Marquis?

   c. What reference is made to Madame Defarge at the top of page 101?

14. The Monseigneur who held the reception is higher in social rank than the Marquis. In what ways are the Monseigneur and the Marquis similar?

15. On what earlier occasion did we meet Gaspard, the father of the dead child? What had Gaspard written on the wall?

16. How does Charles Darnay continue to show a sense of decency and real social concern for the needs of the poor?

17. What is Gabelle's attitude toward the Marquis? (page 104, line 1)

THE SOCIAL AND HISTORICAL SETTING

18. How does the Monseigneur's reception make clear the pointless luxury of the wealthy?

19. Why did the Monseigneur marry his sister to the tax collector, the Farmer-General? How did the Monseigneur's sister make clear that she considered herself above her husband?

20. Why does Dickens say that the Farmer-General was "at least the greatest reality among the personages who attended"? (page 94, lines 28–29)

21. What was the attitude of aristocratic mothers toward having children?

22. Why was the Marquis able to get away with the killing of the child? How did he think he could make amends for the death?

23. How does Dickens explain, in part, the poverty of the people? (page 102, lines 5–13)

24. What two alternatives were there for the poor? (page 102, lines 14–18)

25. The Marquis complains that things were better in the old days. (pages 109–110) What does he mean? Better for whom? If conditions are so bad at the time of the story, what might be said for conditions a generation earlier?

READING IN DEPTH

26. Dickens again uses foreshadowing as he prepares us for events to come. How does each of the following quotations foreshadow the future?

   a. "The sunset struck so brilliantly into the travelling carriage when it gained the hill-top, that its occupant was steeped in crimson." (page 101, lines 21–22)

   b. "The red glow departed quickly; the sun and the Marquis going down together." (page 101, lines 28–29)

27. How does the author use symbolism in each of the following?

   a. "It would have been of as much avail to interrogate any stone face outside the château as to interrogate that face of his." (page 113, lines 19–20)

   b. "In the glow, the water of the château seemed to turn to blood, and the stone faces crimsoned." (page 114, lines 32–34)

   c. "It portended that there was one stone face too many, up at the château." (page 116, lines 10–11)

28. Irony is a strong weapon in the author's attack on the social structure of France at the time of the story. How is it illustrated in each of the following?

   a. "Military officers destitute of military knowledge; naval officers with no idea of a ship; civil officers without a notion of affairs." (page 94, line 39–page 95, line 2)

   b. "Who . . . could possibly doubt that a system rooted in a frizzled hangman, powdered, gold-laced, pumped, and white-silk stockinged, would see the very stars out!" (page 97, lines 2–6)

   c. "But for the latter inconvenience [the rearing of the horses], the carriage probably would not have stopped." (page 98, lines 27–28) *d.* " 'One or the other of you is for ever in the way. How do I know what injury you have done my horses?. See! Give him that.' " (page 99, lines 19–21)

    e. " 'My friend, I will die, perpetuating the system under which I have lived.' " (page 111, lines 36–37)

29. What does Dickens mean when he says, "The leprosy of unreality disfigured every human creature in attendance upon Monseigneur"? (page 95, lines 37–38)

30. How does Dickens poke fun at the absurdity of the social structure in describing the Monseigneur's need for four men to serve him chocolate? (page 93, lines 8–22)

31. Why is Chapter 9 called "The Gorgon's Head"?

WORDS IN THEIR CONTEXTS

  1. *dispense with* (page 93, line 18)

    A. "It was impossible for Monseigneur to *dispense with* one of these attendants on the chocolate. . . ."

    B. The corporation decided to *dispense with* its own research division and to rely on outside consultants for research.

       a. rely upon   *c.* get along without
       b. emphasize   *d.* advertise

  2. *abominable* (page 98, line 39)

    A. " 'Why does he make that *abominable* noise?' "

    B. One of the most urgent problems of modern times is the *abominable* conditions found in big-city slum areas.

       a. very loud   *c.* most obvious
       b. hateful   *d.* sarcastic

  3. *vendor* (page 100, line 12)

    A. "He looked to the spot where Defarge the *vendor* of wine had stood a moment before."

    B. A *vendor* was crying his wares along the narrow street of the old city, but there were no buyers.

       a. seller   *c.* consumer
       b. advertiser   *d.* discoverer

4. *obsequiousness* (page 103, line 35)

A. "[Gabelle] had come out with great *obsequiousness* to assist at this examination. . . ."

B. *Obsequiousness* was not one of his characteristics for he was loud and overbearing.

a. hustle and bustle   c. vigor
b. seriousness   d. excessive humility

5. *diversified* (page 107, line 4)

A. "The fashion . . . was *diversified* by many objects that were illustrations of old pages in the history of France."

B. The school curriculum in its rich offering of a variety of subjects is much more *diversified* now than it was ten years ago.

a. made rich   c. illustrated
b. made less   d. varied

6. *imperturbable* (page 107, line 33)

A. " 'Good,' said the *imperturbable* master. 'Close them again.' "

B. Despite the noise of the small children all around him, Mr. Porter remained *imperturbable*.

a. excitable   c. calm
b. irritable   d. interested

7. *diminished* (page 108, lines 1–2)

A. "He had *diminished* the distance rapidly, but not so rapidly as to come up with Monseigneur on the road."

B. The quarterback's bruised thumb *diminished* the team's chances in their bid for the championship.

a. increased   c. made more clear
b. lessened   d. reflected

8. *ominous* (page 108, line 38)

A. "The deepened marks in the nose, and the lengthening of the fine straight lines in the cruel face, looked *ominous* as to that."

B. *Ominous* black clouds in the west cut short the picnickers' gaiety.

a. threatening   c. cutting
b. mild   d. dark

9. *terminate* (page 111, line 6)

A. " 'Shall we *terminate* our conference for the night?' "

B. Both sides agreed to *terminate* the contract and end the relationship altogether.

    a. expand   *c.* end

    b. renew   *d.* discuss

10. *rational* (page 111, line 40)

A. " 'Better to be a *rational* creature . . . and accept your natural destiny.' "

B. If we are to be *rational,* we must find solutions for the continuing destruction of our natural environment and the consequent threat to our own welfare.

    a. relevant   *c.* courageous

    b. reasonable   *d.* unchanging

Unit 6: Lucie's Suitors
Book the Second, Chapters 10–13

FITTING THE JIGSAW TOGETHER

1. How long a time has passed since the death of the Marquis?

2. How much does Lucie know of the circumstances of Charles's visit to the Marquis?

3. What job has Darnay found to support himself in England?

4. Of what subject does Darnay speak to Dr. Manette? What is Dr. Manette's reaction as he listens?

5. Darnay says, "Like you, a voluntary exile from France; like you, driven from it by its distractions, oppressions, and miseries." (page 121, lines 1–2) Why does Darnay mention this fact?

6. What does Darnay ask of Dr. Manette? How does Dr. Manette accept this request?

7. Why does Dr. Manette ask Darnay not to tell his real name?

8. What happens to Dr. Manette after Darnay's visit? What might be the reason for this reaction?

9. Whom does Stryver intend to marry? Why has he chosen her?

10. To what other person, besides Carton, does Stryver reveal his matrimonial plans? What advice does this person give Stryver?

11. What decision, about his marriage plans, does Stryver make at last? Why?

12. Why does Carton visit Lucie? What promise does he make?

THE CHARACTERS AND THEIR MOTIVES

13. A major contrast in this unit is between Stryver, "the fellow of delicacy" (as he thinks), and Carton, "the fellow of no delicacy."

    a. How does Stryver reveal his character again in giving his reasons for marrying?

    b. Of the Stryver-Carton pair, one member rather clearly understands the other, though the reverse is not true. Which is the perceptive member of the pair? Prove your point by referring to the conversation.

c. Stryver and Carton have contrasting attitudes toward Lucie. What are they?

d. How does Stryver's attitude toward his defeat in love further reveal his character?

e. Why does Carton often wander around near Lucie's house?

14. How does Darnay, in his interview with Dr. Manette, show a consistent characterization with the Darnay we have already met?

15. How does Dr. Manette further reveal his own character in the interview with Darnay?

16. How does Mr. Lorry show himself a perceptive old man in his advice to Stryver?

17. Why does Lucie weep during the interview with Carton?

THE SOCIAL AND HISTORICAL SETTING

18. Why does Darnay speak first to Dr. Manette before proposing to Lucie?

19. Why does Stryver feel his marriage venture will prosper, even though there hasn't been the slightest romantic association with the girl he'd like to marry?

20. What does "these days when it is mostly winter in fallen latitudes" (page 117, line 17) mean? Do we tend to think of other days as better days?

READING IN DEPTH

21. Stryver presents first to Carton and then to Lorry his intentions to marry Lucie. There is much irony, quite unintended by Stryver, in his own words and thoughts concerning himself. Why? Give some examples.

22. How does Carton react to Stryver's announcement? Lorry?

23. Dickens's special brand of humor usually depends upon characterizing the foibles and vanities of human beings. Stryver looks upon his marriage plans in legal terms.

"As to the strength of his case, he had not a doubt about it, but clearly saw his way to the verdict. Argued with the jury on substantial worldly grounds—the only grounds ever worth taking into account—it was a plain case, and had not a weak spot in it. He called himself for the plaintiff, there was no getting over his evidence, the counsel for the defendant threw up his brief, and the jury did not even turn to consider. After trying it, Stryver, C.J., was satisfied that no plainer case could be." (page 128, lines 1–8)

What basic element has Stryver not taken into account?

24. Some critics feel that Dickens is more at home when he is writing about less idealized characters than Lucie and Dr. Manette. Chapter 11, with its snappy dialogue between Carton and Stryver, can be contrasted with Chapters 10 and 13, where Darnay converses with the Doctor and where Carton converses with Lucie. Which chapter seems to you to present the more realistic dialogue?

25. We display different personalities when we are with different people. When Carton is talking to Stryver or Darnay, he speaks quite differently from the way he does when he is talking to Lucie. Which picture of Carton do you prefer? Why?

26. In Chapter 13 there are several hints about the role Carton may play in the future in the life of Lucie—for example:

" 'No, Mr. Carton. I am sure that the best part of it might still be; I am sure that you might be much, much worthier of yourself.' " (page 135, lines 27–28)

" '. . . When you see your own bright beauty springing up anew at your feet, think now and then that there is a man who would give his life, to keep a life you love beside you!' " (page 138, lines 14–16)

Can you think of ways in which Sydney Carton might help Lucie or her family?

27. One technique of evading a question is to ask a question in reply. When Stryver asks Carton whether or not Carton approves of Stryver's marriage plans, Carton replies, "Why should I not approve?" How does Carton really feel about the plans?

28. What does Dickens think of the law in this quotation:

"Everything was got rid of until November should come with its fogs atmospheric and fogs legal, and bring grist to the mill again." (page 124, lines 11–12)

WORDS IN THEIR CONTEXTS

1. *shrewd* (page 124, line 25)

A. " 'I am going to tell you something that will rather surprise you, and that perhaps will make you think me not quite as *shrewd* as you usually do think me.' "

B. The chess master made a *shrewd* move, after which his opponent resigned.

   a. clever   *c.* offbeat and impractical
   b. highly emotional   *d.* colorful and exciting

2. *intelligible* (page 125, line 2)

A. " 'Sydney, I rather despair of making myself *intelligible* to you, because you are such an insensible dog.' "

B. The student writes so carelessly his papers are barely *intelligible*.

   a. appreciated   *c.* free of restrictions
   b. understandable   *d.* enjoyable

3. *moroseness* (page 125, line 21)

A. " 'Why, I have been ashamed of your *moroseness* there!' "

B. Paul's unusual *moroseness* is due to a disagreement with his fiancée.

   a. talkativeness   *c.* cleverness
   b. arrogance   *d.* gloominess

4. *ostentatious* (page 126, line 10)

A. ". . . Mr. Stryver [prepared] him with *ostentatious* friendliness for the disclosure he was about to make. . . ."

B. All that extra jewelry made Leona's outfit seem too *ostentatious*.

   a. noisy   *c.* showy
   b. appropriate   *d.* restrained

5. *magnanimous* (page 127, line 27)

A. "Mr. Stryver having made up his mind to that *magnanimous* bestowal of good fortune on the Doctor's daughter, resolved to make her happiness known to her before he left town for the Long Vacation."

B. Giving the proceeds of the Harvest Ball to the neighborhood free-breakfast program was a *magnanimous* gesture.

    a. generous   *c.* unexpected
    b. belated   *d.* thoughtless

6. *dubiously* (page 129, line 18)

  A. " 'Oh dear me!' cried Mr. Lorry, rubbing his chin, and looking at his visitor *dubiously*."

  B. The house-to-house salesman approached the front door *dubiously,* as if he expected a rebuff.

    a. curiously   *c.* uncertainly
    b. boldly   *d.* fiercely

7. *crestfallen* (page 130, line 5)

  A. " 'Then what on earth is your meaning, Mr. Lorry?' demanded Stryver, perceptibly *crestfallen*."

  B. The pitcher was *crestfallen* as he walked slowly off the mound to make way for his replacement.

    a. outspoken   *c.* excited
    b. carelessly dressed   *d.* depressed

8. *explicit* (page 131, line 36)

  A. " '. . . It might be very painful to Miss Manette to have the task of being *explicit* with you.' "

  B. The directions were *explicit* so we had no trouble in finding our way.

    a. unintentionally confusing   *c.* agreeable and respectful
    b. clear and straightforward   *d.* doubtful but kindly

9. *reiterate* (page 133, line 4)

  A. " 'My opinion is confirmed, and I *reiterate* my advice.' "

  B. The judge asked the witness to *reiterate* the statement since it could not be heard the first time.

    a. reject   *c.* amplify
    b. repeat   *d.* quietly suggest

10. *remorse* (page 136, line 17)

A. " '. . . I have been troubled by a *remorse* that I thought would never reproach me again. . . .' "

B. Afflicted by *remorse* for his angry words, he apologized and promised never to speak that way again.

    a. anguished regret   *c.* annoying uncertainty
    b. light-hearted joking   *d.* feeling of relief

Unit 7: Jerry Cruncher's Profession
Book the Second, Chapter 14

FITTING THE JIGSAW TOGETHER

1. Whose funeral passes Tellson's Bank?

2. Why does Jerry Cruncher leave his favorite spot outside Tellson's Bank?

3. Why is Jerry interested in the funeral?

4. Why does Jerry call upon "his medical adviser," the surgeon?

5. Why does Jerry leave his house late at night?

6. Judging by Jerry's ill humor the following day, how successful was his "fishing expedition"?

7. This chapter seems to be an interlude in the main thread of the story. Yet, what one connecting link is there with an earlier important event in which Darnay, the Manettes, and Mr. Lorry were involved?

THE CHARACTERS AND THEIR MOTIVES

8. How does young Jerry again attempt to imitate his father?

9. Why does young Jerry follow his father on his expedition?

10. Why is Jerry's wife so upset by Jerry's activities?

11. How does Jerry again show his tendency to bully?

12. Why does Cruncher look at young Jerry with pride at the end of the chapter? In what way is he even more justified than he knows?

THE SOCIAL AND HISTORICAL SETTING

13. What was a "resurrection man"? Why did this "trade" exist?

14. What does Dickens think of the behavior of the mob at the funeral? Give examples to prove your point.

READING IN DEPTH

15. Throughout this chapter, the joke about Jerry's "fishing" is maintained. How do the following sections show the author's sardonic humor in his references to Jerry's profession?

" 'I'm going—as your mother knows—a fishing.' " (page 143, line 11)

" 'Your fishing-rod gets rayther rusty; don't it, Father?' " (page 143, line 13)

Jerry "opened a locked cupboard, and brought forth a sack, a crowbar of convenient size, a rope and chain, and other fishing tackle of that nature." (page 144, lines 17–19)

Jerry "was joined by another disciple of Izaak Walton, and the two trudged on together." (page 144, lines 32–33)

"They fished with a spade, at first. Presently the honoured parent appeared to be adjusting some instrument like a great corkscrew." (page 145, lines 22–23)

16. How does Dickens poke fun at Cruncher's "gallantry" in escorting women from one side of Fleet Street to the other?

17. An author may portray a character for us by showing what the character does, leaving us to draw conclusions. Or he may comment on the character directly. The former method is sometimes labeled "objective" and the latter "subjective." Which method is used in each of the following?

  a. Mrs. Cruncher—page 143, line 7.

  b. Jerry Cruncher—page 146, lines 21–23.

18. Why does Dickens use the word *moral* in the sentence, "Mr. Cruncher was soothed, but shook his head in a dubious and moral way"?

WORDS IN THEIR CONTEXTS

1. *mused* (page 139, line 7)

  A. "Time was, when a poet sat upon a stool in a public place, and *mused* in the sight of men."

  B. The visitor to the museum sat quietly before the sculpture and *mused* on its beauties.

    a. considered thoughtfully   *c.* hoped expectantly

    b. disagreed strongly   *d.* won decisively

2. *exultant* (page 139, line 22)

A. "The young gentleman uttered this *exultant* sound with mysterious significance."

B. There were *exultant* cheers from the stands when the winning run was scored.

a. noisy

b. joyful

c. weepy

d. surprising

3. *cavalcade* (page 141, line 20)

A. "A bear-leader . . . was impressed as an additional ornament, before the *cavalcade* had gone far down the Strand."

B. The long *cavalcade* of marchers and bands moved along at a brisk pace.

a. news

b. leader

c. selection

d. procession

4. *condole* (page 142, line 7)

A. "Mr. Cruncher . . . had remained behind in the churchyard, to confer and *condole* with the undertakers."

B. Relatives tried to *condole* with the survivors of the disastrous flood who had lost so much.

a. sympathize with the grief of

b. ask a favor

c. tell a light anecdote

d. explain

5. *dejected* (page 142, line 30)

A. "The *dejected* Mrs. Cruncher shook her head."

B. The team was not *dejected* by their defeat; they simply determined to win the remaining games.

a. easily led

b. peaceful

c. depressed

d. slow-moving

6. *feint* (page 144, line 22)

A. "Young Jerry, who had only made a *feint* of undressing when he went to bed, was not long after his father."

B. General Lee made a *feint* at the center of the line and then, instead, attacked both flanks simultaneously.

a. dash

b. deceptive motion

c. noisy announcement

d. excuse

7. *laudable* (page 144, line 28)

   A. "Impelled by a *laudable* ambition to study the art and mystery of his father's honest calling, Young Jerry . . . held his honoured parent in view."

   B. How *laudable* is the work of those who devote themselves unselfishly to helping the poor and the sick!

     a. well-advertised   *c.* laughable
     b. praiseworthy   *d.* feeble

8. *incessantly* (page 146, line 13)

   A. "All this time it was *incessantly* hopping on behind and gaining on him. . . ."

   B. Some people talk *incessantly* and become awfully boring.

     a. loudly   *c.* without stopping
     b. intelligently   *d.* with vigor

9. *altercation* (page 147, line 4)

   A. "The *altercation* was conducted in a low tone of voice. . . ."

   B. After a brief *altercation* about whose fault the slight accident had been, the two motorists drove their separate ways.

     a. announcement   *c.* harmonious discussion
     b. excessive violence   *d.* quarrel

10. *recompense* (page 148, line 7)

   A. " '. . . That boy will yet be a blessing to you, and a *recompense* to you for his mother!' "

   B. In *recompense* for shoveling the driveway, the boy was given a dollar.

     a. payment   *c.* expense
     b. blessing   *d.* recognition

Unit 8: In Paris

Book the Second, Chapters 15 and 16

FITTING THE JIGSAW TOGETHER

1. What account of the fate of Gaspard is given to Defarge and the other Jacquerie by the mender of roads?

2. Who are doomed to destruction by the revolutionary group that uses the name *Jacques*? Why?

3. What petition did Defarge present to the King? What was the result?

4. Who records the names of those who have been condemned by the revolutionaries? How are the names recorded?

5. Who has come to spy on the poor of Saint Antoine? How are the Defarges warned against him?

6. What surprising news does the spy bring to the Defarges?

7. How did Charles Darnay get his last name?

THE CHARACTERS AND THEIR MOTIVES

8. The Defarges are both bitter revolutionaries, but they differ in many ways.

    a. How do the two Defarges differ in their attitude toward the coming revolution and their patience in waiting to see it come?

    b. How do the two Defarges differ when they hear the news about the coming marriage of Charles Darnay to Lucie?

    c. How does Madame Defarge show an aspect of her character in the fear she inspires in the road mender?

    d. How did Defarge show courage on Gaspard's behalf?

    e. What traits do the two Defarges seem to have in common?

9. Now, long after the trial of Charles Darnay, John Barsad appears again on the scene.

    a. How does his present occupation resemble his occupation as revealed at the trial?

b. How does Barsad try to trick the Defarges into an admission of sympathy for Gaspard and the oppressed?

c. What one penetration does Barsad make in the armor of caution of the Defarges?

10. Dickens succeeds in bringing even very minor characters to life for his readers.

a. What kind of person is the road mender? What are his weaknesses?

b. How does Gaspard keep a certain dignity to the end of his poor life?

c. How are Jacques One, Two, and Three differentiated?

THE SOCIAL AND HISTORICAL SETTING

11. There are a number of indications of the injustice and cruelty of the times, of the oppression of the poor and the weak. Dickens portrays the root causes of the revolution to come.

a. How did the treatment of Gaspard show unusual cruelty on the part of the authorities?

b. How did the reception of Defarge's petition reveal the King's indifference to the wrongs committed by his nobles?

c. How did the treatment of the prisoner Damiens (page 154, line 8) show the evil of the society?

d. What sign is there, also, that the organization of the Jacquerie has penetrated deeply into the social structure?

12. What does Dickens intend to suggest by this description?

"Soon the large-faced King and the fair-faced Queen came in their golden coach, attended by the shining Bull's Eye of their Court, a glittering multitude of laughing ladies and fine lords, and in jewels and silks and powder and splendour and elegantly spurning figures, and handsomely disdainful faces of both sexes, the mender of roads bathed himself" (page 157, lines 18–22)

13. Why do the peasants shout, "Long live the King," if they are so oppressed?

READING IN DEPTH

14. Dickens sometimes shows us people playing games with each other. Each plays a role. How does the dialogue between John Barsad and the Defarges in the wine-shop demonstrate some of the "games people play"? (See pages 164–167.)

15. Answering a question with a question is a time-tested method of evasion. How does Madame Defarge use this technique on page 165?

16. The revolutionary group in the wine-shop, the Jacquerie, uses secret signals for various purposes. What is the significance of "Jacques"? The rose?

17. Why does Dickens again bring in the stone faces at the château?

18. What does Madame Defarge mean by the dolls and the birds she talks about on page 158?

19. Despite the difficult times, the residents of Saint Antoine occasionally enjoy a bit of wry humor. How does Defarge show this trait while the men are waiting for the road mender to tell his story?

20. Dickens again uses foreshadowing to suggest events that are coming to the story.

　　a. How does Madame Defarge foreshadow revolution in her description of the earthquake and the lightning?

　　b. How does Madame Defarge ominously foreshadow the use of the knitting in her answer to Barsad's questions? (page 163, lines 34–36)

　　c. Reread the last paragraph on page 168. How does this paragraph suggest the revolution to come?

21. Dickens may, on occasion, use an illiterate, unschooled person for a description of great beauty and insight. Point out the sensitive touches in the following description by the road mender.

> " 'As they approach, I see no more than that they are six soldiers with a tall man bound, and that they are almost black to my sight—except on the side of the sun going to bed, where they have a red edge, messieurs. Also, I see that their long shadows are on the hollow ridge on the opposite side of the road, and are on the hill above it, and are like the

shadows of giants. Also, I see that they are covered with dust, and that the dust moves with them as they come, tramp, tramp!' " (page 151, lines 29–37)

22. "A suspended interest and a prevalent absence of mind were perhaps observed by the spies who looked in at the wine-shop, as they looked in at every place, high and low, from the king's palace to the criminal's gaol." (page 149, lines 3–6) Why was there such a lack of interest everywhere in Saint Antoine?

WORDS IN THEIR CONTEXTS

1. *sallow* (page 148, line 9)
   A. "As early as six o'clock in the morning, *sallow* faces peeping through its barred windows had *descried* other faces within, bending over measures of wine."
   B. Paul's complexion looked *sallow* from too much study indoors.

   a. rosy red   c. showing pain
   b. unhealthily yellow   d. puffed from exhaustion

2. *descried* (page 148, line 10)
   A. See 1A above.
   B. The hikers *descried* a hawk wheeling and gliding far above the lonely valley.

   a. visited   c. observed
   b. called to   d. overlooked

3. *inaudible* (page 149, line 10)
   A. ". . . Madame Defarge . . . saw and heard something *inaudible* and invisible a long way off."
   B. Traffic noises were *inaudible* inside the soundproof television studio.

   a. invisible   c. not able to be heard
   b. not able to be re-   d. unusually loud and boisterous
      corded

4. *infallible* (page 150, line 34)
   A. ". . . It had been the *infallible* resource and *indispensable* entertainment of his village during a whole year."

B. The judgment of no one man, even the President, is *infallible*.

   a. unfailing   *c.* apparent
   b. insecure   *d.* cherished

5. *indispensable* (page 150, line 34)

A. See 4A above.

B. Those who find bodily comfort *indispensable* should not plan long hiking trips.

   a. desirable   *c.* insupportable
   b. lively   *d.* essential

6. *insolent* (page 158, line 2)

A. " 'Then, they are the more *insolent*, and it is nearer ended.' "

B. The *insolent* manner of the child showed a basic hostility.

   a. courteous   *c.* sleepy
   b. offensive   *d.* physically violent

7. *retribution* (page 161, line 17)

A. " 'Vengeance and *retribution* require a long time.' "

B. Hamlet considered the death of Claudius just *retribution* for the crimes Claudius himself had committed.

   a. repayment   *c.* excitement
   b. legal action   *d.* analysis

8. *docile* (page 162, line 2)

A. "[Defarge stood] before her like a *docile* and attentive pupil before his catechist. . . ."

B. Before the ride, Marcia's horse seemed *docile* enough, but, once mounted, he was almost unmanageable.

   a. wild   *c.* vigorously active
   b. quietly obedient   *d.* intelligently alert

9. *assiduously* (page 162, line 29)

A. "Next noontide saw the admirable woman in her usual place in the wine-shop, knitting away *assiduously*."

B. By applying himself *assiduously*, Jerry was able to raise his grade from a C to an A.

   a. off and on   *c.* shyly
   b. persistently   *d.* cleverly

10. *habitual* (page 168, line 9)

  A. ". . . The wine-shop recovered its *habitual* aspect."

  B. The lad had to forgo his *habitual* practice of taking a midnight snack because the refrigerator was empty.

    a. colorful   *c.* lively

    b. gloomy   *d.* customary

Unit 9: Lucie's Marriage
Book the Second, Chapters 17–21

FITTING THE JIGSAW TOGETHER

1. What happens to Dr. Manette after Lucie and Charles leave on their honeymoon?

2. How do Mr. Lorry and Miss Pross try to help?

3. How does Mr. Lorry get advice from Dr. Manette about Dr. Manette?

4. Who first appears to offer congratulations on the married pair's return home? Why does Dickens bring him into the story at this point?

5. How does Chapter 21 tell us that time has passed since the preceding chapter?

6. Why is Mr. Lorry upset at the news from France?

7. What is happening in France? Who is helping to direct the events there?

8. What is the significance of "One Hundred and Five, North Tower"?

THE CHARACTERS AND THEIR MOTIVES

9. Lucie is again referred to as the "golden thread" (page 190, lines 6, 31), as we see the effects of her influence upon others.

    a. How does she show her devotion to Dr. Manette? Should Lucie be so concerned for her father as to put her own happiness second to his?

    b. How does Lucie show compassion for Sydney Carton?

    c. How does Lucie prove to be a good homemaker?

10. Dr. Manette continues to grow in strength—with a brief exception.

    a. What clues do we find in the following quotation as to the reason for the illness that suddenly afflicts Dr. Manette?

      "The door of the Doctor's room opened, and he came out

with Charles Darnay. He was so deadly pale—which had not been the case when they went in together—that no vestige of colour was to be seen in his face." (page 175, lines 15–18; also page 123, lines 19–21)

   b. Why is the doctor reluctant to give up his shoemaker's bench? Why does he finally agree to have it taken away?

   c. Why does the doctor like to keep very busy?

11. Charles Darnay feels secure in his life. Simplicity and conventional sincerity are characteristic of him.

   a. How does he react to Carton's request to be his friend?

   b. How does he later describe Carton? How would Lucie's news of Carton differ from Darnay's?

   c. What is Darnay's attitude toward Lucie?

12. Sydney Carton is a continuing contrast to Darnay.

   a. Which of the two is more sensitive, Carton or Darnay? Which of the two appeals to you more?

   b. Why does Carton come around at odd times to see Lucie and her family?

   c. Why does Dickens call Carton a "forlorn wanderer"? (page 189, line 37)

   d. Darnay feels Carton can make something of himself still. Lucie and Carton disagree. Which viewpoint do you agree with? Why?

13. How does Mr. Lorry continue to show himself a devoted friend of the family?

14. Miss Pross thinks, almost to the very end, "that her brother Solomon should have been the bridegroom." Why? (Dickens doesn't let us forget that Miss Pross has a brother.)

15. How does the dialogue between Miss Pross and Mr. Lorry (page 174) show an easy, friendly relationship between them?

16. How does Stryver continue to act in characteristic fashion? Why does Darnay rebuff Stryver's offer?

17. What qualities, only suggested before, do the Defarges now display?

THE SOCIAL AND HISTORICAL SETTING

18. Why did the revolutionists attack the Bastille first?

19. How do the revolutionists treat the guards at the Bastille? Why?

20. How does the mob behave during the attack on the Bastille?

21. " 'Kill him!' croaked Jacques Three." (page 197, line 19) What does this cry tell us about the tenor of the times?

READING IN DEPTH

22. How does the following quotation possibly reveal one aspect of the author's philosophy of life?

"In the moonlight which is always sad, as the light of the sun itself is—as the light called human life is—as its coming and its going." (page 169, lines 26–28)

Do you agree with this philosophy? Why or why not?

23. Many great writers have had difficulty portraying children; for example, Shakespeare, in *Macbeth,* portrays a child who is really a small adult. Reread page 191, lines 7–11 and 38–39. Does Lucie's dying son sound like a real-life boy? What do you think?

24. Dickens enjoys introducing little touches that reveal a sound observation coupled with a skill with words. Mr. Lorry says, " 'I must look in at Tellson's.' " (page 176, line 16) Dickens adds, "It was easier for Mr. Lorry to look in at Tellson's than to look out of Tellson's. He was detained two hours." What does Dickens mean here?

25. The revolution in France is referred to as a "great storm . . . with a dreadful sea rising" (page 193, lines 12–13) and "a sea of black and threatening waters" (page 200, line 3). Do you consider this an appropriate metaphor? Why or why not?

26. Dickens is at his best in bursts of vivid description that capture an entire scene in a few words. What are some of the vivid images in the following quotation?

"Saint Antoine had been, that morning, a vast dusky mass of scarecrows heaving to and fro, with frequent gleams of light above the billowy heads, where steel blades and bayonets shone in the sun. A tremendous roar arose from the throat of Saint Antoine, and a forest of naked arms struggled in the air like shrivelled branches of trees in a winter wind: all the fingers convulsively clutching at every weapon or semblance of a weapon that was thrown up from the depths below, no matter how far off." (page 194, lines 26–33)

Why does Dickens personify Saint Antoine? Point out other examples of vivid description in the account of the mob's actions.

27. Why do the revolutionists show the same cruelty to the jailers as some of the authorities had shown to their fellows? Were they justified? Why or why not?

28. What might be the purpose in mentioning "some discovered letters and other memorials of prisoners of old time"? (page 200, lines 23–24)

29. Why does Dickens again bring in the footsteps as he describes Lucie's circle in London?

"Headlong, mad, and dangerous footsteps to force their way into anybody's life, footsteps not easily made clean again if once stained red, the footsteps raging in Saint Antoine afar off, as the little circle sat in the dark London window." (page 194, lines 22–25)

When did he mention these footsteps previously?

30. Chapters have tended to deal with events in London or events in Paris (the "Two Cities"). Chapter 21, however, deals with events in both cities. What is the advantage of having such a chapter at this point?

WORDS IN THEIR CONTEXTS

1. *lethargic* (page 170, line 34)
   A. " 'I have looked at her, in a state so dull and *lethargic*. . . .' "
   B. The lost explorer became *lethargic* with lack of sleep and food.
      a. nervous and excitable   c. drowsy and listless
      b. gloomy and hopeless   d. lively and optimistic

2. *vestige* (page 175, line 17)
   A. "He was so deadly pale . . . that no *vestige* of colour was to be seen in his face."
   B. Did the archeologists find any *vestige* of a lost civilization in the jungles of Honduras?
      a. memory   c. intense degree
      b. trace   d. repetition

3. *detained* (page 176, line 20)

   A. "He was *detained* two hours."

   B. Stop off at the photographer's for the pictures; you won't be *detained* long.

      a. pictured   *c.* scolded

      b. spoken to   *d.* delayed

4. *submissive* (page 177, line 7)

   A. "He obeyed, in the old mechanically *submissive* manner. . . ."

   B. The subjects of the tyrant were kept *submissive* through fear of torture and even death.

      a. obedient   *c.* oppressive

      b. offensive   *d.* openly pleased

5. *allusion* (page 180, line 33)

   A. "An incidental *allusion* . . . to the day of the week, and the day of the month, set him thinking and counting. . . ."

   B. Your *allusion* to the labors of Hercules was a wasted reference because your audience knew nothing about him.

      a. deception   *c.* denial

      b. counting   *d.* reference

6. *malady* (page 183, line 11)

   A. " 'I believe . . . that there had been a strong and extraordinary revival of the train of thought and remembrance that was the first cause of the *malady*.' "

   B. I'm afraid Jimmy is perfectly healthy and his *malady* is imaginary—brought on by the coming test in geometry!

      a. brain damage   *c.* feeling of well-being

      b. illness   *d.* tale

7. *diffidence* (page 184, line 22)

   A. "He spoke with the *diffidence* of a man who knew how slight a thing would overset the delicate organisation of the mind. . . ."

   B. Terry's *diffidence* was shown in the way he became completely embarrassed in the presence of other people.

      a. shyness   *c.* arrogance

      b. confidence   *d.* terror

8. *oblivion* (page 187, line 24)

A. " 'But, Mr. Darnay, *oblivion* is not so easy to me, as you represent it to be to you.' "

B. Many books written in the past twenty-five years have been consigned to *oblivion* but a few will be long-remembered.

    a. disrespect   *c.* thoughtfulness
    b. forgetfulness   *d.* fame

9. *pensive* (page 192, line 32)

A. "These were among the echoes to which Lucie, sometimes *pensive*, sometimes amused and laughing, listened in the echoing corner. . . ."

B. When you are in a *pensive* mood, you want to be alone with your thoughts.

    a. lively   *c.* surprisingly brief
    b. sarcastic   *d.* sadly thoughtful

10. *detested* (page 195, line 28)

A. "With a roar that sounded as if all the breath in France had been shaped into the *detested* word, the living sea rose, wave on wave, depth on depth, and overflowed the city to that point."

B. To the participants in the Boston Tea Party, the tea was a *detested* symbol of the British power to levy taxes arbitrarily.

    a. obscure   *c.* hated
    b. often repeated   *d.* well advertised

Unit 10: Revolution!

Book the Second, Chapters 22–24

FITTING THE JIGSAW TOGETHER

1. Why do the spies disappear from Saint Antoine?

2. Why does the mob kill Foulon? What signal sends the mob on its way?

3. What happens to the château of the Marquis? Who is responsible?

4. Why doesn't Gabelle prevent the action?

5. Why does Gabelle write the letter? To whom is it addressed?

6. Why does Charles Darnay take the letter?

7. What had Charles Darnay told Dr. Manette on the wedding day?

8. What does Darnay resolve to do?

9. Why is Mr. Lorry going to Paris?

10. Why doesn't Darnay tell Lucie of his plans?

THE CHARACTERS AND THEIR MOTIVES

11. The revolutionary group is vividly described for us. The various leaders become individualized.

    a. Who is The Vengeance? What kind of person is she?

    b. How does Madame Defarge continue to display a blood-thirstiness in attacking the members of the old power structure?

    c. What kind of person visits the village of the Marquis? What is his purpose?

12. When did we first meet Gabelle? Was the government unjust in seizing Gabelle? Explain your point of view.

13. How does Mr. Lorry show a great deal of courage in his plans for visiting France?

14*a.* Why does Darnay feel he should go to France? Do you agree with him? Why or why not?

    b. How is Darnay contrasted with Stryver?

    c. Should Darnay have told Lucie of his plans? Why or why not?

d. Why does Darnay feel he can help put the revolutionists on the right track?

THE SOCIAL AND HISTORICAL SETTING

15. Revolution is not a matter of a day. There were steps in the growing intensity and success of the French Revolution, as we see it depicted in the novel.

    a. How does Foulon symbolize the causes of the Revolution?

    b. Were the lives of the peasants materially improved by the death and destruction they dealt in these early days of the Revolution? Explain.

    c. "The fierce figures were steadily wending east, west, north, and south; and whosoever hung, fire burned." (page 212, lines 25–27; also page 211, lines 29–31) What was the purpose of these "fierce figures" wending their way across France?

    d. "There were other villages and townspeople less fortunate than the mender of roads and his fellows, upon whom the functionaries and soldiery turned with success, and whom they strung up in their turn." (page 212, lines 22–25) Why were the arsonists, those who started the fires, sometimes less successful than in the village of the Marquis? Why did the soldiers of the Marquis allow the damage to be done?

    e. In the years 1789 to 1792, what had happened to the Revolution? (See especially the beginning of Chapter 24.)

16. Why did so many of the French nobility go to England? How did some of the nobles anticipate the Revolution and plan ahead?

17. Why was Tellson's Bank so important in the life of these displaced nobles?

18. Why does the road mender now wear a red cap instead of his old blue one?

READING IN DEPTH

19. After the destruction of the château of the Marquis, "Monsieur Gabelle came down bringing his life with him for that while." Why is "for that while" so ominous? What event later gives added meaning to the phrase?

20. "Monseigneur was by this time scattered far and wide." (page 213, lines 29–30) What does *Monseigneur* stand for in this sentence?

21. Dickens says, "He took to his noble heels." (page 213, line 18) Who?

22. In the palace at Versailles, adjacent to the king's own chamber, was a room whose window was made of what is known as "bull's eye glass." This room was reserved for the most splendid and favored of the nobles who made up the king's court. Both that room and the nobles associated with it were known as the Bull's Eye of the Court. (see page 157, lines 19 and 27) On page 213, lines 19–25, Dickens again makes this reference, but adds several sharply ironic puns on the term "Bull's Eye." Explain them.

23. Dickens again (page 211) brings in the symbolism of the stone faces. During the blaze, "The stone faces showed as if they were in torment." What do these faces seem to represent or symbolize?

24. Dickens enjoys humorous subtlety now and then, as in his reasons for the disappearance of spies in Saint Antoine. "The lamps across his streets had a portentously elastic swing with them." (page 201, lines 7–8) What is Dickens suggesting here?

25. Reread the description of the mob's actions. (page 202, line 34– page 203, line 19) What vivid touches can you find?

26. Is Dickens sympathetic to the nobility? To the revolutionists? Explain.

27. As he looks at the stranger who has come to the village, the road mender thinks:

"Fortified towns with their stockades, guardhouses, gates, trenches and drawbridges seemed to be so much air as against this figure." (page 209, lines 10–12)

How does this comment suggest the inevitability of revolution?

28. According to legend, the Loadstone (or Lodestone) Rock irresistibly drew toward it ships that ventured too near. The ships were drawn to their destruction. Why does Dickens refer to the return of Darnay to France by the chapter title "Drawn to the Loadstone Rock"?

WORDS IN THEIR CONTEXTS

1. *awry* (page 201, line 13)

    A. "The raggedest night-cap, *awry* on the wretchedest head, has this crooked significance in it."

B. Geraldine's plans had gone *awry*, but she adjusted to the disappointment.

    a. off to one side, wrong   *c.* straight ahead
    b. proud, vigorous   *d.* lively, enthusiastic

2. *contemptuously* (page 202, line 8)

A. " 'How, then?' cried madame, *contemptuously*."

B. Macbeth at first spoke *contemptuously* about the forces that had come against him but his scorn soon changed to fear.

    a. excitedly   *c.* loudly
    b. scornfully   *d.* clearly

3. *adjacent* (page 203, line 29)

A. "They were all by that time . . . overflowing into the *adjacent* open space and streets."

B. The house was *adjacent* to a park which afforded a pleasant view of grass and trees to the occupants.

    a. large and roomy   *c.* uncluttered
    b. distant   *d.* bordering

4. *conflagration* (page 211, line 14)

A. "In the roaring and raging of the *conflagration*, a red-hot wind, driving straight from the infernal regions, seemed to be blowing the *edifice* away."

B. What had started as an untended campfire soon became a *conflagration* roaring through the dry pine grove.

    a. tempest   *c.* great fire
    b. loud noise   *d.* burning tree

5. *edifice* (page 211, line 15)

A. See **4A** above.

B. The Louvre in Paris is an imposing *edifice* in its own right as well as a great treasure house of art.

    a. something very showy *c.* city hall
    b. large building   *d.* jail

6. *dispersed* (page 212, line 17)

A. ". . . The people happily *dispersed*. . . ."

B. After the speaker left, the crowd *dispersed* quickly.

a. spoke up   c. rioted
b. gathered   d. scattered

7. *latent* (page 216, line 34)

A. "And it was such vapouring all about his ears, like a troublesome confusion of blood in his own head, added to a *latent* uneasiness in his mind, which had already made Charles Darnay restless. . . ."

B. *Dr. Jekyll and Mr. Hyde* is a story that warns of the *latent* evil that may be present underneath the surface even in the makeup of a good man.

     a. present but not apparent   c. criminal in purpose

     b. concealed by evil intention   d. lively and unsubdued

8. *indignity* (page 219, line 18)

A. " '. . . I have been seized, with great violence and *indignity*, and brought a long journey on foot to Paris.' "

B. The president of the corporation was subjected to the *indignity* of having to apologize to his assistant.

     a. wounding   c. act of valor
     b. humiliation   d. shrewd policy

9. *fidelity* (page 220, line 15)

A. "The peril of an old servant and a good one, whose only crime was *fidelity* to himself and his family, stared him so reproachfully in the face. . . ."

B. The knights took an oath of *fidelity* to the duke, swearing to be loyal even to the death.

     a. sense of humor   c. cheerfulness
     b. communication   d. loyalty

10. *annihilated* (page 220, line 32)

A. ". . . The events of this week *annihilated* the immature plans of last week. . . ."

B. In Tennyson's poem, the Light Brigade, in the course of its suicidal charge, was practically *annihilated* by artillery.

     a. changed   c. weakened
     b. destroyed   d. deafened

Unit 11: Darnay's Quest

Book the Third, Chapters 1–3

FITTING THE JIGSAW TOGETHER

1. Why is Charles Darnay's journey to Paris so slow?
2. When he arrives in Paris, why is he put into prison?
3. Who finally escorts Charles to the prison of La Force?
4. What does the phrase "in secret" mean?
5. Why is Mr. Lorry in Paris? Where is he staying?
6. Why do Lucie and Dr. Manette come to Mr. Lorry?
7. What is the grindstone used for?
8. Why does Dr. Manette think he can help Charles?
9. Which three revolutionists visit Lucie and her child in the lodgings?
10. Why is Lucie uneasy about the visit?

THE CHARACTERS AND THEIR MOTIVES

11. Why does Charles fail to realize that he is in imminent danger of being killed without trial or any pretense at justice? (See page 231.)
12. What reason is there to believe that Charles would not have come to France if he had truly realized the situation there?
13. The Defarges are important leaders of the Revolution as Charles arrives in Paris and is imprisoned.
    a. Who seems to be the stronger and crueler, Monsieur Defarge or his wife? What indications can you find for your choice?
    b. Why does Defarge continue to tell Charles, " 'I will do nothing for you' "?
    c. How does Madame Defarge react to Lucie's pleas as a "sister-woman"?
14. How does Mr. Lorry continue to show resourcefulness, courage, and determination in his efforts to help Lucie and her family?

15. Dr. Manette becomes a new man, filled with great courage and strength. What is responsible for his change?

16. How does Lucie react to Madame Defarge?

THE SOCIAL AND HISTORICAL SETTING

17. Why is travel so slow in revolutionary France?

18. How does the following description suggest what the French countryside looks like: "Impoverished fields that had yielded no fruits of the earth that year, diversified by the blackened remains of burnt houses"? (page 228, lines 1–2)

19. How just does the legal system in France seem to be at this time? One officer tells Charles, "Emigrants have no rights." Why not?

20. What news about France, the king, and the nobility does Charles pick up on his way to the prison?

21. Who or what is the "sharp female newly born, and called La Guillotine"? Why did the guillotine ultimately become a symbol of the French Revolution?

22. How does the following quotation suggest the restlessness and danger of the time?

"Every town-gate and village taxing-house had its band of citizen-patriots, with their national muskets in a most explosive state of readiness, who stopped all comers and goers, cross-questioned them, inspected their papers, looked for their names in lists of their own, turned them back, or sent them on, or stopped them and laid them in hold, as their capricious judgment or fancy deemed best for the dawning Republic One and Indivisible, of Liberty, Equality, Fraternity, or Death." (page 224, lines 7–14)

READING IN DEPTH

23. How are we told that there is no turning back for Charles, that he must go through with his quest to whatever end is in store?

24. How does the expression, "Peace, aristocrat!" (page 225, line 23) give Charles a strong indication of his new status?

25. What law was passed on the day Darnay left England? Why is the coincidence an example of irony?

26. There are suggestions of Darnay's likely fate in Paris as he rides toward Paris. What are they?

27. How does Darnay's imprisonment resemble that of Dr. Manette many years earlier?

28. Lorry says, " 'Thank God . . . that no one near and dear to me is in this dreadful town to-night.' " (page 236, line 39—page 237, line 1) Why is this statement so ironic?

29. Another vivid sketch is the description of the activities around the grindstone. (page 239, lines 2—29) How does Dickens feel about the activities?

30. Dickens compares the grindstone with "the great grindstone, Earth." What does this comparison seem to suggest?

31. The mob at first greets Dr. Manette with enthusiasm and vows to free his kin. (page 240, lines 11—14) Why is this not a particularly reassuring fact?

32. "The shadow attendant on Madame Defarge and her party seemed to fall so threatening and dark on the child, that her mother instinctively kneeled on the ground beside her." (page 244, lines 15—17) What shadow? What condemnation had Madame Defarge promised for *all* the Evrémondes?

WORDS IN THEIR CONTEXTS

1. *retarded* (page 225, line 2)

A. "This universal watchfulness not only stopped him on the highway twenty times in a stage, but *retarded* his progress twenty times in a day. . . ."

B. The stone fire wall *retarded* the progress of the blaze.

   a. departed   *c.* speeded up

   b. delayed   *d.* made an example of

2. *decree* (page 227, line 5)

A. " 'He is a traitor since the *decree*.' "

B. By imperial *decree* the slaves were declared to be completely free.

   a. slaughter   *c.* progression

   b. order by authority   *d.* disapproval

3. *stolid* (page 229, line 32)

A. " 'Emigrants have no rights, Evrémonde,' was the *stolid* reply."

B. The defendant could gain no clues to his fate from the expressionless, *stolid* face of the jury foreman.

  a. lively   *c.* solid
  b. bitter   *d.* unemotional

4. *entreat* (page 231, line 3)

A. "Charles Darnay felt it hopeless to *entreat* him further, and his pride was touched besides."

B. The driver tried to *entreat* the policeman not to write a ticket, but his pleading was of no avail.

  a. beg   *c.* persuade
  b. force   *d.* punish

5. *noisome* (page 232, line 18)

A. "Extraordinary how soon the *noisome* flavour of imprisoned sleep becomes manifest in all such places that are ill cared for!"

B. The *noisome* odors of the chemical plant found their way into every house in the village to the disgust of the home-owners.

  a. loud   *c.* offensive
  b. distinct   *d.* noisy

6. *commiseration* (page 233, line 37)

A. "There was a murmur of *commiseration* as Charles Darnay crossed the room to a grated door where the gaoler awaited him. . . ."

B. The playwright received many friendly expressions of *commiseration* after his play closed the first week.

  a. sharp criticism   *c.* jealousy
  b. sympathy   *d.* loud disagreement

7. *prematurely* (page 236, line 15)

A. "The blighted and unfruitful year was *prematurely* cold."

B. Ed's friends congratulated him *prematurely* on a promotion that didn't materialize.

  a. unusually   *c.* too late
  b. thoughtlessly   *d.* too soon

8. *impetuous* (page 240, line 4)

A. "His streaming white hair, his remarkable face, and the *impetuous* confidence of his manner . . . carried him in an instant to the heart of the concourse at the stone."

B. Despite his seemingly *impetuous* manner, Mel really considers his actions carefully beforehand.

a. impulsive   c. colorless
b. fierce   d. unforeseen

9. *doleful* (page 242, line 2)

A. "A disturbed and *doleful* mind he brought to bear upon them, and slowly and heavily the day lagged on with him."

B. The *doleful* expressions on the faces of the mourners revealed their sadness of heart.

a. cheerful   c. fixed
b. excited   d. sad

10. *acquiescence* (page 243, line 35)

A. "Defarge looked gloomily at his wife, and gave no other answer than a gruff sound of *acquiescence*."

B. Having received the *acquiescence* of the stockholders, the corporation went ahead with its plans for expansion.

a. disappointment   c. negative action
b. agreement   d. uncertainty

Unit 12: Darnay's Fate
Book the Third, Chapters 4–7

FITTING THE JIGSAW TOGETHER

1. What is Dr. Manette's main purpose in staying in Paris? What contribution does he make to the cause of humanity, also?

2. How long does Charles stay in prison before his trial?

3. Why does Lucie stay outside Charles's prison two hours each day? Who constantly observes Lucie in her lonely vigil?

4. What is Charles charged with?

5. Which two witnesses appear in his behalf?

6. What has been the fate of the first witness?

7. Who saves Charles during this first trial?

8. Why don't Lucie and Charles immediately flee from France?

9. How many people denounce Darnay and have him brought back to prison? Who are the two actually named? Who might the third denouncer be?

THE CHARACTERS AND THEIR MOTIVES

10. Dr. Manette is a transformed man as he moves around among the wretches who need medical assistance.

    a. Why is he so changed?

    b. What do these changes consist of?

    c. It is sometimes said that people have within them hidden resources that they can call upon in times of difficulty. Do you agree? Can you provide examples to prove your point?

11. How has Lucie been affected by the ordeal of waiting?

12. What tribute does Dickens pay Mr. Lorry on page 256?

13. Why are Jerry's fingers now free of rust?

14. How does Miss Pross remain in character even amidst the great dangers she is surrounded by? How does she manage her marketing in France?

417

15. "When he and Dr. Manette emerged from the gate, there was a great crowd about it, in which there seemed to be every face he had seen in court—except two, for which he looked in vain." (page 261, lines 37–39) Who were the two missing ones? What is suggested by their absence?

16. "Among these last was one with a spare piece of knitting under her arm as she worked. She was in a front row, by the side of a man whom he had never seen since his arrival at Barrier, but whom he directly remembered as Defarge. He noticed that she once or twice whispered in his ear, and that she seemed to be his wife; but, what he most noticed in the two figures was, that although they were posted as close to himself as they could be, they never looked towards him." (page 258, lines 23–30) What does Madame Defarge probably whisper to her husband? Why do they refuse to look at him?

THE SOCIAL AND HISTORICAL SETTING

17. How just were the trials to which the prisoners were subjected? (page 246)

18. The guillotine claimed many victims, but the raging populace claimed many others.

"She only knew that there had been an attack upon the prisons, that all political prisoners had been in danger, and that some had been dragged out by the crowd and murdered." (page 246, lines 9–11)

Why are the people able to kill many prisoners without even the semblance of a legal trial?

19. In describing those who were guillotined, Dickens mentions "gentle born and peasant born." What does that phrase tell us about the progress and direction of the revolution?

20. What inconsistent actions are demonstrated by the mob before and after Darnay's trial?

READING IN DEPTH

21. How did the people, in talking about the guillotine, demonstrate a capacity for "sick humor"?

22. What was the Carmagnole? For Dickens what did it symbolize?

23. Comment on the foreshadowing and symbolism in the following passage.

> "A footstep in the snow. Madame Defarge. 'I salute you, citizeness,' from the Doctor. 'I salute you, citizen.' This in passing. Nothing more. Madame Defarge gone, like a shadow over the white road." (page 255, lines 29–32)

24. When Miss Pross asks Dr. Manette whether she can ask him a question, he replies, " 'I think you may take that liberty.' " (page 265, line 27) Why does Miss Pross reply, " 'For gracious' sake, don't talk about liberty; we have quite enough of that' "?

25. Dickens has an acute sense of the dramatic, especially the dramatic sequence of events. When Dr. Manette reassures Lucie, " 'My love, the staircase is as still as Death' " (page 266, line 32), a blow is struck on the door. What is the dramatic effect of placing the statement and the event so close together?

WORDS IN THEIR CONTEXTS

1. *resolute* (page 248, line 1)

   A. ". . . Jarvis Lorry saw the kindled eyes, the *resolute* face, the calm strong look and bearing of the man whose life always seemed to him to have been stopped, like a clock. . . ."

   B. We need leaders who are *resolute* in their goals but flexible enough to change when change is called for.

   a. constant and steady   *c.* glum and serious
   b. cheerful but subdued   *d.* bright and alert

2. *sagacious* (page 248, line 22)

   A. "This new life of the Doctor's was an anxious life, no doubt; still, the *sagacious* Mr. Lorry saw that there was a new sustaining pride in it."

   B. The *sagacious* young man used a clever combination of flattery and subtle persuasion to convince his friend.

   a. shrewd   *c.* talkative
   b. lean   *d.* depressed

3. *eloquent* (page 250, line 12)

A. "It hushed the *eloquent*, struck down the powerful, abolished the beautiful and good."

B. However convincing their words, the *eloquent* do not always represent what is right or good.

   a. noisy rioters   *c.* quiet rebels

   b. fluent speakers   *d.* proud rulers

4. *calamity* (page 251, line 11)

A. "If the suddenness of her *calamity*, and the whirling wheels of the time, had stunned the Doctor's daughter into awaiting the result in idle despair, it would but have been with her as it was with many."

B. In times of *calamity* and distress we need patience, courage, and positive action.

   a. fire   *c.* disaster

   b. peace   *d.* mild sickness

5. *inclement* (page 252, line 18)

A. "When it was not too wet or *inclement* for her child to be with her, they went together."

B. If we have *inclement* weather, the outdoor art show will be postponed until the following day.

   a. fair   *c.* stormy

   b. hot   *d.* changeable

6. *jocosely* (page 252, line 35)

A. "The wood-sawyer . . . cast a glance at the prison, pointed at the prison, and putting his ten fingers before his face to represent bars, peeped through them *jocosely*."

B. Although the professor seemed to speak *jocosely*, there was an undercurrent of deep seriousness in his message.

   a. rapidly   *c.* seriously

   b. slyly   *d.* humorously

7. *inquisitive* (page 253, line 21)

A. "He was an *inquisitive* fellow, and sometimes when she had quite forgotten him in gazing at the prison roof and grates, and in lifting her heart up to her husband, she would come to herself to find him looking at her. . . ."

B. Great scientists are gifted with *inquisitive* minds which do not permit them to be satisfied with accepted theories.

    a. curious   *c.* underhanded

    b. open   *d.* shrewd

8. *staunch* (page 256, line 15)

A. "The *staunch* old gentleman was still in his trust; had never left it."

B. The *staunch* supporters of the United Nations have stuck to their beliefs despite all the difficulties and opposition.

    a. unsteady   *c.* firm

    b. careful   *d.* physically powerful

9. *pestilence* (page 258, line 2)

A. "In seasons of *pestilence,* some of us will have a secret attraction to the disease."

B. Man has waged a steady war on *pestilence* and some of the worst diseases have been conquered.

    a. famine   *c.* death

    b. disease   *d.* poverty

10. *hazard* (page 260, line 10)

A. "He had come back, to save a citizen's life, and to bear his testimony, at whatever personal *hazard,* to the truth."

B. Soon there may be as little *hazard* in a jaunt to the moon as in a walk around the block.

    a. danger   *c.* disagreement

    b. distance   *d.* gaiety

Unit 13: Carton in Paris

Book the Third, Chapters 8 and 9

FITTING THE JIGSAW TOGETHER

1. Pieces of the "jigsaw puzzle" now fall into place in startling ways and the amazing overall design of the story begins to reveal itself.

   a. Whom does Miss Pross unexpectedly come across in Paris? What is his job there? Who first recognizes Solomon in his other identity?

   b. Who else plays a key role in pinning down Solomon's identity, in informing Mr. Lorry of Darnay's latest arrest, and in being able to gain the upper hand over Solomon? How does all this come about?

   c. What is learned about Cly's "funeral"? How? Where is Cly now? Who was the mourner at Cly's "funeral"?

2. What indications are there that Carton has some definite plan in mind?

3. For the third time, Darnay is on trial for his life. New developments are unfolded.

   a. What early association was there between Defarge and Doctor Manette?

   b. Who is named the third accuser of Charles Darnay? How is this possible?

THE CHARACTERS AND THEIR MOTIVES

4. This unit further explores the character of Sydney Carton and reveals the reality beneath the mask.

   a. How does Carton show a deep understanding of human nature in this handling of Miss Pross's brother?

   b. How does the following quotation further reveal Carton's state of mind at this time?

"There was a braced purpose in the arm and a kind of inspiration in the eyes, which not only contradicted his light manner, but changed and raised the man." (page 273, lines 8–10)

c. Why was Carton "contemplating the walls" of the prison at the time he saw Miss Pross's brother?

d. How does Dickens contrast Carton and Miss Pross's brother in this comment?

"The smooth manner of the spy, curiously in dissonance with his ostentatiously rough dress, and probably with his usual demeanour, received such a check from the inscrutability of Carton—who was a mystery to wiser and honester men than he—that it faltered here and failed him." (page 276, lines 36–39)

e. How does Carton further reveal his character and his feelings when he asks about Lucie, " 'How does she look?' " (page 283, line 15)

f. Carton says, " 'I can't sleep.' " Then Dickens adds:

"It was not a reckless manner, the manner in which he said these words aloud under the fast-sailing clouds, nor was it more expressive of negligence than defiance. It was the settled manner of a tired man, who had wandered and struggled and got lost, but who at length struck into his road and saw its end." (page 287, lines 1–5)

How do these lines give us insight into Carton's present feelings?

g. How does Carton's gallantry in carrying the little girl across the muddy street (page 288, line 1) reveal another facet of his character?

5. How is Barsad portrayed for us? Is this portrayal consistent with the picture of him given earlier?

6. Mr. Lorry's steadfastness and loyalty are again important elements in the story.

a. How does Mr. Lorry's treatment of Jerry Cruncher show his characteristic kindness?

b. Mr. Lorry has always been spry and alert; yet Dickens comments, "He was an old man now." (page 282, line 27) What has brought on this change?

7. How do Jerry Cruncher's actions after the revelation of his former profession further reveal him to us?

8. Do we side with Carton or the wood-sawyer, the "grinning little man"? (page 286, lines 4–6) How does this dialogue with Carton reveal the character of the wood-sawyer to us? Has the wood-sawyer (formerly the road mender) changed since our first meeting with him? How?

9. Minor characters constantly come to life through Dickens's skill in catching representative actions. Jacques Three, described for us earlier on page 153, is again singled out at the trial: "The craving man on the jury rubbed his hands together, and restored the usual hand to his mouth." (page 290, lines 29–30) He is also called "life-thirsting, cannibal-looking, bloody-minded." (page 289, line 23) How much justice might a prisoner expect from someone like him?

10. How does The Vengeance contribute to the uproar against Darnay? Are her actions here consistent with those described earlier? Why or why not?

11. As Defarge begins to speak (page 291, line 10), he looks down at his wife. Why is this a significant action?

12. Why does Barsad fear Madame Defarge?

THE SOCIAL AND HISTORICAL SETTING

13. When Miss Pross and Jerry Cruncher went marketing, they "turned out of their road to avoid any very excited groups of talkers." (page 268, lines 15–16) Why? What do their actions tell us about the times?

14. Jerry says that he was poorly paid and considered disreputable for being a body snatcher. Yet the doctors who used the bodies for research were well paid and highly reputable. Does Jerry have a point in his criticism of the entire setup? Explain your point of view.

15. Explain Dickens's point in the following passage and comment on it.

"There could have been no such Revolution, if all laws, forms, ceremonies had not first been so monstrously abused that the suicidal vengeance of the Revolution was to scatter them all to the winds." (page 289, lines 14–17)

16. The President at the trial rebukes Dr. Manette by saying:

" 'If the Republic should demand of you the sacrifice of your child herself, you would have no duty but to sacrifice her.' " (page 290, lines 24–25)

Who or what was "the Republic"?

READING IN DEPTH

17. In talking to Miss Pross's brother, Carton says bluntly, "I could not better testify my respect for your sister than by finally relieving her of her brother." (page 276, lines 32–33) Explain the paradox.

18. Dickens dramatically tells us of Jerry's surprise by calling its result a "remarkable goblin shadow on the wall." When Mr. Lorry looks further, he realizes that it has been caused "by a sudden extraordinary rising and stiffening of all the risen and stiff hair on Mr. Cruncher's head." (page 277, lines 32–33) What accounts for Jerry's strange appearance?

19. Jerry has been engaged in an illegal enterprise, body snatching; yet he looks upon it as any "honest tradesman" might look upon his job. Given Jerry's assumptions, we must agree with him. Point out the humor in Jerry's indignant attack on Barsad. (page 278 and following)

20. Darnay's second trial in Paris seems to be over before it starts. What indications are there, even before the trial starts, that he will be found guilty?

21. Why is each person looking at a particular person in the following paragraph, and how does it sum up the major currents and crosscurrents in the novel?

"In a dead silence and stillness—the prisoner under trial looked lovingly at his wife, his wife only looking from him to look with solicitude at her father, Doctor Manette keeping his eyes fixed on the reader, Madame Defarge never taking hers from the prisoner, Defarge never taking his from his feasting wife, and all the other eyes there intent upon the Doctor, who saw none of them—the paper was read, as follows." (page 291, lines 26–32)

WORDS IN THEIR CONTEXTS

1. **vexed** (page 269, line 30)
   A. " 'What is the matter?' said the man who had caused Miss Pross to scream; speaking in a vexed, abrupt voice (though in a low tone), and in English."
   B. The passenger was vexed at the failure of the airline to notify him of the flight cancellation and expressed his irritation in a letter to the company.
   - a. startled
   - b. irritated
   - c. charmed
   - d. impressed

2. **furtive** (page 269, line 36)
   A. " 'Don't call me Solomon. Do you want to be the death of me?' asked the man, in a furtive, frightened way."
   B. The furtive manner of the stranger made the villagers wonder what he was up to.
   - a. secretive
   - b. pleasant
   - c. uncertain
   - d. weary

3. **abhorrence** (page 273, line 30)
   A. "Mr. Lorry . . . regarded his new visitor with an undisguised look of abhorrence."
   B. The pacifist expressed his abhorrence of war.
   - a. delight
   - b. surprise
   - c. indifference
   - d. hatred

4. **consternation** (page 273, line 36)
   A. "Struck with consternation, the old gentleman exclaimed, 'What do you tell me! I left him safe and free within these two hours, and am about to return to him!' "
   B. To the consternation of the Cubs' fans, the Giants got five runs in the first inning.
   - a. delight
   - b. indecision
   - c. dismay
   - d. recklessness

5. **composure** (page 276, line 17)
   A. " 'You scarcely seem to like your hand,' said Sydney, with the greatest composure."

B. The panelist lost his *composure* and became excited and incoherent.

   a. calmness   *c.* sense of suppressed excitement
   b. eagerness   *d.* friendly attitude

6. *elongate* (page 278, line 1)

A. "Here Mr. Lorry perceived the reflection on the wall to *elongate*. . . ."

B. As the sun approached the horizon, the shadows of the trees began to *elongate*.

   a. thicken   *c.* wear down
   b. become longer   *d.* magnify

7. *elicit* (page 283, line 27)

A. "His indifference to fire was sufficiently remarkable to *elicit* a word of remonstrance [protest] from Mr. Lorry. . . ."

B. The reporters tried to *elicit* an expression of opinion from the Mayor but that official could not be brought to make any comment.

   a. emphasize   *c.* bring out
   b. deny   *d.* shut in

8. *surmise* (page 288, line 37)

A. ". . . It was easy to *surmise* where the good old man was gone."

B. Not knowing all the facts, we could only *surmise* the reasons for his hasty departure.

   a. state   *c.* repeat
   b. guess   *d.* call out

9. *tranquil* (page 290, line 18)

A. " 'Citizen Manette, be *tranquil*. To fail in submission to the authority of the Tribunal would be to put yourself out of law.' "

B. After the wild storm had passed, the forest glade was again *tranquil*.

   a. lonely   *c.* unchanged
   b. alert   *d.* calm

10. *expounded* (page 290, line 32)

    A. "Defarge . . . rapidly *expounded* the story of the imprisonment. . . ."

    B. Dr. Martin Luther King *expounded* the doctrine of nonviolence.

        a. set forth   *c.* took back

        b. denounced   *d.* canceled out

Unit 14: Out of the Shadow
Book the Third, Chapters 10–15

FITTING THE JIGSAW TOGETHER

1. With the reading of Doctor Manette's paper, all—except one—of the remaining pieces of the "jigsaw puzzle" click into place to complete the intricate and powerful entanglements of this tale.

- a. Who were the various persons in Dr. Manette's narrative? Identify the two nobles, the dying peasant woman, the dying peasant boy, the distraught woman member of the nobility, her son, the doctor's servant.
- b. Why was the doctor called in?
- c. How had the nobles killed the peasant woman's husband?
- d. For whom was the wife of the Marquis St. Evrémonde so concerned?
- e. Why did the doctor write the letter to the Minister? What was the result of his efforts?
- f. When the doctor wrote, " 'I denounce them to Heaven and to earth,' " to whom was he referring?

2. The final piece of the puzzle—having to do with the true identity of Madame Defarge—shapes all the dread and ominous aspects of the story to their terrible summit. Explain.

3. Now, like flood waters bursting through a dam, the great forces that have been building up release themselves in a final onrush of dramatic events.

- a. What does Carton say to Lucie when he kisses her for the last time? How do these words relate to something in the past?
- b. What last effort does Dr. Manette make on behalf of Charles? Why does this effort fail? What change comes over Dr. Manette?
- c. Why does Carton go to Defarge's wine-shop? Why does he refrain from strong drink at this time? Who is impressed by the resemblance of Carton and Darnay?

429

d. What additional plots does Madame Defarge have against the family of Dr. Manette? Whom would she destroy? Who will give the additional evidence against Lucie and her family? Why does she not consult her husband at this point? Why does Carton say, " 'It [the exit certificate] may soon be recalled and, I have reason to think, will be' "? (page 315, line 11)

e. What is Sydney Carton's plan for saving Darnay? What are some of the obstacles in the way of its successful completion?

f. How does Carton get Darnay to do his bidding in the prison? How is Darnay removed? Who has to help? Why does this person provide the help?

g. Who recognizes that Carton is not Darnay? Why doesn't this person tell the authorities?

h. Why do Miss Pross and Jerry plan to leave after the rest of the party?

i. Why is Miss Pross left alone in the apartment?

j. Who arrives before Miss Pross leaves? Why does Miss Pross try to detain the visitor?

k. What is the result of the struggle between Miss Pross and the visitor?

l. Why is Barsad so concerned about finding Carton in the tumbrils?

m. For whom is The Vengeance waiting so patiently? Why is she doomed to disappointment?

n. How does Miss Pross save the day?

o. Whom does Carton comfort to the very end?

p. Why is Carton content to make the sacrifice?

q. In the vision on the last two pages, we learn the probable fate of various characters in the story. What is to happen to Barsad, Cly, Defarge, The Vengeance, Dr. Manette, Mr. Lorry, Lucie, Charles?

r. Who is mentioned on page 345, line 21, as "the foremost of the just judges"?

THE CHARACTERS AND THEIR MOTIVES

4. Carton becomes fully realized in these last chapters—in his actions and in his thoughts.

a. Again Carton is on the scene, rushing from an obscure corner. (page 307, lines 3–7) What does that tell us about Carton's personality? When, earlier in the story, did Carton show his keen attentiveness toward Lucie?

b. Why does Carton try to show himself so poor in French and so naive in his encounter with Madame Defarge in the wine-shop? What role is he playing?

c. When Carton enters the prison to talk to Darnay, there is "something bright and remarkable in his look." (page 320, line 35) Why is Carton, who is so close to death, so bright and apparently elated?

d. How do Carton's actions at the very end of his life give us some insight into what his life might have become in other circumstances?

e. Carton doesn't want to die. He hopes, for a moment perhaps, that Dr. Manette will be able to save Darnay. But when the time comes, he is fully resigned and courageous. Why?

5. Madame Defarge's bitterness and burning hatred do, in fact, bring on her death, just as Carton's love brings him to his death—but with different results for others.

a. Darnay's mother would have helped Madame Defarge as a child, if she could. Charles Darnay himself gave Madame Defarge no harm and even disowned all that his family stood for. Why then is Madame Defarge so bitter toward Darnay? And why so bitter toward Lucie, young Lucie, and even Dr. Manette —himself the innocent victim of the original tragedy? What does Dickens seem to be saying here about blind hatred?

b. Madame Defarge and her husband, up to now, have worked together. But now she draws apart and plans her own course. Why?

c. Madame Defarge provides a clue to her course when she says, " 'Tell wind and fire where to stop, but don't tell me.' " (page 312, line 22) Why does she compare herself with these two forces?

d. Why is Madame Defarge so beloved of The Vengeance and Jacques Three?

e. "Imbued from her childhood with a brooding sense of wrong, and an inveterate hatred of a class, opportunity had developed her into a tigress. She was absolutely without pity. If she had ever had the virtue in her, it had quite gone out of her." (page 332, lines 2–5)

Is Dickens forgiving Madame Defarge for her qualities here? Explain.

f. What positive qualities does Madame Defarge have?

g. Love and hatred meet again when Madame Defarge confronts Miss Pross. Why is Miss Pross a match for this woman who is much bloodier and crueler than she?

6. What additional clues to Defarge's character do we get from these chapters?

7. How does Darnay remain in character to the end?

8. What causes Jerry Cruncher to repent his former ways? What resolutions does he make?

9. The three minor characters—The Vengeance, the wood-sawyer, and Jacques Three—come more chillingly to life.

a. How does The Vengeance encourage Madame Defarge in her worst impulses?

b. How does Jacques Three reveal his character when he says, " 'No one must escape. We have not half enough as it is. We ought to have six score [executions] a day' "? (page 329, lines 26–28)

c. When the wood-sawyer was a mender of roads, he followed the crowd blindly. (page 157) He was terrified of Madame Defarge. (page 156) Has he changed in either of these particulars? Explain.

10. What kind of person is the little seamstress? Why is she introduced into the story?

THE SOCIAL AND HISTORICAL SETTING

11. What evils of prerevolution France does Dr. Manette's manuscript reveal?

12. What does revolutionary justice seem to depend upon? (page 308, lines 31–34)

13. According to Dickens, what are the roots of revolution? (page 340, lines 14–17)

14. America is going through a period that many have labeled a kind of revolution. Are there resemblances between America of the 1970's and France of the 1790's? Are there lessons we all can learn from this book?

READING IN DEPTH

15. Chapter 10 is called "The Substance of the Shadow." What is the meaning of this title?

16. Suspense is a major ingredient in this final unit. Carton has planned "an impossible mission." Everything has to click. There are many obstacles and near disasters as we follow the story line to its conclusion.

 a. How does each of the following present a possible obstacle to Carton's plan: Dr. Manette's condition, Lucie's upset, Darnay's probable unwillingness to change places, Madame Defarge's unyielding hatred, Barsad's noted unreliability, the difficulties of traveling in revolutionary France, the possibilities of being found out and overtaken?

 b. How does Carton plan to get Lucie to agree to leave Paris?

 c. There is also suspense in the execution. How does Darnay prepare himself for his death?

 d. " 'Are we not going too slowly? Can they not be induced to go faster?' " (page 327, lines 11–12) How does Mr. Lorry answer Lucie? How does his answer add to the suspense? (Reread pages 327–328 for insight into how Dickens builds suspense skillfully.)

 e. One of the last delays is provided by the guard who asks how many are going to the guillotine. How does this provide a bitter touch at the end?

 f. As Darnay revives in the fleeing coach, "He thinks they are still together; he asks him, by his name, what he has in his hand." (page 328, lines 16–17) Where does Darnay think he is? What is he referring to?

17. How does little Lucie foreshadow Carton's plan in her plea to him, "Now that you have come, I think you will do something to help mamma, something to save papa!" (page 307, lines 21–22)

18. " 'Yes. He will perish; there is no real hope,' echoed Carton." (page 309, line 6) What double meaning is there in these words?

19. How does Dickens provide an ironic comment in Darnay's last preparations? (page 319, lines 11–15)

20. At the side of the guillotine, The Vengeance calls Madame Defarge by name, but she doesn't answer. A woman suggests The Vengeance call louder. "Aye! Louder, Vengeance, much louder, and still she will scarcely hear thee." (page 342, lines 28–29) Why not?

21. What are the strong and striking qualities of these last words of Sydney Carton and of the story?

> "It is a far, far better thing that I do, than I have ever done; it is a far, far better rest that I go to than I have ever known." (page 345, lines 26–27)

WORDS IN THEIR CONTEXTS

1. *apprehensive* (page 292, line 24)

   A. " 'As I stood aside to let that carriage pass, *apprehensive* that it might otherwise run me down, a head was put out of the window, and a voice called to the driver to stop.' "

   B. Hearing that many employees were going to be dismissed, the clerk became *apprehensive* about his own job.

      a. cheered   *c.* careful
      b. fearful   *d.* interested

2. *prodigious* (page 300, line 25)

   A. " ' "There is *prodigious* strength . . . in sorrow and despair." ' "

   B. The climbing of Mount Everest required *prodigious* stamina, strength, and courage.

      a. sorrowing   *c.* lessening
      b. enormous   *d.* cruel

3. *accessible* (page 308, line 15)

   A. " 'There is a celebration in the streets, and no one will be *accessible* until dark.' "

B. The mountain cabin is isolated, being *accessible* by only a single, narrow trail.

   a. visible   *c.* able to be approached

   b. able to be counted   *d.* at home

4. *assented* (page 312, line 5)

A. " 'It is so,' *assented* Defarge."

B. When asked to help push the car, the passerby *assented* and joined the others in their efforts to get the vehicle moving.

   a. grunted   *c.* agreed

   b. denied   *d.* listened

5. *fervent* (page 316, line 6)

A. "His manner was so *fervent* and inspiring, that Mr. Lorry caught the flame, and was as quick as youth."

B. Despite a *fervent* plea by the officers of the senior class for cooperation, the students continued to show little interest in class activities.

   a. short   *c.* unexpected

   b. announced   *d.* impassioned

6. *comprehended* (page 317, line 27)

A. "He had fully *comprehended* that no personal influence could possibly save him. . . ."

B. Although the traveler had taken Italian in college, he barely *comprehended* the directions given to him so rapidly by the Florentine policeman.

   a. understood   *c.* read

   b. hinted   *d.* advertised

7. *resignation* (page 318, line 6)

A. "There was a hurry, too, in all his thoughts, a turbulent and heated working of his heart, that contended against *resignation*."

B. As the ship began to sink rapidly, the hopes of the crew were replaced by *resignation* to their certain fate.

   a. struggle   *c.* confusion

   b. acceptance   *d.* brooding

8. *eccentric* (page 320, line 9)

A. "After a hard contest with that *eccentric* action of thought which had last perplexed him, he had got the better of it."

B. His *eccentric* ways were in marked contrast to the conventional habits of the rest of the family.

a. unusual

b. concentrated

c. commonplace

d. exciting

9. *impaired* (page 322, line 34)

A. "As if his memory were *impaired,* or his faculties disordered, the prisoner made an effort to rally his attention."

B. The vacuum cleaner was *impaired* beyond mending so we had to get a new one.

a. worked

b. damaged

c. affected

d. true

10. *alacrity* (page 331, line 22)

A. " 'I willingly obey the orders of my chief,' said The Vengeance with *alacrity,* and kissing her cheek. 'You will not be late?' "

B. Summoned by a whistle to his meal, the hungry dog responded with *alacrity*.

a. bitterness

b. insincerity

c. regret

d. eagerness

Benji

Benji

Benji

Benji

Benji